CALCULATED FLIGHT

George K. Gosché III

Calculated Flight: a novel / by George K. Gosché III

ISBN-10: 0-692-68732-7
ISBN-13: 978-0-692-68732-1

Cover art and IT assistance by Silvia Dominguez
Technical advice by Capt. Richard Schauwecker

The names of the people in this story have been changed.
Not to protect the innocent, nor even the guilty.
They've been changed to protect me.
All names but two:
the Ashby family, with my thanks for her trifles and his whiskey,
and my great friend Paul Bisno—an undisguisable classic,
who took his life in 2011.

The places are real.
I've been there. I've eaten there. I've drunk there. I've slept there.
Each and every one.

The things are real, too—I know them all.
I've touched them, flown some, flown in the others, driven some,
owned some.
Each and every one.

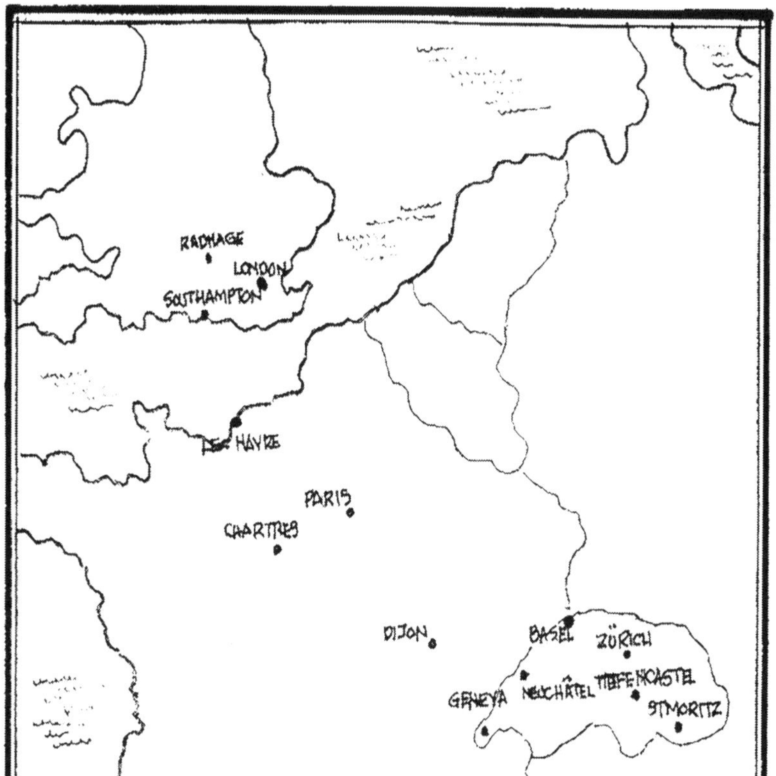

RADHAGE
•
LONDON
•
SOUTHAMPTON
■

HAVRE
■

PARIS
•
CHARTRES
•

DIJON
•
BASEL
■ ZÜRICH
■
GENEVA ■ NEUCHÂTEL TIEFENCASTEL
■ ■ ■
ST MORITZ
■

MONACO
■

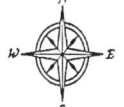

CALCULATED FLIGHT

<u>Chapter One</u>

Over the Atlantic

Thursday, 13 July 2000

If one is fortunate, a few times in life it is possible to chance upon the joys of that limbo existing between the departure from the known negatives of the last assignment and the optimistic and naïve prospects for the next. I was currently luxuriating in one of those rare and wonderful intervals. Sadly, things change. In three days, my closest friend would be murdered, and within ten, I would be wanted in two countries on a series of criminal charges too numerous to fathom.

"Good afternoon, ladies and gentlemen. Captain Mulholland speaking. As may be observed on the cabin displays, we are presently traveling at Mach point nine five, or six hundred and thirty miles per hour, at an altitude of thirty-one thousand feet. In a few moments we will initiate our engines' afterburners, at which time you will feel our aircraft's most impressive acceleration as our cruising speed rapidly climbs to slightly over twice the speed of sound. Thank you for your attention, sit back and enjoy your flight, and I'll be speaking with you again shortly."

The powerful thrust from the ignition of the four afterburners planted me back in my seat with a pressure similar to that experienced on the takeoff roll. I glanced at the digital readouts on the bulkhead several rows ahead of mine: We'd seamlessly transitioned through the sound barrier and we were now accelerating through Mach 1.15. The adjacent altimeter was clicking through 35,000 feet. Within a minute, I could feel the warmth on my hand as I held it against the uncommonly small window, where, only inches away, the outside skin temperature of the aluminum alloy was pushing 250 degrees Fahrenheit. Looking out, the infinite sky appeared deep cerulean, almost indigo.

"Your captain again," the Scottish-accented pilot announced several minutes later. "As you may observe on the cabin displays, with the help of our four Rolls-Royce Olympus engines generating over one hundred and fifty thousand pounds of combined thrust, we have now passed through Mach two point one, or thirteen hundred and eighty miles per hour. That's equivalent to approximately two thousand feet per second, roughly the speed of a bullet exiting a rifle barrel. We have reached our trans-Atlantic cruising altitude of fifty-nine thousand feet, and as you look out your windows, you will see a phenomenon only witnessed by astronauts, a few select military pilots, and your fellow Concorde passengers: the curvature of the earth. Viewing from left to right, we can see over seven hundred and fifty miles between horizons. Thank you for flying British Airways and Concorde this afternoon, and I'll be speaking with you a bit later to advise of our flight's progress."

Within minutes after leveling off, the captain started his meet -and-greet walk down the aisle of the two-by-two configured nine-foot wide cabin. With today's less than forty percent load factor in the one-hundred-seat aircraft, he would have ample opportunity to welcome a good number of the passengers in the two uniclass cabins. Upon noticing the ancient C-47 pilot's operating handbook on the tray next to my drink, the pilot leaned across the empty aisle seat next to me and with a growing smile said, "Now that was a truly great airplane. May I ask where you found your flight manual? I'd like to buy one for my collection if they're still available."

I explained I was simply the courier pigeon. "My father asked me to pass this along to an old friend of his in England, a former RAF pilot. But tell you what I'll do if you're interested, Captain: Before I deliver the book to its new owner, I could arrange to have it copied. Let me have your card and I'll send it to you."

He beamed, accepted, and thanked me. "May I presume you're also a pilot, sir?"

"Not anymore. I flew C-130s in the Air Force. Nothing very sexy. But that was over thirteen years ago. Now, your airplane, this is exotic."

"Ah, you were on the Hercules. First-rate aircraft. I'll show you our flight deck a bit later if you'd care to have a look. I'm sorry, my name is Hamish Mulholland," he said, extending his hand.

"Dane Baron. Pleased to meet you, Captain. And that would be outstanding."

The pilot excused himself as a flight attendant placed an iced glass of Stolichnaya on my tray, along with an ample portion of Beluga caviar in a bed of crushed ice. Lemon, diced onion, chopped egg, and blinis surrounded the presentation. I had no regrets for having treated myself on this final trip to the twenty percent fare upgrade from first class to Concorde. Vodka in hand, I began drifting back to the captivation out the window and reflected on my last three years' work.

* * *

I had agreed to get together with my Swiss former boss in Paris in two days to settle accounts, though I saw no real purpose in it other than Arnaud liked to meet people in Paris. Our only remaining business was my collection of Arnaud's check for my share of the buyout proceeds. I told him bank transfers worked quite well for that, but I sensed he wanted one last shindig. Not one to disappoint, and not requiring any arm-twisting, I naturally acquiesced. Paris it happily would be.

I first met Arnaud Laurent at the invitation of his son, Luc, whom I knew from the waterfront tiki bars of Sarasota. I met some of my favorite people at tiki bars. Luc was in his early thirties, a quiet, skinny kid, with a wisp of a hopeless mustache above his lip. Though I guessed I was about eight or ten years his senior, we had become friendly at the outdoor boozers primarily due to the goodly amount of time I'd spent in Europe; the young Swiss had found a comfort zone with me. Early on, I'd made the mistake of confessing I could still speak fairly fluent French and he rarely spoke English to me again. I seldom experienced headaches from hangovers, but force me to speak French for a couple of hours and, zap! a near migraine.

Luc had shown more than a casual interest in my international trading background. In passing, I'd mentioned I'd been involved with various export activities, ranging from used sports cars to refurbished MRI machines and a myriad of goods and commodities in-between. When not asking about my projects, he would entertain me with stories about his father's watch manufacturing company in Neuchâtel, Switzerland, little histories which I found genuinely interesting. Luc explained how his father, frustrated over their lack of other than European sales outlets, had sent him packing to travel haplessly around the world for a few years in search of importers, to date with limited successes.

I learned Luc had been more or less drafted into the family business following his university years—and he hated it.

"Dane, I'm nothing like my father. He has a true passion for the watch business. He's good at it. He loves it. He's the most creative designer in Switzerland. But that's not me."

"What would you do if you left your dad's company?"

"You'll think it's ridiculous. My father does. I want to get into my own business, nothing to do with watches."

"And that would be?"

"I want to be a professional fisherman. A charter boat captain."

Oh boy, perfect. Pop sends the kid off to Florida to open some U.S. and Latin American markets and junior decides to go fishing.

"I told my father about you, about your international marketing business, and how you might be of some help to him. He was very receptive to the idea, particularly when I told him you spoke French. Like many Swiss, he speaks French, German, and Italian, but his English is quite limited."

I had no idea how I could possibly help the owner of a Swiss watch company, especially while conversing exclusively in French.

"He asked me to invite you to meet with him in Paris for a day

5

or two to maybe get some ideas from you. At your convenience, of course. Naturally, he'll be paying your travel costs and a consulting fee."

I'd heard worse offers, and I had absolutely nothing on my plate for the next several weeks, nor the foreseeable future. "Luc, I appreciate your confidence in me, but I've got kind of a hectic schedule right now. I really don't know when I could break free, even for a few days," I answered before remembering he'd seen me around the coastal drinkeries every afternoon this week.

Luc flashed a grin. "I should mention he'll pay for first class passage, and your choice of hotel."

The kid clearly wanted me to meet his father, and he was hitting all the right buttons for me to do exactly that. A little jaunt to Paris was becoming quite doable. Before I could ask about fees, he stepped right into my office.

"My father asked me to tell you he'd be pleased to pay you one thousand dollars per day—travel time included—if you could meet with him at your earliest convenience."

A first class trip to Paris for a long weekend, and four or five grand for my trouble? Yup, in a hot second. My daybook was magically clearing itself.

"How's your father's schedule for this Saturday, Luc?"

* * *

The dramatic deceleration was impressive. The cabin instrument displays were now indicating our speed had dropped to Mach 0.5, something around 330 miles per hour at our present altitude. The chief steward approached my seat. "Mr. Baron, the captain asked me to inquire if you would be interested in taking the cockpit jump seat for landing?" he whispered.

I smiled broadly and nodded.

"Please follow me, sir."

He opened the door to the flight deck, stepped back to let me pass, and gestured toward the empty seat on the left behind the captain. While the passenger cabin offered adequate clearance for my six-foot-two, two-hundred-and-ten-pound body, I now found myself hunching over a little.

A formidable array of instruments and switches were crammed above and below the windshield, as well as on both sides of the surprisingly narrow cockpit area. The pilots' instrument panel had displays completely foreign to me; it might as well have been a space vehicle for as much as I recognized. Droop nose and visor selector, G-meter, center of gravity indicator, Machmeter—all very cool stuff.

I secured my shoulder harness and the flight engineer silently pointed to the audio jack on my left as he reached across, handing me a headset. Captain Mulholland's voice came through the intercom.

"Welcome to our office, Mr. Baron. We thought you might enjoy seeing our approach from up here. We're presently thirty-five miles out from Heathrow. Ivor will be taking this landing," he said, nodding toward his first officer in the right seat.

I had a reasonable view of things over the captain's right shoulder but still found myself leaning forward and farther to the right for a better look. The moveable nose cone had already been lowered, affording fairly unrestricted forward visibility.

"Captain Mulholland, when the droop snout is raised up, when you're at altitude and cruise speed, how can you see your traffic through what I imagine is nothing more than a little slit?"

"Mr. Baron, you're a pilot, think about it." He shifted in his seat to face me. "At almost sixty thousand feet, our only possible traffic would be a westbound Concorde or a military jet, and air traffic control keeps us well separated, both horizontally and vertically. But should there be a target approaching, it likely also would be traveling at Mach two. Possibly faster. Therefore, our closing speed on the other aircraft would be about one mile per second. In other words, once you recognized something out that windscreen, by the time you could take evasive action, you'd already have collided with it. So it really doesn't matter that we can barely see a damned thing out there. Reassured?"

"That was undoubtedly my dumbest question since flight school. Sorry, I'll shut up now."

"Speedbird Concorde zero zero two, Heathrow approach. Report localizer established Nine Left," I heard through my earphones. I assumed Speedbird was ATC's call sign for British Airways.

"Heathrow approach, roger. Speedbird Concorde double oh two, localizer established Zero Nine Left."

"Speedbird zero zero two, contact Heathrow tower on one eighteen decimal seven."

"One one eight decimal seven, Speedbird two. Cheers."

We were now set up on a long straight-in approach for landing from the west, and from what I'd read about Concorde, anything but a straight-in this evening could become rather sporty. In the race to beat the Russian's Tupolev to fly the first operational supersonic transport, certain compromises had been required on the Concorde project. The consortium of four British and French engineering and manufacturing firms had crossed into a frontier of aircraft development never before explored, resulting in many concessions, not the least of which was the airplane's limited fuel capacity. Having taken off three hours and twenty minutes ago, we were beginning to push the envelope on Concorde's airborne endurance—I was confident Concorde had never been stacked in a holding pattern for landing.

"On speed, sinking eight hundred," Capt. Mulholland called out, indicating Ivor's approach speed was normal, and we were descending at eight hundred feet per minute.

"Gear down," the F.O. requested.

The captain moved his right hand to the copilot's side of the center control panel and pulled down on the landing gear selector. I strained to get my first glimpse of the runway.

"Gear down," the captain confirmed.

"Speedbird Concorde double oh two, Heathrow tower. Wind zero five zero degrees at ten, gusts to fifteen. You are number one, cleared to land Zero Nine Left."

"Roger, tower. Double oh two cleared to land Zero Nine Left."

Now four or five miles distant, the runway slowly began to grow larger through the windshield.

Ivor subtly applied a slight back pressure on the yoke to begin his minimal flare from our already high angle of attack as the aircraft approached the airport fence. Seconds later, we gently touched down on the concrete like a butterfly with burnt feet, and almost instantly, reverse thrust was initiated on all four engines. The deceleration was unlike anything I'd ever experienced; we slowed from 180 miles per hour to less than 50 in short seconds.

The airplane seemed to stand on its nose before the thrust reversers disengaged and the noise level dropped.

"Speedbird double oh two, vacate Left and turn right for reverse turnoff Taxiway Bravo. Contact ground decimal niner. Good evening, sir," the tower transmitted. The captain read back his taxi instructions and switched the radio to ground control frequency 121.9 as advised.

Capt. Mulholland turned back toward me. "And that's how that's done, Mr. Baron. Will you be taking Concorde back to America on your return?"

"I really don't know yet. I'm off to Paris on Saturday afternoon and things are kind of open after that. I think a return flight on Concorde might be a little disappointing after sitting up here with you guys. Many thanks. Really enjoyed the ride. Now I'd better get back to where I belong. And Captain, I'll send that manual off to you in a day or two."

* * *

The thirty-some minute ride into the Mayfair district passed quickly and quietly in the rear seat of the hotel's Bentley Brooklands. We turned off Park Lane into Grosvenor Square, past the massive eagle over the American Embassy, and finally into Brook Street, where, a block away, I recognized the hotel's canopy by the flags flying above it.

"Good evening, Mr. Baron. Welcome back to Claridge's," the fortyish reception manager greeted me from his side of an oversized Victorian mahogany desk. "Our records indicate it's been only three months since your last visit. I trust you've been well, sir?"

"Yes, thanks very much. Always a pleasure to return to the hotel." I handed him my passport and signed the register.

"We've reserved the same room for you in which you stayed on your last visit, sir—overlooking Brook Street. We've noted you would like the International Herald-Tribune at your door in the morning, along with the Financial Times, and no starch in your shirts. Also, a bottle of Black Label and an ice bucket have been placed in your room. Unless your preferences have changed, I trust this meets with your requirements, Mr. Baron?"

"Uh, yes, thanks. That's perfect."

As I followed my bellman to the elevator, I took a glance back at the revolving glass entry door to see a tall, beaming, honey-haired beauty opening her arms as she rushed toward me across the lobby. In three weeks, she'd jolt my world with the force of an eight-point earthquake.

Chapter 2

London

Three months earlier—Friday evening, 14 April 2000

Regina Domenico had been referred to me soon after I assumed responsibilities for Arnaud's United Kingdom sales. An account manager for a medium-sized English advertising firm, she'd approached Arnaud several years ago in an attempt to assist in his local marketing efforts. While Arnaud ultimately chose not to pursue this avenue, he told me Regina had greatly impressed him with her creativity. He hadn't mentioned her looks.

I arrived at the subtly impressive China Tang Bar in the Dorchester on Park Lane a few minutes past five to see what I hoped was a Regina, sitting alone, waving from one of the cocktail tables. She looked to be in her early thirties . . . and she was elegant. Her loosely cascading below-shoulder length reddish-blonde hair perfectly complemented her tanned face. The epitome of understatement, she wore no jewelry and I perceived only the slightest touch of make-up, a delicate suggestion of coral lipstick. Standing, her impeccably tailored pure white suit exquisitely highlighted the alluring lines of her chest and hips. She was stunning. I was smitten.

"Dane?" she asked, here generous lips revealing the finest white smile I'd ever seen in England. Approaching me in her stilettos, she was nearly six feet tall.

"Regina, it's great to finally get together." I was trying not to swoon, stutter, or sweat as we shook hands. "I've been looking forward to meeting you ever since I heard Arnaud's glowing endorsements."

"Don't embarrass me. I blush easily," she said with a hint of a demure wink from her dazzling neon blue eyes. "And please, call me Gina."

"All right." My God, the woman was gorgeous. "Please, sit. How do you maintain such a beautiful tan here in England?" Ever the master of the suave small talk.

"Oh, thank you. I've only just returned from a fortnight's skiing holiday on the Continent. My family has a little chalet in Celerina, near to St. Moritz. We had a brilliant time. But the two weeks seemed to have passed far too quickly."

We? "Let me order us some drinks from the bar. What would you care for, Gina?"

"A cassis would be lovely. Thanks."

The slightly built Asian waiter whom I hadn't seen standing directly behind me repeated Gina's order. "I understand a cassis for the lady, and what may I bring for the gentleman?"

"Good afternoon. Johnnie Walker Black, please. Large glass, lots of ice."

The waiter offered the slightest of bows and departed for the bar.

"Are you staying here at the Dorchester, Dane?"

"No, I'm at Claridge's, a few blocks up the road. But I prefer the bar here at the China Tang. A little more relaxed. Have you been here before?" Damn, why not just say, *do you come here often?* So much for suave.

She raised one eyebrow. "Oh, Claridge's. Very posh. I've had tea there several times with my mum. They serve the most delicious scones and savories. Sorry, no, I haven't been in this room before, but I will again. I love the decor."

"Does your mother live here in London?" I asked, thinking inquiring about mom would deftly ease into her personal life. I was still wondering about the *we* she'd mentioned earlier.

"No, she's in Cambridge, actually. I was born there. Both my parents teach at the University."

I was trying to pin down her accent: English "public" school with Continental overtones, I concluded. "Tell me more. Sounds like an interesting family."

Gina hesitated while the waiter carefully and silently placed our drinks on the table. With her glass raised, she offered, "Cheers. Here's to our finally meeting. All right, a short bio, if you're really interested. But stop me if I start to ramble.

"My parents moved to the U.K. from Switzerland shortly before I was born. My father comes from Lugano, in the Italian-speaking canton of Ticino, in the south of the country. My mother's from Luzern, in the central Swiss German area. I went through my early schooling here in England, until my early teens, when my parents packed me off to Switzerland to live with my aunt in Luzern for my final four years of school. On graduation, I was, of course, completely fluent in English, as well as the three main Swiss languages, German, French, and Italian. Then I came back to England to attend the University of Cambridge—naturally Cambridge, where else would I go?" With an exaggerated eye roll, she reached for her cassis.

"I'm embarrassed to say that's far more than I've ever revealed to a prospective client on a first meeting. Now let me hear a little about you. All Arnaud told me was that you've been in charge of his international marketing and sales for a few years, you're from America, and I would like you. And so far, I concur on the latter point."

She returned her drink to the table and leaned forward, coquettishly laying her chin onto her down-turned clasped hands and gazing at me through exaggerated wide-eyed blinks. She knew she was destroying any protective reservation I could possibly summon up.

"Go ahead, your turn," she coaxed as she seductively tongued her lips.

"Okay, but it's not nearly as interesting as your story," I started hesitantly. "And I *will* be brief. First generation born in the U.S., my father Hungarian, my mother Danish. When I was eleven, I moved to Paris with my parents for my father's work and lived there for six years, through high school. I returned to the States for college, and after graduation from the University of Miami, I joined the Air Force, went through Officer Training School in Alabama, and then on to flight school in Texas. I received my wings and was assigned to C-130s, a four-engine turboprop cargo airplane. Real airplanes have propellers, you know.

"After three years serving as copilot, I was promoted to captain and moved over to the left seat. For reasons I won't get into right now, after almost seven years of driving airborne semi-trucks, I

15

stopped flying and was reassigned to an embassy job in Paris, only because I could still speak fairly acceptable French. My job there was to attend embassy parties and write reports about what I'd heard. They even gave me a cost of living pay increase. So, better pay, living in Paris, and going to parties, yeah, I had a pretty good gig for a while. Three years to be exact.

"I resigned my commission after ten years in the Air Force, returned to Florida, and through various accidental but happy circumstances, I found myself involved in the export business, usually working with different overseas partners. We exported Corvettes and Harley-Davidsons to France and Belgium, gray market software to Scandinavia, zero-timed used MRI machines to the U. K. and Ireland. You name it, I tried to move it. For the most part, it was a lot of fun, and on a good day, fairly profitable. The tax situations were also attractive. And that, in a nutshell, is the name of that tune."

Her focus was seductively transfixed on my eyes as I recited my little history—she was flirting with me.

Our waiter reappeared in a most timely fashion, our glasses now nearly emptied.

"The same?" I asked.

"Uh, no. I'll have a Pimm's Cup this time. Thanks."

"Another Scotch, please."

The waiter nodded before retreating with his little bow.

"Now, your Christian name and your sandy hair obviously come from your Danish mother, but your surname of Baron, with an Hungarian father?"

"One of those Ellis Island screw-ups. Ellis Island's located at the mouth of the Hudson River in New York Harbor, where

16

European immigrants arrived for their processing. My grandparent's real Hungarian name—Bárány—was apparently too weird or had too many accent marks for the immigration agent and he changed it on the spot. Baron's easier to pronounce, so it's probably a blessing it was changed to make everyone's life simpler."

"Interesting. I envy your flying background," Gina commented as the waiter returned with our cocktails. "I took my first lesson down in St. Moritz in a Cessna only last week. I absolutely loved it. Now, before you get me overly refreshed with these drinks, let's talk about how I'm going to land your U.K. advertising account."

With her head slightly tilted and her cobalt eyes continuing to laser mine, she reached down to retrieve the art portfolio resting next to her chair.

"I've brought along some very rough preliminary layout ideas for you to look at, Dane. Before I have our artsy people get into anything too specific, of course, I'll need to see some more of your product line. Maybe you can give me some more background on the firm itself," Gina requested as she unzipped her case.

She laid out a stack of sketches, most showing eye-catching females prominently displaying watches on their wrists as they lolled across the hood of an Aston or a Rolls. Some were lounging in negligees on animal skin covered beds. Fifteen minutes passed before I realized I hadn't a clue as to why I was here.

"Gina, you've clearly gone to a great deal of time and effort in putting all this together, but I have a minor problem: You could show me your most creative ideas for the rest of the evening and I still wouldn't know which way to go on this thing. Let me try to describe some of Arnaud's concepts and maybe it'll give you a better notion about what we're doing."

"Perfect, although I should mention I must be off by half six. I'm so sorry. I have something I must do. But please, continue."

I shouldn't have been surprised she had something to do on a Friday night, but it did bring me back to the sad reality that this was a business meeting, not a date for drinks. And I would be sleeping alone tonight.

I took a glance at my watch. "All right, I promise to get you out of here in a half-hour, but let me order us one last round before you go." Our Asian waiter was already walking toward our table.

"We'll have two more, please."

"I think I'll change again. A Campari and soda, please."

"Yes, madam, and another Black Label for the gentleman," he confirmed politely but matter-of-factly, turning back to the bar.

I was more than curious about her eclectic drink orders but I didn't comment. The first two had no apparent effect, and unfortunately, I wouldn't be around later to see the results of the third.

"When we have a little more time, I'll show you my sample case," I said, and immediately kicked myself, thinking, Jesus, that came out a lot like, *let me show you my etchings*. "Most watch companies' lines have the usual large Rolex chronometer styles, the French Cartier tanks, et cetera. But Arnaud's designs are truly unique."

"How much longer will you be in London? I'd love to see them. It'll obviously help me to see what he's done."

"I'm leaving for Basel tomorrow morning. I told Arnaud I'd help him with his sales stall for a few days at the Watch and Jewelry Fair. Are you familiar with it?"

"Dane, have you already forgotten I'm Swiss as well as English?" she smiled. "Of course I know about the Watch Fair. It's the biggest expo we have in Switzerland, but there most of us call it the Müstermesse. I've been through it a once or twice with my parents, years ago. It was fascinating. I'd love to see it again some time."

Oh, really?

"Gina, I just had a thought, and please take this as it's meant. How about flying down to Basel with me for a quick look at what we're doing. I'll be paying, of course."

Her smile grew as she leaned forward to retrieve her Campari. She turned and looked vacantly toward the bar. Then back to me. "I told you I must be off by half six. I'm taking my son up to Cambridge by train so he can stay with his grandparents this weekend. I wanted to free up a day or two in case we needed more time together to discuss your project."

"Great. Does that mean you'll fly down to Basel?"

"Is your invitation dependent upon my sleeping with you once we get there?"

I couldn't accuse her of not being direct. "Not at all. Strictly business," I answered with my best shot at a straight face.

"I'd love to check out the expo again, especially as an insider this time. And I haven't seen Arnaud in years. Okay, I'll do it. But I think I'll only fly down for the day. I'm sure hotel rooms in and around Basel are booked a year in advance for the Fair."

"Don't worry about a room. Arnaud and I have reservations at the Drei Könige for a two-bedroom suite with a living room. I'll take the fold-out couch in the center room and you can have one of the bedrooms. There, it's settled." I leaned back and crossed my arms, most pleased with my prospects.

"The Drei Könige?" she repeated, raising her eyebrows again in mock affectation. "My, you do have good taste in hotels. But I couldn't relegate you to a roll-out bed in your own suite."

"Well, there are other options if you feel that strongly about it."

"Okay, you've got a deal. And thanks for taking the roll-out." Her eyes twinkled.

"Not a problem. And I agree: The Drei Könige is an incredible place. But in our case, it's more of a utilitarian choice. We try to set up appointments with a few key prospects at the show and invite them over to our suite for hors d'oeuvres and drinks in the evening."

"Sounds promising. So when do we leave?"

"I have reservations on BA tomorrow morning at nine. I'll call later and get you a seat. When would you like to return?"

"It will have to be Sunday, I'm afraid. I'll have my parents put my son on a Sunday evening train back to London and I'll have to be here to collect him. My car's been at the mechanic's in Cambridge all this week. I'll drive it down early tomorrow morning. What time should I come round to Claridge's?"

"About seven-thirty, if that's not too early."

"Not a problem. I'll meet you in front of your hotel. Now, I must be off or we'll miss our train from King's Cross." She rose to organize her belongings, then, extending her hand to shake mine, she pulled me slightly closer and kissed my cheek. "Till tomorrow, then. Bye, Dane."

"Okay, see you in the morning, Gina. By the way, is your son a skier?" I asked as a none too subtle afterthought as she was starting to leave.

She stopped and slowly turned back toward me. "Yes, Dane, he is. And he was also my traveling companion on my holiday, if that's what you're asking. Cheerio," she answered with another wink before walking toward the door with an ever so slightly exaggerated hip swing.

I motioned for the waiter. "I'll do one more, please. And this *will* be my absolute final, final."

Chapter 3

London to Basel

Saturday morning, 15 April 2000

The male flight attendant wished us good morning, glanced at our boarding passes, and gestured toward our seats, one row back on the right, numbers 2 A and B.

"Dane," Gina said after taking the window seat, "this is so good of you to treat me to this weekend. This working weekend, I should say. I only hope something constructive comes of it and you haven't wasted your money."

I withheld my temptation to reply with some cute and other than subtle risqué response.

"Please, you're doing me a huge favor. I'm sure you'll come up with all kinds of creative ideas."

"I'll do what I can, but I must say this is the first time I've ever traveled with a client. I'm sure it will be the big gossip amongst my colleagues when I return to the office Monday," she said, lightly touching my arm on the console between us.

The steward approached our seats holding a silver tray upon which were placed flutes of bubbly Mimosas and almost look-alike plain orange juices. We each happily accepted the former.

"Now, before we start working, and to change subjects a bit, I didn't have a chance last evening to ask much about your flying career. Tell me more. I'm really quite interested."

Crap. I didn't want to get into the whole nasty story with her but I couldn't think of a way of politely dodging it; it wasn't one of the proudest junctures in my life.

"All right, if you insist. After I graduated from Undergraduate Pilot Training at Sheppard Air Force Base in Wichita Falls—that's in Texas—the Air Force approved my dream sheet request to get in the track to train on C-130s. I saw an air show when I was a kid in Paris where one of the acts was a C-130 Hercules taking off with JATO rockets—that's Jet Assist Take-Off—strapped on the rear of the fuselage. The airplane flew off the runway like a popping Champagne cork. It was about the coolest thing I'd ever seen. I guess I just kind of naturally gravitated to the plane after that. I never considered flying anything else. Most guys put in for fighter training, so getting my first pick on C-130s was a snap.

"As I mentioned yesterday, after three years of flying copilot, I was promoted to captain and moved over to the left seat as aircraft commander. A year later, I was reassigned to Ramstein Air Base in Germany, about sixty miles south of Wiesbaden. It was a great assignment: Just keep the pointy end of the airplane into the wind, and transport bodies, beans and bullets to and from contingency locations. Life was good. Then one clear, sunny day a couple years later, I destroyed one of their airplanes and one of their men."

Gina's expression turned to unsettled concern. She placed her drink on the console between us. "What happened?"

"Well, briefly, I was assigned a newly minted butter bar second lieutenant, fresh out of flight school. He was to do his on-the-job training under me. I knew after the first few minutes of flying with him he wasn't anything close to being a natural pilot. He struggled with everything. He was always behind the airplane instead of thinking a few steps ahead.

"On a routine training flight several days after he came aboard, I gave him the airplane, meaning it was his to land on the approach we were shooting at Ramstein. He was doing fine; he had the airplane perfectly trimmed up, on glide slope, and on speed. Everything was cool, up until we crossed over the perimeter fence just before the runway. I still don't know how the hell he did it, but he inadvertently yanked up on the throttles, which immediately reversed the pitch on the props. I should have been watching him even closer than I was.

"I guess we hit a little turbulence before he started his flare for landing, and maybe that jarred his arm. Anyway, all hell broke loose. You're coming in over the fence, on speed, then the pitch on the props is reversed, so now you're down below stall speed—and bam! The C-130 simply stopped flying twenty-five feet over the runway threshold. We augered in and literally belly flopped onto the concrete. The thirty million dollar-plus aircraft was totaled, and my loadmaster—Senior Master Sergeant Robert Washington—broke his back on impact. He's now a paraplegic. Fortunately, there was no fire, and the other crew members weren't too badly injured.

"After a brief inquiry, the Air Force decided they didn't want me to break any more of their airplanes, so they sent me to our embassy in Paris where I couldn't smash anything. Just keep my eyes and ears open and speak French at diplomatic parties and write reports on what I'd heard."

Gina was listening intently without interruption. "But it wasn't your fault. Why would the Air Force ground you and not the young lieutenant?"

"Oh, believe me, they took his ticket on the spot. But as aircraft commander, everything that happened on a flight was my responsibility. I understand they had to bust me: I screwed the pooch. One very expensive airplane was totaled under my command, and one very good guy had his life ruined on my watch."

She gently took my left arm with both of her hands. "Dane, what a horrible story . . . for everyone involved."

"Yeah, that incident really messed me up for a while. It still does. Anyway, that's the last time I flew an airplane. Never again. I've got no problem being a passenger on the bus now . . . as long as it's in the front of the bus."

I think Gina was sensing this was a delicate subject and she considerately didn't pursue it. She turned to look out her window for a few moments before changing the conversation. "I told my son a bit about you. He couldn't stop asking questions: 'Where does he live in America? Does he play American football? Has he ever been to Texas?' Et cetera, et cetera. I told him you're a big man, and therefore you probably had been a footballer, you now live in Florida, and I was sure you'd been to Texas at some point. My God, he's fascinated with anything American these days, especially Texans. Too many hours spent watching the telly, I'm afraid. Fortunately, he's not too envious of my going to Switzerland this weekend since we were just there for his spring holidays. In fact, I think he's jolly well happy to be back with his mates and away from mum for a bit. And he does understand it's a business trip."

Gina had a breezy, yet poised, demeanor about her as she spoke. It was a facile, freewheeling attitude, not the least bit pretentious. For as beautiful and confident as she was, she evidenced not a hint of conceit or arrogance. I was fully enjoying her company and let her go on, surprising myself with how entertaining I found her stories about her son.

"What's your boy's name?"

"Willie. Actually, it's William. When I chose his name, my mother was pleased to no end, thinking I'd named him after the legendary Swiss, William Tell. I never told her I hadn't considered that connection. I was thinking of William the Conqueror. After all, Willie was born in England. He's just turned ten. He's a wonderful boy. I love him to death. And he's a great sport: My flat's so small, Willie's on the living room sofa at night. But I'm hopeful someday soon, I'll be able to afford to buy something larger and give him his own room. I want to put him into a preparatory school this fall, followed by public school—which would be known as a private school in America—and finally, university after that. I'm going to need a great deal of money in the near future, Dane, so hopefully you'll like what I'll be able to do for the Laurel Watch Company."

I smiled without comment. Subtlety wasn't her strong suit, but nor did she make any attempt at it.

"I'll bet he really misses you when you're away."

"Not that much, I afraid," she answered with a great laugh. "Willie absolutely adores staying with his grandparents. He has several young friends in their neighborhood in Cambridge and he's always quite keen to go up there. He loves my parents' cooking— my father making him Italian dishes, and my mother the Swiss

German stuff. Sadly, I normally don't make the time to do a lot of cooking myself. During the week, I'll usually pick up takeaway at a chippy or curry house or something. When I do cook, I'll throw together a bubble and squeak, or bangers and beans or something. But it sustains life, and Willie continues to grow. Unfortunately, I possess none of my parents' culinary skills," she said with a small shrug and a grin.

The flight attendant returned, offering a second round of drinks. Gina requested a coffee, saying, with a busy day ahead of her, one "Buck's Fizz" was more than ample at this hour.

I called them Mimosas, and had another. It was too early for Scotch.

Chapter 4

Basel

Saturday afternoon, 15 April 2000

Though most of the population in Basel speak German, the Swiss Germans consider themselves to be a cut above their German neighbors to the north (which takes some doing). The Swiss French lust to be Parisians, and the Ticinesi, the Swiss Italians, are envious of both the Swiss Germans and the Swiss French, but are mostly pleased they weren't born in Italy. The Romansch don't count; they'd been all but absorbed by the Swiss Germans in the eastern canton of Graubünden.

Maybe I hadn't spent enough time here, but as European, or for that matter, as Swiss cities went, Basel wasn't on my hit parade. However, Basel hosted the annual Watch and Jewelry Fair, and that made me money.

The city's massive convention center, Basel's primary *raison d'être* with well over a million square feet of exhibit space was only a short cab ride from the airport. But then, every drive in Switzerland is a short ride—it's a short country. Equipped with a map of the multi-block center, I started to lead Gina past countless watch manufacturers' stalls, all seemingly amping out cacophonous Eurodance waves of synthesizers and electronic rhythms. Slowing to recheck my map, I noticed the Laurel signage brightly displayed in gold on black amidst a wreath. Laurel was the Anglicization of Arnaud's surname, Laurent.

His stall was slightly larger than last year's, having grown to maybe five hundred square feet. As we entered, a dazzling young female model type in a tight black sweater and a red leather mini was playing bartender to a heavyset Arab visitor with two plastic goodie bags in his hands. Arnaud was seated twenty feet away, opposite a man and a woman in an offset conversation area. Seeing us wave, he nodded slightly and continued on with his meeting.

Arnaud had opted for one of the likely more expensive decor packages the expo offered its exhibitors: black carpeting complemented by mirrors and black-and-gold striped wallpaper to match his logo colors. With muted Bach harpsichords pleasingly audible in the background, it was all quite elegant and successfully reflective of the Laurel marque. He had done a magnificent job. Again.

Arnaud had designed many attractive new pieces over the winter and I noted he'd kept with his successful and distinctive unisex theme throughout the collection. They were stunning, and unlike anything I'd seen previously. One particularly striking example featured an octagonal gold case with a dial of midnight blue lapis lazuli stone; only the gold Roman numerals *XII, III, VI,* and *IX,* and a gold wreath enclosing the word *Swiss* appeared on the face. Arnaud did things with geometry and colors few artists were capable of conceiving, let alone designing. He was a true architect of watches. No chronometers or sport watches here. Not a sweep-second hand in the entire line. Not a single knock-off of the industry standards. And not a bracelet in the lot; Arnaud eschewed metal bracelets in favor of only the warmer leather and hide straps —pig, cow, croc and gator.

I found myself smiling as I recalled a moment from last year's show when I'd greeted a white-robed Arab accompanied by his two praetorian guards. After extending my hand and, in my best Arabic, I offered, "*Salaam aleikom. Neek hallak?*"— Hello. How are you?—the bodyguards stiffened in unison before the sheik returned my smile, shook my hand, and replied in perfect British public school English, "I believe you meant to say '*Kaifa haloka*,' sir, and I'm fine, thank you. Not to embarrass you, but you told me to go shag myself." So much for picking up my linguistic tips from a Bedouin bartender at the Cairo Marriott.

Gina rescued me from my inattentive reverie. "Dane, I think I'll take a stroll around the hall if you don't mind. It'll give you some time alone with Arnaud when he breaks free."

"Sure, no problem. Have fun."

I turned to see Arnaud had stocked his little bar with all top shelf brands. Nice touch. Expected, but nice.

"Monsieur, may I offer you a drink while you're waiting for Monsieur Laurent?" Arnaud's hostess asked me in French.

I approved of his Scotch selection. And his hiring policy. "Yes, please. I'll have a Black Label, with lots of ice." Arnaud's young temp—Veronique, according to her name tag—added a bright and energetic touch to the room, something definitely lacking at last year's show when Arnaud and I alternated at playing bartender.

Veronique and I chatted casually for several minutes until Arnaud rose and escorted his guests to the door where cards, smiles, and handshakes were exchanged. Arnaud then turned and said, in French, to my frustration, "Dane, it's good to see you, my boy. You're looking well."

"And you. Arnaud, the stall looks terrific. Much better than last year."

He nodded graciously and reached across to open a small green Perrier bottle, emptying it into a crystal tumbler. "I'm so pleased Regina was able to come along with you. She's a wonderful girl. Listen to me—I should say she's a wonderful woman. I've known her for so long I still think of her as a little girl."

"I wasn't aware you'd known one another that long. I thought you only met a few years ago over your advertising issues, before I came on board."

"No, no. I've known Regina all her life. Her father and I went to university together in Zürich, at the Federal Institute of Technology. Did Regina tell you that he and his wife Juliette are professors at the University of Cambridge in England?"

"Yes, she did. And I'm glad she came with me. She's very pleasant to be around. She's also very quick on the uptake."

Arnaud chuckled. "Dane, you forget: She's Swiss. She may have been born in England, but she's still Swiss, through and through. And all self-respecting Swiss have a latent passion for the watch business. It's our heritage. Come, let's sit and get caught up on things," he said, gesturing toward the sitting area.

Arnaud Laurent was of average height and weight, in his late fifties, as fit as a man fifteen years younger, and blessed with the quintessential eye for fashion. Everything about Arnaud exhibited a certain brio and élan; at times, his breezy smile reminded me of Maurice Chevalier. Today he even made the standard navy blazer and gray trousers ensemble appear stylish with the addition of a dark blue knit tie over a broad striped red on white shirt. A very snappy looking guy. I wasn't so sure about the tan suede loafers, but he was the fashion guru, not me.

"So, Arnaud, how goes the show?" I asked, switching to English; it was work speaking French. Arnaud had forced me to learn how to field strip a watch and know every part name in French, but it was still a pain in the ass for me to speak it for hours on end.

"The European business is still quite good," he responded in French, not skipping a beat. "I have my old and steady clients of years and years. Thankfully, they're still loyal to me, and the high end of this business, our product line, for example, hasn't been overly affected by this global economic slowdown. Your American and Arab exports should be very strong, I suspect."

While the least expensive Swiss watches retailed for around $200 and change (versus $40 for the Japanese competition), our Laurel products ranged between $2,000 and $3,000. Not nearly top end, but certainly in the better-kept slums of the neighborhood. The Japanese had yet to tap the upper end market, so far having left that specific business to the masters in Switzerland. And there was still a monumental difference in those five little letters on the bottom of a watch face: *Japan*, or *Swiss*.

"Your clients are loyal to you because of your designs and your quality. You're a lot more creative than you give yourself credit for, Arnaud. So, have you picked up many new clients in the last few days?"

The Basel Fair extended for more than a week, including the days allotted for the press and the public. The four or five days in-between were the meat of the show for the manufacturers, the period during which they pushed their new lines to their traditional customers and sought new sales outlets.

"It's been fine. Nothing spectacular, but more than acceptable," he said. "And I think you're starting to know me: You know I don't want to get deluged and be forced to take on bigger facilities and more staff. I'm a simple engineer turned watch designer, not a hungry businessman. I'll leave that to the larger and better known marques and the young lions. It's not my niche."

Arnaud's small offices and assembly rooms were located outside the French-speaking town of Neuchâtel, near the lake and in the canton of the same name, to the north of Lake Geneva. The nearby centuries old watchmaking towns of La Chaux-de-Fonds and Le Locle were big local draws for tourists, as this was the traditional home and the heart of the Swiss watch industry.

Most of Laurel's competition manufactured many times more units than Arnaud's facility. He had only increased his annual output beyond his normal 10,000 or so units in the past three years, since I'd joined him and found successes in increasing his international sales.

In many ways the consummate traditionalist, Arnaud religiously tried to stay with the classical mechanical jeweled movements, reluctant to cave to the mid- and late-twentieth century advent of quartz movements which now represented over ninety percent of all production in Switzerland. Only in the recent past had he acquiesced to some of his importers demands for more quartz.

"Quartz movements are pieces of electronics," he often said. "A true watch utilizes jeweled mechanical systems. I'm not an electrician or a computer scientist—I'm a watchmaker."

World demand be damned.

"Now that we have a little time to ourselves, I have a question for you, Dane. I was a little confused when you phoned and said you were bringing Regina with you from London. She's most welcome, of course, but I must say I was somewhat surprised. Let me be direct, if you don't mind: What are your intentions?"

I was hoping the phrase implied something different in French than it did in English. I couldn't resist: "Strictly honorable."

"Let me be more direct: Are you sleeping with her?"

Nope, wrong. It meant the same thing in French.

"No, and I'll admit it's a little unusual to bring along one's advertising rep after only one short meeting. But over drinks yesterday evening, I had an idea, an idea she doesn't know about yet." I paused until I'd regained his eye contact. "And it has absolutely nothing to do with romance. I want to bring her into my operation, as my importer for the U.K. and Ireland. Again, she has no idea that's why she's here."

Arnaud slowly rubbed his face with both hands and shook his head. He rose from his chair, went behind Veronique's bar, and returned with a double measure of Remy Martin. Both of his large manicured hands engulfed the cut crystal snifter while he swirled the Cognac and focused on me for several seconds, seconds which felt like endless minutes.

"Dane, I'm aware I have no say as to how you conduct your operations outside continental Europe. That's your territory now. I understand that. Nevertheless, on this issue of Regina Domenico, I don't think it's a good idea. She knows nothing about our business."

"Arnaud, you know I have nothing but total respect for you—as a friend, and as a master in the profession. However, when you say your objection to my giving importation rights to Gina is because she has no background in the business, you might recall that three years ago, I barely knew the difference between an atomic clock and an hourglass, and yet your importations outside Europe have been booming since I came aboard with you. Gina's a bright lady. She'll be a quick study. And just as importantly, and as you pointed out, she's Swiss. This business is part of her soul."

"I'm aware you didn't have a great deal of knowledge of my products when we first got together, but you already had well established international contacts you could exploit from the very beginning. That's why I wanted to work with you."

"Arnaud, you also wanted to work with me because I gave you two hundred and fifty thousand dollars for your international rights." The instant the words were out, I cringed, knowing his sensitivities would be stunned with such bluntness. "When your son Luc first approached me in Florida, it was ostensibly to set up a meeting for two or three days of consulting to advise you on tapping more international markets. But after you and I met and I delved a little deeper, I told you I'd like to have some type of involvement with your company. I'm sorry, my earlier comment was rude. But you know conversing in French is tough for me."

"Your French is fine, and I appreciate you not forcing me to speak in my terrible English. Your directness has nothing to do with speaking in a second language. We're friends, but we're also both businessmen, and sometimes directness is called for. No apology required. However, I think you know by now I didn't need your investment—I merely wanted to assure myself of your undivided attention to the task at hand. I still do. That's my prime objection here. And as a small point of correction, you did not *give* me two hundred and fifty thousand dollars—I *sold* you ex European distribution rights for that sum. Just to be clear."

"Point taken."

"All right, do as you will. I won't bring it up again." He looked across to Veronique, and with a circular wave over our two empty glasses, he motioned for refills. "You indicated Regina knows nothing of this offer yet. Why do you think she'll accept it? She already has a career in advertising."

"I can be very convincing . . . you may have seen that in me before. I have a vague guess as to what she's making now in the U.K. She'll jump at my offer."

In typically Gallic fashion, Arnaud shrugged his shoulders and opened his hands, palms out. "I've said what I had to say on the subject. Now, what do you think of the new designs?"

I was grateful for the change of gears and I complimented him generously on his new work. Arnaud sojourned alone for three weeks each winter while he worked on his designs for the April Basel exhibition. He kept a standing reservation at the Hôtel de Crillon in Paris for a one-bedroom suite the last three weeks of January. The hotel fronted on the place de la Concorde, where, when weather permitted, Arnaud would walk past the square into the Tuileries and sit for hours sketching watch designs.

I could imagine the sitting room of his suite in the Crillon, littered with sketches and balled up paper discards which had missed the trash basket. The maid service was likely restricted to only the bedroom and bath areas. However it happened—and whatever occurred in Paris—Arnaud would return to Neuchâtel the first of February refreshed and replete with twelve to fifteen new designs, a number which would be whittled down to six or seven after he and his craftsmen would make and reject some of the new prototype models. Demand at the Basel show would further narrow the year's new designs.

Arnaud's wife had never quite adapted to his private stays in Paris for these periods of epiphanous creation, and twenty years ago, they separated. Madame Laurent remained châtelaine of what I suspected was their grand house in La Chaux-de-Fonds, while Arnaud lived in an apartment he'd purchased for himself in Neuchâtel.

With a tone of resignation, Arnaud was discussing the increasing demand for more quartz movements from his established European clientèle when I saw Gina rushing down the concourse. I instinctively glanced at my watch and realized Arnaud and I had been talking for more than an hour without a single prospect having visited the Laurel displays.

Gina chatted briefly with Veronique, and then, armed with a frosty bottle of Evian in one hand and an oversized shopping bag hanging from the other, she joined us at our table.

With a broad smile, she said, "Gentlemen, I think I've made myself rather useful. I've taken the liberty of buying you a laptop computer, Arnaud. I can say with certainty yours is the only firm in this massive exhibition hall without one. And whilst you two are working away for the rest of today and tomorrow, I'll set you up with client contact lists, product pricing, ordering data, et cetera."

I looked at Arnaud and made no attempt to minimize my gloating grin.

Gina continued: "I also spent a bit of time chatting up several potential buyers as I was circulating. I invited those who showed more than a casual interest in the brochures up to your suite this evening. I should think we may have as many as fifteen or twenty turn up if they're good to their words. Mostly Europeans, but a few Yanks and Arabs may drop by as well. Oh, and one Japanese chap for sure."

Arnaud leaned back in his chair, locked his fingers behind his head, and smiled at me for the first time since we'd started our discussion. He hadn't seen fifteen prospects all day, let alone in a sales environment as captive as his hotel suite.

"Dane, I have a question for you," Gina said, her demeanor taking a more animated turn. "Are you personally handling the Laurel business in the U.K.? I ask because you haven't mentioned working with any importing firms."

Could it be? This was going to be simpler than I'd hoped. And possibly cheaper. "No, no importer yet. So far, I haven't exploited the area very effectively. Why do you ask?" I was doing my best not to break into a Mexican hat dance around the table.

"Well, if I may be a bit forward, I was rather expecting you to offer me the job before I flew home. I'm assuming you didn't bring me down to Basel just so I could gather ideas for an ad campaign. That made no sense. As I also assumed your intentions were professional and not personal, why else would I be here?"

Her logic was Sherlockian, with the exception of my not having a personal interest in her; I normally had all the subtlety of a bulldozer.

"I've been thinking about getting out of the advertising trade for a bit now. I want to become involved with something of my own, something more lucrative. So, yes, I accept your offer, with the possibly gross presumption it was going to be tendered, *and* knowing you will offer me a sizable increase over what I'm now earning with my present firm. After all, I am genetically Swiss, and what could be more natural than my working in the watch business?"

In less than thirty seconds, Gina had managed to cut through all my angst about convincing her to leave her job and accept my offer.

"Was I that obvious? Welcome aboard, Gina. And I'm sure I speak for Arnaud as well when I say that."

Chapter 5

Saturday evening, 15 April 2000

By seven o'clock, the living room of our suite in the Drei Könige was bustling with new prospects; I counted eight potentials from a quick scan of the room. Gina was smoothly shifting into hostess mode, occupying the new walk-ins with her friendly chatter until she saw either Arnaud or me become available.

I'd finished wrapping up an agonizingly boring conversation with one of Arnaud's long-established clients, an elderly woman from Stockholm, when I noticed Gina tending to a Japanese gentleman. He was typically conservatively dressed, and I guessed him to be his early sixties. I quickly leafed through my collection of business cards I'd had printed in English on one side and in the client's language on the reverse. Gina introduced the man as Mr. Toru Jioruji, correctly placing his last name first. After shaking hands with the requisite mini bow, mine slightly deeper than his, I presented my card with the Kanji script side up. I held out the card with both hands, having learned this little nicety on my previous trips to Japan. Toru reciprocated, and we each spent more than a moment respectfully and carefully reading each other's card before filing it away, another most civilized Japanese business tradition. Director of European Operations, Kizoku Holdings, Ltd., his card read, followed by an Osaka address and phone and fax numbers.

I vaguely recalled the Kizoku name from my earlier research. I only remembered Kizoku translated to *aristocrat* in English, they were involved in a myriad of different products and commodities —including the manufacturing of modestly priced watches—and there had been a hint of scandal several years earlier, the details of which escaped me.

Slowly and distinctly, not knowing how well—or if—my Japanese prospect spoke English, I said, "Toru-san, thank you for coming to our little reception." Gina handed him a snifter containing one ice cube and a large measure of what I presumed to be Cognac.

"Thank you for the invitation, Mr. Baron. I was planning on meeting with you at the Fair today but Miss Domenico invited me to your suite before I made it that far," he replied, his English most accomplished. Toru's carriage suggested he was at ease dealing with Westerners, a poise likely acquired from years of international contact. Raising his snifter, he added, "And my thanks for the fine Cognac. Exceptional. Remy Martin Louis the Thirteenth, if I'm not mistaken."

Impressive. Earlier this evening, before our visitors arrived, I watched as Arnaud poured the Louis XIII out of its original Baccarat crystal and into a nondescript squarish glass vessel. He explained, at almost $1,000 a bottle, his guests tended to request it less frequently when it came from a plain decanter. "But at the end of the week, I pour it back into its Baccarat and usually have more

41

than a half bottle remaining for myself . . . and it's tax deductible," he'd said with a sly smirk of contentment.

Toru was a short, thickset man. His shaved head barely reached my shoulder height. His attire was standard Japanese business, and clearly expensive: dark gray suit, starched white shirt with straight collar and button cuffs, solid navy blue tie, and shiny black plain toe shoes. In consummate contrast to his staid apparel, he was carrying a thin, dark green crocodile briefcase with gold finish hardware.

"Mr. Baron, I was very impressed with the Laurel brochures Miss Domenico gave me earlier today. Unfortunately, I am leaving tomorrow, but I am quite interested in speaking with you regarding some possible business between us."

"I'd be pleased to acquaint you with our new collection this evening if you have a little time. Are you flying back to Japan tomorrow or are you staying on in Europe for a while?"

"I've arranged a few days of vacation time for myself before I return to Osaka. I'm stopping off in Monaco for a bit of gambling. It's my one passionate vice. Do you know Monaco, Mr. Baron?"

I'd been traveling to Monaco almost annually for over ten years for my passion, the Formula One races. I knew the Principality's five hundred square acres intimately, and I immediately seized upon this most serendipitous icebreaker.

"Yes, I go there nearly every year, but not for the casinos. I'm a big fan of Grand Prix racing, and I try to make it down every spring. I could live there year round if I could figure out how to afford it," I laughed. "But I've heard one must have an eight digit dollar equivalent deposit on account with a Monégasque bank to gain permanent residency and I don't think I'll make that cut until at least next Thursday." My comments received a slight amused smile from the Japanese.

"Ah, so. An automobile aficionado. Are you a collector?"

"Sadly, no. I have a '78 308 GTS Ferrari at home, but usually I drive my motorcycle, an old Triumph Bonneville. I live on a little island in Florida a mile off the Sarasota coast called Lido Key where the speed limit's only twenty-five miles per hour, so the Ferrari's engine tends to get gummed up since it's seldom out of first or second gear. Seems I can only do about a thousand miles or so in it before it wants to visit the mechanic for a few days." In an attempt to move the conversation back to my guest, I asked, "Where are you staying in Monaco, Mr. Toru?"

"I've been at the Hôtel de Paris in the past, across from the casino. But since you obviously know the town much better than I, what is your preference?"

"The Hôtel Hermitage. It's directly behind the Hôtel de Paris, and since it's off Casino Square, it's a little quieter. I guess you could say there's more of an intimate feel to the place, and the Belle Époque architecture is every bit as impressive. Either way, they're both great places. They're both owned by the Société des Bains de Mer, same folks who own the casino."

"I will take your suggestion," Toru replied. "I'll see if I can change my reservations."

The requisite chitchat had served its purpose, and with luck, this was the contact I needed for my biggest and most dormant outlet. The Japanese market was the oyster I'd long been trying to crack, but after three exploratory trips there in the past three years since joining Arnaud, I'd had zip for success. My previous experiences in my meetings with the Japanese had been frustrating: extreme initial civility, followed by month after month of delays and untold further inquiries. I'd lost my patience with them; I'd had it with all their screwing around resulting in no action. But Toru coming to our little sales reception boded well. And I felt particularly grateful for whatever circumstance required his departure tomorrow, meaning we might actually get something accomplished tonight. Drinks in hand, I steered Toru to the couch facing one of our display tables.

"Mr. Baron, we are very familiar with your watches. As I would have expected, Monsieur Laurent's new offerings are exceptional. His designs have what we call *shibui* in Japanese—a thing of great elegance and simplicity completely devoid of any extraneous elements; concepts which are aesthetically pleasing to the eye. As Leonardo wrote, 'Simplicity is the ultimate sophistication.'"

"Thank you. I'll pass along your compliments."

"Mr. Baron, I must tell you my company has been following Laurel for several years now. No need to spend time showing me your collection. We know your product. Speaking for my fellow directors at Kizoku, I will pay you another compliment by being direct: We are not interested in buying your timepieces—we want to buy your company." Toru's focus didn't shift from me. "I particularly wanted to speak directly with you, Mr. Baron, in this regard."

Toru had blindsided me but I managed to muster my best aplomb and not spill any Scotch on my shoes. I pushed myself to say something before the silence grew too pregnant.

"Correct me, but I'm assuming you don't speak French or German, and therefore you'd prefer to speak with me rather than

Monsieur Laurent. But Mr. Toru, unless you're aware of something that I'm not, the last time I checked, Monsieur Laurent hadn't hung a for sale sign on his front door. Why would you possibly envision our company being interested in selling?"

"Mr. Baron, for over two years our group has been, should I say, investigating—and please excuse me if I am not using the right word here—investigating smaller Swiss watch manufacturers for the purpose of investment."

"It sounds as though you're more interested in acquisition than investment," I threw out to confirm we were on the same page. Given my personal history with the Japanese, I could fully appreciate it had taken Toru's team a couple of years to make this move, and I was grateful I hadn't approached them instead and been messed with for that long. I only hoped if something were to happen, the Japanese had finished their homework and were now ready to get off the pot.

"All right, acquisition, if you prefer," Toru replied.

"Well, if you're talking about buying our company, then I guess I would prefer the word acquisition since that's what it appears to be. But why are you particularly interested in the Laurel marque? There are dozens of other small companies here in Switzerland we compete with that you must have considered and researched." I was testing the water a bit here.

"A most reasonable question, Mr. Baron," Toru started, leaning back into the suede couch and crossing his legs to expose a chalk white shin above a too short black sock. "Naturally, my group has been most impressed with the Laurel design work. As you are well aware, a timepiece is valued for only three reasons, none of which is its accuracy. A watch is prized for its manufacturer's reputation, its attractiveness of design, and its precious metal or gem content. Everyone assumes a watch will keep the proper time, for as you know, this has been the case for over a hundred years since the jeweled movements were perfected. And that, coupled with the advent of quartz mechanisms more recently, has made accuracy a non-issue.

"People buy flash. Flash which happens to keep perfect time. Monsieur Laurent's new artistic designs are what keep his customers buying new watches they don't need. After all, who really needs jewelry? We are interested in your company because the Laurel brand is without parallel in design concept and reputation. We would like to add a company with Laurel's prestige to our group. Our company, Kizoku Holdings, is only interested in being associated with enterprises which share our own level of reputation for excellence and quality."

After three years of charging around the world finding successful importers, I'd achieved a reasonable level of good fortune, but it was fast becoming tedious. More to the point, it had become a real job, something anathema to my life's design of passing my days in tiki bars overlooking warm sandy beaches. My uniform days should have long since passed, but now I was back to wearing suits and ties and keeping appointments. If Toru's proposition had any worth to it, and knowing Arnaud would treat me fairly, this could be my out.

With the presumption the Kizoku group's offer was to be a serious one, convincing Arnaud to accept it would be one colossal undertaking. But he was a realist. He knew his forte was solely in design; he dreaded the business side of the operation. He didn't like it, and he knew he wasn't good at it. Hell, he'd only entered the computer age less than six hours ago.

I was eager to hear Toru's pitch. "Very well, Mr. Toru, I'll listen to your proposal, but I'm giving you absolutely no assurance Monsieur Laurent will have any interest whatsoever. Now, I assume you're aware of the difficulties involved with the Swiss government in regard to foreign ownership of Swiss companies, particularly in regard to the watch business? They're rather protective of their own."

Toru leaned forward and spoke quietly. "Yes, our legal staff has researched this potential problem quite thoroughly. Their recommendation is for our group to become an outside investor in your company, with Monsieur Laurent technically retaining titular ownership of Laurel. Of course, we would insist he stay on indefinitely in a design consulting capacity. That is why I initially called our proposal an investment, as opposed to an acquisition."

"So your plan is to continue to manufacture Arnaud's designs here in Switzerland, and not simply replace the word *Japan* with the word *Swiss* on the bottom of the dials of the watches you're presently producing?" I asked, perhaps somewhat gracelessly.

"Mr. Baron," Toru began to reply, outwardly untroubled by my comment. "Our current watch products will continue to be made in Japan, and continue to be marketed under the Kizoku brand. Our name carries considerable positive market recognition in Japan. Should we become involved with Laurel, the two companies would remain totally separate entities, but under one umbrella, if you will. Kizoku's interest in Laurel is purely for expansion into the upper end of the business."

"I think this conversation may be starting to get out of my pay grade, Mr. Toru," I said, feeling more confident about his command of English. "My professional association with Monsieur Laurent is strictly related to the international markets, exclusive of continental western Europe. I have absolutely nothing to do with the day-to-day business or financial affairs of the Laurel company. Monsieur Laurent continues to, and always will, retain complete control over those matters."

By now, the other remaining prospects—our "valued guests"—had left the suite, and in the background, over Toru's shoulder, I caught Arnaud's glacial glare. He was leaning against the portable bar, swirling a partially filled brandy snifter. I knew he had a problem with the Japanese, and I assumed that was the reason behind the contentious evil eye he was giving me. In years past, he'd had encounters with the Japanese, ostensibly buyers, who would come into his stalls at the Basel show and attempt to photograph his collections. He claimed one character had the audacity of trying to set up some macro-photography paraphernalia lest he miss any details. He threw out the "buyer" without a return invitation, complaining that at least he could buy the damned watch if he wanted to make a knock off of it. There was no paranoia here; Arnaud's concern over these scam artists was well-founded—they truly were trying to steal his designs. Though this was all several years back, he was still wary of the Japanese. Fortunately, he didn't know yet that Toru wasn't here merely to rip him off—he was here to take him out.

His voice now almost muted, Toru said, "Mr. Baron, we are aware of your situation with the Laurel company, that you are strictly involved in other than European operations. You are naturally concerned that should my group eventually reach a successful agreement with Monsieur Laurent, you would be out of a job. And that, unfortunately, would likely be true. But I have come to you for your help in facilitating our approach to Monsieur Laurent, and I am prepared to offer substantial compensation for your efforts in bringing our plan to fruition."

"Let me stop you right here, Mr. Toru," I jumped in, not hiding my irritation. The guy had balls of iron to think I'd hustle Arnaud. "Arnaud Laurent is not only my boss, he's my very good friend. I don't appreciate you attempting to have me influence him by my subliminal promotion of your company's goals. If you want to buy his company, pitch him, not me."

Ignoring my comment, Toru slowly cleared an area on the glass-topped table before him where he positioned his briefcase. With two audible clicks from the gold locks, he opened the case and withdrew a thin black leather binder, extending it across the table.

The file was only five pages in length, which I scanned in less than a minute. After skimming past the brief introductory boilerplate, I saw that the Kizoku group's proposal was basically quite succinct. They were to pay Arnaud $7 million within three months of his acceptance of their offer to purchase ninety percent of new stock to be issued by Laurel. Arnaud was to be paid an additional $250,000 for each of the next four years for design consultation. The Neuchâtel offices and assembly rooms were to be leased by Kizoku for a like period, four years, for an amount to be determined by professional survey of current market leases. At the end of the four years, the land and the improvements thereon would be purchased by Kizoku for a price ten percent over the appraised value at that time. And in a nutshell, that was that. Very straightforward, clear, and cut to the bone.

Arnaud had never confided in me regarding his profit margins, nor had I ever felt it was my place to ask. But I guesstimated he was personally grossing close to a million dollars a year, based on his current 20,000 unit annual production schedule, and after paying commissions on my sales of roughly half of the company's total output.

Toru's pitch was compelling, but I knew that regardless of the amount of their offer, Arnaud would likely reject it summarily, especially since it was coming from the Japanese.

"Mr. Toru," I finally said after several minutes of rereading the paperwork without expression, "obviously I will have no comment on your proposal. As I mentioned earlier, Monsieur Laurent's company is not for sale. But I will show this to him later tonight or tomorrow. I feel obliged at least to inform him of your interest."

"Thank you, Mr. Baron. That is all I can ask. Your courtesy is most appreciated. And to demonstrate our appreciation, I have been authorized to transfer one million U.S. dollars to an account of your choosing, subject to our offer being accepted by Monsieur Laurent . . . and the sale being consummated," he smiled.

A million bucks. Almost four years' worth of commissions in one shot. And back to wearing flip-flops, shorts, and tacky Hawaiian shirts for a while. It had a nice ring to it.

"I'll pass along your offer to Monsieur Laurent. And I'll take the liberty of adding your generous finder's fee to the bottom line and let him decide what to do with it."

The Japanese nodded, rose, gave me a slight bow, and departed after thanking me for our meeting. I turned to look at Arnaud, who was still working on his crystal snifter of Louis . . . and still giving me the hairy eyeball.

"Cheer up, Arnaud," I grinned as I watched Gina conjure up a Scotch for me. "You've got some new fans. Apparently, you're a big hit in Japan."

"I noticed. What was all that?" Arnaud asked with more than an edge to his voice, seamlessly switching the conversation back to French. Unconsciously, I had spoken to him in English, and it just hit me he had transparently and perfectly understood me.

"Oh, he was just exploring some ideas with me. Nothing that will ever come to anything. Remind me later and I'll tell you about it," I casually threw out, satisfied I was not lying to either of them; I didn't want to get into my session with Toru in Gina's presence. She'd only come aboard a few hours ago, and it was pointless to concern her with a buyout offer Arnaud most likely would never seriously entertain.

"It just occurred to me we haven't seen food all day—let's get some dinner. Should I call downstairs to the Cheval Blanc for reservations?" I asked, referring to the hotel's signature gourmet dining room.

"Good idea," Arnaud quickly replied, evidently now more hungry than upset. "But let me call. The maître d' knows me. He'll find us a nice table on the terrace overlooking the Rhine."

* * *

Arnaud took control of the menus once we were seated at the candlelit table near the terrace's rail. A pair of nearby decorative gas heaters warded off the evening chill. Addressing the waiter whom he apparently also knew, he said, "Marcel, we'll start with a bottle of the Krug Rosé, and some Beluga. For dinner, we all shall have the *Menu des Rois*, served along with a . . . " he paused, running his finger down a selected page of the wine carte. "Please ask the sommelier for a bottle of the '83 Château Margaux, to be served with the venison."

"*Très bien, Monsieur Laurent. Je reviens dans un instant,*" replied the glowing waiter, promising to return immediately, and obviously approving of Arnaud's selections.

Our host (or at least I hoped he was hosting after ordering the Krug, caviar, and Margaux) chatted about his relative successes at this year's Fair without interruption for several minutes after the Champagne was sampled, approved ("*Formidable!*"), and poured. Then, without anything close to a bridge, he said, "Dane, I appreciate you helping me here today, but I don't see any reason for you to stay on for the rest of the weekend. Tomorrow is a day for the public, and little ever comes from those. I have a suggestion: Why don't you take Regina down to our offices in Neuchâtel tomorrow? It would no doubt be of some benefit for her to see our facilities now that she'll be covering your British activities. You can change her air reservations to fly home out of Geneva tomorrow afternoon after you finish up in Neuchâtel, and you and I will have dinner tomorrow night when you return."

I wasn't sure who he was trying to get rid of most, Gina or me. He'd been crapped on all day, and he clearly wasn't in for a rerun tomorrow. After finally resigning himself to the idea of Gina working with me, Arnaud's disappointment had been obvious when I followed that act with my lengthy conference with the Japanese. At this point, I suspected he just wanted us out of his hair for a while.

"It sounds fun," Gina chimed in. " And I'd enjoy the ride along the lakes if you wouldn't mind all that driving."

"Not a problem. I'll rent a car in the morning and leave it at the airport in Geneva when I drop you. I'll take the train back up here to Basel tomorrow afternoon and catch up on some sleep."

"Good, it's settled then," Arnaud said. "A couple of the men will be working tomorrow even though it's Sunday. I asked them to put in some extra time to start getting out my new designs. You met Klaus on one or two of your trips. He'll definitely be there."

Swell. With the personality of Vlad the Impaler, Klaus Schulrat was possibly the most disagreeable, miserable, and malodorous individual I'd ever come across. I supposed he was likely around eighty, but with a face looking like something between a gargoyle and a walnut shell's innards, he appeared to have been prematurely taxidermied. Klaus had started working in the Laurent family business over sixty years ago, before the war, in the late 1930s, originally having been taken on by Arnaud's father. Arnaud had kept Klaus working long past the normal Swiss retirement age not solely out of loyalty: He needed Klaus's master goldsmith talents. Arnaud claimed the ornery old Swiss German could take one look at one of his boss's larger than life-size design renderings and create the requisite gold casting molds in mere hours. No computer-aided design programs here. Klaus was irreplaceable in Arnaud's non-computerized operation, a leverage factor the old boy surely relished.

Though Klaus had lived in the French-speaking canton of Neuchâtel for most of his adult life, he stubbornly only spoke to Arnaud in thick Schwyzerdütsch, his native provincial Swiss German dialect, to which Arnaud would respond in French. They both understood one another perfectly, but neither would cave.

"Sure, Klaus and I are old buddies," I teased. Arnaud was continually embarrassed by Klaus's foul temper and behavior toward others, including this non-Swiss foreigner. He'd also given up on commenting to Klaus about his rancid fetor. "But give him a call in the morning and tell him we'll be touring his domain so he doesn't pull out a crossbow when he sees me."

Arnaud smiled and nodded with a resigned shoulder shrug.

Gina and Arnaud fell into a discussion about Swiss politics, what there was of it, happily leaving me to savor the magnificent six-course chef's menu Arnaud had selected for us: paté de foie gras with peppered pineapple slices, coquilles Saint-Jacques, filet of sole with peanut and curry sauce, and saddle of venison en croûte accompanied by pumpkin sauce. Our desserts of sliced caramel pears arrived with the perfect wine complement, glasses of sweet Château d'Yquem, courteously comped by the maître d'. And finally, the obligatory chariot of cheeses. Methought my Swiss friend was enjoying more than a mildly prosperous week.

After a full and eventful day, generously punctuated by multiple Scotches and a half-dozen glasses of superlative wines before, during, and after dinner, I was ready to go upstairs. What would have been yesterday's odds of my having this gorgeous woman across from me in my bed tonight? With me in the other room . . . on a Hide-A-Bed.

Chapter 6

Neuchâtel

Sunday afternoon, 16 April 2000

Gina dressed casually for her travels on this chilly and rainy day: jeans (uncreased—a good thing), a mauve Oxford cut shirt, navy blue beret, and a powder blue leather jacket. Whatever she'd worn the last three days, I'd remembered each of them. A personal first. I also opted for jeans, along with a snappy sweater (the only one I owned) and a pair of well broken-in deck shoes.

Neither of us said more than a couple of words for the first half-hour of our late morning drive; the bucolic Swiss countryside was almost a curative for the after-effects of last night's alcohol. Ever-present off the highway stood tidy three-storied squarish chalets interspersed along the hillsides below the line of pines. Complementing each of these oversized gingerbread structures were the requisite wooden geranium planters, either hanging from the windows or placed symmetrically along the balcony railings. Most properties displayed the red and white Swiss flag in their yards, and many residences, of course, had their share of fabled belled cows meandering in the nearby fields.

I must have been smiling or subconsciously humming when I heard Gina say, "You really do enjoy coming to Switzerland, don't you?"

"Yeah, I do. It shows, does it? It's a good gig, working with Arnaud and all. It gives me an excuse to come back several times a year. The money's good, I get along very well with Arnaud, and I meet interesting people . . . like you." I was almost thankful for my booze-induced slumber last night which had kept me from any thoughts of a late night knock on her door.

"If I may ask, do I understand correctly you're a part owner of Laurel?"

"No, no ownership. Only certain geographic sales rights I purchased a few years ago. But Arnaud and I have a perfect relationship which doesn't require a written contract: We both need one another."

"It sounds perfect. Let me ask you something else I've been curious about: How are Mr. Toru and his Japanese group going to fit into this happy relationship between you and Arnaud?"

Jesus, she was unambiguous and blunt. I stared down the road in silence for several seconds while I thought about how I was going to field this one. I didn't want to get into last night's discussion with Toru before I first presented his proposal to Arnaud, even though I was confident he would reject it. Nevertheless, Gina had offered to quit her job in favor of working with me and she deserved my honesty. Or a form of it. Though honesty was the best policy, unfortunately it wasn't always the only policy. "You're perceptive—what do you think Toru and I were talking about last night?" I asked, hoping her suppositions were tangential to the facts and I could deny everything with a clear conscience.

"All right," she said, playfully licking her lips. "But I do hope I don't offend you with my prying. Whilst you and Arnaud were both involved in your respective discussions last night, I became curious about the Japanese gentleman. Since I had nothing better to do after most of the clients had gone, I took the liberty of doing a bit of computer searching, and the results of my little surfing expedition were fascinating. I found Kizoku Holdings is involved in the manufacturing of a broad range of products in Japan. It seems they're into everything: paper products, small kitchen appliances, electronics, even inexpensive watches. The key word in this you'll note is *manufacturing*—not representation, not import —solely manufacturing. Therefore, I naturally assumed they're not interested in importing Arnaud's watches—they want to make them."

"Anything else?" I asked, trying for cool curiosity in my voice, and pressing a little to see what more she'd found. She was good.

"Something a bit dodgy perhaps; possibly nothing. A little over a year ago, Kizoku was in the news for a few days in Japan concerning some tax related issues. After a brief investigation, the Japanese government levied some penalty fines on the firm for a series of failures to correctly report certain income figures. Something about large flows of capital in and out of the firm which weren't properly accounted for. Fines were paid, a couple of staff accountants were sacked, and that was that. At least that's all I could find."

So that was likely the crux of my half-recollection regarding Kizoku's difficulties. It must have occurred during one of my trips to Japan and I'd read about it in the English language *Japan Times*.

Whatever, that nagging little thorn which had been needling my suspicious mind was now removed.

I didn't want to continue to hide what apparently was now obvious to her. "I guess I should tell you Toru's group is making an offer to buy Laurel. I'm going to tell Arnaud about it at dinner tonight. Gina, if I'd thought there was any real possibility of Arnaud being the least bit interested, I'd have told you before now. But there's no way he's going to sell his company, especially not to the Japanese. He's got a real thing about them getting into his shorts. Don't stress over it. Laurel's not going anywhere. As far as I'm concerned, the British and Irish markets are yours."

After a half-minute's pause, she asked, "Why are you so certain Arnaud won't be interested in their offer? Why wouldn't he accept it if the financials are substantial enough?"

"You're a Swiss, Gina. My guess is some things here just aren't for sale, not even for a pile of money. Laurel is his Swiss heritage. Arnaud is second generation in his father's business, and nothing would please him more than to see his son Luc return to the fold and perpetuate the family's involvement in the company. Arnaud already has more money than God, and I really don't think he'd bail for a few more million. The preservation of the family's connection to the Laurel marque is more important to him. Unfortunately, I don't think there's any chance of Luc coming back." But the more I thought about it, the more plausible it became: Lay enough money on him and possibly he would sell.

"I understand what you're saying. When I was chatting up Arnaud last night whilst you were talking with Toru, I asked him about Luc. Did I mention I met Luc a few times when I was here for my secondary schooling? Anyway, Arnaud seems to be rather sad about Luc dropping out of the business. He told me he was hearing from Luc now and then, but only when he needed money. He indicated they don't communicate at all anymore."

"Yeah, that sounds about right. I only know Luc from seeing him at happy hours around Sarasota. He's a likable kid," I said, immediately regretting calling him a kid. While he and Gina were both in their early thirties, Gina had a sophistication and levelheadedness years beyond Luc's. She impressed me as knowing exactly what she wanted, and nothing was going to stop her from attaining it. Luc was still playing with his childhood fantasies.

Twenty miles northeast of Neuchâtel, we passed through the town of Biel, or Bienne as it was known in French, and our conversation was continuing to revolve around the Laurent family. I asked Gina what she knew about Arnaud's wife.

"I think I may have seen her many years ago, when I was a child. My father told me he suspects if Arnaud and his wife weren't both such good practicing Catholics, they'd have divorced long ago. Apparently, she lives in their house in the Jura hills above Neuchâtel, in La Chaux-de-Fonds, and he lives in an apartment he owns in town. Her name is Sandrine, I believe."

"That's about what I would have assumed. About their living situation, I mean. So it goes. I guess you call that a marriage of convenience."

"Are you married, Dane?"

I was beginning to notice she had a habit of throwing out these little gems without a hint of foreplay. But this one didn't require a nanosecond's hesitation.

"Nope. Tried that a couple times, and finally decided I wasn't good at it. I married women hoping they'd never change, but the women I married both thought they could change me. Yeah, right. My last divorce was over five years ago, and so far, so good. I think I've got this singlehood thing wired again, and my happiness is no longer manipulated by other people's moods. Maybe you could call me socially deficient, but I want happiness that lasts, without a preordained expiration date. So now I just buy stuff. There's an expression: After you've been disgraced and financially screwed, you can live freely. So, between totaling an Air Force transport plane and my two divorces, I guess I must be living pretty damned freely now. How about you?" I ventured, seizing the opportunity I'd been looking for since our first meeting.

Gina turned her head away to gaze out her window in silence for several seconds before answering, "No, Dane, I'm not married. It took you a bit to get around to asking, didn't it? I'm not divorced, not widowed, not engaged . . . not anything. I'm just a single mum with a smashing great son. I've basically stopped dating because I'm tired of blokes thinking I owe them a quick shag if they buy me dinner."

"But you came to Switzerland with me."

"You came with good references," she grinned. "And I must say, you've been the perfect gentleman."

"Oh, trust me, I was thinking about knocking on your door last night."

"Oh were you, then? You cheeky little bugger. Are you hitting on me, Dane?"

"It's my duty—it's a male thing. Anyway, you were flirting with me a tad in London."

"Was I? Then maybe you should have knocked me up . . . uh,

60

knocked on my door," she said—then translated—before turning toward me with that fetching wink and smile. If this was what was known as sexual tension, I liked it.

It was closing in on 12:30 when we passed through Le Landereon on the southwestern end of the Bielersee, the narrow, placid lake extending to the south of Biel. Seven miles farther, I slowed the rental Audi to turn off the main road onto the smaller Route de Neuchâtel leading into the village of Hauterive, one of the small northern environs of Neuchâtel, and home to the Laurel Watch Company.

Arnaud's one-story building was sited on the street side of a flowering field and was likely no larger in total area than some of the grander chalets we'd passed along our morning's route. Houses and small light industrial buildings extended down the road on either side of Arnaud's facility, with ample spaces of open land in-between. Laurel's steel and brick building was painted a midnight blue, so dark it appeared black when not fully sunlit. Over the double glass front entry doors hung the stainless steel signage displaying the words *Laurel Luxury Watches* in gold relief lettering. I pulled in next to the only two vehicles parked in the lot: a dirty white Fiat van, and a spotless dark green '60s vintage Volkswagen Beetle. I would have laid odds Klaus owned the van.

Arnaud had tastefully furnished his relatively small reception area with Scandinavian blonde wood chairs and a pair of overstuffed black leather couches surrounding a glass coffee table. Beyond the lobby, at the end of a thirty-foot hallway, was the door to the main assembly area. Once inside the shop, I spotted Klaus and another workman—Didier, I remembered Arnaud calling him —sitting on stools opposite one another facing an elongated raised metal table covered with small tools and buffing wheels. Shafts of sunlight streaming through the windows radiated off the ten or more gold watch casings laid out between them on black velvet. The only noise in the cavernous room was the sound of clicking blades on the heater fans suspended from the fifteen-foot high ceiling.

The younger man was pale and thinnish. He was nearly bald, but sported long sideburns and a black goatee, in contrast to the slightly overweight Klaus, who still had all his graying black hair and evidenced a four-day beard stubble. Neither man said a word when they looked up from their work.

As I was preparing to greet them in my best and well-rehearsed five words of Schwyzerdütsch, Klaus slammed his hand down on the table, jumped up, and gruffly spat out a string of guttural mumbledegook and unintelligible bon mots in a language totally foreign to me. I did assume, however, he was indicating he was other than gruntled to see us. Gina gave a quick squeeze to my hand before releasing it, and then with a big toothy smile, she stepped forward, and in her softest of tones, she spoke to Klaus in a dialect sounding similar to the one he'd used. Klaus's focus immediately went directly to Gina's chest, her shirt now opened to the fourth button. When she finished speaking, Klaus gave her a curt nod and returned to his work without further comment. A curt nod from Klaus was possibly equivalent to gyrating wahines greeting one with scented orchid leis.

"I knew I kept you around for some reason," I whispered to Gina, my new lion tamer guardian. "What the hell did you say to him? And what language were you two speaking?" I asked, slowly leading her away.

"Romansch. It's our fourth official Swiss language, but now only about fifty or sixty thousand people in the eastern part of the country still speak it. I apologized to him for stumbling in unannounced, that we'd stopped in on our way to the airport in Geneva from the Müstermesse so you could show me where the world's finest watches are made. Since I heard him speak to us in Romansch, I knew he must be from the canton of Graubünden. I told him I had relatives from a small town called Celerina near St. Moritz in the same canton."

"Yeah, that might have had something to do with it, too." I was pointing to her décolletage which was now exhibiting an abundance of breast. "You cheated. You had him as soon as you took off your jacket. Hell, you could have spoken to him in Swahili after that."

With the outside possibility of Klaus giving us a quick tour of his shop clearly out of the question, I attempted to explain the various production stages to Gina as I walked her past rows of assembly tables and light machinery. Large wire and plastic meshed bins were filled to the top with watch bands . . . black and brown, leather and reptile. Arnaud refused to use metal or jeweled bracelets, shunning any extraneous components which could detract from the innate aesthetics of his designs. Or, as Toru had so perfectly described, their *shibui*.

Turning back toward the front of the shop, I was surprised to see the door to the gold vault half-opened, something I'd never seen before in my many trips to Neuchâtel. The vault door was always closed and locked.

"C'mon over here. This is the first time I've seen the safe open. It's where they store the stash—the little gold bars they melt down for the cases."

I pulled the vault chamber door open wider. Recessed a step behind it was an open steel and concrete safe, painted black, all of six feet high, roughly four feet wide, and almost as deep. The interior glittered with gold bullion. Neatly stacked in piles of twos along the top metal shelf were eight gold kilobars, a not unusual on-hand quantity to be expected at this point in the production year. Each of the 32 troy ounce bars appeared to be a little less than four inches long, two inches wide, and maybe an inch high. But on the lower shelving was the mother lode: I quickly counted 20 LGD bars, the long-established gold bar standard used in transactions between refineries, major gold dealers, bullion banks, and governments.

"Jesus Christ! Can you believe this?" I almost shouted. I instantly turned to see if Klaus had heard me, but he hadn't budged from his head down position at the workbench across the room.

"Oh, my God!" Gina whispered, her hand moving to her mouth.

Examining both stacks, the London Good Delivery bars dwarfed the kilobars which were cast primarily for jewelry and industrial usage. Though I'd never seen one before, I'd read a fun fact once which reported an LGD bar weighed approximately 400 troy ounces, or about 27.5 pounds. They were each about nine inches long, over three inches in width, a little less than two inches tall, and stacked two high, they stretched the complete width of the safe. After a brief mental calculation, I figured at the current gold value of around $280 per ounce, we were looking at something on the north side of $2 million, not counting around $100,000 in pocket change for the kilobars.

I felt as though I'd been staring at the gold for several minutes, but more likely, within seconds of my opening the vault door, I heard Klaus's heavy-booted approach. Without a word or a look toward us, he pushed past Gina, slammed the safe doors shut, twirled the combination dial, and exited the vault, banging closed and then locking the outer doors behind him. He muttered something, this time in Schwyzerdütsch, which I assumed included his feelings about these damned tourists. He stormed back to his workbench but his ripe stench lingered.

With a schoolgirl giggle, Gina said, "I get the impression we weren't supposed to be looking in there. I think I just lost whatever marks I made earlier with Klaus."

"Don't worry about it. If you're lucky, you'll never see the bastard again. It was incredible though, wasn't it? I have no idea why Arnaud would keep that much gold on hand. And twenty of them! Those big suckers are for institutional and central bank transfers. They have nothing to do with manufacturing watches. I'm very confused. Why the hell would anyone keep that kind of stockpile on premises?"

"Well, we are in Switzerland, Dane. It's not unusual for people here to keep a lot of money in their homes, or in this case, in their office vault. But that was a lot of gold, wasn't it? How much do you think it's worth?"

"I figure something over two million dollars, give or take a quarter mil."

"Are you going tell Arnaud what we saw when you meet him for dinner tonight?"

For whatever reason all that gold was here, Arnaud had never mentioned it. "I have to," I reasoned. "Klaus will let him know what just happened. It'd be best if I bring it up tonight before Arnaud does. I'll let you know what's up after I find out."

I led Gina back through the corridor connecting the workshop to the front offices and locked the entry doors behind us. "Before we go, I have one last thing to show you."

I guided her to the opposite side of the building from where I'd parked the Audi. Fifty or sixty yards to the rear of the shop was another structure, this one significantly smaller than the main building, but of similar design and color. We walked past its locked aircraft hangar-like sliding metal doors and continued around the side to a pair of small windows.

"Go ahead, take a peek inside," I offered. "The longer of the two machines is one of three of the world's rarest automobiles. And one of the most expensive. It's called a Bugatti Type 57SC Atlantic. The smaller one is also a Bugatti, a Type 35B. In its era, Bugatti produced the most technologically advanced and most expensive automobiles in the world. I think the Atlantic represents the absolute pinnacle of design—it's an incredible work of art. I think the Bugattis—both *père* and *fils*—were more sculptors than automobile designers. Nothing made before or since can match it. It's truly amazing."

"They're beautiful. They belong to Arnaud?"

"Yup, and I'm trusting you to keep this a secret, Gina. This Atlantic isn't supposed to exist."

"I promise," she replied, zipping her lips with her forefinger. "I should think if you can trust me not to mention two million in gold bars, you can trust me with a couple of cars. But what do you mean, it isn't supposed to exist?"

She saw me shudder. *A couple of cars?* She immediately

66

dropped a half point from her original nine and a half on my admittedly chauvinistic female rating scale.

I moved closer to the window to ogle the two machines through the glass for a few moments. Appearing to be traveling fast while sitting still, the aerodynamically curvaceous fastback Atlantic coupé was painted an elegant two-tone burgundy and black. Extending down the center and the full length of its elongated hood, and splitting the windshield and the teardrop two-seat passenger compartment, was the Type 57SC's signature dorsal ridge. A little more than an inch high, the flange was the meeting point of the two halves of the body which had been riveted together. Similar ridges were centered along the four protruding fenders. The massive external headlights were basically freestanding between the fenders and the trademark arched Bugatti radiator. With a 130-inch wheelbase, and a supercharged inline 8 cylinder engine producing 220 horsepower, the Atlantic would have been a most formidable automobile in its day. Today, it was irreplaceable.

"There were only four Atlantics made by Bugatti, all between 1936 and 1938. They were actually designed by his son, Jean. Collectors now own two of them, one by a man named Dr. Williamson, and the other by a guy you've probably heard of: Ralph Lauren, the clothier. A third was destroyed in a collision with a train in 1955 and later rebuilt, but because of a lot of part substitutions in the rebuild, that Atlantic's not considered authentic anymore. This one in front of us, Arnaud's, was sort of the factory demonstrator, which is thought to have been lost during the German occupation of France during World War Two. Arnaud's father, Édouard Laurent, bought this Atlantic directly from old man

Bugatti in late 1939 at the factory in Molsheim. That's near Strasbourg, about seventy-five miles north of Basel. Édouard knew Bugatti—Etorre was his first name—from the early days, when they both were inventing various machining tools.

"Etorre Bugatti told him he was afraid the Germans would soon liberate his factory and automobiles; he said he'd rather destroy his machines than see some Nazi general abscond with them. He then offered to sell this Atlantic to Édouard, who'd always had a love of automobiles. Édouard jumped at the offer. Arnaud told me his father paid something around the franc equivalent of fifteen thousand dollars for it at the time. Neither Édouard, nor later Arnaud, had any interest in either displaying the Type 57 at shows or selling it, so the mystique of the *lost Atlantic* has been perpetuated over the years. And mostly out of amusement, neither of the Laurents ever did anything to squelch it."

"Fifteen thousand dollars was a lot of money for a car sixty years ago, wasn't it?" Gina asked.

"You're damn right it was. I'd guess that'd be around an inflation-adjusted equivalent of a hundred and fifty thousand dollars today. Maybe more. But guess what it's worth now?"

She shrugged her shoulders and shook her head.

"Subject to the fluctuations of the classic automobile market, this Atlantic could bring in something around five or six million dollars."

Gina moved away from the window. "Bloody hell! At least he keeps the two million in gold in a safe vault. What's the little blue one worth, then?"

"The little blue one, as you call it, is a 1927 Type 35B Bugatti, once an awesome racing machine. It's a two-seater, because, in the old days, they raced with a driver and a mechanic. It's what? seventy-three years old? With a top end of a hundred and thirty miles per hour, and a seven second zero to sixty. Impressive stuff. The Type 35 has always been my favorite, possibly because I still have a glimmer of hope that someday I'll be able to afford one." I continued to drool over the supercharged 2.3 liter, 140 horsepower, open-wheeled racer until Gina interrupted my daydreaming.

"Okay, go ahead, I'm waiting," she grinned. "How much?"

"On a good day, and if you got lucky at a slow auction in a soft year, maybe around a million, a million and a half. Dollars, that is. Back when it was new in 1927, it only cost about sixteen hundred dollars."

"You boys and your expensive toys," Gina said with another headshake. "If his owning the Atlantic is such a secret, isn't he concerned about people around here finding out about it? He never drives it?"

I nodded and started to walk her back to our car. "Yeah, he drives both of them . . . regularly. Short jaunts in the countryside around here to keep the juices flowing—his and the Bugattis'. I guess he thinks if people see the Atlantic, they won't know what they're looking at anyway. Come on, let's get going. I'll buy you a late lunch on the road before your flight."

"Good idea. I'm starved. Oh, what time is my flight this afternoon?"

"Five twenty-five, and my train leaves at five thirty-six from the airport station. Plenty of time for a two bottle lunch."

Chapter 7

Basel

Sunday evening, 16 April 2000

I was able to sleep for most of the three-hour ride back to Basel despite waking at each of the five or six en route stations when the train braked to a stop. And I found myself smiling every time the train departed precisely as the second hand hit twelve on the oversized platform clocks. Not give or take a few seconds—on the dot. They're Swiss.

Arnaud was to meet me at the Stucki Restaurant in the wooded Basel suburb of Bruderholz, less than a five minute drive from both the hotel and the station. The Stucki had been my suggestion, via the recommendation of my crackerjack Drei Könige concierge. If my man suggested it, I had total confidence it would measure up to Arnaud's lofty gastronomic standards.

The maître d' informed me his old friend Monsieur Laurent had already arrived. He escorted me to a window-side table where Arnaud greeted me with a raised glass of white wine.

"Is there anyone in this town you don't know?" I asked, lowering myself into the chair withdrawn by the maître d'. "I bust my ass to find someplace to retaliate with after your extravaganza last night, and I take you to a place where you probably went to school with the owner or something."

Arnaud laughed. "Switzerland's not a very big place. Live long enough and you'll possibly meet everyone in the country. But I certainly didn't want to quarrel with your choice of restaurants when you suggested the Stucki on the phone this afternoon. Good pick, lad."

"I think I'm going to try to get something simple. Maybe some good Swiss peasant food," I proposed while perusing my menu. "I know it's a cliché, but do you think you could use your juice around here and have them make me a schnitzel with some rösti?" Rösti, the Swiss butter fried riced potato, onion, and bacon dish, was one of my absolute favorites and I'd found it impossible to replicate outside Switzerland.

Arnaud was smiling as he laid his menu on the table. "Dane, we have no peasants in Switzerland. And no, I'm sure it won't be a problem. I'll ask. I think I'll have a little paté and some sweetbreads. For wine, a Fendant is all right?"

Fendant was first described to me by a bartender I'd come across on a trip to Zermatt: "It's a local wine from the Vaud and Valais areas. It's a mild, white wine, low in alcohol content, and completely lacking in character." He was French.

"Sure. Never met a Fendant I didn't like."

After some brief instructions to the waiter, Arnaud leaned forward slightly and studied me for a moment before speaking. "Did you find your trip to Neuchâtel interesting this afternoon?"

"I presume Klaus called you about the vault?"

"Yes, he did. I think you would care to ask me some questions,

71

no?"

"Nothing you don't want to tell me. But if you're asking if I'm curious, hell yes."

"This is a most private conversation we are about to have," Arnaud started. "Also, I'm a little concerned about Regina's discretion in this matter."

There was no way I could guarantee Gina's silence, but I trusted her. "Arnaud, you've obviously known Gina a lot longer than I have, but I wouldn't expect a problem there. I think she was more impressed with the value of the Bugattis than with what she saw in the shop."

"Ah, she saw the Bugattis as well, eh? I do hope she's discrete. We'll see." He reclined back in his chair and paused while the waiter opened our bottle of Fendant, pouring a small measure into Arnaud's glass for his sampling pleasure. Noting the silent nod of approval, the pudgy black-vested waiter decanted an appropriate portion for each of us and withdrew.

Arnaud inspected the tables closest to ours and seemed to satisfy himself that everyone was rapt in their own discussions. "It's a long story, but I'll abbreviate it the best I can."

He paused as he swirled the chilled white wine in his glass before taking a long taste.

"During World War Two, my father, Édouard, and Klaus Schulrat were posted together near the German border, to the north of Schaffhausen. Schaffhausen is on the Rhine, about forty kilometers north of Zürich. As you may recall, Klaus worked for my father before the war as an apprentice machinist and they somehow worked it out to remain together during most of the war years—my father, a sergeant, and Klaus, a corporal, in the Swiss

Army."

The waiter silently placed a plate of foie gras before Arnaud and departed with a "*Bon appétit, monsieur.*"

"But first I must regress," Arnaud started again once we were alone. "During the war, as you know, Switzerland was neutral to both the Axis and the Allied powers. However, an agreement was struck between the Swiss and the Germans, wherein German trains could cross through Switzerland on their route between Italy and Germany provided all the cars remained sealed for the duration of their Swiss transit. One night, in February of 1945, just months before the close of the war, my father and Klaus were on duty at the railway border crossing north of Schaffhausen. The trains were required to stop there for a short time for formalities before entering Germany. After one of the trains departed into Germany, my father and Klaus were walking back along the tracks from the border when one of them spotted someone hiding in the woods. They shined a light and saw a German soldier sitting on a snow-covered mound, his hands held upright in the air. When they drew closer, they recognized by his uniform and the eagle and *Totenkopf* —or skull—on his hat he was a major in the *Schutzstaffel*, the *Waffen-SS* to be exact."

With a small shake of my head, I declined Arnaud's offer to share a portion of his paté starter, finding myself completely engrossed in his story and satisfied with sipping my *characterless* wine.

"The major wanted to surrender, and he asked not to be sent back to Germany after the war for fear of facing the inevitable justice the Allies would impose upon all SS officers. He told them he'd been in charge of security for the small three-car train's consignment. When his train reached the border stop, the Nazi major said he gave his three guards permission to go inside a little workman's hut for a few minutes to warm themselves. Once they were gone, he went to the other side of the train, and using his keys, he opened one of the car's doors, found his target boxes, and managed to move twenty gold bars into the woods lining the tracks before ordering his troops back to their sentry positions on top of the railway cars. After he instructed the engineer to proceed, he succeeded in jumping off the train without being seen before it crossed the border into Germany. He collected all the bars, placed them together, and covered the small pile with dirt, snow, and pine needles."

Arnaud paused his monologue when our dinners arrived. Whatever my friend had told the waiter, he'd missed the part about my desire for a smaller portion. The breaded veal cutlet topped with a fried egg and caviar completely filled one plate. A second plate was nearly overflowing with a skillet-sized round of rösti. A little squeeze of lemon over the schnitzel and I was chowing down before the waiter left the table.

For the next half-hour, Arnaud continued his retelling of his father's narrative without a word of interruption from my side of the table. Without telling them where he'd hidden his treasure, the German offered the two Swiss a share of the gold if they would take him to the American consular office in Zürich. He claimed to have information that would be of vital interest to the Americans, which he would exchange for not being tried for war crimes after the suspension of hostilities.

"So they actually split up the gold?" I finally interrupted.

"Yes, fifty-fifty," Arnaud replied between bites.

"I'm missing something. The only reason I can see for them to split it with the German was if they couldn't get to the gold until after they'd offered him up to the Americans. Is that what happened?"

"Not exactly," Arnaud answered calmly, but unable to contain a hint of a smile. "Before my father could decide what to do, Klaus stabbed the Nazi in the left eye and killed him. Klaus never cared much for officers, especially German officers. My father and Klaus split the gold fifty-fifty."

"But how did they find the gold after Klaus killed the guy?" I asked, probably with my open mouth dropping bits of veal onto my lap.

"Simple. In his haste, one of the wooden boxes had broken open and the German hadn't covered the gold completely. When Klaus and my father had their torches and lanterns on him, they both saw some glints of the gold shining through the leaves and snow he'd used to try to cover it."

"What did they do with the German's body?"

"They moved it farther into the woods and left him for the wild boar and wolves to eat. A fitting demise for a *Waffen-SS* officer, don't you think? Then they burned his uniform. Nothing was ever discovered, or at least they never heard anything about it," Arnaud calmly replied, reaching for another forkful of sweetbreads.

Arnaud's mini-history lesson staggered me. I'd finished less than half of my delectable schnitzel and potatoes, but I'd lost interest in eating. I beckoned the waiter for a Scotch.

"Are you telling me these gold bars have been sitting in your factory ever since the war?"

"No, absolutely not. Until last month, they were at Klaus's little farm in the canton of Graubünden, in eastern Switzerland. My father and Klaus left the hidden gold in the woods near the rail tracks that night in 1945, and it remained there for several days until my father was able to requisition a small army truck. They came back, uncovered the bars, drove the two hundred kilometers to Klaus's place outside the village of Tiefencastel, buried the gold in a meadow next to his house, and then returned to their post near Schaffhausen before sunrise. The gold wasn't moved to my vault in Neuchâtel until several weeks ago, which was the first time I'd ever seen it. You see, last month the electric utility officials advised Klaus they needed to erect a tower in his meadow to support some new power lines. They showed him a map indicating where the tower would need to be positioned."

"Where they'd buried the gold, right?" I shook my head. "What are the odds?"

"Precisely the spot," Arnaud answered, finally letting go with a laugh and a resigned shrug. "So we immediately dug up the bars and transferred them to my offices, where we plan on keeping them for several months until the electric people are finished. Only four people ever knew of the gold's existence. Now it seems there are six, thanks to Klaus's stupidity and carelessness."

"Six? I count five: your father, Klaus, you, Gina, and me."

"And my son, Luc. I told him about the gold several years ago, but he's never seen it."

"What about Didier? I assume he also saw the bars in the shop if we did."

"No, I considered that, but Klaus assured me Didier didn't have a view of the safe from the side of the table where he was working."

"Why did Klaus open the vault in the first place? They were only doing some polishing work when we saw them."

"The oaf claimed he'd left some of his own valuables in the safe and he forgot to close and lock the doors after he went to retrieve them. The whole episode was a combination of bad luck and carelessness."

We sat staring at one another for several seconds, likely thinking the same thing: A secret of more than a half a century revealed by one absent-minded momentary slip.

"But I don't understand why you still have the bars, Arnaud. They're obviously burdensome to store. Why didn't your father and Klaus sell the gold years ago? Or use it in your manufacturing?"

"Think about it, Dane. London Good Delivery bars are used for transfers between financial institutions, like central banks . . . and countries. Far too many questions would be raised if an individual were to try to exchange them for cash. Not impossible, but most awkward. As far as melting them down for making our watchcases, that would create unpleasant questions from the tax people. If we were audited, I would have no purchase receipts for the gold we supposedly used in manufacturing, so on a purely business level, I wouldn't be able to deduct the material cost from our profits. Either way, the best option was to keep the bars and hide them. We've been fortunate in that neither Klaus nor my father nor I have ever needed the money the gold represents. Keep in mind, in 1945 gold was only worth 37 dollars an ounce. Last Friday it was over 280 dollars an ounce. As you can see, hoarding has had its inflationary benefits."

"Klaus has never asked for his share of the money?"

"No. He has no relatives, I pay him well, and he owes nothing;

he doesn't spend but a fraction of what he earns," Arnaud explained. "His farm near Tiefencastel has been in his family for generations, so he has no debt there either. Klaus is a simple farmer who also happens to be one of the best in the country at what he does for me. The subject of physically splitting up the gold has never been broached by either of us."

As bizarre as it was, it all made perfect sense the way Arnaud calmly explained it. A dead Nazi, over two million dollars worth of unusable gold, and total reliance upon an individual Arnaud himself described as a careless oaf. Perfect sense. But as an other than perfect finish to the evening, I still had to present the Japanese proposal.

"That's an incredible story. Let me call for the check if you don't mind, Arnaud. I have something to show you from Monsieur Toru which I'd rather go over with you back at the hotel."

"I was wondering when we would get to your discussion with the Japanese. My compliments on a fine dinner. I only hope it isn't spoiled when I hear what you have to tell me."

Chapter 8

Sunday evening, 16 April 2000

We located a pair of overstuffed leather chairs near the fireplace in the hotel's elegant and still lively Les Trois Rois Bar and stuck with our usuals when the bar waiter took our respective orders: Louis XIII and Johnnie Black.

"So, Dane, what do you have for me?" Arnaud asked, happily reflecting a pleasant mood from dinner and numerous glasses of wine.

I handed him Toru's papers. "Don't shoot the errand boy. Oh, and add one million dollars to the top number on the second page. I'll explain when you've finished."

Arnaud stared at me for a moment before taking the proposal. He read the five pages slowly, then reinspected them for several minutes, flipping the pages back and forth without expression or comment.

"All right, I've read it." Arnaud lowered his reading glasses farther down his nose and looked up as our drinks materialized. "You had something you wanted to explain?" he asked casually.

"For some reason, Toru felt he stood a better chance of success if he had me as an ally in presenting the Kizoku Holdings proposal to you. He offered me a million dollars if I was able to convince you to sell. Add that chunk to their seven million purchase price and you have their starting point."

An amused expression began appearing on Arnaud's face as he sipped his Cognac. "A million, likely in cash, eh?" he mused rhetorically. "I appreciate your honesty. My good judgment of character proves itself once again. So, what do you think of their offer?"

Jesus, he was really considering this thing? I was stunned.

"I have no opinion," I replied flatly and candidly. "Nor am I entitled to one. It's your company, Arnaud. I'm only the highly paid foreign peddler. But am I sensing you're actually giving this some thought?"

Arnaud leaned back into the soft leather, Cognac snifter in hand. He was gazing directly ahead into the fireplace. "You mentioned their *starting point* a minute ago. Explain that if you will, please."

"Arnaud, I've dealt with the Japanese for the better part of ten years now, for Laurel, as well as in some of my earlier ventures, and I think I've developed a pretty clear understanding as to how they operate. Overall, I've found them to be rather honorable, but it takes them eons to reach a decision. It probably took the good folks at Kizoku over a year to work out their game plan on this approach. I'll guarantee they wouldn't spend that kind of time and energy on something to see it go up in smoke if you didn't jump at their first draft. Makes sense, right? But let's back up for a minute. Are you seriously considering selling the company? I'm shocked."

I looked at Arnaud and could envision a twenty-five jewel watch movement efficiently clicking away in his head. He was most certainly thinking about the fact that his family's business of over sixty years had no possibilities of continuing operations into its third generation of family stewardship now that Luc was out.

"I think I should at least listen to what they have to propose," he started, somewhat philosophically. "I'll be in my sixties soon, Klaus is about twenty years older than that, and my son Luc has obviously shown no interest in continuing in our business. Moreover, I have a certain sense of loyalty—no, I have an obligation—to my employees. I must assure their livelihoods are preserved after I'm no longer active in Laurel. Dane, you've had twenty-four hours to mull over their offer. What's your opinion?"

I hesitated, strangely realizing I was truly ambivalent. I could be content to continue to expand the international markets for Arnaud for a few more years, or alternatively, I was confident he would fairly compensate me should he choose to accept the Japanese offer. I concluded I could be completely objective in my counsel.

"First off, I have to ask you a question: Is the eight million dollar figure at all reasonable? I haven't a clue as to what your business is worth."

"That's a little on the high side, I would think," Arnaud replied with a slight eyebrow raise and a typically Gallic lip puff. "It's a difficult number to establish, obviously, but I would have estimated something closer to six. Maybe a little less. That's for the business only, you understand. Including all inventories, but excluding the buildings and the land. And their offer to pay me ten percent over the appraised value for the latter two would certainly be acceptable. But I think we should try for an immediate sale of the real property, not in four years as they propose."

I picked up Toru's papers from the table and fumbled in my pockets for what proved to be a nonexistent pen.

Arnaud chuckled and handed me his gold Montblanc. "Remind me to buy my *consigliere* a writing instrument before he goes off to bargain with Monsieur Toru."

"Thanks," I smiled, thinking about his last words. So that's it. He was going to sell, and I was to negotiate the deal.

"Okay, let me get some of this down. Their terms for the real estate portion would be acceptable, subject to an outright purchase to coincide with that of the business, the sale price for which is eight million," I said aloud while I jotted in the column of the top page of the Japanese proposal. "How do you feel about the consulting situation they're offering? They've indicated they want you to stay on for at least four years in a design capacity."

"Do you seriously think they want my business for the artistry I put into my products?" Arnaud asked with a sense of amusement in his voice. "My presumption is they simply want controlling ownership of a Swiss watch company in order to gain an aura of quality for their own watches."

I found it interesting Arnaud had quickly come to the same estimation as I had in regard to Kizoku's motivation. "I considered that, and you could be right," I said. "But I'm guessing they want to buy some time, like four years, in which to try to hone the design skills of their own personnel. And you get a fat expense account to cover all your overhead in Paris for a while, not to mention a quarter of a million a year for your trouble."

"What expense account?" Arnaud asked, reaching for the

paperwork. "I didn't see that."

He seemed more excited about the possibility of being toked for room, food, and beverage in Paris during his yearly design sojourns than he did about the likely ten million dollar-plus total package.

"Don't bother looking. It's not in there. But it will be," I said, rather enjoying a bit of bluster. "They need you a hell of a lot more than you need them. And they're well aware of that fact, Arnaud."

We were quickly progressing beyond the stage of merely looking at their offer—we were now in the process of tweaking the details of the contract. I could only assume Arnaud must have been examining the possibilities of retirement for a few years, and the Toru approach had proved to be of fortuitous timing.

I leaned over the table, pen in hand, lest any pearls be forgotten. "You've always stayed at the Hôtel de Crillon during your Paris trips. Interested in moving around the corner to the Ritz? I don't think we'll have a problem with them on a little change of venue if you'd care to try for an upgrade."

Arnaud took a draw from his snifter. "I appreciate the direction you're taking here, Dane, but I've been staying at the Crillon for over thirty years now. They treat me as though I've returned home every January when I come back. No, it's a superb hotel and I'll continue to stay there, but I like your thought process."

"Fine, your choice. How do you feel about the two hundred and fifty thousand dollars per annum they're offering for your design work?" I asked, continuing to work down Toru's bullet-pointed checklist.

"My preference would be to have no further contact with these people once they purchase Laurel," Arnaud replied. I sensed he was starting to enjoy his new prospects. "But if they insist upon subsidizing an annual trip to Paris for me, I would have no problem with the figure they've offered. In reality, I already have several dozen new design sketches I haven't put into production. So, yes, I'll accept their hospitality in Paris for a few years at the numbers mentioned."

We started on our second round of drinks, continuing into another hour of discussion. "Arnaud, it's starting to sound as if you've just sold your business." I raised my glass to toast.

"*Santé*," he responded. "Now, we need to cover your interests."

Strangely—and most unlike me—I hadn't really given my own situation a lot of consideration. This was all moving so unexpectedly fast. For the moment, I was more stressed over what I'd tell Gina. It didn't sit well with me to bring her down to Switzerland for the weekend to pitch her on a job, and then renege within days of her acceptance.

"We'll get around to me in a minute. Right now, I have more than a bit of a problem with what I'm going to do about Gina. I didn't have the slightest idea you'd seriously consider Toru's offer. Now she's flown out of Geneva today thinking she has a new job with me. If you don't object, I'd like to insert something in the paperwork saying she either retains her rights of exclusivity for British and Irish imports or they buy her out."

"I have no problem with that. But do you think she'd actually consider working with the Japanese?" Arnaud asked, appearing completely incredulous at the option.

"Hell, Arnaud, if she can get along with Klaus, dealing with the Japanese would be an afternoon tea party." I briefly related the story of Gina taming Klaus in the workshop. "You should have seen her this afternoon. She was masterful. She damn near had the old bastard cooing."

Arnaud laughed wildly, slapping the leather arm of his chair. I could only fantasize as to the image of a cooing Klaus he was conjuring up in his mind.

"Let's try this," Arnaud suggested, gathering himself. "The Japanese either agree to extend Regina a five-year contract for her exclusive territorial rights or they purchase those rights from her for a hundred thousand dollars."

"*A hundred grand*?" I repeated. "Christ, Arnaud, I appreciate the thought, but she's only been working for me for a day."

"If they balk, settle for fifty, or she keeps her new job and works with them. You know better than I that they won't walk away from this negotiation over a paltry little payout such as this. Now, again, let's discuss your situation."

"The more I think about it, the more I think I'm going to be out of a job," I conceded. "Kizoku will likely be handling its own marketing and sales. But I suppose I could convince them of my usefulness for a year or two."

"You'd work for them?" Arnaud asked, seemingly gagging on the concept.

"If I had to, yes. You know I'm in a totally different situation than you."

Arnaud nodded, indicating he understood my circumstances, and I began to sense he was already working out a suitable resolution. "Dane, through your efforts, my small watch company has basically doubled its sales in the past three years. Without you, we both know Monsieur Toru's offer might not have been forthcoming, but if it had been, it would not have been nearly as generous. Therefore, I propose the following: five hundred thousand dollars reimbursement of your initial investment, and a million for making this sale possible. Would you find that acceptable?"

I sat stunned, completely bowled over by Arnaud's offer. I'd expected far less, perhaps less than half that figure, inclusive of the return of my original investment.

"Acceptable, and greatly appreciated. You know it's too much, but I'm not going to draw this out by arguing with you," I grinned. "You do remember I only paid you two hundred and fifty thousand, don't you?"

"Let's call it interest," he replied with a wink. "And it makes for a nicer round number, wouldn't you agree?" He extended his snifter to clink with my glass in salute.

"You're more than generous. Many thanks. A million and a half should take the edge off things for a few weeks."

Arnaud nodded agreeably, sat back in his oversized chair, staring into the fireplace once more, momentarily retreating to his thoughts. "I have two other issues I'd ask you to present to the Japanese, if you don't mind," he mused aloud, his gaze fixed on the fire. "First, I'm thinking this may be a most serendipitous and profitable opportunity to dispose of our LGD bars. Why don't we propose that Kizoku's purchase of the LGDs is integral to my sale of the business? And shall we say, at a ten percent premium over Friday's market settling price of $281 an ounce? A concern as large as Kizoku shouldn't have any difficulty in converting them to cash whenever they choose."

Very slick. No nasty questions from the taxman. No more need to stress over the gold's mere existence. And why not ask for the ten percent bump? The Japanese had already opened that can in trying to sweeten the deal by offering to pay a premium for Arnaud's real estate. "Sure. Let's give it a shot. I'm sure they left themselves some wiggle room in their first pitch. What's your second issue?"

"I would insist upon some assurance my employees remain with the company for at least a reasonable future period. Shall we say for a minimum of two years? Or insist Kizoku agree to pay a full year's wages in severance to any employee they terminate before that."

"Done," I said, returning to my note taking. "I assume you'll want to run all this past your attorney before we present your counter to Toru?"

"Dane, we Swiss are not as intrigued with nor as reliant upon lawyers as you Americans seem to be. I believe our thoughts can be clearly expressed to our buyers without any need for my lawyer friend in Geneva to complicate our words with a lot of redundant and needlessly expensive clauses. If it makes you feel better, I'll have my lawyer look over things after we've spoken to the Japanese."

I liked the way Arnaud thought, but it wasn't my ten million bucks on the line. "All right. If you feel comfortable with that, I'll type up our response on Gina's new laptop tomorrow morning. How do you want to handle the counter presentation?"

"Do you know if Monsieur Toru is still here in Basel?"

I got a kick out of Arnaud's style: not Toru, but Monsieur Toru, despite his utter contempt for him. But I never would have expected less.

"He's in Monte Carlo as we speak," I said, not in the least

displeased with the direction this seemed to be going. It was headed south—due south, to Monaco.

"How do you know?"

"It came up in our conversation last night. He'll be registered at the Hermitage. Would you like me to call him tomorrow or would you prefer to deal with him yourself?"

Arnaud turned to face me, unable to contain his broad grin. After three years, he had my number. "Dane, I have no desire to speak with these people, but may I assume you would be available for a brief visit to Monaco? Possibly tomorrow? I'm paying, of course."

"If I must. And since you asked nicely."

Chapter 9

Monte Carlo

Monday/Tuesday, 17/18 April 2000

Within thirty minutes of my Swissair Airbus touching down in Nice, I was buckled into the front left seat of a Heli Air Monaco jet helicopter awaiting our takeoff clearance for the short hop to Monaco. The helo transfer cost only a little more than twice the cab fare, yet permitted one to avoid the ever-present traffic congestion on the fifteen mile coast road between Nice and the Principality. I looked at helicopters as I looked at 12-year-old peaty Scotch whiskey: While neither was required to sustain life, both were reasonably affordable and definitely most pleasurable.

After receiving clearance to depart over the two parallel runways, the right-seated pilot climbed his machine to 500 feet over the placid Mediterranean and flew east toward Cap Ferrat, only six miles distant and the halfway point to our destination. Each time I took the brief seven-minute flight to Monaco, I found myself wishing it lasted a little longer: the spectacular craggy hillside landscapes, the rocky shoreline, and the mammoth yachts in the marinas—all warranting more than a passing glance at over a hundred knots.

I'd phoned Toru at nine this morning and we'd agreed to meet at three o'clock in the ground floor bar of the Salon Europe in the casino. I presented my passport, paid the forty franc entry fee at the casino entrance, and proceeded into the world's hub of ornate, marble, and gilt.

Toru waved and rose to greet me the moment he saw me approaching the cocktail table he'd staked out for our meeting. "Mr. Baron, I'm so pleased to see you again. I very much appreciate you taking the time to travel down to Monaco this afternoon to meet with me."

"Good to see you too, Mr. Toru," I replied, shaking hands and returning his modest bow. "Coming to Monte Carlo is always a welcome diversion."

A waiter arrived, carrying two partially filled brandy snifters and a small ice bucket.

"I recall from our meeting on Saturday evening, you're a blended Scotch drinker, Mr. Baron. I've taken the liberty of ordering my favorite for us. One ice cube only, I recommend."

"Yeah, I gave up on single malts when the yuppies kept whining every time I'd add ice." I knew the purists would never consider corrupting a fine whiskey with ice, but whatever I lost in depth of flavor, I made up for in refreshment.

The unique peaty taste was extraordinary, one I'd only sampled a few times previously. At $40 a pop, it was hard to forget. I raised the crystal snifter, swirling its contents to view the smoky, golden amber color reflecting from the light of the chandeliers.

"Johnnie Walker Blue Label. A complex and rare mix of blends ranging between twenty and sixty years old," I grandstanded. "You have excellent taste, Mr. Toru. It's also my favorite. Thank you. And here's to a successful meeting."

"*Kampai*," Toru toasted.

After a somewhat lengthy and embarrassing stare down which I refused to lose, the Japanese finally opened: "Am I correct in assuming Monsieur Laurent has found my group's offer to be of some interest?"

"He wasn't particularly taken with your proposal at first, but after several hours of examination and discussion, he's decided, subject to some minor revisions, of course, your offer would be acceptable," I replied coolly.

I reached across the table and handed Toru my paperwork. Before he had a chance to begin reading, I couldn't resist stirring the pot a little.

"Also, I should tell you, Monsieur Laurent said his counter offer is valid for twenty-four hours only, and his revised terms are nonnegotiable. If I don't report back by this time tomorrow and advise him your company has agreed to his conditions, no further approach by Kizoku will be entertained in the future."

Toru stared at me blankly before sitting back in his chair to examine my five amended pages. I was looking for a tell, but his deadpan expression didn't give me a hint as to his thoughts.

"You realize, of course, Mr. Baron, I am not in a position to authorize these changes to our original offer. Unfortunately, with Osaka being eight hours ahead of us, our corporate offices are now closed. But if I may be frank," he continued, "we both know everything in life is negotiable. I honestly don't know how my superiors will react to your offer, but I would hope for a little flexibility on Monsieur Laurent's part."

Flexibility? To a point. "I'm merely passing along Monsieur Laurent's instructions," I lied. "And don't forget, Mr. Toru, he's not actively soliciting buyers for his company. You came to him."

"I understand that." Small beads of perspiration were beginning to form on Toru's brow despite the massive room's adequate air conditioning system. "Without getting into the purchase price yet, let's talk about a few new issues I see here. Specifically, the items concerning the expense account in Paris, Miss Domenico's situation, the simultaneous purchase of the property, and the matter of the gold inventory. As far as a closing date of July 14th, I don't think my company will have a problem with that."

Okay, here it comes. I knew I could handle the property issues, but Gina, the expense account, and the gold—especially the gold —might get a little dicey.

"Regarding the purchase of the real property, Monsieur Laurent was clear it makes no sense for him to sell his business and the property separately over a four-year period. He feels if he's to sell, he wants to sell everything at once, not piecemeal. If you want the business, you buy the buildings and the land along with it. I would encourage your group, Mr. Toru, to hire its own commercial appraiser. We'll do the same, and the purchase price will be ten percent over the mean value of the two reconciliations."

The Japanese made some notes on his paperwork before finally nodding. "I believe I may speak for my company on this point: The earlier purchase of the real estate would be acceptable to us. Now, the other items I mentioned?"

"All right. First, in regard to Monsieur Laurent's expenses, it's only normal business practice for the contractor to pay its subcontractor's expenses. We'll offer a *not to exceed* figure of fifty thousand dollars for each of Monsieur Laurent's annual design trips to Paris."

Toru was again retreating to his note taking which I now took to be a good sign. "Agreed. Now, to the subject of the gold. What quantity are we discussing?"

I summoned up my calmest of voices. "8,040 troy ounces," I stated, thinking I should be nominated for an Oscar in recognition of my deadpan tone and expression. "At today's price of $283.50 an ounce, and adding a ten percent premium, it totals a few pennies over $2,500,000." Before entering the casino, I'd handwritten in today's gold settling price above the blank line I'd typed in earlier. The difference between Friday's close and today's represented a $23,000 surprise for Arnaud, or more than $25,000 if Toru went for the ten percent bump.

Toru matched my wooden face. Inscrutable, I think was the appropriate cliché.

"Interesting," he responded impassively. "I would not have suspected a watch manufacturer with Laurel's production volume to require such a large gold inventory. But for what possible reason would my company pay a ten percent premium over market price?"

"Because they want to buy Laurel. That small premium would represent the seriousness of their intentions toward this negotiation, as well as showing evidence of their respect for Monsieur Laurent. Let's call it a signing bonus," I returned, amazing myself with how good that crap actually sounded.

"As to Miss Domenico's situation," I continued, "we assume you'll be using your own international marketing resources, and, therefore, I'll be bowing out of my position with the company. However, with our confidence that Miss Domenico's close contacts throughout the United Kingdom and Ireland would yield more sales in the short term for the new ownership, we'd like to see her continue on for several years. She's exceptionally persuasive. Monsieur Laurent and I can both attest to that."

"How long has Miss Domenico been with your company?"

How about, *officially, she hasn't started quite yet?*

"Oh, I couldn't tell you exactly, but I know she and Monsieur Laurent go back a long way. Personally, I can vouch for her work ethic and organizational skills. Her contacts are something I believe Kizoku would find well worth exploiting."

"I believe my company plans to start fresh with our own marketing and sales staffs, but possibly something can be worked out financially for her if we choose not to retain her services."

"That certainly would be your option," I responded, rather pleased with myself at the ease with which I'd dodged that one. "I believe Monsieur Laurent would find one hundred thousand dollars to be a minimum amount due Miss Domenico should you chose not to avail yourselves of her services."

Toru shook his head before returning to his notations. "I'll fax your numbers to our Osaka offices this evening and ask them to telephone me at my hotel tomorrow morning."

This was probably as good a time as any to double down. "That'll be fine. Oh, there is one other item we didn't discuss," I said. "You understand, of course, for obvious reasons there is no mention in those papers of my, shall we say, my *expediting* fee, which you offered in Basel."

I looked for a reaction. Nada.

"I naturally assumed your counter offer of eight million dollars for the Laurel purchase included the one million I offered for your assistance, that it was a measure of your candor with Monsieur Laurent," Toru replied with deadly calm and the slightest hint of smugness.

"Be assured, Mr. Toru, I am always candid with Monsieur Laurent," I answered, starting to feel myself getting annoyed. "I told him about your offer to pay me a fee and he has no problem with that. He simply insists if he was to sell Laurel, his price would be eight million dollars."

Toru shook his head from side to side in frustration. More money and a twenty-four-hour deadline. His body language was undermining his stated position of being outside the loop on his company's bottom line offers.

"Mr. Baron, I am very doubtful my superiors will authorize a payment of one million dollars to you now with Monsieur Laurent having raised his number by that amount."

I was growing tired of Toru's act. He was reneging. Not really, but I easily rationalized he was hustling me. Regardless, it was now time for him to grasp what was about to occur. Screw all this civility.

"Listen well, Mr. Toru." I leaned forward and placed my drink on the table. "And make sure you understand something very important: As quickly as I put this deal together for you people is about twice as long as it would take for me to make it go away. Now let's cut the crap. You've just pissed off the wrong guy. I suggest you follow closely what's going to happen."

I snatched a paper drink napkin from the small stack on the table, took out my loaner Montblanc, and jotted down my numbers from memory.

"This is my account number with Credit Suisse in Neuchâtel. I'm leaving now, but I'll be back at this same table at three o'clock tomorrow afternoon if my bank confirms a wire transfer of five hundred thousand dollars into my account by two o'clock. And if I am here, I will also expect our revised contract to have been approved. The closing date of this sale will be in three months, on Friday, July fourteen, in Neuchâtel, assuming an additional five hundred thousand dollars has been deposited to my account not later than one hour before close of business on Thursday, July thirteen. Have a good evening."

I rose and parted without our customary handshake or little curtsy, but as I walked briskly across the casino floor and out the entrance, I had a bad feeling I'd pushed too far. We'd both been playing some very high stakes poker, and only tomorrow would tell which one of us had been bluffing.

I didn't want to risk even the slimmest of chances of running into Toru for the next twenty-three hours. The Hermitage, even the Hôtel de Paris, would remain off limits tonight. I opted for a safer choice: La Réserve, in Beaulieu-sur-Mer, where I'd stayed once during race week, about a fifteen-minute cab ride back down the coast road toward Nice.

* * *

After a short midmorning jog followed by orange juice and a couple of croissants, I phoned my account manager at Credit Suisse in Neuchâtel to leave a number where he could notify me when, or if, my funds had been received. I was still fairly secure in my thinking the Japanese hadn't spent this much time and research on Arnaud's company to have the deal go away over a ten or fifteen percent goose in our counter.

"*Bonjour*, Monsieur Baron," Louis Andrésy greeted me. "I assume you're inquiring about the wire transfer we received for you this morning?"

"Yes, I am, and good morning to you, Monsieur Andrésy. So funds have been placed in my account?" Hot damn!

"*Oui, monsieur*. We are in receipt of an overnight transfer for you from the Mitsui Bank in Osaka in the amount of five hundred thousand U.S. dollars. It is from the account of Kizoku Holdings, Limited," Andrésy advised.

"And the funds are considered good at this time?"

"Definitely, monsieur. You have my personal assurance everything is in order. May I assist you in any other way this morning?" the efficient Swiss banker politely queried.

"No, but thanks for your help, Monsieur Andrésy. Have a good day."

I began to feel a tad guilty about yesterday's curt lecture to Toru and my other than polite leave taking. But only a little guilty, not a lot. I'd get over it.

I held off on calling Arnaud until later in the day lest anything get screwed up in the next few hours, two or three of which I was planning to spend luxuriating by the hotel pool. A half-hour of swimming laps, a poolside salade niçoise with a split of Pouilly Fumé, a brilliant sunshiny day . . . I was only sorry Gina wasn't here.

* * *

At precisely the assigned hour of three, I walked across the casino floor and greeted Toru. This time he didn't rise from the table where we'd met yesterday. And today, the table was devoid of drinks. No Blue Label, no ice bucket, no water, no nothin'. He clearly was still miffed over yesterday's episode.

"Good afternoon, Mr. Toru." I extended my hand which he hesitantly shook. "I trust you had a pleasant evening."

"Yes, thank you. By your presence here today, I assume you've verified our deposit to your account?"

"Everything is in order. Thank you. And I will therefore assume your people in Osaka have approved our contract amendments?"

Placing his briefcase on his lap, Toru clicked open the two gold latches and withdrew his paperwork. In a quiet and controlled voice, he said, "In concept, yes. Only one or two small details which I trust will be agreeable to Monsieur Laurent. We transferred the requested sum to your bank as a gesture of our good faith, and as such, we would expect a small measure of reciprocity on some minor issues.

"First, we are electing to utilize our own marketing and sales personnel in the United Kingdom and Ireland. Therefore, we agree to pay Miss Domenico your proposed hundred thousand dollar sum as severance."

"Very well, if that's your decision," I said, restraining myself from rolling my eyes at Gina's windfall. "I'm sure she'll be disappointed with her separation from Laurel, but that option is certainly yours. Next?"

"The outright purchase of Monsieur Laurent's real estate in lieu of an initial lease has been approved. The timing of this transaction will coincide with the closing date of the business purchase." Toru's focus remained fixed on the papers in his hand. "The expense account for Monsieur Laurent in Paris is also acceptable. The only remaining issue is the purchase of the gold inventory."

Damn, here it comes. We were no longer picking nits, and dumping those LGDs was important to Arnaud.

"We will buy your entire gold stock. However, Monsieur Laurent's signing bonus, as you put it, has been included in our offer to pay ten percent over appraised market value for his real estate, not to mention raising our purchase price of the business by one million dollars. Our offer is this: We will pay ten percent below yesterday's market settling price of $283.50 per troy ounce for the bullion."

"Below market? What the hell are you talking about?"

"Mr. Baron, my company believes we have been quite generous in our offer to purchase Laurel and the related property. And we both know that an individual attempting to dispose of London Good Delivery bars would face a series of embarrassing questions and unwanted scrutiny as to how they had come by the bars originally—twenty of them, no less. Therefore, and as a concession to Monsieur Laurent, we will buy all his LGDs, but at ninety percent of the $283.50 per ounce figure." He quickly searched through his paperwork. "That calculates to 2,051,406 U.S. dollars."

I hadn't given him enough credit. He knew he had me.

"Speaking for Monsieur Laurent, and in the spirit of reciprocity, I think we could go along with that," I returned after several moment's reflection, more with relief than anything else.

"And finally, one last item, which I do not think Monsieur Laurent will object to," Toru added, this time clearly more relaxed than he'd appeared for the last two days. "The purchase of the gold will not appear in the final contracts between Kizoku and Monsieur Laurent. And the agreed upon price for the bullion will be paid in cash. I assume these conditions would be acceptable?"

This one came out of left field. Why the hell would a company the size of Kizoku pay cash for anything? I immediately recalled Gina's brief research having revealed some past financial hanky-panky—this outfit was still cooking the books. However, since Arnaud's gold stash technically wouldn't exist, neither would the two million in cash.

A quick calculation of two times twenty-two pounds per million dollars, another fun fact I'd stored away hoping for a day just like this: forty-four pounds of hundred-dollar bills! I was looking forward to Arnaud's reaction to a suitcase or two filled with C-notes.

"Cash works. Acceptable."

Chapter 10

London/Radnage

Three months later—Thursday/Friday, 13/14 July 2000

You bloody bastard!" Gina shouted.

Echoing like the crisp and rapid reports of an M16, her high heels clattered noisily across the marble checkerboard lobby floor as she raced toward me, leaping into my arms in front of God and the entire morning suit attired hotel staff.

"You drop me at the airport in Geneva three months ago and I kiss you goodbye thinking I'm about to start a new career, you call the next morning to tell me not to quit my old job, and then two days later, you invite me to fly to Paris with you in three months for a belated Bastille Day party and a big surprise. And in all our nightly phone calls since, not a word about what the hell's been going on in Switzerland."

"I didn't want to jinx things. But apparently you know it's going to be a good thing or you wouldn't have your legs wrapped around me in the lobby of Claridge's."

She self-consciously uncoiled herself; I sensed she was pleased to see me. I've always prided myself on my ability to instantly grasp the subtleties of a woman's body language.

"Let's get a drink." I turned to the wide-eyed bellboy, handed him a ten-pound note, and added, "If this gentleman wouldn't mind taking my bags to my room."

The silver leafed ceiling in Claridge's Bar effectively complemented the single red rose atop each of the highly polished dark wood cocktail tables. We slid into the first available red leather banquette.

"Perhaps we should celebrate with a bottle of Champagne?" Gina suggested as the waiter took up a parade rest posture several feet from our table lest he interrupt our conversation by approaching closer. God forbid—this was Claridge's.

"The day after tomorrow in Paris will be the celebration." I turned to the waiter, now freeing him to advance another step toward our table. "A Champagne cocktail for the lady. I'll have a Black Label. Lots of ice, please. And let's try a small sampling of your sushi. Enough for two." I looked to Gina after the waiter departed. "You know, since I've known you, I don't think you've ever had the same drink twice. Is this a superstition or something?"

"No, but possibly a bit capricious, I suppose. Perhaps someday, after I've sampled everything life has to offer, I'll stop flitting from one thing to the next. We'll see," she added with a smooth double entendre and that wink I'd been missing for three months. "Now, before you fill me in on all that's been happening, tell me about your flight today. I'm so jealous. I've always wanted to fly Concorde," she exclaimed, squeezing my hand.

"Sensational. That's one very special airplane, one hell of a sweet ride. I'm still stoked about flying over Mach two today— almost fourteen hundred miles per hour. An amazing three and a half hours. I'll tell you all the details later. Now, how have you been? And how's your son Willie doing?" Yeah, don't forget about Willie, I reminded myself.

"Oh, everything's been good with us. And thanks for asking about Willie. He's really looking forward to meeting you. So, tell me, how's Arnaud reacting to selling Laurel?"

"Mixed feelings, I sense. We both know the only part of the business he really enjoyed was the design end, and he'll still be doing that. At least for another few years anyway. He'll be fine."

"I'm happy for him. Now tell me, what exactly is going to happen in Paris on Saturday?" Gina asked. "You've been keeping me in the dark far too long."

"I won't tell you everything, but suffice it to say for now I'm collecting a check from Arnaud for a ton of money, and the three of us are going to go out and spend a conspicuous amount of it on dinner and what you Brits call a great piss up. And anything else your little heart desires."

She put down her Champagne flute, slid across the banquette, and threw her arms around my neck.

"I think I'm happy I met you, Mr. Baron." She pulled my head toward hers, slowly kissing me on the lips for the first time. But as quickly as she'd attacked me, she returned to her original spot a foot away.

"Now . . . tell me about the sleeping accommodations in Paris," she asked in a most deliberate tone, eyebrows furled, arms crossed below her breasts. "I trust you've made the proper arrangements? I *am* British, as you might remember."

Swell. "Uh, well," I started cautiously, "I reserved a suite for us at the Royal Monceau. But if you prefer, I can switch it to separate rooms. Sorry, I guess I was being a little presumptuous."

"I should say so. I didn't realize going to Paris was dependent upon my sleeping with you," Gina huffed. She paused for my reaction, and then, with a big grin, she blurted, "You really are an idiot! Of course we're sleeping together. I was just winding you up. I didn't realize how gullible you could be."

"Good one." She got me. I shrugged and shifted gears. "Gina, I have to go out to Buckinghamshire tomorrow, to a village in the Chiltern Hills, about halfway to Oxford. My father has an old friend from the war who lives out there and my dad asked me to personally deliver a book to him."

"That wouldn't be a burden. I'd love to go with you," she said before I could finish. This was going smoother than expected.

"The fellow I'm meeting—Paul Bisno—lives in High Wycombe. We've arranged to meet for drinks at a little inn called the Three Horseshoes. I've stayed there a couple of times before. It's just outside a village called Radnage, not far from where Paul lives. I thought you and I might stay over at the Horseshoes tomorrow night and come back to London on Saturday before our flight to Paris. Maybe yes?"

Gina placed her hand over mine, with her face wearing one of those "*I'm so sorry, but . . .*" expressions. "That sounds lovely, Dane, but Willie isn't with his grandparents this weekend. He's home at our flat now, with my landlady who's minding him. It's a bit complicated, actually. My parents popped down to Switzerland this afternoon to look in on my aunt who's been quite ill. I'm to collect them at Heathrow tomorrow evening when they fly back. They'll stay at my place with Willie until I return from Paris. Am I being at all clear?"

"Crystal." I needed a program.

Evidently believing me, she continued, "Good. So, could we take Willie along? I'll drive us out to Bucks tomorrow morning and we can come back after lunch. Would you mind terribly?"

Terrific, a romantic day in the countryside with junior. Would I mind terribly? Yeah, I would.

"Sure, that'll be fine. I should have thought of little Willie," I fudged after an embarrassingly long pause.

"Thanks awfully. That's our plan, then. This'll be fun."

"Is your minder lady in for whole night?" I ventured. Might as well give tonight a shot.

Gina playfully slapped my hand: "Slow down there, cowboy. You've kept me waiting for three months, and now you can't wait another two days till we get to Paris?"

She's been waiting three months? "Just looking for a reaction. But I hope you've arranged to stay out a little later tonight. We have reservations at Le Gavroche in twenty minutes."

* * *

Good morning, sir," the chauffeur greeted me as he held open the Bentley's rear left door.

"Morning," I returned. "We'll be making a quick stop in South Kensington along the way to pick up our other passengers. Queensbury Mews West, just below the Cromwell Road. Do you know it?"

"Yes, sir. We should be there in less than ten minutes."

I reach some of my better decisions in the shower: Within five minutes of calling the concierge this morning, he'd phoned back to confirm my request for a helicopter charter from the nearby London Heliport. Fifteen minutes flying time to Radnage, max. The thought of driving doubled over in Gina's Mini through the one lane hedgerow-lined roads of the Buckinghamshire countryside terrified me. I was a quick study; the drive to Heathrow with her three months ago had cured me.

"Look for the blue door on the left when you enter the mews," she'd instructed when I called. She'd sounded confused but open to a change in plans.

We turned into the cobbled dead-end street to see Gina waving from her front door. The driver slowed the ash gray Bentley to a stop at the base of her steps.

"Willie, this is my friend Dane I've told you so much about. Dane, meet Willie," Gina said once I'd stepped out onto the sidewalk.

As he looked past me to the Bentley, the wide-eyed young man said, "How do you do, sir?" With his mother's good looks and the red from her strawberry blonde hair, Willie bore more than a slight resemblance to a young Prince Harry. Turning to look back at me, and then Gina, he said, "But mum, he's not black."

Gina burst out with a laugh before holding a finger to her lips to shush Willie.

"Why did you think I was a black man?" I asked the boy, thinking this ought to be interesting.

Gina leaned down to hear Willie whisper in her ear. She let go with another laugh, wiped her eyes, and then composed herself enough to explain what was going on. "You remember, I told you I originally described you to Willie as being a big man, and you were from America. Then he asked if you were a footballer. I told him, yes, you'd probably played at some point. Well, he seems to have assumed from watching American football on the telly that you were black."

"I was the kicker." The chauffeur's smile told me he was the only one of the three of them who got it.

Clearly disappointed, Willie turned back to his mother and asked, "Mum, may I sit in the front?"

I immediately opened the front passenger door for the boy before he changed his little mind. The driver tipped his cap, still grinning over my kicker line.

Once seated in the rear next to me, Gina turned and said, "You get full marks for this one, Dane, even if it is a bit over-the-top."

"Wait, it gets better."

The chauffeur smoothly guided our car south through the moderate Chelsea traffic toward the Embankment. Once across the Thames on the Battersea Bridge, the Bentley continued south for a few moments before turning right to parallel the river. The helipad jetty, overhanging the Thames on its support pilings, came into view a minute later. As we neared, the pungent smell of exhausted Jet A fuel filled the car's interior.

"Bloody hell, Dane. I already told you I'd sleep with you, and you had Willie the moment the Bentley rolled up," Gina softly whispered in my ear, kissing my cheek.

"Well, we only have a few hours till your folks arrive so I thought this might be a little more expedient," I said with a Cheshire grin. "And, anyway, I like helicopters. So there."

Our pilot was doing his paperwork in the front right seat of the dark blue helicopter, a twin jet engined Aérospatiale 355, I recognized.

"Willie, why don't you take the front left seat, next to the pilot," I offered, watching the little fellow's eyes and mouth grow wider. This was better than the circus. "Go ahead and get in, Gina. I'll be right back. I have to take care of a little business inside for a minute."

A large wall mounting in the office displayed the helicopter company's logo above the words, "We don't need no stinkin' runways!"

"Good morning, Mr. Baron. I understand you'll be returning this afternoon?" the young woman behind the counter asked.

I handed her my American Express Platinum card. "Good morning. Yes, this afternoon. Can you arrange to have us picked up, uh, collected, sometime around four?"

"Very well, sir. At four it will be, then. Here's your card back."

I steadied my hand as I signed the charge slip for the £1,400 round trip charter fee. 2,100 bucks. What the hell? Tomorrow was payday.

The main and tail rotors were already spinning when I climbed in next to Gina and onto the helicopter's plush rear bench seat. A ground crewman latched my door, slapped the aluminum side of the sleek machine twice with his palm, withdrew several steps, and gestured to the pilot with a thumbs up.

"Good morning, sir," the pilot turned to welcome me in a loud voice, looking back over his left shoulder. "As I've already told your wife and son, if you'd care to put on the headset, you'll have a bit of a better idea of what we're doing. When you want to communicate, simply press the push-to-talk switch on the electrical cable. We'll be off momentarily."

Willie turned to the pilot and said over the intercom, "He's not married to my mum. They're just friends for now." The pilot smiled back at Willie and appeared to be ever so pleased to have been included in that essential bit of intelligence.

The increasing whine of the two Allison jet engines and the sound of the spinning rotors were blessedly dampened somewhat by the noise-canceling headsets. Looking between the front seats, I watched the pilot almost imperceptibly pull up on the collective pitch lever with his left hand; the helicopter got light on its skids before rising to a hover ten feet off the landing pad. I could see him inputting slight movements with his right hand to the cyclic stick between his knees to steady and level the machine, while his boot deftly pressed on the left tail rotor control pedal to compensate for the increasing torque and keep our craft pointing straight ahead.

The intercom crackled with the pilot's voice. "We're cleared to follow the Thames upriver for a mile or two before we turn north toward the A40. Please feel free to ask questions along the way. And remember to key your microphone button before you speak. Tally ho."

He smoothly eased forward on the cyclic stick, the helicopter's nose lowered slightly, and our forward speed began to increase. Seemingly simultaneously, he applied more upward pressure on the collective to gain altitude.

A glance at the altimeter showed we had quickly passed through 500 feet while we followed the western London meanders of the Thames. Our altitude continued to climb until we leveled off at 1,000 feet, still low enough for an amazing view of the city gradually disappearing off our right side. Somewhat typically for summer, the clouds were scattered, perhaps 2,000 feet above us, as we flew west toward more pastoral landscapes.

"Dane, I think you've earned yourself a little something extra when we get into our suite in Paris tomorrow night," Gina purred through the headset.

"Madam, I should advise that any communication on the intercom is received by all aboard," the pilot deadpanned into his microphone. "Something I thought you might want to be aware of."

Gina slapped my leg while mouthing a silent "Oh, shit!" She leaned forward, her chest down to her knees, and mockingly beat the back of her head.

The helicopter held steady at 1,000 feet, passing over the large town of High Wycombe off to our right. My sightseeing was interrupted by the pilot's voice on the intercom.

"Mr. Baron, uh, I think I'll need your help in finding our exact landing location, sir. I'm descending a bit as I think we're getting close now. Do you have your destination in sight yet?"

I leaned forward and took hold of the back of Willie's front seat for better support and forward viewing. I toggled my mic.

"Sure, not a problem. And no, I don't see it yet. Continue following this road below us. I'm pretty sure that's still the A40. Okay, I think I see Stokenchurch dead ahead. See it? That small village about three miles out."

"Roger, I've got it, sir," the pilot confirmed.

"All right, start slowing and bank off to your right about thirty degrees. I think I've got it in sight now. Maybe two miles."

The helicopter descended to what appeared to be about 100 feet above ground level as we slowly approached the Horseshoes. "Sir, do you know if there are any power lines near our landing area? If so, please advise location."

"No, I don't think there are. Or at least none that I recall, but I'll be looking. There's your landing zone now, in that field just to the east of the inn. Got it?"

"Yes, sir, I see it now. Thanks. I think we'll put down a bit farther away from the building so we don't annoy those people outside with our rotor wash." The pilot was kicking in a little right pedal to bring the machine into the wind before setting up a hover a few feet off the ground in the field behind the Three Horseshoes. The ground effect of the air forced down from the main rotor made our touchdown on the dirt field a seamless transition from air to land.

With the main rotor now idling above us, the pilot turned to face Gina and me in the rear seat. "Hope you both enjoyed our short flight, and I'll see you back here at four. Have a good afternoon."

I held Gina's left hand and she used her right in a vain attempt to hold her hair in place as we jogged under the still spinning main rotor and its downwash. Willie jauntily walked backward toward us while giving a thumbs up to the departing pilot. He'd probably been waiting to try that since he saw the assistant do it at the heliport.

A few of the early lunch crowd on the pub's rear patio waved, some stood to clap, before the Aérospatiale became airborne again and flew off in a sweeping low turn to the east. Young Willie precociously stopped and took a deep bow. The kid showed a little panache; I kind of liked his flair.

A scripted black on white wood sign affixed to the exterior of the building's brick chimney claimed to offer *Real Ales and Hot and Cold Food since 1645.* The slate roofed flint and mortar structure had been enlarged over the years, a commercial kitchen and some additional guest rooms having been masterfully added by landlord Tim Ashby's own hand. He had successfully merged the new construction with the original in keeping with the authentic rural seventeenth-century style.

"This is lovely," Gina commented. "How did you first discover this place?"

"I met the landlord, Tim, down in Monaco at my favorite little bar and grill there—Sam's Place. I'd met up with some friends of mine from the States for the Grand Prix and Tim was with a mob of his buddies from this area."

"After you," I gestured as we approached the front door. I remembered to duck as we entered the snug, the smaller and more rustic of the two bar areas. I normally smacked myself once or twice a day on the pub's overhead blackened beams and low lintels when I stayed here, more if a session wore on late into the night.

"Dane! You're getting to be a right toff, you old flash bastard. You and your bloody helicopters. How are you, mate?" Tim called out from behind the bar, pulling a couple of pints from one of the taps. He was wearing one of his typically gaudy ties over a black dress shirt with neatly rolled up sleeves. At a well-proportioned five and a half feet tall, Tim had no difficulty navigating under the pub's low beams without nicks to his balding pate.

"Hi, Timmy, good to see you. It's been a while", I returned. "I'd like you to meet my friend Gina, and her son Willie. Gina, Willie, this is our host, Tim Ashby."

Gina and Tim exchanged greetings while Willie scoped out the little room. He quickly settled on a chair next to Winston, the house bulldog, curled up by the inglenook fireplace.

"What would you care to drink, luv?" Tim asked Gina between his other bar orders.

"I'll have a shandy, thanks, Tim. And an orange squash for Willie, please."

Before I could get my order in, Tim said, "Right, a shandy, a squash, and a large measure of Black Label with ice. Do I still have it right, Dane?"

"Guilty as charged. Hey, Tim, we're expecting to meet a gentleman driving in from High Wycombe. Any chance he's already arrived?"

"That would be the gentleman in the corner, I believe," Tim gestured with his free hand. "Cheers," he said, passing the three glasses across the bar.

I led Gina across the room, possibly the size of a large parlor, and still floored with the original stones, now highly polished with over three centuries of wear.

"Mr. Bisno?" We approached the single man who was working on a pint of stout at one of the small and well-distressed wooden tables.

"Please, call me Paul. And that would make you Dane," the elderly and heavyset man replied. He unsteadily rose to greet us. I assumed him to be in his early eighties, given my father's age, but once he stood he still bore the erect carriage of the classic British military veteran officer.

"How do you do, sir," I introduced myself. "This is my friend Gina, and the young man over there with the house mascot is her son Willie. Please, sit down. Sorry to have kept you waiting."

"Not at all. I've only just finished playing nine holes nearby with some friends and came directly here."

Oddly contrasting his years, Paul was raffishly clad in yellow pants, a light blue and red argyle sweater, and topped with a cap which could have fallen out of Ben Hogan's bag.

"My father didn't tell me you were a professional golfer. I assume this is your second career?"

"Hardly," Paul chuckled. "I'm still active with our auction house activities in London. I'm a regular on the train into the city two or three days a week."

"Oh, you're *that* Bisno," I said in honest awe. "I'm familiar with Bisno's Auctions. You're involved mostly with the fine arts as I recall?"

"Mostly, yes, and I'm very flattered you've heard of our small firm over in the States. For the past fifteen or so years, we've expanded our little bailiwick into some other areas as well: estate liquidations, numismatics, philately, and once a year we put on a classic automobile auction."

"Where do you hold it? In London?"

"No, in Monaco, actually, each July. In fact, our next one is in two weeks' time, the twenty-eighth of this month. I hired a young woman four or five years ago who's quite knowledgeable about the classic automobile markets. She's been able to generate a handsome little business for us. She contacts owners whose cars didn't make reserve in Monaco during race week in May or June with the Christie's, Barrett-Jackson, or Brooks people. She's been quite good at securing a rather large percentage of their left-overs, machines whose owners are willing to give auction sale one more go since their cars are already down there."

"Sounds fascinating," Gina commented. "How long have you

been in the auction business, Mr. Bisno?"

"Please, it's Paul. I got into this shortly after the war. And by that, young lady, I mean the big one, World War Two," he laughed. "But it's been a good living. I can't see myself ever completely retiring from it."

Gina began to answer Paul's questions about her background when I took the opportunity to excuse myself to retrieve the small package containing the C-47 manual I'd left on the bar. I'd given the book to the concierge at Claridge's last night, and by ten this morning, it had been returned back to my room along with a spiral bound copy for my Concorde captain.

"Here's the manual my father asked me to give you, Paul." I placed it next to his beer. "And I'm delighted to report this old book got me onto the Concorde flight deck yesterday."

That door now opened, Paul and I enthusiastically talked airplanes, with Gina showing a remarkable and unexpected interest and knowledge for a non-pilot.

Before I could order another round, Paul emptied his second pint, insisting he still had a drive ahead of him and his third was better consumed at home. "I must be off now, but here's my card," he offered. "Let me know when you're back this way again, Dane, and we'll have that third pint or maybe play a few holes at my club if you have the time. I'll send a note off to your father tomorrow to thank him. Cheerio for now."

The lunch patrons had cleared out by three o'clock when we heard a loud "*Pull*!" An ear-thumping blast, the report of a shotgun, followed almost instantly. I'd failed to warn Gina of the occasional impromptu afternoon trap shoot off the rear patio. It was Friday afternoon, and some of the lads had decided to call it a week—shoot a few clays, and enjoy a few more pints.

"*What the hell was that*?" Gina yelped, reaching for Willie.

"Oh, just some of the regulars popping off some clay pigeons over the back field. Sorry I didn't warn you." I wasn't really sorry. It was always funny as hell watching the reaction of first-timers to the pub when artillery practice started.

"I jolly well hope they run out of ammunition before the helicopter comes back," she said, feigning a snit. Willie jumped up and squirmed to rid himself of his mother's clutches.

"Please, Dane, could we have a go?" the boy asked excitedly.

"I think those twelve-gauges they're firing out there might be a little hefty for you, Willie," I responded, looking for a sign from Gina.

"We call those twelve-*bore* on this side of the Atlantic," Tim pointed out from across the small barroom. He was finishing cleaning the last of the empty glasses. "And with mum's permission, I have one I could loan young Will if he'd care to have a crack."

The boy was ready to wet himself.

Gina leaned closer and whispered, "Do you think it's all right? Dane, these chaps have been drinking all afternoon."

"They're all very careful with their guns. In fact, I think they're better shots with a couple of pints behind 'em. It steadies 'em down —like throwing darts. Tim'll show him what to do. Up to you," I shrugged. I knew she'd cave.

Sensing a half nod from Gina, Tim said, "Come on then, lad. Let's find you a shotgun before all the clays are gone. Dane, you and Gina are self-serve now. Honor system, old boy."

Gina took my hand and we looked at one another in silence for a few moments, punctuated only by the explosions of shotguns for that special touch of ambiance.

"I think you've made quite a hit with the little guy," she finally said. "Bentleys, helicopters and shooting—what else could a boy ask for?"

"I like him. He's a good kid. And he has a touch of the theater in him. Did you see that bow for the folks when we got out of the helo? What a little ham. But I'm afraid I'm not going to miss him when we get to Paris."

"Oh, God," she giggled, sliding her chair nearer. "I can't believe I was such a prat, forgetting Willie and the pilot were listening on the intercom when I was trying to talk sexy to you. What a bloody twit I can be sometimes."

"Did you see Willie snickering? He was chuckling away for a couple minutes after that one."

Gina scanned the small room, confirming it was empty but for the two of us and Winston. Draping her arms around my neck, she drew closer.

"Dane, I can't tell you how much I appreciate you taking Willie and me with you today. Quite the second date. Or is this our third? I think I'm discovering that behind that rather blasé exterior, you're actually a bit of a romantic."

Ever since my last divorce, I'd become a little gun-shy of most women. Or maybe I'd simply had it with being screwed over—financially and emotionally. I now prided myself on my knack for staying aloof from any who started getting too close. *Please, stay the night, maybe the weekend, but don't even think about leaving those things in the closet or the bathroom.* But this was different: Gina was getting to me, and surprisingly, I was okay with that. Our almost nightly phone calls since dropping her in Geneva back in April had given me a far deeper insight into her than could have been expected from the actual time we'd been together. Still, I was also starting to feel a little twitchy with all this gushy and gooey-eyed staring stuff.

"How long did you tell your parents you'd be in Paris?"

"I've left it a bit open. They're on holiday for another month. They're taking Will out to the West Country the week after next for a few days of trout fishing near Bampton along the River Exe in Devon. I only hope you haven't spoiled him after today."

"Hey, I've got an idea I'd like to lay on you. Can you get away from your office for a couple of weeks?"

"*A couple of weeks*? What are you dreaming up this time?"

"Well, uh, I saw an ad in a magazine on the Concorde yesterday. There's a German travel outfit that's chartering one of the Air France Concordes on the twenty-fifth of July, a week from Tuesday. The package includes flying to New York from Paris, then hooking up with a ship called the MS *Deutschland* for a sixteen-day cruise to South America. Sounded kind of fun. What do you think?"

"That sounds brilliant. I'd love to go. But this is going to take some real juggling, my parents looking after Willie and all."

"Fantastic. I'll check to see if there's any availability left. Maybe hold off on any announcements till I call Germany tomorrow."

"Okay, but if we do this, the timing couldn't be better, especially with both my parents and Willie on school holiday. And as far as my job, Dane, well, that's something I was going to tell you about later, perhaps in Paris when we'd have more time. Oh, hell, I'll just come out with it: I've left my firm. Last Friday was my last day. I've enjoyed advertising but I've started to feel a bit burned out with it the last few years. It's time for a change. And as I mentioned before, I need to make a lot more money in the very near future. So whether we go or not, I'm now a woman at liberty."

"That's kind of a shocker. I knew you were thinking about it in Basel, but— "

I was interrupted by the first *wop-wop-wop* sounds of an incoming helicopter's rotors. Willie came running back into the empty pub, rubbing his obviously sore right shoulder.

"Dane, may I sit in the front next to the pilot again? Please?"

Chapter 11

Paris

Saturday, 15 July 2000

I loved Paris. Whenever I returned, I recalled Gertrude Stein writing, "America is my country, and Paris is my home town."

Paris had the frenetic energy and vibrancy of New York, with its millions of residents busily charging from one place to the next. And typically, more than a few newcomers to Paris found the bustling citizenry brusque and rude. I didn't agree. Similar to New Yorkers or Londoners, Parisians knew exactly where they were and where they were going as they walked and drove quickly through their city, and simply did not have the time for a smiley chat with lost strangers. Just keep up, folks. After all, how many Americans at home would offer more than a shrug before walking away after ignoring a tourist's request for directions in a language other than their own? I'd encountered more than a few assholes in Paris over my lifetime—nearly as many as I'd come across in the States—but generally, I rather enjoyed Parisians.

My years of schooling in Paris and my subsequent Air Force posting at the embassy had given me not only an adequate command of the French language, but just as importantly, I'd developed an understanding of the Parisians themselves—Parisians, as differentiated from the rest of the French. Similar to the American or British visitor feeling unwelcomed, I was confident the poor schmuck from Avignon also returned home after his short stay in Paris wondering why he hadn't been made to feel more loved. Jesus, it's their city, and it's to the visitor to adapt. Or don't. Nobody cared. I simply had grown tired of listening to all the bitching about my home town.

Our taxi turned right into the avenue de Messine toward the Parc Monceau, followed by a left and a quick right to the avenue Hoche; the Hôtel Royal Monceau was visible at the end of the block. Once registered, I figured we had a little time to enjoy a pair of friendly barstools before meeting Arnaud for dinner. We strolled down the avenue Hoche toward Étoile.

"I sense this is more than a leisurely walk before dinner. You wouldn't be taking me to one of your locals would you?" Gina asked.

"Well, since you mentioned it, and if you don't mind a short hike, I'll take you to my world's favorite bar. A proper whiskey and gin martini saloon, with none of that dinner mouthwash called wine. In fact, I'll bet it's the only watering hole in all of France that doesn't serve wine . . . and definitely no coffee. Tends to keep out the amateur status riffraff. It's between the Ritz and the Opéra, maybe two miles, but it's mostly downhill. You up to it?"

"I wouldn't miss it."

In less than thirty minutes, we walked the length of the Champs-Élysées to the place de la Concorde, where, on the northern corner, we approached the entrance to the American

Embassy. Two U.S. Marine sentries were standing guard at the front gate.

"Isn't this where you were worked when you were in the Air Force?"

"The very place." I gazed through the wrought iron fence and could still picture my blue captain's uniform with my shiny—yet indelibly tarnished—silver senior pilot wings pinned above the left breast pocket. "This was an assignment most guys would have killed for. The only problem was I was always broke. A young captain's salary without flight pay didn't go very far in a place as expensive as Paris, even with a cost of living allowance. But I still had a great time here. Hell, my job description essentially consisted of going to foreign embassy cocktail parties and writing reports on what I'd seen and heard."

"So you were really a spy?"

"I guess, of sorts. Basically just a low grade spook with a sexy security clearance who sucked up free booze and canapés but never came across anything nefarious enough to fill a chapter in a spy novel."

We continued on, along the north side of the Tuileries, up the rue de Castiglione, and across the tony rue Saint-Honoré, which, even I could appreciate, made Beverly Hills' Rodeo Drive and Palm Beach's Worth Avenue appear to be gaudy afterthoughts. Another block and we passed the Hôtel Ritz in the place Vendôme before turning right into the rue Daunou.

"Thar she blows," I said, pointing at the diminutive red neon "*Harry's Bar*" sign hanging out from above the bar's entrance. The saloon's street frontage was minimal, possibly no more than fifteen feet.

We seated ourselves at the near end of the long wooden bar. "What's it to be?" I asked Gina.

"What's the house specialty? I suspect you may just have a little local knowledge here."

A white-aproned bartender with the size and heft of a rugby player approached, his ruddy face becoming more familiar the closer he came. I finally recognized the name Gilles embroidered on his white barman's jacket. Without looking at me, he asked Gina, in English with only a trace of a French accent, "Mademoiselle, what may I get for you?"

"Your Bloody Mary comes highly recommended. Please."

Gilles nodded silently and retreated to his mixing station several feet away. When he returned with her drink, he reached behind and pulled down a bottle of Johnnie Black. "With lots of ice, no?" he deadpanned while pouring a most healthy measure over the rocks.

"How have you been, Gilles?" I asked, now fully recalling a past session or two. I shook his extended hand across the bar top.

"*Ça va*. Welcome back to Harry's. My memory's still not too bad, no?" he said before returning to his earlier mid-bar location and his chat with three of the other patrons in the long and narrow room. I was always amazed at a professional bartender's ability to remember your drink though he most likely had forgotten your name.

"So how long have you been a regular here at Harry's? The barman obviously remembers you quite well."

"Since I was thirteen," I answered with a straight face.

"*Thirteen*? Are you serious? My God, I knew the French were somewhat enlightened, but thirteen's a bit over-the-top, isn't it?"

"No, it's true. My dad would take me here almost every other Saturday afternoon. He'd play chess for a couple of hours with a friend of his and I'd wander around looking at the college pennants on the walls and eat hot dogs and drink Cokes or a small beer." I pointed down the bar toward the 1930s vintage hot dog and bun steamer. "I was easily amused."

After several more minutes of filling in Gina on the history of Harry's New York Bar, our conversation drifted to our upcoming Concorde flight and the South American cruise. I'd phoned the German travel agency before leaving London and was told the best they could do was place us on a stand-by list, the tour having sold out several weeks earlier.

"That's disappointing," she frowned. "Stand-by doesn't sound very promising."

"We'll see. Here's the deal: The agent indicated there's still a strong possibility a certain couple may cancel. Apparently, there's an older fellow whose doctor has recommended against his going. But the tour operator may not know till the last minute."

"I don't understand. Are we supposed to just turn up at the airport Tuesday week and see if there are any empty seats?"

"Basically, yeah. But if this all sounds too insecure for you, we can always do something else."

Gina took another sip of her drink and leaned back, nearly falling off the backless wooden stool before I caught her. "That's embarrassing," she laughed. "Sorry. I usually hold that act until after midnight. No, let's give the Concorde trip a go."

"Okay. Look, if we don't make the flight, we'll be at Charles de Gaulle anyway and we can pick somewhere else to go. I don't really care where. I suspect we'll have a good time wherever it is."

Gina leaned closer. "Hey, Yank, we haven't even slept together yet. You sure you want to be stuck with a bad lay for two weeks?"

"Yeah, right. I have a feeling I'm in for a personal best tonight. C'mon, let's finish up here and go walk around a little till we meet Arnaud."

"You never told me, where are we dining?" she asked as Gilles handed me a small piece of cash register tape which served as our bar check.

"A surprise, but you'll be pleased. In my opinion, it's the best restaurant in Paris. They also claim to have one of the most significant wine cellars in town."

"The Taillevent?" Gilles commented, picking up my cash.

"Bingo! How the hell did you know that?"

"*Et voilà*. The best restaurant in Paris?" he pondered with a shrug. "Perhaps. Possibly among the top four or five. But the best *cave*, or cellar as you say? Either the Taillevent or the Tour d'Argent. And you seem more like an Eighth Arrondissement type than a *rive gauche* kind of guy, so I reasoned the Taillevent. *Bon appétit. À demain?*"

"See you then. *Au revoir, Gilles. Merci.*"

* * *

I'd been to the Taillevent only twice before but I instantly remembered the displays of contemporary oils suspended on oak paneling throughout the restaurant. The impeccably set white linen covered tables were barely half occupied, the eight o'clock hour still being somewhat early for the Parisian clientèle. Over the chinks of fine silverware touching finer china, conversations were carried on in soft tones by the swells and the upscale foodies alike. Dining here was how I imagined spending an evening at a gentleman's club which also happened to serve the absolute best in classical French cuisine. And the Taillevent was priced accordingly, proudly one of the most expensive tables in town.

Arnaud looked up from the massive wine tome before him (no mere list here) and rose to take Gina's hands and kiss her on both cheeks. As expected, he was dressed impeccably: double-breasted charcoal suit with the subtlest of pinstripes, light blue shirt with white French-cuffs and detachable collar, and a snazzy dark red paisley tie with a matching silk foulard cascading from his breast pocket. So much for my spiffy new pinkish Brooks Brothers seersucker jacket; Arnaud had a knack for making me look like the before photo in a before and after ad.

A waiter withdrew Gina's chair for her as I shook hands with my Swiss friend. We passed on the kiss-kiss.

"How is your hotel? The Royal Monceau, no?" Arnaud asked.

"Yes. We haven't been to the room yet, but I'm sure it'll be more than agreeable."

A bottle of 1982 Taittinger Brut Blanc de Blancs Comtes de Champagne appeared for Arnaud's inspection. After first displaying the label side for several seconds, the sommelier then deftly removed the cork with a sound more like a cough than a pop. After a discerning taste and a soft "*Oui, merci*," Arnaud nodded his approval.

"Here's to you successfully driving me out of business, Dane," Arnaud toasted. "Seriously, I want to thank you for all you've done. You did a masterful job with the Japanese. Now, before I forget, let us take care of a few small matters of business right off so we may enjoy our meal without it being tainted with the vulgarities of money."

Arnaud reached into his suit coat pocket and withdrew two small monogrammed off-white envelopes. He briefly glanced at the names on each before handing one to Gina and the other to me.

Gina looked at me with a growing question mark in her expression before turning to Arnaud.

"What's this? My birthday's not until November."

"Open it, my dear. And you may thank Dane."

She ripped open the envelope, unfolded its contents, and stared at the check. "Bugger me! A hundred thousand dollars? I'm gobsmacked! Lovely jubbly!" she burst out before covering her mouth. "What the hell is this for?"

"Dane and I thought you should be entitled to a small something to help compensate for losing your new job with us. After all, you brought Monsieur Toru to our little reception in Basel."

"That's absurd. I didn't do anything of the kind. He was looking for your stall at the Müstermesse and I simply chatted him up a bit." She shook her head. "But since you two are apparently serious, I'll put this away before you come to your senses. You're both clinically daft, you know. Thank you ever so much . . . both of you. " She was beaming.

I looked down and opened my envelope: a cashier's check from the Union Bank of Switzerland for $1,500,000. Not a shabby bonus for three year's work. I folded the check, put it in my wallet, and withdrew a personal check I'd filled out Thursday after I'd confirmed the second wire transfer from Kizoku into my Credit Suisse account.

"Thanks very much, Arnaud. I appreciate this. And I agree with Gina: You're too generous. Now I have a little surprise for you." I passed my check across.

Arnaud stared at it blankly for a moment, then at me. His confusion was genuine. "I don't understand. A million dollars? What's this?"

"My kickback from the Japanese for making this thing fly for them. As I flat out told Toru in Monte Carlo, they wanted you a lot more than you wanted them. I threatened him, saying that without a million going in my direction, the deal was dead. Enjoy."

Arnaud shook his head back and forth, turned the check over a couple of times, finally placing it in his pocket without saying a word. He pulled out his checkbook, scribbled quickly, tore out a check and placed it in front of me.

"Eight hundred and fifty thousand Swiss francs?"

"A half-million dollars. Look, I'm not particularly clever at the workings of business, but I assumed you would include, shall we say, a small gift for yourself in your negotiations. That's normal, no? Your honesty is appreciated, Dane, so let's split it. Fair?"

"Fifty-fifty, eh? Like your father and Klaus? You're way more than fair. Not at all necessary, but thanks very much."

With all our newly acquired swag safely stowed away in our respective purses, wallets, and pockets, Arnaud nodded to the nearby waiter. I guessed correctly he had pre-ordered for the table despite my earlier insistence this was to be my treat. After a foamy lemon mousse amuse-bouche, our first course of mushrooms in near transparent ravioli arrived and our Champagne flutes were refreshed.

"Arnaud, how did Toru get over two million dollars in cash

delivered to you for the LGDs? I multiplied it out, and that's one hell of a pile of money."

Arnaud laughed and sat back in his chair. "You're right—it is a lot. Before I put it in safe deposit boxes at my UBS branch in Neuchâtel, I actually weighed it on my bathroom scale. Slightly over twenty kilos of American hundred-dollar notes. Apparently, they openly brought the money into Zürich without a problem. Monsieur Toru said he and his associate flew in from Osaka in the Kizoku company's Sabreliner business jet. Thankfully, we Swiss have never asked a lot of questions of people bringing money into our country," he grinned and reached for his wine.

"Did the Japanese indicate whether or not they plan to keep your staff?" I asked.

"Yes, they're keeping most of them. Monsieur Toru did comment about purchasing some computerized equipment for the casting operations. He explained Klaus would be leaving."

"I kind of thought that might happen. Does Klaus know you sold the LGDs to them?"

"No, I didn't want to say anything prematurely in case the sale wasn't finalized."

"You didn't talk to Klaus before you left?"

"No, but I plan to. I cleared out my personal effects and moved the Bugattis from my office on Thursday. I returned for the last time yesterday to close on the sale, but I didn't see Klaus. I would have called him yesterday evening but he doesn't have a telephone at his place in Neuchâtel."

"I'm shocked." I couldn't resist. "Here we are about to enter the twenty-first century, and Klaus is still kicking and screaming over leaving the nineteenth."

Arnaud smiled and shrugged. "I stopped by his apartment on my way to Cointrin Airport in Geneva this afternoon. He wasn't there but I left a note telling him I'd see him after I return from Paris."

"Did you mention in the note that you sold the gold?"

"Of course. When I return to Switzerland next week, I'm going to drive down to his farm in Tiefencastel and give him his little gift. To use your expression, Dane, I think that should take the edge off his disappointment for a while."

I hadn't liked Klaus from the moment we'd first laid eyes on one another three years ago, but strangely I felt a small pang of pity for the old curmudgeon. Without a family, Laurel had been his whole life. It had been all he'd known since World War Two.

"Good luck with that," I said. "I'm serious. I think he'll need a friend now that he's lost his job in your shop after all these years."

Arnaud nodded. Gina patted my hand.

Our fish course arrived—lobster in a chestnut sauce—for which Arnaud had chosen a '95 Domaine Leflaive Puligny-Montrachet as an accompaniment—an impeccable choice, I assumed. (I didn't have a clue.)

"So, Arnaud, where are you storing those beautiful Bugattis I saw in Neuchâtel?" Gina asked.

"I moved them to my house in La Chaux-de-Fonds," he replied casually. He glanced at me for a reaction; he hadn't lived in that house with his wife for two decades.

"You have news? Apparently a lot more has happened in the last three months than the sale of Laurel," I pried.

"Ah, yes, things change, don't they? My wife and I have always been fond of one another, but we had, shall I say, differing opinions on our lifestyles? She's older now, and, I suppose, a bit more understanding."

"What are you talking about, Arnaud?" I teasingly pushed him, knowing full well what he was saying though the subject had never been broached between us.

"Well, we've both agreed to make a better effort to get along and be less critical of one another's little peccadilloes."

I couldn't resist. "Does that mean madame will be joining you in Paris next January?"

"Dane, we're civilized people. Of course she won't. Now, enough about me. Tell us about the lunch plans for tomorrow you mentioned on the phone."

"We have reservations at the Pré Catalan, in the Bois de Bologne. But before that—"

"I accept. Also one of my favorites," Arnaud interrupted. Appearing relieved at the change in conversation, he probably would have jumped at going to Burger King at this point.

"But *before* that, I've arranged for a cruise on the Seine tonight after dinner."

"Dane, that's brilliant!" Gina gushed, wiggling in her chair like a kid who'd just seen Santa Claus. "But it'll be near on eleven by the time we finish here. Won't it be too late?"

"Nope. I've chartered a cabin cruiser. The captain and his boat are ours for the night."

"I'm not sure if three of us cruising the Seine tonight may not be one soul too many," Arnaud mused. "Why don't I bow out after dinner and meet you two tomorrow for lunch?"

"Absolutely not. This party's just getting started. After the cruise, we have reservations at a little night club I know off the avenue Georges V called the Sheherezade. I figure that ought to keep us going till four or five tomorrow morning."

"Again, Dane, you can be most convincing. And since apparently you insist, I can't think of a better way to spend my last night in Paris with you."

Chapter 12

Sunday, 16 July 2000

The sun's glare streaming through the bedroom's open windows awakened me. My mouth tasted like something between kimchi and rabbit droppings (I guessed). I cracked open my right eye—the left one was still stuck shut—rolled over in the king-sized bed, and looked down at the sheet of paper sticking in my side.

"*D. — I'm downstairs in the restaurant having coffee. Join me if you're still alive. Don't forget we're collecting Arnaud at 1:00 for lunch. Cheers. G.*"

The clock on the nightstand read 11:47. As I began to sit up, I realized I was still almost fully clothed; only my jacket, tie, and shoes were missing. Damn it! Three months of chatting her up for last night and I pass out. This was beyond being an idiot, this was downright humiliating. I showered, dressed, and hustled down into the restaurant within twenty minutes to find a grinning Gina waving from across the room.

"Good morning, cowboy. And how do we feel this morning?"

"Jesus. I feel like I fell into a vat of Kickapoo Joy Juice. Did I do what I think I did last night?" I asked, my head down.

"If you mean did we make love, no, we didn't. If you're asking if you passed out the moment your face hit the pillow, yes, you did."

I killed off my glass of orange juice in two long gulps and caught the waiter's attention to bring another. "How bad was I? At least you didn't go back to London. Or are you?"

"Of course not. You weren't that bad . . . unfortunately," Gina winked and patted my cheek. "And here I thought you arranged for that hundred thousand last night so I'd sleep with you. But then you got all blindo and legless and crashed out on me instead."

"Oh, man. I'm sorry. I hope I didn't make a total ass of myself."

"Not at all. At least not until the taxi ride back from the night club."

"Oh, Christ. What'd I do?"

"Actually, you were quite sweet. You told me how much you loved me, that I was the only woman in the world for you. You were starting to become rather amorous in the back seat and had my bra half off when the driver told you to restrain yourself till he dropped us at the hotel."

"Please, no more. God, how much did I drink?"

"I would guess between the boat and the Sheherezade, you did in the better part of a bottle of whiskey. And that's not counting Harry's, or the champers and wines with dinner, plus a couple shots of old vintage Calvados after dessert."

"No wonder I feel like crap. I think I'll stick with Coca Colas for the rest of the day. Do I get a rain check?"

"I'm not quite sure what that is, but I'm not going anywhere. How could I after you bared your soul to me last night?"

I shook my head. "What about Arnaud? How'd he do?"

"Stop worrying, Dane. We all had a brilliant time last night. Arnaud stayed in there until after three at the nightclub. He was keeping up with you drink for drink all night. He took a taxi back to his place less than an hour before we left. Speaking of Arnaud, don't forget we're meeting him at the Crillon in thirty minutes. We're still on for our lunch in the Bois, I hope?"

"Yeah, I'll be fine. And food's an excellent idea. I wonder if it's legal in France to drink Coke with a four-course lunch?"

"You may want to consider going a bit slower, but you don't have to stop drinking. Bloody hell, you're so damned good at it. I don't think a glass or two of wine will hurt."

"I don't want to chance it. This stud ain't passing out on you again tonight. Alrighty then, let's do this," I said, rising slowly, and already feeling a tad better now that it was past noon.

* * *

The cab made a U-turn from the hotel, circled the Arc de Triomphe, and proceeded down the Champs-Élysées toward place de la Concorde and Arnaud's hotel. Traffic was somewhat lighter than usual, even for a Sunday, perhaps due to some of the locals already having left town in advance of the traditional first of August mass exodus for the annual month of vacation—*la grande vacance*. I recalled from my years of living in Paris how difficult it was to get the smallest thing accomplished here in August. The town was almost literally turned over to the tourists and those who couldn't afford a month's holiday in the country or at the shore.

Our timing was perfect: It was exactly 1:00 when our taxi

rounded the obelisk in the center of the square and stopped in front of the Crillon.

"Wait here a second, Gina. I'll go find Arnaud."

After a cursory and unproductive scan of the lobby, I asked a clerk at the reception desk to phone his room.

"Are you a friend of Monsieur Laurent, monsieur?" the expressionless yet mildly attractive forty-something woman asked.

"Uh, yes. Why? I just want you to let him know I'm waiting downstairs," I answered, a little miffed at her prying.

Somewhat literally translated from her reply in French, she said, "Well, monsieur, we have experienced some grave unhappinesses this morning."

"What the hell are you talking about?" I felt my frustration level rising.

"May I have a moment, monsieur?"

I turned to the voice from my left to see a shortish, beige-suited man with a black mustache and goatee, both of which needed trimming. He discreetly displayed his plastic encased police I.D.

"My name is d'Aubigne, of the *police judiciaire*. Your name, monsieur?" he inquired in French. His breath shot up at me reeking of a melange of garlic and tobacco.

"I'm Dane Baron. What's going on?"

"Please come with me, monsieur. Let's sit over here for a moment." He led me across the ornate chandeliered and marble-floored lobby to a small Louis XV table surrounded by four matching period chairs. Before I sat, it hit me I'd abandoned Gina in the cab.

"Excuse me one second. I have a friend outside waiting in our taxi. I'll be right back."

"Very well, monsieur. I will go with you," he stated, apparently uncertain if I'd return for our little chat.

I paid the driver and helped Gina out the rear door. "Something's wrong," I whispered. "This guy's with the police."

"Mademoiselle," my official escort nodded to Gina after a quick glance at her naked ring finger. "Please follow me inside."

"Now tell us what's happening. Is Monsieur Laurent all right?" I asked upon returning to our seats.

"In a moment. But first, your name, mademoiselle?" He withdrew a small plastic covered notebook and a blue capped Bic from his shirt pocket.

"Regina Domenico."

"And your relationship with Monsieur Laurent?" he asked with a growing bureaucratic demeanor. The French cops, *les flics* as they were less than affectionately known locally, had a reputation for rudeness and even brutality, but so far, our guy d'Aubigne was acting civilly.

"We're friends of his," I answered curtly, growing more worried and impatient. "I've known him for over three years through our business, and Mademoiselle Domenico has known him, well, her entire life through her family. Please, what's going on?"

"Monsieur, mademoiselle, sadly, I have very bad news for you today. Monsieur Laurent is dead. His body was discovered in his suite only an hour ago by the chambermaid."

Gina grabbed my arm with one hand, buried her face in the other, and started to cry. I felt gutted; my whole body went taut. This was the first time I'd ever physically felt grief.

"*What?* How?" I remotely heard myself asking.

"I cannot give you details, but, shall we say, it was not of natural causes. Now, unhappily, I must ask you some questions. What are your nationalities? Both American, I presume?"

"No, I'm British and Swiss. I carry dual citizenship," Gina quietly responded without raising her head.

"American," I said, handing the detective my passport which he briefly thumbed through. "You're probably already aware Monsieur Laurent is, uh, was, Swiss."

"Yes, monsieur." He jotted down a few more lines in his book before returning my passport. "You are not staying here at the Crillon, correct?"

"No, we're at the Royal Monceau, in the avenue Hoche."

"Yes, monsieur, and I know where the Royal Monceau is located," he said, beginning to stray from his initial cordiality. "When were you last with Monsieur Laurent?"

Before I could answer, Gina replied, "Last night. No, I mean early this morning. We were out quite late. Arnaud took a taxi back here by himself from the Sheherezade around three this morning."

"The two of you are, uh, together? You were in the same room last night at your hotel?"

"Yes, all night," I answered with the presumption Gina hadn't crept out during my booze-induced coma and shot Arnaud.

"Are you aware of any other people Monsieur Laurent knew or was planning on seeing in Paris during his stay?"

"To the best of my knowledge, he was only in Paris to see us. He'd recently sold his watch company in Switzerland and we were tying up some last pieces of business."

"What exactly were you tying up?"

"We met with Monsieur Laurent to settle our financial affairs.

Mademoiselle Domenico and I were both owed monies from the proceeds of his sale."

"How much money?"

Our detective was quickly starting to become an officious pain in the ass. "That doesn't concern the Paris police. It's a private matter. We finalized our business early last evening."

"I'll be the judge as to whether or not it concerns us. I'll ask you again: How much money was involved?" He hadn't raised his voice, but I was sensing he didn't want to ask a third time.

I stared at him for a moment before responding, finally deciding it would be simpler to answer than to prolong his questioning. "My proceeds were two million U.S. dollars. Mademoiselle Domenico received a hundred thousand."

The detective let go a soft whistle and returned to his note pad to scribble down the numbers.

"Look, can we take this conversation into the bar? I need a drink."

"As you wish, monsieur," d'Aubigne obliged, rising to help Gina from her chair.

Gina lifted her head and gave me an understanding nod of approval, her eyes still watering. "I don't blame you. This isn't the day to stop drinking," she murmured without a hint of a smile.

We walked across the lobby to a vacant lounge, literally only the bartender and ourselves. D'Aubigne motioned for Gina and me to sit together on a dark purple sofa a few feet from the bar while he took the adjoining matching chair. A single Asian man took a seat at the rail shortly after we arrived, but other than the five of us, the room was empty.

"I'll have a tea, with milk, please," Gina requested from the barman.

I looked over to the detective, who'd pulled out a somewhat crumpled blue pack of unfiltered Gitanes Brunes cigarettes. Whenever I rode the Métro, I could still remember their distinctive pungent smell from my school days in Paris.

"Would you care for a drink, detective? Or coffee or something if you're on duty?"

"If I wasn't on duty, I wouldn't be here asking you questions. I'll have a pastis," d'Aubigne brusquely replied and retrieved his note pad.

"Black Label, with lots of ice, please," I requested. The waiter responded with a simple "*Merci*" and retreated behind his bar.

"Has Arnaud's wife been notified?" Gina asked the detective.

"I don't know, but I'll ask. If she hasn't been contacted, would you prefer to speak to her first?"

She looked at me, shaking her head. "I'm sorry, Dane, I can't. Would you mind?"

"No, I'll call. But I don't have her number," I said, turning to the detective.

D'Aubigne pulled out a cell phone from the inner pocket of his unpressed suit coat and placed it on the marble-topped table between us. "This is Monsieur Laurent's. I would assume her number is in it. And write down any other names you see that you may be familiar with."

"Gina, I forgot—what did you say her name was?"

"Sandrine, I think."

I recognized only four entries from the lengthy contacts menu: Sandrine, the Laurel offices, Klaus Schulrat, and myself. I assumed the number for Klaus was for his place in Tiefencastel since Arnaud had mentioned he didn't have a phone at his Neuchâtel apartment.

"I can't help you with many of these," I told the detective as I wrote down Sandrine's and Klaus's numbers for myself. I made a duplicate note of the names and handed it and the phone to d'Aubigne. "I'll call his wife as soon as we're through here."

"Very well," the detective said, looking down at the paper. "Who is Schulrat?"

"Klaus Schulrat. Klaus has been working for the Laurel Watch Company since the late '30s, back before World War Two. He first started with Arnaud's father. For lack of a better term, he's something between a tool and die maker and a goldsmith. And before you ask, I barely know him. I've only seen him a few times at the company's facility in Neuchâtel." I opted not to get into an irrelevant commentary about my personal feelings toward Klaus.

D'Aubigne snuffed out his cigarette, killed off the last of his milky-colored Pernod, and rose to leave. "Thank you for your courtesy, mademoiselle, monsieur. Please write down your permanent addresses and telephone numbers," he droned in a bored voice which had obviously repeated the same request countless times before. "How much longer will you be at the Royal Monceau if I have any further need to speak with you?"

"I don't know yet. Anything from a day to another week or so," I answered. "We're taking an Air France Concorde charter to New York to meet up with a cruise ship on the twenty-fifth. Here's our contact information." I passed the numbers to him.

D'Aubigne nodded, lit another Gitane, exhaled from both his mouth and nostrils, and departed without additional comment. Just another day at the office.

Chapter 13

Monday, 17 July 2000

*B*onjour? Monsieur Baron?"

I correctly assumed the voice on the phone was Sandrine Laurent's but I was surprised it had taken her until this morning to return my call.

"Thank you for your message yesterday afternoon, monsieur. The Paris police notified me of Arnaud's death before I had an opportunity to see you had called. I'm sorry, but I needed some time to myself before I telephoned you. The police told me Arnaud's body will be released at some point tomorrow after they perform an autopsy. I've made arrangements for the funeral service here at my church in La Chaux-de-Fonds on Thursday morning." Both her words and her tone had a calm and dispassionate quality, likely a reaction to many recent hours of anguish and tears.

"I understand. How may I be of any assistance, madame? Possibly I could take care of transporting Arnaud back to Switzerland?"

After a brief discussion of logistics, it was agreed I would escort Arnaud's coffin to the funeral home on Wednesday. Before saying our goodbyes, I told Madame Laurent I would call immediately should I become aware of any details from the police, details I seriously doubted would be coming my way.

"That's very good of you, Dane. I'm sure Madame Laurent appreciates it," Gina said. Her breakfast setting from room service two hours earlier remained basically untouched; only the sterling silver teapot had been moved to the end table closest to her. She hadn't budged from the couch all night.

"Would you like to fly down to Madame Laurent's place with me on Wednesday?" I asked from my still singly-occupied bed across the room.

In a barely audible and cracking voice, she replied, "I'm afraid I'm not up to it. God, he was such a sweet man." Our conversations since leaving the Crillon yesterday afternoon were bordering on the nonexistent. I'd been careful not to push. Gina wasn't handling this well, and I could only give her some time and space. "I think I'll fly back to London. I'm sorry I'm not better company, but I can't go to Switzerland and I don't want to stay here in Paris by myself right now. I do hope you understand."

I understood perfectly, but I didn't like it, and there wasn't a damned thing I could do about it. I had plunged from possibly the happiest day of my life to one of the worst in less than twenty-four hours. My good friend—my best friend—had been murdered, and my new almost-girlfriend had turned into a basket case and was going home. Still dressed in the skirt and top she'd worn yesterday, Gina sat up from the couch, walked to the bed, and curled up next to me.

"Are you still up for the Concorde next week?" I ventured.

"I think so. But I need a bit to work through all this by myself."

* * *

By half past ten, Gina was in a cab back to Roissy, the town northeast of Paris where Charles de Gaulle is sited. As much as I enjoyed her company, her return to England for a few days was probably best for both of us. Overnight, my initial and profound sadness over Arnaud's death had turned to anger, and I knew I wasn't good enough to deal with that and Gina's problems at the same time.

I put in a call to Air France to check on the formalities and document requirements for transporting Arnaud's coffin to Geneva. Expectedly, I was advised of the various forms and releases that required the widow's signature, all of which, I was informed, could be faxed. After noting all the necessary certifications, I phoned Madame Laurent with the information, for which she thanked me and promised to have everything faxed back to my hotel within hours. I advised her I would be arriving in Geneva on Wednesday at 2:10 P.M. on Air France and she assured me the funeral home people would meet me there and then.

It was after one by the time I'd finished with my calls, showered, thrown on some casual clothes, and finished off the other than fresh remains of Gina's croissants and fruit plate. I phoned d'Aubigne for an update, only to hear him say he'd be in touch if anything developed—I sensed he was yawning as he lied. Just then, that normally dim light in my head switched on: Marie-Claude Perrin.

Marie-Claude, or Clyde, as I'd nicknamed her, was an old friend from my Air Force days in Paris. A mid-level detective with the Paris police, she had worked in a liaison capacity with the U.S. Embassy, helping out when Yanks found themselves in trouble with the French cops. While our jobs never overlapped, Clyde was always a willing volunteer whenever I needed a date for an evening on the embassy cocktail circuit. We'd had our little fling for a few weeks, but her part-time affinity for the ladies proved to be too rough on my touchy male ego. Though I hadn't seen her since leaving the service, we were both reliable for a yearly Christmas card.

"*Allô? C'est Perrin,*" Marie-Claude gruffly answered my call.

"Hey, Clyde. What's up? Dane Baron here. I'm in Paris for a couple of days and I was hoping I could buy you a drink."

"*Putain de bordel de merde!*" she shouted into my earpiece—I hadn't forgotten her partiality toward tangy vocabulary. Her idiomatic greeting didn't translate well (whore of a shitty brothel?) but it did seem to cover most of her displeasure regarding my absence in one short phrase. "Definitely I want a drink. Where are you?"

"I'm at the Royal Monceau right now. What's your schedule like this afternoon? Can you spare an hour or two for an old friend?"

"*Mais certainement.* I could meet you at, uh, is four all right?"

"Four's perfect. I thought we might meet at Harry's Bar in the rue Daunou?"

"*Et bien.* Of course at Harry's. I don't think you ever took me anywhere other than Harry's or the embassies. Okay, I'll see you shortly. Bye bye. *Ciao.*"

"Clyde, before you go, have you heard about the murder of a Swiss national in the Crillon yesterday?"

"But of course. A murder at the Crillon makes big news around here. Why do you ask? Did you know him?"

"Yes, very well. We had dinner together the night before he was killed. I have a favor, Marie-Claude. Before we meet, could you possibly make a call and see if there's any progress on the investigation? I'm getting stonewalled by one of the detectives who's involved, and I was hoping to be able to give my friend's widow some news when I see her in Switzerland on Wednesday."

"D'Aubigne, you mean. Yeah, I saw he was working the case. He always wants everyone to think he's the smartest guy in the room, but basically, he's just a pompous asshole. Let me put in a call or two and see what I can find. And by the way, you never call me Clyde when you want a favor," she pointed out in that same husky voice I remembered. "Bye bye. *Ciao*."

* * *

Clyde was waiting outside the door smoking a cigarette when I rounded the corner off the avenue de l'Opéra, less than fifty yards down the street from Harry's. Approaching, I saw that little had changed in her appearance since I'd last seen her. She wasn't a showstopper, but she'd aged attractively. The subtlest of lines around her jade green eyes hinted at her forty and a few years; her raven black hair was now cropped shorter than mine, yet still exuded a raw sexiness which was evidently as attractive to women as it was to men. Dressed in a navy blazer and untucked white shirt over a pair of tight Levi's and three-inch black heels, she looked her same tough and lusty self. I reached to kiss her cheek, but I couldn't remember: was *la bise* right cheek, left cheek, right cheek,

146

or the other way around? Whichever, Clyde followed my lead, appearing pleased with the process.

"So, how many times have you been in Paris without calling me since you left the Air Force?" she needled. We grabbed a pair of bar stools nearest the door, the same two Gina and I had used Saturday. "Life is good with you?"

"Yeah, everything was perfect—until yesterday. But we'll get to that later. I was half-surprised to see you're still with the police. Don't you French have a twenty-year retirement or something?"

"Dane, I only have eighteen years in, thank you very much, and even with a twenty-year plan, I still can't get out—I'm always broke. I need a sugar daddy . . . or maybe a sweet mama. *Un vieux protecteur,* as we say in French. Anyway, I'm a lieutenant now, working in the *milieu* unit—the organized crime squad—of the *police judiciare's brigade criminelle,* or *la Crim'* as we affectionaely call it. I've been in it a little over four years. It's the most interesting work I've ever done. But enough about career talk. We had some good times when we were at the embassy, no?"

"Yeah, it was fun. I don't see a ring, so I guess you're still breaking all the little boys' hearts?"

"And a few little girls," she replied in her best Marlene Dietrich while exhaling toward the ceiling and wagging her non-filtered Gauloise. "You know, I've never slept at the Royal Monceau. I hope you called me for more than a drink and information on an on-going and most confidential murder investigation."

"Uh, sure. I wanted to catch up on your life and career and things. But I guess I should tell you: I'm kind of, uh, well, I'm seeing someone."

"Relax. I'm only messing with you. Has anyone ever told you how gullible you can be?"

"Yeah, as a matter of fact, they have. Gina—the lady I'm seeing —she was accusing me of that a few days ago. You two should meet. Scratch that. I don't want us fighting over the same woman. And I'm offended: Did you know that in English gullible means stupid like a seagull?"

"Perfect," Clyde teased. "And not to worry: I don't mind sharing." She let go with a raucous laugh that caught the attention of the group at our end of the rail. She didn't appear to give a damn; Clyde was the same brassy and self-assured cop I'd remembered.

Nervously, I said, "Okay, enough on that." I hoped my face wasn't as red as it used to become when Clyde threatened to pull out her cuffs. "Can you tell me anything about my friend's murder? Have they made any progress?"

With only the slightest change of expression, Clyde replaced her Jack Daniels (neat) on the bar top. She reached down for her scuffed brown leather satchel and pulled out a notebook and reading glasses. "So I don't waste our time, how much do you already know?" she asked, perusing her notes without looking up.

"Nothing, other than d'Aubigne said Arnaud died of other than natural causes. And I'm more or less aware of his time of death since he left us at the Sheherezade around three in the morning and they found him murdered sometime before noon. That's it."

"Well, we don't know a hell of a lot more than that yet ourselves, but I'll give you what I was able to find. First off, he was stabbed. One time. And the killer left the knife in, uh . . . the wound. You know I shouldn't be telling you any of this," she warned, sliding her glasses farther down her nose and raising her head.

"If you didn't trust me, Clyde, you wouldn't be here."

"True. But not a word. Understood?"

I nodded.

"*Bien*. Second, and as you'd expect, the Hôtel de Crillon has a quite sophisticated surveillance camera system. We have time-stamped tapes showing the victim exiting from a taxi in front of the hotel at three twenty-seven Sunday morning. But before he entered the hotel, another man, wearing a broad brimmed hat, a dark raincoat and gloves, approached the victim on the sidewalk. Unfortunately, the camera doesn't show his face. The two shook hands and appeared to speak to one another briefly before they walked into the hotel together, took the lift to the third floor, and entered Monsieur Laurent's suite."

"So Arnaud knew the guy," I commented, never one to shy from exhibiting my keen perspicacity.

"*Oh, là là*, I envy your brain. You don't have to be hit in the face with a shovel to get it, do you?" Clyde sighed, rolling her eyes before continuing: "The only other thing we have are tapes showing the suspect leaving the suite one minute later, walking quickly to the staircase, and then out through the lobby to the front entrance on the place de la Concorde. Did you know that Laurent, I'm sorry, your friend, was meeting someone after he left you?"

"No, I'm sure he was headed straight for bed when he left us. Or so Gina told me. I was pretty drunk by that point. But I'm very confident he was only in Paris to see me . . . and Gina."

"Why were the three of you here?"

"Didn't you already read that in the statement I gave to

d'Aubigne?"

Clyde suddenly shoved her things back into her bag. "*Putain!* Listen carefully, Dane," she said while maintaining riveted eye contact. "I'm here to see an old friend, and help if I can, though I shouldn't. I could be heavily disciplined if anyone ever found I'd discussed these things with you. And for your information, I don't have access to d'Aubigne's notes. Now, if you want to continue with this, tell me why you were meeting with Monsieur Laurent in Paris."

"Sorry, Clyde. I thought you were changing hats there for a second. I'm still pissed at d'Aubigne, but I didn't intend for it to carry over to you. In answer to your question, Arnaud was settling accounts with Gina and me. He recently sold his watch company in Switzerland and he was paying us our proceeds from the sale. Before you ask, I received two million dollars. Gina got a hundred thousand."

"*Merde alors!*" Clyde blurted as she did that back and forth limp-wristed hand and finger flip the French exhibit when impressed. "You've come a long way since we used to split our drink checks. I should have worked on you a little harder."

"Yeah, well, uh, things change, I guess," I shrugged. "I worked with Arnaud for over three years, handling all of his ex European sales. A few months ago, a Japanese group came along and made him an offer he . . . well, you know. My two mil was mostly for putting the sale together for him. Anyway, I take it you people have no idea as to the murderer's identity yet?"

"No, *we people* don't, but am I sensing you might?" Clyde asked with more than a little edge to her voice. "Even though you thought he wasn't meeting with anyone here other than yourselves, he obviously knew the man who met him in front of the Crillon. Who else knew he was here?"

"It would be a short list, and you're right, I think I do know who killed Arnaud. But before I start guessing, is there any way I could get a look at some of those hotel tapes? I don't want to start accusing people if the image doesn't fit."

Clyde stared at me, hesitated, then reopened her satchel. "This'll be my job if it gets out I've shown you these." She was whispering as she visually swept the bar again to confirm no one was interested in our little chat.

I took the three 5 x 8 glossies Clyde handed me beneath the bar. The black-and-white prints from the video were of high resolution, clearly showing Arnaud's face in two of the three. As Clyde had indicated, the other man had his back to the camera in all three photos, but . . . .

My mind flashed back to Arnaud's tale of the murdered SS officer near Schaffhausen during the war.

"Arnaud was stabbed in the left eye, wasn't he?"

Clyde jerked her head away from her bourbon glass. "How the hell could you possibly know that?" she asked, appearing stunned, and confirming what I suspected.

"A wild shot. I need you to trust me, Clyde. If I can confirm my suspicion, I promise to tell you everything on Thursday afternoon after I fly back from Geneva. I need to look up someone while I'm in Switzerland."

"No, tell me now. You obviously know more about this case than the police do. Friends or otherwise, you're not going anywhere until you explain how you knew how he was killed."

"Why? 'Cause I took a lucky stab? Sorry, bad word choice.

Look, Clyde, I'm not saying anything unless I'm sure whom I'm accusing. Bear with me for a couple of days? One for the old times?"

"I don't have a hell of a lot of choice, do I? Okay, I've shown you mine, but I want to see yours on Thursday. Can you give me anything? What, are we looking for someone with a modus operandi of running around France or Switzerland stabbing people in the left eye?"

"Maybe not running around, but you're closer than you think."

Chapter 14

La Chaux-de-Fonds

Wednesday, 19 July 2000

The Air France people in Paris and Geneva performed their jobs with gratifying efficiency and courtesy. Within short minutes of landing at Geneva's Cointrin Airport, Arnaud's coffin was placed expeditiously, yet carefully and respectfully, into the hearse from La Chaux-de-Fonds. I explained to the funeral director I wouldn't require a ride, having decided earlier to hire a rental car for my short stay in western Switzerland.

It was going to be a busy twenty-four hours. First, a courtesy visit with Madame Laurent this afternoon; I phoned her from the airport once I'd picked up my Hertz Mercedes. She guesstimated I could cover the 140 kilometers to her house within two hours, allowing for the midweek traffic on the windy route up the foothills of the Juras. A quick stopover at the Laurel offices was only a four or five mile deviation, but I'd see Toru tomorrow, after the funeral, on my way back to Cointrin.

*B*ienvenue, Monsieur Baron. Welcome to my home. Thank you so much for all you have done, helping me with the formalities in Paris and all. My husband told me how much he admired and trusted you. He considered you to be one of his closest friends."

"Thank you, madame. Very kind words. It's a pleasure to meet you, but I'm so sorry it had to be under these circumstances. Again, you have my sincerest sympathies. Arnaud was probably my best friend. His loss is devastating to all of us. And please, call me Dane." I knew she wouldn't, any more than she'd ask me to call her Sandrine. The Swiss and most other Europeans of her generation and social standing maintained a rather strict unwritten code about such things.

Madame Laurent was several inches shorter than Gina, and thinner. Not skinny, just not as curvy. She wore a black below-the-knee dress, with a fit which made me think it wasn't an off-the-racker. Her pulled back hair was shiny ebony black without a single gray. The softness of her features made her appear to be in her early forties, though logically she was well over fifty, or more politely, *a woman of a certain age*. Clearly, life had been kind to Sandrine Laurent.

She took my arm and led me from the rustic tiled entrance foyer into the great room, an area truly deserving of the name. Possibly twenty feet high, the pale blue plaster ceiling was suspended on rough-hewn oak logs spaced three or four feet on center. The focal point of the room was the stone fireplace of palatial proportions at the far end of the space. A seven seat copper-topped bar, constructed of provincial masonry similar to the fireplace, highlighted one of the adjoining walls. The furnishings resembled the countrified look found in high-end resort ski lodges. Arnaud's flair for the comfortably simple, yet artistic, was clearly in evidence.

From a quick scan of the room, I was guessing there were at least forty people in attendance. Some were seated and quietly chatting and drinking in the subtly designed conversation areas; others had gravitated to the tended bar.

"A glass of wine for Monsieur Baron, please," Madame Laurent requested of one of the two circulating waiters. "As you can see, Arnaud had many friends. I'm gratified so many were able to come to our little memorial gathering this afternoon."

I removed a glass of red wine from the passing tray. I'd have preferred a Scotch.

"Madame, please let me not keep you. See to your other guests. I'll be fine. I think I'll walk around outside for a while if you wouldn't mind."

"*Mais absolument.*" Her face then turned disquietingly serious; she guided me to a nook off the large room. "Monsieur Baron, I must speak with you in private about a very serious and personal matter. But after our friends have gone. Could you possibly stay for another hour or so?"

"Certainly, madame. Just let me know when it's convenient to talk."

I downed my wine (while collecting a second), and went outside to survey the grounds of the Laurent estate. To the rear, and on higher ground than the main house, a three-car garage and a red brick barn were set into a level area surrounded on three sides by pines. The barn door was identical to the aircraft hangar type at

Arnaud's facility in Neuchâtel. Unlike the Neuchâtel garage, however, these sliding sheet metal doors weren't locked or bolted. I carefully placed my glass on the gravel and slid open one side of the door along its rails.

Voilà—the Type 57SC Atlantic and its smaller brother, the Type 35B. Parked several feet from one another, and facing out on the painted and polished white concrete floor, both appeared to have been recently detailed—not a speck of dust anywhere. This had to be the second finest sight I'd ever seen, with the third being so far distant as to not count.

While the Atlantic's classic styling was generally considered to be without peer in the automotive world, I still was drawn to the French racing blue Type 35B. With the recent deposit of Arnaud's check into my Credit Suisse account, owning a Type 35 was now becoming less of a remote adulthood dream. The one before me was in perfect restored condition—a true 100-point concours specimen, as was the untouchable Atlantic.

I made numerous slow laps around both machines, wondering what madame had in mind for their futures. I seriously doubted she had any idea of their worth, let alone an appreciation of their intrinsic purity. And since Luc had never mentioned his father's Bugattis, I assumed he shared her lack of interest. Pity. I only hoped these beauties would someday find loving (and nutty) new owners.

"Monsieur Baron?" I turned to see a gray-jacketed young man standing at the half-opened barn door. "Madame's guests are departing. Whenever convenient, madame would like to speak with you."

"Thank you. Please tell her I'll be right in."

* * *

Please, Monsieur Baron, take this chair," Sandrine Laurent motioned when she saw me enter the great room once again. Beethoven strings were playing softly in the background. "Would you care for a drink?"

"A Scotch would be nice," I said hopefully, turning to the lad who'd summoned me from the Bugatti barn.

"Monsieur Laurent has a rather deep collection, monsieur. Do you have a preference?"

"Any dark blended would be fine. Lots of ice, please."

I found myself leaning forward in my overstuffed leather chair, expecting madame to open the conversation, but she sat silently across from me, demurely gazing out the nearby window with a serene wisp of a polite smile, her hands folded in her lap, apparently waiting for the help to return with my drink . . . and depart.

"Johnnie Walker Blue Label, monsieur. It was Monsieur Laurent's favorite," he pointed out, almost whispering, as he placed the bucket glass on a linen cocktail napkin. "Will there be anything further, madame?"

"No, thank you, Antoine. And I appreciate your fine staff's efforts this afternoon. I'll phone you the first of next week about the charges. *Bonsoir.* "

Madame Laurent absently stirred her tea while she waited for the server to close the front door behind him. "Monsieur Baron, I had a most disturbing meeting several days ago. Klaus Schulrat.

Do you know him?"

Jesus. Why would the old bastard have come here?

"Yes, madame, I do, slightly," I answered, incredulous at what I guessed I was about to hear. "I've seen him at Arnaud's offices in Neuchâtel several times. We've never spoken."

"*Et bien*, so you know whom I'm about to discuss with you. I've known Klaus for well over thirty years, ever since Arnaud and I were married. He came to talk with me on Sunday evening—within hours of my learning of Arnaud's death—and he related a most bizarre series of events. Klaus told me he knew Arnaud was going to Paris after the sale of the business was completed, and Klaus drove there to see him concerning some gold from the Laurel offices. He said they met late on Saturday night. Were you aware of this meeting?"

"Uh, no. Not at the time, anyway. But I later suspected Klaus had been to Arnaud's hotel."

"Why did you suspect this?"

"Let me get into that later with you, madame. As I indicated, I only suspected he might have been there, but I wasn't sure. Please, continue."

She stared at me for several moments with fixed dark eyes. "Very well. Klaus told me, with few specifics, mind you, that he had made a terrible mistake. He said he'd thought Arnaud had cheated him out of a great deal of money when he sold some gold to the Japanese which partially belonged to Klaus. He claims to have phoned Arnaud for an explanation, but when he could only reach his message recording, he drove to Paris to see him. When he returned to his apartment in Neuchâtel the next day, he told me he found a note from Arnaud explaining the sale of this gold to the new buyers. Evidently, my husband left the note on his way to the airport in Geneva on Saturday afternoon when he flew to Paris, but Klaus had already departed by that point. Arnaud wrote he would be giving Klaus his share of the proceeds when he returned from his trip." She became silent and returned to stirring her tea.

"What else did he tell you, madame?" I urged, a little surprised at her composure. She knew.

"He said he'd been very angry with Arnaud for selling the company—and his gold. But then he returned home and read the note. This is when he stated he realized he'd made a horrible mistake. You worked with Arnaud. What is this gold Klaus was talking about?"

It was now clear Klaus hadn't believed Arnaud's explanation of the gold sale when they talked for that brief minute in Arnaud's suite before Klaus stabbed him. It was also clear Arnaud had told me the truth when he said Gina and I were only the fifth and sixth people to have knowledge of the bars' existence. He'd told Luc about the gold, but not his wife. Strange . . . or maybe not.

"Madame Laurent, I only know Arnaud and Klaus shared ownership of a significant number of gold bars, gold which was not obtained for the purpose of casting watch cases. These bars went to the Japanese as assets of the business."

Kinda.

"I also know Arnaud was planning to see Klaus when he returned from Paris to settle accounts with him. He told me that over dinner the night before he was murdered."

"Klaus killed my husband, didn't he, monsieur?"

"That's my guess, yes. Klaus was likely distraught over losing his job and he thought Arnaud had swindled him out of his share of their gold. But the French police have no evidence of Klaus even being in Paris, let alone connecting him with the murder. Right now, all they know about Klaus Schulrat is his telephone number."

Madame Laurent rose from her seat on the couch and slowly walked to the fireplace. She stopped and turned to face me. "Klaus has the gold bars?" I thought I heard her ask. I could barely hear her soft voice across the room.

She was obviously confused. "No, madame. They're in the vault at Laurel. Or at least they were when the Japanese took over last Friday."

"You didn't understand me, monsieur. I wasn't asking—I was *telling* you: Klaus now has the gold."

Christ! What the hell had he done? The fool. "Klaus told you this? He said he took the gold from the safe?"

"Exactly, monsieur. It would seem the Japanese terminated his employment last Friday afternoon, the very day Arnaud sold the company to them. Klaus said his gold was still in the factory safe and Arnaud hadn't paid him for his share. He said the new owners hadn't changed the locks or the safe combination yet, so before dawn last Saturday morning, he went to Laurel and simply used his old key. He took the gold to his apartment, and then drove directly to Paris to have it out with Arnaud for stealing from him. After he met with Arnaud, he drove his van back to Neuchâtel, collected the gold bars, and took them to his farm in Graubünden."

The anger I'd felt in Paris over Arnaud's death was suddenly resurfacing. A careless afterthought of a note left on Klaus's door, a phone call not returned, a paranoid and vindictive old Swiss farmer. Klaus meets Arnaud at his hotel, doesn't buy his story of the note in Neuchâtel explaining the situation, thinks Arnaud's ducking his calls, then stabs him in the eye and kills him. Sweet Jesus. It sickened me even to consider the disastrous and fatal chain of events. Without the slightest thought of asking permission, I walked to the bar and poured myself a double.

"Madame, I need to see a man named Jioruji Toru. Immediately. He's the new Japanese director of Laurel. I need to explain what's happened to his gold. Then I'm going to the police about Klaus."

"I don't think that will be necessary, Monsieur Baron. About Klaus, I mean."

"Why?"

"It's irrelevant now. And you may want to rethink seeing the Japanese."

"I'm sorry . . . what do you mean?"

Without comment, she reached to the end of the oak table between us and passed me a newspaper, *L'Express à Neuchâtel*. She pointed to an article above the front-page fold.

"As you see, the cantonal police found Klaus dead in his apartment yesterday morning."

I was in semi-shock as I carefully read the newspaper story. The reporter wrote that police had told her there was evidence of torture and one fatal gunshot wound. Time of death approximated to be Sunday night or early Monday morning. He was 81 years of age. No suspects. Motive unknown. No family had been found to contact. The apartment building owner said the victim had been employed by the Laurel Watch Company for many years.

Toru.

"Monsieur Baron, from what you've told me today and from what Klaus related on Sunday, I am now assuming the new

Japanese owners of Laurel killed Klaus for stealing their gold. Or they arranged for it. Would you agree?"

"Likely. But as far as I'm concerned, if they did, I'm not going to grieve over it. There's now no question in my mind Klaus killed your husband in Paris. Madame, your husband was my friend. If the Japanese killed Klaus, they simply saved the authorities the trouble and expense of caring for him until he died in prison."

"Monsieur, at this moment I still feel total hatred for Klaus," Madame Laurent asserted somewhat loudly, her serene exterior momentarily unveiled. "But I am a devout, practicing Catholic woman, and in time, and with God's help, I will learn to forgive Klaus's soul." She picked up the newspaper again, her finger now stabbing at the article. "I can conceive of their anger over Klaus's theft, but killing him? And the torture. Why torture him?"

I hesitated until she sat back and regained her poise.

"Let me ask you something, Madame Laurent." I spoke slowly, vacantly running my finger around the rim of my Scotch glass. "Why do you think Klaus came to see you?"

She stared blankly at the table. After a brief pause, she responded pensively, calmly, somewhat ethereally. "He was an old man. A lonely and foolish old man. He was in tears when he all but admitted killing my husband. In retrospect, I think he came to apologize, but he couldn't bring himself to do it."

"He was a murderer, madame. And he wasn't here to apologize. He was here to buy your forgiveness. Why else would he have told you he'd taken the gold bars to his farm? I think he'd decided either to turn himself in, or more likely, to kill himself. In an attempt to assuage his guilt, he wanted you to have the gold. The Japanese tortured him to find out what he'd done with it, but I seriously doubt he would have told them anything."

Half expecting her to dismiss my theory with a hand wave or a shrug, she surprised me. "Do you have any idea how much these gold bars are worth?" she asked in a flat voice, almost businesslike.

"Yes. Exactly, actually, since I negotiated their sale. About two million U.S. dollars." I saw by her blank expression she wasn't used to thinking in dollars. "Somewhat less than four million Swiss francs," I helped. "The price of gold has dropped a smidgen since the sale, but not much."

"And this amount was paid to Arnaud?"

She'd clearly hopscotched a few squares past her stress over the subjects of murder and torture.

"No, madame. He was paid slightly more than the dollar equivalent of three point four million francs. In cash. It's difficult to explain, but basically, Arnaud settled for less than the gold's true worth in order to sell the business and the property for considerably more than their market values."

"I see . . . I think. Do you know what Arnaud did with this cash?"

"Yes, I do. He mentioned in Paris he'd put it into safe deposit boxes at his bank in Neuchâtel," I answered, revealing confidences deemed sacrosanct only four short days ago.

"I have another question, if you will indulge me." Her facial expression was now completely free of emotion. "My husband's cars, the four in the rear garages. Do you have an opinion as to their worth?"

The cars? A valid question, but oddly timed.

"I have a rough idea. Of the Bugattis' values, I mean. What

other two automobiles?" I asked, my mind still on the two vintage machines I'd lusted over earlier.

"The Mercedes and the Facel Vega."

Right, those minor leaguers. I hadn't considered Arnaud's modestly impressive daily transportation.

"Well, only guessing, the Facel would probably be worth something between seventy-five and a hundred thousand francs. Maybe about half that for the Mercedes," I ventured after a quick mental calculation, remembering to multiply by one point seven to bring my dollar estimate into her currency. "As far as the Bugattis, their values greatly depend upon the strength of a somewhat volatile classic automobile market. Since they would be sold most efficiently at auction, it would also depend upon the skills of the auction people in hyping the sale. And luck."

"Your estimate?" she pressed.

"All right, keep in mind I'm only guessing here, but since I'm a Bugatti fan, I do follow their prices occasionally. I'd say in the current market, the Atlantic could fetch between ten and twelve million francs. This is an extremely rare and significant automobile. And Arnaud's is unique because it was thought to have been lost during the war. The smaller one, the Type 35, which, by the way, has always been my personal favorite, is possibly in the neighborhood of two million francs."

Madame Laurent rose again and silently retraced her steps toward the fireplace, her head down and her arms folded across her chest as she slowly paced. I played with my ice cubes and watched two minutes tick away on the grandfather clock next to the bar.

"Monsieur Baron," she started, "my husband recently returned to our home. He may have told you, we lived apart for many years

—since the early eighties. However, even while we were separated, I believe Arnaud loved and respected me as much as I did him. I was so looking forward to our future years together. But that has all been taken from me now. Monsieur, if these Japanese had never entered Arnaud's world, I would still have my husband with me. Even Arnaud despised these people. I can't tell you how many times he told me the Japanese manufacturers had tried to steal his designs.

"As Arnaud's sole beneficiary, all his assets are now mine, including these things of which we've spoken today—his automobiles and the contents of his safe deposit boxes. You will think me a vengeful woman, but I want something more: I want to hurt the Japanese who killed him, however indirectly. Though it is of little significance when compared to my other assets, I want their gold. And yes, I want it strictly out of spite. I want them to lose what matters most to them."

While her comments about the past industrial espionage may have been true, I was damned if I could get behind her fuzzy, circuitous illogic in holding the Japanese responsible for Arnaud's death. Or just maybe, perhaps those little peccadilloes on Sandrine Laurent's side of the ledger Arnaud had alluded to in Paris included a wee touch of avarice.

Evidently sensing I couldn't think of an appropriate response, Madame Laurent continued: "Let me suggest an idea to you, Monsieur Baron." Her inscrutable calm was starting to scare me. "There are two things here I'm incapable of doing, and I can't think of anyone to ask to help me do them, other than yourself. I would like you to arrange for a fair price in the disposition of Arnaud's automobiles . . . and I want the gold the Japanese purchased from

165

him.

"Before you say anything, Monsieur Baron, this is my proposition: If you can sell the cars, with the Atlantic bringing a minimum of ten million francs, and if you find the gold bars and convert them to cash for me, I will give you title to the Type 35 Bugatti."

I reflected carefully for seven weighty seconds. Paul Bisno could likely handle the automobile part of the equation. And as for the gold, who truly owned the LGDs? In reality, they belonged to the untraceable heirs of whomever Mussolini or the Nazis had stolen them from some sixty years ago, and since then, they had belonged to whoever had the right of possession. Technically, the Japanese had purchased stolen goods. So maybe it was a bit of stretch, but if I did find the bars, and knowing Toru and friends had committed torture and murder, I had minimal qualms about not returning them to the Laurel safe. Possibly pushing the limits of rationalization, I quickly concluded helping Madame Laurent wouldn't be committing a mortal sin or make me a generally bad guy. And I wanted a Bugatti.

Chapter 15

London

Thursday, 20 July 2000

The Laurent family had a mastery for gaining my attention. The earlier magnanimous gestures by Arnaud, initially via Luc in Sarasota, and later personally in Basel, had been interesting financial inducements for me to help expand, and later sell, the Laurel Watch Company. However, the latest offer of the Type 35 by Sandrine Laurent was different. Earning my keep this time could prove to be most unhealthy. Someone, or some people, perhaps Toru himself, were starting to kill folks they suspected of stealing their LGD bars. But logic and sensibilities be damned: Put a million dollar classic Bugatti at the end of a stick and I'm your guy.

Prior to the funeral, I explained to Madame Laurent I needed to leave for Cointrin immediately after the services to make my 1:40 British Airways flight to London to get started on her assignment.

"I fully understand, Monsieur Baron. However, I'm curious: Why are you going to England? The cars and the gold are here, no?"

"The gentleman I know who owns an auction house, and who I hope may be instrumental in selling the automobiles and gold for us—that's *if* I find the gold—has his offices in London. This business isn't something I can effectively deal with over the telephone. Also, I meant to tell you: I have a personal commitment for a couple weeks starting next Tuesday, the twenty-fifth. It's something I promised my girlfriend. We're taking a charter flight to join up with a South American cruise, so unfortunately the dates are rather inflexible. But be assured, madame, your situation will have my undivided attention for the few days I have remaining before that. And afterward, if necessary. Hopefully, I can find your gold and dispose of it before I leave. The automobiles may take a little longer, but possibly only another week if we're lucky."

* * *

Gina met me at Heathrow for my 2:25 P.M. local time arrival, despite my pleadings not to. Her driving scared the hell out of me.

"I'm so glad you're here," she yelped before jumping into my arms and laying a big wet one on me. "I'm sorry about my behavior in Paris. It's just that it hit me so hard. But I'm better now, now that you're with me. And as you can see, I hired a car you can fit into a bit better than my Mini."

"Hey, that wasn't necessary. I'm just happy to see you. How are young Willie and the folks?"

Gina turned to face me for a moment before steering her rental Vauxhall through the light drizzling rain toward the M4 and the West End. "I'm sure they're all fine." She hesitated. "I haven't seen them, Dane. That's the real reason I couldn't drive my Mini. I checked into the Hyde Park Hotel when I flew back on Monday. I needed some time to myself. I've been there the last three nights, and it seems to have worked. But I'm staying at my flat with them tonight. I want to spend a little time with Willie before we fly down to Monaco tomorrow."

"What are you talking about, Gina? It's *I* am going to Monaco tomorrow—not, *we* are going. Look, I want to find Toru to see if I can figure out how involved he is in all this."

"That's complete rubbish. Why can't I go?"

"As I told you on the phone last night, Klaus was tortured and murdered. There's some very nasty shit going down over this gold and I don't want you mixed up in it. Got it?"

"I'm not going to sit on my backside here in London like a bloody potted plant whilst you're cavorting around the South of France. Dane, you know you absolutely adore me, and if you ever want to have sex with me, you'll jolly well take me with you. Got *that*?"

"You make an excellent argument. Okay, you're going. Now that we have that out of the way, what was that about staying at your place tonight? You've been here in a hotel by yourself, and now that I show up, it's back to the family? I thought we'd finally be together tonight. Well, you know."

"Yeah, I know," she grinned with her now patented wink. "Tomorrow night, in Monte Carlo. And by the way, squire, it's not as if I haven't given you your chances, you know."

"Oh, Jesus," I groaned. "Please, that still hurts. All right, tomorrow. Now, do you know how to get to Bisno's Auctions in Knightsbridge? I told him we'd be there around three-thirty."

"Yeah, I looked it up after you rang me last night. It's just down the road a bit from Harrods. No worries—we'll make it in time," she said, placing her left hand on my upper thigh and her right foot on the accelerator.

* * *

Paul Bisno's inner office furnishings were something out of a period movie set: The Victorian era meets the Art Nouveau movement. I first checked out the pair of Tiffany lamps atop his Queen Anne partners desk and the complementing table. Turning, I noticed the dark mahogany walls were almost completely covered with Rococo through Impressionist period oils, two of which I actually recognized. Paul struggled to rise from behind his desk.

"Good afternoon, Paul. Please, don't get up," I offered, attempting to save the old RAF pilot from the obvious effort. "It's good of you to see us on such short notice."

"Good afternoon to you, Dane. And Gina, you're looking even more lovely than when last we met. You're a fortunate man, Mr. Baron. I was most happily surprised when you rang up yesterday, Dane. I didn't think we'd be meeting so soon after our pints in Radnage last week. And I appreciate you possibly bringing a Bugatti Atlantic to our house for auction. I must say, a most formidable offering. Please, sit," he motioned.

I continued to scan the august room while none too subtly examining the inventory of wall art.

Paul caught me and chuckled. "Magnificent, aren't they? But please, don't be overly impressed. They're not ours. We're simply the minders until we can find them a good home. Now, to business. I'm sorry, but I have another appointment at half four, which, unfortunately, I was unable to reschedule. You mentioned in addition to the Atlantic, Madame Laurent also wanted to sell two, shall we say, somewhat less interesting specimens?"

"Since I phoned you, she's decided to ship the Mercedes to her son in Florida. The remaining car is her late husband's '57 Facel Vega HK 500."

Raising a finger to put me on hold, Paul picked up his desk phone and punched in three numbers. "Portia, dear girl. Paul here. I need a realistic target price for a 1957 Facel Vega HK 500." He cupped the mouthpiece with his right hand after listening for a few seconds. "She's asking about condition. Have you seen the car?"

"Yes. In fact, I rode in it a few months ago. From what I've seen, it's certainly less than concours condition, but excellent. I checked it yesterday afternoon and the odometer shows forty-eight thousand kilometers and change, which I assume to be correct since Arnaud was the original owner."

Paul repeated my comments to his specialist and replaced the phone in its cradle a half-minute later. "She thinks somewhere in the vicinity of forty thousand pounds. Around sixty thousand U.S.," he stated without a moment's hesitation in conversion. "Dependent upon the interest we can generate, of course. Now, Dane, the Atlantic. What can you tell me about it, other than it is thought not to exist?"

I related the Bugatti's provenance, retelling Arnaud's story of the machine slipping between the cracks of history in 1939 pre-war France and thereby avoiding certain *liberation* by the Nazis.

"I see. Does the owner, or do you, have proof of the transfer from Etorre Bugatti to the senior Monsieur Laurent?" Paul asked, rocking in his chair, rubbing his chin.

"Madame Laurent gave me this bill of sale, or title transfer, I guess you could call it. It's signed by Bugatti. She also provided these photos of the Atlantic." I placed the items on the desk.

After a careful inspection of the yellowed document, Paul let out a soft whistle and pressed a button on his intercom. "Pepperdine, please ask Portia to come up." He remained fixed on the paper and the photographs. "Portia Trickelbank, she's the young lady I mentioned to you in Radnage who heads up our automobile section. When you rang up earlier, Dane, I asked Portia to start researching the Atlantic. I believe this machine will generate astonishing interest in the markets."

Portia tapped twice on the oversized mahogany doors and entered without waiting for a response. Paul made the introductions before directing the woman to a seat next to Gina's. Portia had most unfortunate features for a female, though she would have made for a reasonably handsome man (despite her pasty white skin and lusterless brown hair that screamed out for a good washing and styling). The more I looked at her, the more I could see a curious facial resemblance to a young Frank Sinatra. I'll never forget her outfit: a loose fitting beltless red on white polka dotted dress and red high top tennis shoes. She sat erect in her chair, hands crossed atop the briefcase in her lap.

"So what have you found for us, Portia? And, not to worry: I know I've only given you a few hours to do your research, but how does it look?" Paul inquired.

"Well, sir, initially, I'm assuming the Type 57's provenance can be authenticated?"

Paul leaned forward across his deck and carefully passed her the paper bearing Etorre Bugatti's hand written and signed details

172

of the sale to Édouard Laurent, along with the interior, exterior, engine, and undercarriage photographs. After opening her case to withdraw a notebook and magnifying glass, Portia scanned back and forth between the original paperwork and her files in an apparent attempt to verify the signature and script. The office fell silent for several minutes while the three of us watched as she continued to examine the Laurent Atlantic's document.

Shifting in her chair to face her boss, she said, "I believe this to be authentic, Mr. Bisno, and therefore, this may be one of the most significant automobiles ever to come to auction. Mr. Baron, as you may know, we have four things to consider in the classic automobile markets. First, the vehicle itself, as in, intrinsically, is it an attractive and timeless design? Second, its condition, third, its rarity, and finally, its provenance.

"Here, with this Type 57SC Atlantic, we have possibly one of the most aesthetically beautiful machines ever built. As far as condition, and only judging from these photos, mind you, I see no flaws to detract from a hundred-point motorcar. As far as rarity, well, with only four ever manufactured . . . enough said. And as to its provenance, an original owner, or father and subsequent son owners, if you will, who purchased the automobile directly from the owner of the factory—this is truly quite extraordinary.

"However, of prime importance in the case of this Atlantic, only two were known to still exist—I'm not counting the one involved in the train wreck in central France in 1955. Finding this fourth of only four produced by Bugatti, well, I don't think I can recall another offering quite like it. This is an amazing find, Mr. Baron. Again, you may have one of the most important automobiles ever to go to auction."

Paul was now leaning forward, his arms extended flat on the desk, his interest obvious. "What value would you assign to it, Portia? A preliminary number, of course, until you can finish your work."

After buying a moment or two to think, she replied, "Very difficult, sir, obviously. Are you offering the automobile on a reserve or no-reserve basis, Mr. Baron?" she queried.

Placing a minimum sale price, or reserve condition, on the classic could possibly result in a no sale, forcing Sandrine Laurent to wait another year or two before offering the Atlantic again if her "not less than" number wasn't reached at the auction.

"Unfortunately, no-reserve. Madame Laurent wants her deceased husband's things liquidated as quickly as possible. But for my own very important personal motives, I can't tell you how much I'd like to see the Atlantic sold for not a penny less than 3,993,000 pounds." I was ready for this one, and I'd rounded £984 high; I'd committed to memory the British pound equivalent of Madame Laurent's 10,000,000 Swiss franc bottom line figure.

"Right. Rather queer number, but I'm sure you have your reasons," Portia commented, noting the figure on her scratch pad. "Now, please don't hold me to this, but I should think three and a half million pounds would not be an unreasonable expectation. Possibly more, considering the automobile's original ownership pedigree."

"Not 3 point 5 million, Portia; 3 point 993 million," I corrected.

"Hmm, quite, and without reserve. Curious. Were you thinking of putting the Atlantic in our upcoming sale in Monte Carlo next week?" she asked, appearing to dread the painful and obvious answer.

"That's correct," Paul answered for me. "I realize that doesn't give us much notification or advertising time, but I'm sure you'll get your team right on it. I have full confidence you'll do the best you can. Thank you, Portia."

Taking her cue, Portia collected her paperwork, shook her head, said her goodbyes, and as she walked past me, I overheard her mumbling, *sotto voce*, "Right, eight bloody days." I could only guess at the intense inner conflict she was feeling: She'd been offered to represent the automobile of a lifetime, but with only a little over one week to do six month's worth of bush beating and marketing.

"Good lady," Paul said after Portia closed the door behind her. "By the time you leave my office, I dare say she'll have communiqués out to every Bugatti owner in the world, and those who would like to be. I have full confidence she'll fetch the best possible price for us. Thank you for bringing this to us, Dane."

"No, thank *you*. I have one other item I'm hoping you may be able to help me with, Paul. Do you have any way of selling some London Good Delivery bars? Are you familiar with them?"

"Yes, of course. LGDs. 12.5 kilo bars. Minimum 99.5 percent gold purity. How many, and may I ask where you obtained them?"

I was afraid he'd ask me that. How the hell could I explain this one? My buddy's dad and another guy shived a Nazi, stole his loot, hid it, son inherited dad's share, son and other guy both murdered last week, and I'm on a treasure hunt to find where it was last stashed?

"Twenty bars. How I obtained them is a tad complicated, I'm afraid. You see, I don't actually have them . . . yet."

Paul gave me the hairy eyeball. "I see. Well, let me ask you this: When you do acquire them, will you do so legally?"

His questions were getting tougher. Would I acquire them legally?

"Yes, more or less. Sort of. Well, it really depends on how you look at it. The previous owners, three generations of owners ago, were the Third Reich, so I guess we can't really assume they came by them completely legally either."

That got a chuckle out of him. "Quite. Look, Dane, in answer to your question, yes, I can easily dispose of the bars for you. However, since LGDs do not have ownership paperwork associated with them, I need your assurance—your word—that you will come by them legally. You see, I'll personally be guaranteeing their integrity."

I chose my words carefully. "How about if I assure you I arguably have as much right to them as their owners of the last fifty-five or sixty years have had? And my promise that no one will ever come back claiming the bars were theirs."

Paul gazed at me across the massive desk as he pressed the fingers of both hands against one another, resting his chin on the steeple they formed. If he could have risen from his chair without the strain involved in so doing, I could imagine him pacing a couple of laps around the office while he considered my request.

"Right. We'll do it. When will you have the gold in your possession?"

"Hopefully within a few days. Now, maybe a stupid question: Do you need the LGDs here in England or could you arrange to sell them in Switzerland?"

"Sorry, my boy, but unfortunately, I would require possession of them here in London. I wouldn't have any idea as to whom to contact in Switzerland for something of this nature. Is that going to be a problem?"

Without a thought as to what the hell I planned to do, I knee-jerked, "No, no problem at all. It just would have been a little easier, that's all." No shit.

I'd covered two of the three points for which I needed Paul's help: Bugatti and LGDs were mentally checked off. But after his questions about the gold, and in large part due to my impeccable sense of timing, I prudently decided to pass on the third—I'd find a gun elsewhere.

* * *

Things had just become a whole lot tougher; I wasn't prepared for this. There was no way I'd be able to get those LGDs into England. And that was assuming I'd even find them.

"Let's take this one step at a time. Yard by yard, it's hard—inch by inch, it's a cinch. We'll figure something out," Gina remarked, grasping my hand as we walked down the Brompton Road, now crowded with the after-workers. "Look, the pubs will all be chock-a-block now; it's almost five. Let's take a stroll over to Hyde Park. We can talk a bit there before I have to meet my parents and Will for dinner."

Within minutes, we covered the four blocks to the park where Gina led us to a vacant bench overlooking the Serpentine, Hyde Park's great artificial lake. A Scotch would have been nice right about now.

"Dane, I think I may have a plan."

"Great. As Mike Tyson once said, 'Everybody's got a plan till they get hit.'"

"I'm serious. It may sound a bit wild at first perhaps, but stay with me. I think this'll work."

"I'm all ears." We should have gone to a pub. I didn't recall ever sitting in a park during happy hour.

"First off, tell me again why you want to see Toru in Monaco tomorrow? What's to be accomplished by that?"

A reasonable question, for which I didn't have a totally reasonable answer. "I want to meet with him, eyeball to eyeball, in a very public place, like Monaco, with its security cameras watching every square inch of the Principality. I'm going to explain to him how Klaus mistakenly stole his gold, thinking Arnaud had screwed him over. I want to make it clear to Toru I didn't have anything to do with it, just in case he was thinking of whacking me next. If I'm convincing, that should at least buy us some time to go to Klaus's place in Tiefencastel and try to figure out what he did with the LGDs."

"Why do you think Toru's in Monaco?"

"Mostly 'cause he's got a gambling jones. But before boarding my flight in Geneva this afternoon, I called to see if he was at the Laurel office in Neuchâtel. The woman who answered told me he'd gone, and he wasn't expected back for at least a week. So I figured either he flew back to Japan or he went to play a little baccarat. I called the Hermitage in Monte Carlo, asked to be connected with his room, and when they put me through, I hung up before he could answer."

"Very clever, luv. But won't he be afraid you'll turn him in to the police if he thinks you know he killed Klaus? Maybe an excellent reason for him to kill you as well, no?"

"Frankly, I couldn't care less if he killed him or not, and I plan to make that very clear."

Squeezing my hand, she said, "It still scares me a bit. All right, would you care to hear how we're going to get the gold into England?"

"Again with the *we*, huh? And that's *if* we find it. But, yeah, shoot. I'm listening."

"I don't know if I told you before, but my parents own a Cessna Skylane, which presently is in St. Moritz. They had some new radios installed last week and they haven't gone down to fly it back to Cambridge yet. So—"

"So I'm supposed to abscond with their plane and fly more than five hundred pounds of gold bullion into the U.K.? And, what, simply declare it at customs? Swell idea, Gina."

If this was her plan, I was almost looking forward to her joining her folks for dinner. I'd down a few stiff drinks and feel sorry for myself over losing out on my Type 35.

"No, listen, Dane, this is doable. And there's no other way we could get that stuff back here, if for no other reason, the sheer weight of it all."

I gazed out over the lake, rubbing my temples while I considered her comments. Problem was, as crappy a plan as it was, I didn't have a better one. I decided to play devil's advocate: "You forget, Gina, I don't fly anymore. I *don't want* to fly anymore. I haven't flown in thirteen years—since I totaled the last airplane I flew. Remember? I don't even have a pilot's license. And God knows when I last flew a small single-engine. I think I'd rather run naked through Harrods than sit in the left seat again."

"I can picture it: you—starkers—dashing though Harrods Food

179

Hall! Now *that* I'd pay to see. Look, if you could captain a huge cargo aircraft like the C-130 Hercules, you could surely handle their little plane. And not having a valid license would be the least of your problems if we're pinched."

True enough. Happy thought.

"I'll think about it. C'mon, let's get out of here. You've got people waiting for you."

And I needed a pop.

Chapter 16

Monte Carlo

Friday, 21 July 2000

I'd spent the better part of last night thinking about it, alone, from the comfort of my red leather stool in Claridge's Bar, a bottomless crystal glass of Black Label in front of me.

The awesome logistics of moving twenty gold bars had me stymied. I'd flown Cessnas in college, before the Air Force, but it had been so long ago I couldn't remember much about them. Could the aircraft handle the weight of full tanks, Gina and me, and an additional 550 pounds of bullion? Did it have the legs to make it from St. Moritz to England without refueling? Could I make the flight without being detected? Where would I land to avoid Her Majesty's Customs? A lot of questions, and few answers. But nor did I have a more viable alternative, even though I got hives merely thinking about flying again.

Gina, her usual (and appreciated) punctual self, met me at the BA check-in counter 45 minutes prior to our 11:40 A.M. departure to Nice. Our time aboard the short flight south to the sunny Côte d'Azur passed quickly, with orange juice, sans Champagne, my beverage of choice. Once aloft, a voice from the flight deck announced we'd be only a few minutes late for our scheduled 2:40 P.M. arrival in Nice—two hours of flying time, plus the one-hour Continental time change.

"Did you think about my idea last night?" Gina asked, her head facing me atop the small pillow she'd wedged between her headrest and the second row window of the Boeing 757.

"Yeah, a lot. And I can also foresee a lot of problems. But I still don't have a better idea. I checked out some of the Skylane's performance and loading parameters on my computer last night, and it is possible, I guess. Did you happen to mention to your folks over dinner last night you planned on ripping off their Cessna with an unlicensed pilot who pranged his last plane?"

"No. I thought I'd save that little surprise for another day."

"Jesus, Gina, we could go to prison over this little caper. Or at least I could. This isn't exactly like pulling the tags off pillows. And I meant to ask you yesterday: Why are you getting involved in all this? You've got Arnaud's check for a hundred thousand dollars in the bank—what's that? Almost seventy thousand pounds? That should make for a nice down payment on a new flat, with lots of change left over for Willie's tuition bills. And anyway, hell, I'm the one getting the Bugatti out of the deal . . . if I don't get dead first."

"Because you need me. And for other reasons which should be abundantly obvious to you, even though you are the thickest man I've ever known."

I left that one alone.

"And by the by, whilst it has nothing to do with anything, even though I'm incredibly grateful to you and Arnaud for the check, I'm afraid my future plans will require a bit more than my recent sixty-seven thousand pound windfall."

I didn't touch that one either—back to topic. "Have you given any thought as to how we're supposed to fly from Switzerland to England without being observed? Countries tend to get a little cranky over folks popping in on them unannounced without clearance."

"Ever heard the expression, 'under the radar?'" she replied with a grin.

"This isn't funny. I'm serious."

"Me too. I'm not a pilot, but isn't it possible to literally stay below the scan of the radar so as not to be seen on their screens?"

I turned away, pushed my seat back to the full recline position, and swirled my flute of virgin Mimosa, a.k.a. plain orange juice. Was this all really worth it? I had a fresh deposit slip in my wallet for two million bucks, a damned good life back in Sarasota, and an incredibly exciting and gorgeous new girlfriend sitting next to me (whom I was finally going to get lucky with tonight). And I was actually considering blowing it all for a shot at a Type 35 Bugatti? Yeah, I was; I had nothing better to do till Tuesday.

"I guess it's possible we could avoid radar detection for the first portion of the flight by staying low until we hit the French coast," I reasoned aloud. "And I mean one hundred to two hundred feet above the ground low— almost smacking into the ground low. But that short leg across the English Channel would be the tough part. That little Channel's always tended to be a hell of a barrier. That segment would have to be flown just above the wave crests— literally on the deck. This is dangerous stuff, Gina. There's also the possibility they, meaning the Brits or the French, have radar buoys in the water for the sole purpose of picking up low-flying aircraft.

"I remember flying a training mission once in a C-130 from Texas to MacDill Air Force Base in Tampa. We were flying low, below the coverage of land radar, but we were picked up by a tethered radar balloon in the northeastern Gulf of Mexico, in Apalachee Bay, off Apalachicola. It was probably designed to find drug runners coming in by go-fast boats or low-flying aircraft. I don't know if they use them in the English Channel, but they obviously wouldn't be shown on any navigational charts if they do."

"Not a lot of drug traffic coming into the U.K. across the Channel from France though," Gina offered.

"*Yeah, right.* Wanna bet? But it is possible they wouldn't have anything out there in the water because of the hazard to shipping traffic. It's the busiest stretch of water in the world. I guess it's a chance we take if we go through with this."

"Right, so you agree, it is *possible* to fly the gold in from St. Moritz. Now, let me ask you: Where could we land without having to go through customs inspections?"

I'd had a couple of Scotches worth dwelling on that one last night. "Two choices," I said, not sure if I was trying to sell Gina or myself on the viability of the developing scheme. "One, since this flight would have to be at night, we could land at an uncontrolled airport, or one where the tower closes down after dark. But there's a big risk with this, because if we were being radar tracked, all kinds of officialdom would be there to greet us when we landed. Definitely not a good thing. My second idea is tougher to pull off, but there's less of a chance of our being popped for smuggling once we did land."

"Drop the bars out of the plane before we land!" Gina

interjected in a loud whisper.

"There you go. Then if we're nabbed when we eventually land, the gold's gone, the plane's clean, and I merely go to the big house for illegal international border penetration, failure to land at an airport of entry, grand theft airplane, and flying without a license. Sounds better every time I think about it."

"Details, my dear. But where would we drop the bars so we could find them again before they're spotted and collected by someone else?"

After hours of reflection last night, I'd had a true light bulb epiphany: a place easily accessible for retrieving the bars, yet seldom visited by hikers or other foot traffic. "The field where our helicopter landed, behind Timmy's pub in Radnage. Remember? The field's bounded by the road in front of the pub on the west, and by a hedgerow on the east which stretches between two narrow roads on the north and south. The field's about 500 yards long. I did a little calculation in my room last night. If I brought the airplane down to barely above stall speed, flaps down, we could pass over the field doing around 50 knots—that's about 57 miles per hour. That means we'd be traveling at roughly 85 feet per second. Are you with me?"

"I'm all yours," she nodded.

"Okay, you'll see why this is important in a minute. At 85 feet per second, I calculated we'd cover the length of the field in about 17 seconds, assuming light or zero wind conditions. Now, if we each drop one bar out of our window every 3 seconds, we'd have dropped 10 bars between us, right? Take a second pass, and all 20 are out."

"That's brilliant! But one problem: How do we find them?

Those bars are heavy and they could bury themselves beneath the crops and soil falling that fast, couldn't they?"

"Possibly, and I thought of that. Sounds kind of sci-fi, but we attach a small homing transmitter to each bar. We drop the bars, and then land the plane at Booker Airpark. That's a small airfield nearby which closes at night. It's about seven miles by road from there to the Three Horseshoes. So, after we land, we walk back to the pub. That'll take about two hours. Later in the day, we rent a car, wait till the pub closes that night, then go out and locate the bars from their transmitter signals, put them in the trunk of the car, and the next day, get them to Paul Bisno. Kind of far-fetched, but I think this might actually work."

* * *

It was approaching four by the time the Heli Air Monaco van dropped us at the Hôtel de Paris. Since Toru-san was registered at the Hermitage, a little distance between us was probably a good thing.

"Toru doesn't know you're coming to see him, does he?" Gina asked as we walked through the hotel's place du Casino front entrance.

"Nope. We're gonna give him a treat and surprise him. I'm laying eight-to-five odds we'll find him across the street at the baccarat tables."

I gave our small carry-on bags to the porter to take to our room, a one-bedroom suite overlooking the square and the casino. I'd been lugging around my two larger suitcases for a week and I was relieved to have finally left them behind at Claridge's for the next few days. With the possibility of flying the Cessna back to England, needless weight wasn't an option; I'd calculated the plane's gross weight would be right at the maximum limit for the skinny-aired high altitude takeoff from St. Moritz.

I presented our passports, paid the casino entry tax, and guided Gina to the same table where I'd met Toru three months earlier. "Do me a favor, Gina. Order me a drink. I'm going to see if our pal is here. Right back."

I walked past a line of nearly empty blackjack and roulette tables before coming to the slightly recessed baccarat alcove. I slowed my approach, making sure I'd see him before he saw me.

"*Bien fait, monsieur,*" the attractive female chemin de fer croupier announced upon observing Toru's cards: a five and a four. He organized his chip stacks, then lit a Marlboro and raised his brandy snifter.

"Congratulations, Mr. Toru," I softly commented from my standing position directly behind his seat.

He almost dropped his glass as he abruptly turned in his chair to face me. His mouth moved, but words didn't follow.

"I'm in the cocktail lounge. Same table as before. When it's convenient, of course." I smiled and slowly walked away.

Thirty seconds couldn't have elapsed after I rejoined Gina before I saw the Japanese practically trotting across the room. His pace slowed when he saw I wasn't alone.

"Miss Domenico, Mr. Baron, such a pleasant surprise," he lied. I motioned him toward the vacant seat at our table. "What brings you to Monaco?" he asked nervously. I'd not seen this twitchy side to his normally tranquil personality.

"Good to see you too, Mr. Toru. I thought it was time we had a little chat."

"Very well. But with no offense to you, Miss Domenico, I think we should speak in private, Mr. Baron . . . just the two of us."

Before she could even think of leaving, I had my hand on Gina's forearm, pinning it to her chair's armrest. "By that, I see you have you a rough idea as to why I'm here. Miss Domenico is completely aware of everything that's happened in the past few days, Mr. Toru, and she'll be staying. We can all speak freely here, and as you can see," I said as I leaned back and gestured at the empty tables nearest us, "our conversation will be private."

A waiter approached and nodded at the new arrival to the table. "Monsieur?"

"Coffee. No sugar. No milk. Black," Toru said, before turning back to me. "Why are you here, Mr. Baron?"

"I think you already know, but okay, let's get into it. Two people have been killed in the past week over the LGD bars. I'm fairly certain Klaus Schulrat killed Arnaud Laurent over a tragic misunderstanding. Then Klaus was killed last Sunday or Monday after being tortured. I think you, or one of your people, tortured him to find out what he did with the gold he stole from you. How am I doin' so far?"

Toru lowered his head and put his hands over his ears, more in despair than in an attempt to silence me. Long seconds passed before he looked up again. "Mr. Baron, there are things underway over which I have no control. I did not kill anyone. I've never harmed anyone in my life—at least not physically. I need you to believe that. Do you?"

"I don't know yet, and it doesn't really make a hell of a lot of difference if I do. What do you mean there are things *underway*?"

188

"Mr. Baron, you must simply trust me on this."

"*Bullshit!* People around me are getting killed," I barked as I leaned forward.

Raising the palms of his hands to calm me, Toru began: "All right. You may know Mr. Schulrat was dismissed from the new Laurel company last Friday, shortly after we finalized our purchase. We're going toward more automation in our production, and as a result, Schulrat no longer fit into our plans. Carelessly, I didn't change the door locks or the combination to the gold vault after he was let go, and obviously he came back later that night or the next morning and stole our LGDs. Strangely, the smaller kilobars were untouched."

I'll be damned. The old Swiss crud had ethics. "Those weren't his," I mumbled aloud without thinking, a dumb gut reaction.

"None of it was his. Why do you say *those* weren't his?"

"Never mind. It doesn't matter anymore. Go ahead. Continue. What's *underway*?"

"Mr. Baron," Toru continued, showing his angst, "I like you. And you, Miss Domenico. I don't want to see any harm come to either of you. However, there are things happening now which I am powerless to stop. I tell you this because you were fair with me in the past and I don't want you hurt. You see, our company, Kizoku Holdings, has been infiltrated in recent years by a group known as the *Yakuza*. Have you heard of them?"

I'd read about the *Yakuza*, though in my several trips to Japan, I'd never heard them mentioned in any of my mundane dealings. "A criminal society of some type. The Japanese mafia? I don't know exactly. Enlighten us." I had absolutely no idea where this was going.

"The *Yakuza* is an organized underworld group which claims to follow the code of the samurai. Their history goes back many centuries in Japan, but I won't bore you with history. Currently, the *oyabun* of the Inagawa-kai family has been pervading large legitimate Japanese corporations."

"What's an *oyabun*?" Gina asked, saving me.

"*Oyabun* literally means father, or patron, in Japanese," Toru explained. "The *oyabun* is the head of a *Yakuza* group—a crime family. In our case, the Inagawa-kai."

"Okay, go ahead. How could this Inagawa-kai family have infiltrated your company?" I pressed.

"The *Yakuza* have been making large investments in legitimate Japanese companies for over two decades. For example, in 1989 the *oyabun* of the Inagawa-kai paid two hundred and fifty-five million dollars for stock in the Tokyo Electric Railway Company. Once they gain an interest in the companies, the *Yakuza* finds ways to blackmail the directors into paying them huge sums of money to keep quiet about various indiscretions the *Yakuza* either discover or set up. It's so bad in some places, the boards actually include these payoffs as part of their companies' operating budgets. The *Yakuza* also extorts money from companies for protection. They are a very powerful force behind many Japanese businesses. Including Kizoku Holdings, unfortunately."

"So you're saying the *Yakuza* family entrenched in Kizoku are really the ones running the show at Laurel? You're merely the front man?"

"Not exactly. I'm responsible for overseeing Laurel until I'm able to hire a plant manager, a local Swiss, who will report to me once I return to Osaka. I'm hopeful of this happening quite soon.

Until then, I have shut down operations in Neuchâtel temporarily and given the staff a two-week holiday during the closure. Only my new receptionist is working during this hiatus.

"At this point, the Inagawa-kai is only interested in Laurel for the gold, though that may change. They have unimaginable amounts of money they've taken in through protection, prostitution, narcotics, and arms dealings, and they need to invest it legitimately.

"When your offer to sell the LGDs came to their attention in Osaka, that proved to be an excellent vehicle for them in which to convert cash into gold. And at an instant quarter-million dollar profit to the *oyabun* when Monsieur Laurent agreed to sell at a ten percent discount to dispose of his most cumbersome commodity. Furthermore, they're speculating the price of gold will escalate in the future above the current two hundred and eighty dollar levels and yield even higher profits."

"Okay, I'm starting to get the picture, but you still haven't told us about these activities which are underway."

"The Inagawa-kai paid Monsieur Laurent two million dollars, rounded off, for those LGDs which were later stolen. They want their gold returned, and people will continue to be killed until they get it."

"Are you talking about me? I had nothing to do with the theft. I've got no idea where the goddamned gold is," I lied, a little.

"I believe you," Toru replied, "but that doesn't matter. The *Yakuza* think you're involved and that should matter to you. These people are totally amoral. A few years ago, a *Yakuza* family member burned down an apartment building in Japan in retaliation for the owner not paying them protection money. Over fifty residents of the building died in the fire. They would kill you if they even suspect you had any knowledge about the theft . . . after trying to convince you to help return it, of course. The individual who flew into Zürich with me last Friday with the cash for the LGDs already knows who you are and where you're going next."

"What? Who is this guy?" Gina chimed in.

"Miura Etsujirou, Miura being his surname. He's been with the *oyabun* most of his life. He's about forty now. Unlike most *Yakuza*, Miura cleans up and dresses in a way to hide his tattoos so he can better blend into the legitimate business world. He's been following you off and on since you were in Paris with Monsieur Laurent last week. He even knows you two are going on a Concorde charter flight to New York next Tuesday."

Now I was starting to worry.

"After Miura and I discovered the gold was missing on Saturday afternoon when we came to the office, we knew Schulrat was the only likely candidate to have stolen it. I immediately tried calling Monsieur Laurent, but only reached his answering message. So Miura went to Schulrat's apartment—we found his address in the personnel files. By the time he arrived there, Schulrat was gone. But Miura told me he saw the note Monsieur Laurent had left on Schulrat's apartment door, and read that Monsieur Laurent had flown to Paris. He then correctly assumed Schulrat had gone to see him, and he'd obviously departed before the note was left. Miura followed them to Paris in our company's Sabreliner. Over my objections, of course."

"Okay, your *Yakuza* guy reads the note, and then flies to Paris to track down Arnaud and Klaus to either get back his gold or his cash. I got it. But how did he know where to go once he got there?

And how does he know about our Concorde flight next week? No one knew about that."

"You told me here in Monte Carlo last April that Monsieur Laurent always stays at the Crillon," Toru answered. "Miura waited in the hotel for several hours on Saturday evening, and finally, around seven or eight, he saw Monsieur Laurent walk through the lobby and enter a taxi."

"How did he recognize him? They'd never met."

"Yes, they did. At the closing, on Friday, in the Laurel offices. When he paid the cash for the LGDs to Monsieur Laurent. I had been instructed to introduce Miura as one of my associates."

"So basically, *you* fingered Arnaud for this scumbag." I was starting to feel a little less licentious about ripping off the *Yakuza's* gold for Sandrine Laurent. "Now tell me how he knew we're taking the Concorde charter?" The little patience I had was waning.

"He saw you being interviewed by the police in the Crillon. That's when he first guessed Schulrat had murdered Monsieur Laurent. You see, after Miura lost track of Monsieur Laurent when he entered the taxi the previous evening, he decided to come back to the hotel the following day and wait for him again. When you moved from the lobby to the bar during the police questioning, he followed your group into the lounge and sat at the bar with his back to you, but within listening distance. He said he heard everything you told the detective, including your mentioning you were leaving on the twenty-fifth on the Concorde charter flight."

"You miserable sons of bitches! So then this Miura character goes back to Neuchâtel for Klaus and tortures him to find the gold. Jesus, man, and you say all this is beyond your control? Bullshit."

Toru was now hunched forward in his chair, head down. "Mr.

Baron, I cannot apologize enough to you for what's happened, even though I had nothing to do with any of it, other than being forced to give Miura the information he demanded from me. He would kill me if he knew I told you any of this. And he will kill you, both of you, if he thinks you have his *oyabun's* gold or arc involved in any way. He cannot return to Osaka until he finds it." He paused and lifted his head to look at me again. "Do you know the word *yubizume?*"

I was almost feeling sorry for him. His neck was out there as far as ours. And I believed him: By merely telling us about Miura, he had no doubt jeopardized his own life.

"No, what's a *yubizume?*" I hesitantly asked, dreading the other bits of good news he evidently had for us.

"If a *Yakuza* man offends his *oyabun* by lying or being deceitful, or displeasing him in any way, he is punished by *yubizume*. The offender amputates the top joint of his little finger and presents it to his *oyabun* as a form of apology. If he commits another act of disappointment to his *oyabun*, the next joint is cut off. And so on. They continue to the next finger if the transgressions continue. Do you understand?"

"Yeah, but so what?"

"Mr. Baron, Miura's fingers are all intact."

Chapter 17

Monte Carlo/Zürich

Friday evening/Saturday, 21/22 July 2000

Toru had duly scared the crap out of me. If, indeed, Miura had been following us, he surely knew by now we were in Monte Carlo, and it was time to get Gina off his radar screen. And once again, I would be sleeping alone. So much for our long delayed romantic evening.

Knowing Gina wouldn't take well to being asked to leave, I decided to subtly skirt the issue until she saw the light for herself and eventually acquiesce.

"Let me try this out on you, Gina. There are a couple things we need right now: I need a gun, and you need not to be in Monte Carlo." I was hoping she hadn't missed the subtle part.

"I'm not going anywhere without you, you daft bastard. And I realize we're in a spot of bother, but a gun?"

A spot of bother? "Gina, we need to split up, and right away. This *Yakuza* guy is looking for me, not you. He's more than likely aware I'm in Monte Carlo, and three-to-two money says he already knows we're staying here at the Hôtel de Paris. Let me put you on a plane tonight for Zürich and I'll meet up with you tomorrow. Okay? Do me this one favor?"

I caught her eyeing the king-sized bed in the next room through the open double doors. "All right, if I must. Where will I see you tomorrow?" she pouted in frustration after thinking for a few seconds.

My mind mulled over the possibilities—the missed possibilities for tonight, and the other than pleasant ones for tomorrow. "Tiefencastel. We'll meet at the train station there. I'll make a reservation for you tonight at the Zürich Airport Hilton and call you there early tomorrow morning once I figure out what we're doing. Give me a second. Let me see if there's still a flight out of Nice tonight."

"Tiefencastel? We're going to do a bit of gold mining at Klaus's place?"

"That's the plan."

I checked my watch as I dialed the concierge: 5:15. He answered my query from memory; there was one last flight to Zürich at 6:40 this evening and we could still make the 5:45 Heli Air Monaco chopper, leaving over a half-hour to connect with the Swissair flight. The shuttle van would meet us downstairs in ten minutes, he promised.

"Listen, Gina: I'm going with you to the airport, and—"

"Dane, don't be a prat. I'm perfectly capable of finding my own way to the airport."

"As I was saying, I *am* going to Nice with you. And when I get back, I'll make some calls and see about tomorrow's schedules. I'll also try to think of some way I can come up with a gun, but I know it's a hell of a lot tougher here in Europe than in the States. If this

Miura character shot Klaus, and he's now looking for me, I want to be holding something other than your hand if we run into him."

Gina paced the sitting room for the better part of a minute, exhibiting that French puffy lip thing. She finally stopped at the glass balcony doors and gazed out over the place du Casino before turning back toward me. "I suppose you're right," she sulked. "And I have one. A gun, that is. It's my father's, actually. In Celerina, at my parent's house outside St. Moritz. All Swiss men are required to serve in the Army reserves until they're fifty, and they keep their rifles at home. My dad kept his after his reserve commitment was up and he stores it in a locker in the basement, along with some ammunition."

"A rifle, huh? I was kinda thinking along the lines of a pistol, but I guess we'll take what we can get. Hell, if I'm stealing his airplane, I don't think your dad would mind if I took his weapon while I'm at it. Man, this just keeps getting better and better."

* * *

Dane, Marie-Claude here. Weren't we supposed to meet yesterday after you flew back from Switzerland?"

"Hey, Clyde, thanks for returning my message so quickly. I'm in Monaco now; I was just walking into my favorite bar here. Sorry about my no-show yesterday, but things have been kind of nuts for the last day or two. I have some good news for you: I think you can close d'Aubigne's case for him. A man named Klaus Schulrat basically confessed to killing Arnaud Laurent in the Crillon. He was the guy you saw in the hotel's surveillance videos. Klaus used to work for Arnaud. He told Arnaud's widow all about it when he returned to Switzerland. I suppose he was looking for her forgiveness or something."

"*Bien fait*! Ever think about becoming a detective in your next life? So, do you think our killer will make life simple for us and sign a confession? Do you know where the Swiss cantonal police can pick him up?"

"Too late, Clyde. Someone already beat you to him. He's no longer of this world."

Marie-Claude hesitated for several seconds on the silent connection before speaking, and then, "*Putain la vache!*" Fucking hell! "Please tell me you didn't do it, Dane."

"No, but I know who did. And I'm told he's looking for me next."

"Who told you that? Come on, talk to me. What's going on down there?"

I figured this one fell into the *need to know* category, and Clyde didn't need to know everything. A juicy two million dollar gold heist—along with a purloined airplane—might be a little more confidence than any good Paris cop should be trusted with . . . pals be damned.

"I don't want to lie to you, Marie-Claude, so I won't get into all that now. I know it's asking a lot, but I need you to trust me a little longer. And I need another favor."

"*Merde alors*! Why is it every time you call me you want something? Can't you call me sometime when you're in Paris and just ask me out for a drink or dinner? Or maybe take me to bed?"

"Clyde, I'm sorry, but I really need this one. I need you to find out what you can on a Japanese national named Miura Etsujirou. Monsieur Miura, first name Etsujirou. He's from Osaka."

"He's the one trying to kill you?"

"So I'm told. He's connected with the *Yakuza*. You know about them?" I asked without thinking.

"Dane, I told you I was now working in the Organized Crimes Unit. Sure, I've heard of the *Yakuza*. They don't operate in France yet, but I know about them. Look, all right, I'll check with Interpol and see what I can find. Happy?"

"I owe you, Clyde. The next time you hear from me, it will be for drinks. And dinner."

"Two out of three's not bad. Not the two I was hoping for, but I'll settle for that. Call me back tomorrow morning. Is there anything in particular I'm looking for on this Miura?"

"His track record, how he operates. See if the Japanese police suspect him of any murders, or torturing anybody. I'd like to know as much as possible about the guy in case I run into him."

"*Oh, là là! Torture? Mon Dieu*! Please, watch yourself, Dane. Talk to you tomorrow morning, *mon cher*. Bye bye. *Ciao*."

I lingered at the bar at Sam's Place until closing, doing in the better part of their last bottle of Black Label before walking the few short blocks back to the hotel. I thought about whether I'd lost all perspective; I'd put Gina at incredible risk. But I could also imagine her reaction if I'd asked her to return to London.

* * *

1 needed to give Gina a head start today. She had to get herself from the Hilton—in the Zürich suburb of Kloten—to St. Moritz by train, hire a rental car, find pop's rifle, check out the plane, and then drive back over the Julierpass to meet me in Tiefencastel a little before six. I decided against cautioning her about being followed as I doubted she could do anything about it if she was.

I also considered the strong possibility of this entire mission turning into a futile exercise; the odds were long on getting lucky enough to find Klaus's cache. But I was on, regardless. Damn the *Yakuza*. Full speed ahead. Yeah, right.

"Good morning. Ready for some action?" I asked when Gina answered on the first ring. It was barely seven A.M.

"Morning to you, and Dane, I've been ready for some action since we first met at the Dorchester. But unfortunately, I assume you're talking about our trip to Tiefencastel. So what's our plan for the day?"

"Okay, this is what I have so far: There's a train leaving from the airport station near the Hilton in a little less than two hours—at eight fifty-five—that'll get you to St. Moritz a few minutes before one P.M. I have a reservation for a Hertz BMW, under my name, which you'll be picking up at Badrutt's Palace Hotel. You know the place, I assume?"

"Badrutt's? Of course."

"Hertz doesn't have an office in St. Moritz, so they're driving the car in from somewhere else. I gave 'em my credit card number over the phone earlier this morning. The agent said he'll park the car in front of the hotel not later than one o'clock and leave the keys in the glove box." I read her the rental's license plate number the agent had given me.

"Fine, I'm with you. I'll go over to my place in Celerina—for you know what—and then about an hour's drive to meet you at the station in Tiefencastel. What time there?"

"I'll be coming in on the train from Zürich at five forty-seven."

"Zürich? Where are you now?"

"I'm still in Monaco. I've got a Swissair flight to Zürich later this morning. Remember, I need to do some shopping before we go to England."

"Shopping? Oh, the transmitters. Right. Dane, this is all moving so quickly."

"If it weren't, I'd have time to really think about this whole deal and probably realize what a crappy idea it is. Oh, I need you to do one more thing before you leave Celerina: Drive over to the airport and check to make sure the plane's fully fueled. My guess is it probably is; pilot's always gas up after they land. We do have keys for this thing, right?"

"Yeah, at the house. How do I check the fuel?"

"Look for the Master Switch. It's a little red plastic on-off switch on the lower left of the instrument panel, on the pilot's left side. Push the top half of the switch to *on*, give it a second, then check the fuel quantity indicators toward the top of the copilot's panel. See that both tanks are reading completely full."

"Okay, got it. What if they're not full?"

"You'll have to come up with something and have one of the guy's in the office fill it up for you. No way we're taking off with partial tanks. Oh, and look in the cabin and see if you can find some charts. For the entire route, obviously. There'll likely be three or four. If you can't find any, you'll have to figure out a line to give the folks in the office as to why you need to buy some."

"Okay, I think I can handle all that. You be careful. Bye, Dane."

"Bye, kiddo. See you this afternoon."

Next call: Madame Laurent in La Chaux-de-Fonds. I'd spent

over an hour on my laptop last night trying to get an exact fix on Klaus's farm near Tiefencastel, with less than sterling results. The property records I'd tracked down had given me information regarding tax assessments, size of his property (6.72 hectares), and size of the improvement to the property (93 square-meter main dwelling). I also noted a barn of undisclosed area. The closest thing I could find regarding the precise location was an image of the surveyor's plat, and that only indicated the lot's juxtaposition to an unnamed road that formed a "V" pointing to his property.

"Madame Laurent, good morning. Dane Baron. Sorry for the early morning call. I hope I didn't wake you."

"*Ah, bonjour*, Monsieur Baron. No, I'm having my coffee. Is everything all right?"

"Yes, fine, thanks. I wanted to tell you I've arranged with my contact in London to have the Bugatti Atlantic and the Facel Vega sold at his upcoming auction in Monaco. The sale will be at the Monte Carlo Grand Hotel on the twenty-eighth, next Friday evening."

"Excellent. But I'm not familiar with the Grand."

"It's the old Loews Monte Carlo, down the hill from the casino, on the seafront. A new group took it over a little over a year ago."

"Ah, yes, I know it now. Well done, Monsieur Baron. You worked very fast, no?"

"Well, yeah, I guess, but we were just plain lucky to coincide with my auctioneer friend's schedule. I've taken the liberty of arranging for the Atlantic and the Facel to be picked up by a special transporter truck next Tuesday morning. I've already paid the shipping fees. I'll only need you to give the driver the ownership papers, access to the automobiles, and sign the limited power of attorney he'll present to you for the eventual sales and title transfers. Will you be able to make yourself available next Tuesday?"

"I'm writing it down in my calendar as we speak. Very efficiently handled, monsieur. Many thanks for all of your efforts on my behalf. How much do I owe you for the transportation fees?"

"Nothing. It's my pleasure, madame. But I do need your help on another matter. Have you ever been to Klaus Schulrat's farm near Tiefencastel? I'm having trouble locating it."

"Are you in Tiefencastel now?"

"No, I'm going there this evening. I thought it would be best to wait until after dark so the neighboring farmers don't see me poking around. I did notice on a surveyor's map that the property abuts a road which makes a sharp hairpin turn at the entrance to what looks like a path leading into his property. My problem is the road isn't labeled, and I don't know where it is in relation to the town."

"Yes, I know the turn you're describing exactly. Arnaud and I stopped at Klaus's place several times when we'd drive back from St. Moritz after a skiing or sailing outing. As I recall, his farm is a short distance, maybe no more than two kilometers, up the hill on the only road leading west out of Tiefencastel. You'll turn up the hill where you see a rather large hotel at the corner of the main road in town."

Clear as Everglades mud.

"Ah, and I remember he had two large white wagon wheels marking the lane into his property. They were on the right as we drove up from the town. But, of course, that was many years ago.

I'm afraid that's all I can tell you. So you're picking up the gold bars tonight?"

Yeah, thought I'd cruise by the place and grab those little babies just sitting there on the front stoop for me.

"Well, I'm going to see what I can find, but it'll take a huge stroke of luck to discover anything. I'll give you a call in the next day or two and let you know how I did. Thanks for your help. *Au revoir*, madame."

"*Merci*, Monsieur Baron. *Bonne chance*."

Not bad. Take the only road leading west out of town, drive up the hill a little over a mile, and then look for a sharp turn and a pair of white wagon wheels. Not bad at all.

Next on my list was a call to Clyde.

"*Entrez*," I shouted after hearing three sharp raps on the door. I nodded to the breakfast room service waiter and pointed to the sitting room coffee table while I waited for Clyde to come on the line.

"Morning, Clyde. Hold on a second, please."

I laid down my cell phone and glanced at the check the waiter was holding out for my signature: 30 bucks—plus tip—for orange juice, croissants and tea. The suite may have cost me over $1,100 for the night, but the breakfast tab pissed me off. That was just downright wrong.

"Sorry. Am I too early for you?"

"No, it's fine. I had to come in early to make my calls for you. I remembered yesterday afternoon Osaka is eight hours ahead of Paris. I had to catch them very early, my time."

"Any success?"

"A little, yes. I went straight to the Osaka police instead of screwing around with Interpol in Lyon—they always ask too many questions, in my experiences with them anyway. Dane, according to the sheets the Japanese faxed me this morning, your friend Monsieur Miura is apparently a very bad boy. Let me read you a few of the highlights I see here: served two years for possession of a silencer, then another three and a half years and a hefty fine for possession of a Glock 17."

"I'm not surprised. The Japanese have some major league gun laws."

"True. I have more. He's definitely *Yakuza*. He belongs to a family called the Inagawa-kai. Ever heard of them?"

"Yup. And I'm not pleased to say you're confirming what I was told yesterday."

"Well, when I was speaking with the Osaka detective, he told me this Inagawa-kai family is big into corporate manipulation and extortion. He said Miura had been arrested in connection with the mutilation and murder of a corporate executive two years ago, but he walked when the witnesses refused to testify. Evidently, he cut out some guy's tongue and castrated him before shooting him in front of one of his associates and two female companions. And that was his second arrest for murder. They couldn't make the first one stick either. Dane, what's your connection with these people? You need to tell me something. *Now!*"

Maybe someday I would tell her an apocryphal story over drinks at Harry's, but right now I needed another forty-eight to seventy-two hours. I'd minimize the lies and shoot for vague.

"Clyde, all I can say now is some people think I know the location of something stolen from them. I've attempted to convince them I've got nothing to do with it, but this Miura guy can't go home till he either finds the stuff or makes somebody pay for stealing from his boss."

"His *oyabun*?"

"Very good, Clyde. You did your homework. But I still can't get into all this with you now. Things would only get messier for me. But if the gods are smiling, I'll be able to stay out of Miura's sights and everyone will go back about their business within a week. Miura-san will be called back to Osaka by his *oyabun*, lose an inch off his little finger, and the world will go on."

"Dane, I'm telling you, you don't want to screw with these people. You don't have the training for it. As a former pilot who wrote reports for the embassy, you're in way over your head here. Are you listening to me?"

She was correct, of course, but as Sherlock would have said, the game was afoot. And that's what it all amounted to: a game, with a million dollar Bugatti as my prize if I succeeded.

"I know. You're right. I'll be careful. How's that?"

"*Imbécile! Tu es fou! Merde alors*. Well, since you're obviously not going to let me help you, I guess all I can do is wish you luck. Dane, do *not* underestimate this guy. And don't do anything stupid and get yourself arrested. Call me next week if you're still alive. Bye bye. *Ciao*."

* * *

It was 9:20 A.M. by the time I'd showered, thrown on some jeans and a sport shirt, put my overnight bag together, and rechecked my laptop to locate the intersection in Tiefencastel Madame Laurent had described. Five minutes for check out, and another ten for the trip down the hill to the helipad for my 9:45 ride to Nice. As I laid down my things in the hallway to close the door behind me, the phone rang in the suite. No one knew I was here except Gina, and she was on the train to St. Moritz.

"Mr. Baron?" the now familiar voice at the other end asked.

"Mr. Toru. Good morning. How did you know I was here at the Hôtel de Paris?"

"Simple process of elimination. I knew you hadn't flown up to Zürich last night, and there are only three or four hotels in Monaco I thought you'd consider staying in."

How did he know about Zürich?

"Zürich?"

"I hesitated to phone you, Mr. Baron, but I think you may be in real danger. I should have told you yesterday Miura was waiting here in Monaco for you to contact me. He guessed correctly you'd come here to talk with me after Monsieur Laurent and Klaus Schulrat were killed. After you and I met in the casino, Miura went to wait for you at the Nice Airport, hoping you'd lead him to his stolen gold. Well, late last night, our corporate pilot called me. He said Miura saw you checking in at the Swissair counter yesterday evening. Apparently, Miura assumed you and Miss Domenico were both flying together to Zürich, so he commanded our pilots to fly him there. They departed shortly before the Swissair flight, and he was already in the Zürich airport terminal when Miss Domenico arrived without you."

"You knew this last night? Goddamn it, Toru! Why didn't you call me immediately? So this *Yakuza* son of a bitch knows where Gina is?" I shouted with a sudden surge of rage.

"I can only assume so. And I'm ashamed I didn't tell you Miura was here but I was afraid for myself. I still am. If Miura finds I've told you about this, I'm certain he will kill me next. I finally decided this morning I must call and alert you. I'm sorry I didn't do it sooner."

My phone hand dropped to my side as I stared out the window. Damn it! What had I done? Gina was only tagging along to please me, and I'd packed her off alone, knowing Miura was out there looking for us. But Toru wasn't the bad guy here. He was scared, but in the end, he'd risked his life to warn me.

"Mr. Toru, I shouldn't have yelled at you, and I do appreciate you calling me. I'm sorry if this gets you into any trouble. I'm obviously very concerned about Gina. Is there anything else I should know?" I stopped before I told him I was running late for my flight.

"I've told you all I know, Mr. Baron. I caution you to be very careful. I assume you're leaving for Zürich now?"

Screw it. Of course he knew I was going to Switzerland. "Absolutely."

* * *

I made it to Zürich uneventfully, though I'd stayed on the lookout for forty-year-old Japanese wiseguys with all their fingers intact and bulges in their suit coats. Yesterday, I'd convinced myself it would have been impossible for Miura to follow us. The short helicopter ride to Nice Airport should have put him off our trail . . . but not if he was camped out in the terminal waiting for us. He didn't want Gina—he wanted me, because he'd assumed correctly I could lead him to his gold. And logically, now he would follow

Gina until she led him back to me. But, while Miura knew I would be coming to Switzerland, there wasn't any way he'd even heard of Tiefencastel. The remote possibility of Klaus giving it up to him would have taken Miura off our backs by now, and according to Toru, that wasn't quite the case.

After landing, I walked to the railway platforms beneath the terminal and waited while the first train boarded and left for the short ride to the downtown station, the Zürich Hauptbahnhof. Fifteen minutes later, and after carefully checking out the other fifty or so passengers, I climbed on the next one. Paranoia runs deep.

While sitting in Sam's Place last night, I'd taken out my laptop which my host Christian had obligingly plugged into his internet router cable behind the bar top. I'd made note of four addresses in Zürich for retail electronics stores which advertised stocking amateur sleuthing devices. Whether they had twenty small transmitters, combined, was another issue. As soon as my Swissair flight had pushed back in Nice, I'd kicked myself for not having checked there as well. Now if I couldn't find them all in Zürich, it was on to plan B . . . the instant I developed one.

"*Guten Tag*," the shop clerk, a goofy-looking kid in his late teens, said when I entered my third Swiss equivalent of Spy vs. Spy meets Radio Shack.

"*Guten Tag*," I replied, nearly depleting my store of German vocabulary. "Do you speak English, or French?" I asked fingers crossed in hopes he could handle option one.

"*Ja, natürlich*. How may I help you, sir?"

"Great. This may be a rather strange request. I'm looking for small radio frequency transmitters. A lot of them."

"Not a problem. What type do you need, sir? Locating devices? Radio control units? RF ID tags?"

"Locating devices . . . I think. I want to attach them to some things so I can find them later. Hopefully with a range of up to a half kilometer," I answered after mentally converting Tim's acreage to metric.

"No, I'm sorry. I cannot help you with that. The locating type transmitters we stock only have a range of about two hundred meters. Nothing more than that."

Another quick calculation while I subconsciously turned to check for anything Japanese and shifty lurking outside the store windows. Two hundred meters, about six hundred and fifty feet. Not the fifteen hundred feet I'd wanted, but they would work with a little luck and possibly more time walking the field.

"Two hundred meters, eh? Okay, those will be fine. I need twenty-five of them," I said, cleverly thinking to buy a few spares in case of some malfunctions. Not a good thing to lose a gold bar worth better than a hundred grand over an electronics glitch. "Can you help me with that many?"

"Twenty-five? I think I can. Moment, please. You would also need a receiver to pick up the signals from the transmitters?" he asked, somewhat rhetorically, before walking to a ladder to check some high shelving behind the counter.

"Yes, thanks, and make that two receivers. I'm curious: Why do you have such a large supply of these transmitters on hand?"

The clerk started to lower some boxes from one of the upper racks. "For the cows, sir. Some dairy farmers are starting to use them instead of the bells to locate their cows after they've wandered off into the woods at night. I suppose the farmers prefer the quiet."

Made sense. Who the hell would want to listen to those damned clanging bells all night? *For the cows.* I stifled a laugh.

He returned to the counter with a large carton and counted out all of my requested twenty-five units. Then another box from which he withdrew two receivers.

"Batteries as well, please," I added. "Oh, and can you help me with two large flashlights?"

The young man nodded, reached behind him, placed two military grade flashlights on the counter, and added enough batteries to last me through a decade of Cat 5 Florida hurricanes.

After a few moments spent punching away on his calculator, he finally announced, "That totals 5,726 francs, sir." Ouch. Over $3,300. Damn. This little escapade was starting to get expensive.

After a relatively brief but thorough tutorial, the clerk packaged up my goodies.

"How would you suggest I attach these to the objects I'll be searching for?"

"The farmers use duct tape on the cow's collars. Here," he smiled, tossing me a roll as I opened the door. "On the house, I believe you say in English."

Duct tape. But of course.

Now laden down with my overnight bag, computer case, and what felt like about thirty pounds of spy gear, I gave zero thought to retracing my mile walk up the Bahnhofstraße back to the main station. Five minutes later, a cab dropped me with thirty minutes to spare for my 3:37 train to Tiefencastel . . . and Gina.

Chapter 18

Tiefencastel

Saturday evening, 22 July 2000

Gina waved from the driver's seat of the rental silver BMW when she saw me step from the first class car onto the concrete platform. If I'd been younger, I'd likely have resembled a college student toting my three bags on a Eurail Pass summer vacation.

Pointing to the oversized station clock suspended between us, she said, "You're spot on time: five forty-seven exactly."

"I thought Swiss trains we're supposed to be on time," I grinned before dropping my impedimenta onto the back seat and climbing in next to Gina.

"Where to?" she asked after leaning over for a kiss.

"Let's find a restaurant where we can settle for a while until it gets dark. Uh, I don't mean to sound melodramatic or paranoid, Gina, but did you happen to notice if you were being followed? In the train, or after you picked up the car?"

She dropped her head and slapped the top of the steering wheel with both palms.

"Blast! I knew it! I'm *not* barmy. After I left the airport near St.

Moritz, when I drove into town—a black Mercedes. I first saw it when I left the office at the airport, then again across the street in St. Moritz when I got out to buy some things. The car followed me out of town for quite a few miles, it seemed, but I lost him in the mountains on the Julierpass when I overtook some lorries. Are you thinking it was your *Yakuza* chum?"

"Yup. Toru called me this morning after you were already on the train from Kloten, so it was too late to reach you. His company pilot phoned him last night from Zürich. Apparently, Miura saw us buying your ticket at the Swissair counter in Nice and he assumed we both flew out last night. He ordered the pilot to fly him to Zürich in their business jet and they landed before your flight came in. And now, evidently, he's been on your tail ever since."

"But how could he have followed me to St. Moritz, Dane? I would have noticed an Asian on the train. They're a bit rare around here."

"He was either on the train, maybe in a different car, or possibly he saw you buy your ticket to St. Moritz and drove there. I don't know. But let's get this car out of sight before he picks us up again."

Without a word between us, we both scanned the main road for a black Mercedes before Gina pulled out of the station and turned left onto the highway. We'd gone no more than a quarter mile when she braked hard, turned right to avoid the main parking lot of the Hotel Grischun, and drove to the rear of the building, out of view from the street. The sign over the rear entrance proudly advertised *Passing Trade Welcome*. I guessed we qualified.

"I should think we'll be all right with the car hidden back here. I've stopped at this restaurant before," Gina said. "Grischun is

Romansch for Graubünden, the canton we're in. The place is simple but serves fairly good local Swiss food as I recall. I'm afraid it's a bit down-market from your usual Michelin three-star fare."

"Some kalbsbratwurst and rösti sound good. So tell me, were you able to check out the Skylane?"

She reached to the floor behind my seat and grabbed a plastic bag. "The requested charts, sir."

"Well done. Was the plane gassed up?"

"Both tank indicators were reading full."

"Perfect. Did you find the rifle?"

"It's in the boot, under the blanket."

I walked to the rear of the car as Gina remotely popped the trunk lid. Without completely raising the weapon out of the well in an attempt to avoid any prying eyes, I felt the hefty weight of what I later learned was a SIG 57. I guessed it was maybe four or five pounds heavier than the M16s I'd fired in basic training. Laying next to the rifle were two curved banana magazines holding twenty-four rounds each, as well as a large box of 7.5-millimeter ammunition. Ample firepower to invade Liechtenstein.

I restowed the weapon under the blanket, returned to the front passenger seat, and opened the bag to inspect Gina's charts—all two of them. What I saw was not what I'd been hoping for: two Jeppesen en route instrument charts. One, a high altitude chart with a 1 inch to 20 nautical mile scale, the other, a low altitude, not much better at 1 inch to 15 miles. I'd been counting on Sectional charts with twice that definition. Nor did the Jepps show any terrain features. As in big, hard mountains. And zip for roads.

"Uh, Gina, I think we might have a little problem here. These charts are designed for en route jet traffic, not small planes flying low and slow. Why would your father have these?"

"He didn't. I looked, but there weren't any charts in the plane. I went to the airport office and told them I needed to buy some new ones for my dad before he picked up his plane, but the girl told me they were sold out of the ones he'd need. She said her new shipment was overdue and these were all she had until then. They won't work?"

Flying my C-130 H model at 27,000 feet, I normally couldn't have cared less what the ground elevation was below me. And I sure as hell didn't need roads to help out my navigator. But flying a single-engined Skylane across half of Europe, in the dark, at less than 200 feet, the en route Jepps were less than ideal.

"Let's just say they won't do a helluva lot to help me avoid low clouds with rocks in 'em."

I studied the low altitude chart a little longer, searching for some nav aids. "At least it does show distances between VORs, and their frequencies. And it's got ATIS numbers, so that'll help."

"What are those?" Gina leaned closer to look at the chart I was holding.

"VOR stands for Very High Frequency Omni-directional Radio Range. They're transmitters that send out radio signals so aircraft can establish their bearings toward or away from the VOR station. You chart out a course showing where you want to go, and then dial in the frequencies and radials of the various VORs between you and your destination. You follow them simply by keeping the needle centered on your on-board instruments. ATIS stands for Automatic Terminal Information Service. They primarily transmit recorded weather conditions for their site."

"Good. Sounds like that's all we'll really need, so we're okay, right?"

"No, not at all good, Gina, but it's all we've got. Some road maps would be helpful, but it's too late for that."

"Maybe not. You mean like Michelin maps, right?"

"Those would be good."

"What would you do for me if I said I had Michelin maps covering our entire route?" she winked.

"You're kidding. You do? Where'd you get 'em?"

"At a travel agency, in St. Moritz, as I was leaving to meet you, the second time I saw the Merc I was telling you about. I thought of the Michelins after the girl at the airport explained the Jeppesen charts weren't designed for local flying since they didn't show ground features."

"Where are they?"

"In the other plastic bag, behind my seat."

I picked up the sack and pulled out three plastic covered folded maps: Switzerland, France, and South East England. Kissing her cheek, I said, "Outstanding! You're right: I do adore you."

"Sometimes, even I love me," she replied with a grin.

"These are all good, readable scales," I noted aloud while briefly scanning the three maps. "Between these and the Jepps, I think we've got it. We're lacking terrain clearances, but at least the Jepps show airport elevations. That'll give us an idea as to how high things are nearby. The toughest part will be seeing all the mountains around St. Moritz. We won't have much light since we're a week past a full moon. C'mon. I'll call weather."

"So I bring you maps and now you adore me? Very flattering," she pouted.

I collected the two plastic bags containing the charts and road maps and walked to the hotel's rear entrance. As I held the door, Gina stopped. "Wait a minute: You're going to call for weather? Does that mean we're flying out tonight? I assumed we were going tomorrow night."

"If we can find the LGDs within a couple of hours, yeah, we'll go tonight. If we can't, we'll try again tomorrow night. The sooner we're out of Switzerland, the sooner Miura will stop looking for us. But even if we do find the stuff tonight, I don't want to take off unless the weather's okay. I want your dad to have his plane and his daughter returned as I found them—in one piece."

Gina opened her mouth, then hesitated; only a shrug with an animated frown, a shake of her head, and a deep sigh. "Not that I'm counting or anything, but do you realize this will be the fourth or fifth night we've been together since you flew to London from Florida, what, eight days ago? and you've yet to take me to bed?"

"C'mon, Gina, all but one of those weren't my fault. Okay, you're on. Let's get a room here before we eat."

"What? A ten-minute quickie before the sauerkraut arrives? I don't think so, squire. I was thinking more of a candlelit room with some Champagne and strawberries, soft jazz playing on the radio, and having a lie-in for at least a day." She stepped through the open door before turning back to face me. "Relax. I'm only screwing with you. God, you're gullible. It's been neither of our faults, merely bad timing . . . except for you getting pissed and passing out on me in Paris. How's this: I'll save you a dance on my card once we're back in England. Now, let's eat."

Without a hostess to seat us, we walked to the table farthest from the front entrance. The spacious and bright casual dining room was overly decorated with local bric-a-brac and gingerbread knickknacks: cowbells hanging from the rafters, at least a dozen wooden cuckoo clocks on three of the walls, and a sun-faded bluish panoramic painting of the nearby mountains completely covering the fourth. I hoped the mural's vertical scale of the peaks was exaggerated; there was no way I could navigate the Skylane around the pictured Alps.

I asked Gina to order me one of whatever she was having. I checked my phone, and not surprisingly, the nearby peaks blocked any semblance of a reception signal.

"Do you happen to remember the registration letters on your dad's Skylane?" I asked as I looked out the windows for a quick reassurance a black Mercedes hadn't parked outside.

"Yeah, HB-GKG. Why?"

"I need it to get my weather." The second the words were out, my brain kicked in. She read my mind.

"You're not really going to give them our true registration, are you?"

"Right you are. I don't know what I was thinking about. Order me a bottle of flat water, would you?"

"This *is* a first. I guess we're definitely flying out tonight," she said a little too loudly to herself as I walked to the pay phone I'd spotted on the way in. I pressed in the numbers for the weather briefing service I'd noted off the computer last night.

"Good evening. This is twin Beachcraft Hotel Bravo Sierra Romeo Quebec," I lied to the answering briefer. HB indicated Swiss aircraft registration, and SRQ popped into my head from the three-letter code for my local Sarasota/Bradenton Airport in Florida. It was a requirement to give the aircraft registration number when calling for a briefing in the States, and I assumed it was a safe bet here as well. I also lied about the aircraft type. He didn't need to know I was actually flying a single-engined Cessna. "I'll be filing IFR from Samedan Airport, St. Moritz, to Redhill Aerodrome in southeast England, near London Gatwick, departing tomorrow morning around 0700 local. Our route will be Samedan, Montana, St. Prex, Dijon, Bray, Paris, Dieppe, direct Gatwick. And I'll need your winds at 3, 6, and 9,000.

The stated route was essentially correct as far as Dijon, but thereafter I strayed a little. My true proposed route through France was 50 or 60 miles to the south and west of the course I'd indicated, but still close enough to receive accurate weather reports from reasonably nearby airports. Nor was I intending to depart at 7 A.M. tomorrow, fly at 9,000 feet, file an instrument flight plan, or land at Redhill Aerodrome.

"Very good, sir, I have your information," the briefer replied after a brief pause. Thank God English was the official international language of aviation. "For most of your route, we'll be expecting fairly clear to scattered skies forecast from now through 0900 tomorrow morning, then becoming broken to overcast with heavy rain likely from that time on for the next forty-eight to seventy-two hours. Presently, surface winds at Samedan/St. Moritz are from 020 degrees at 10 knots. Your winds aloft should be fairly uniform throughout your flight until reaching the French coast. St. Prex is currently reporting winds aloft at 3,000 to be 090 degrees at 15 knots, at 6,000 they're 070 at 20, and 9,000 is 070 at 24 knots. Dijon's winds at 3,000 . . . " he continued with similar information for three other reporting stations, and as he'd indicated, they were all pretty close to the same.

219

"Winds aloft are forecast to be changing tomorrow mid- to late-morning, from the northeast to more of a northwesterly direction, and increasing. Give us a call back closer to your departure time for an update on those. As for the Channel and southeast England, I'm seeing mostly broken clouds at 2,500 feet, with an overcast layer around 6,000. London Gatwick is currently reporting surface winds 010 degrees at 15. Again, check back tomorrow morning and we'll have some updates for you."

I didn't care in the least about the winds over 3,000 feet, but it made things sound a bit more credible asking about them. If the weather was forecast to stay fairly constant from now through the 7:00 A.M. departure time I'd requested, life would be good for our projected midnight takeoff. Overall, I couldn't have asked for a better report: wind almost straight down the runway for takeoff on Runway 03 at Samedan, and clear to scattered skies all the way through Switzerland and France.

"How does it look?" Gina asked the moment I returned to the table.

"Excellent. For tonight, at least. The weather's supposed to start deteriorating late tomorrow morning, but we should be in good shape."

A sturdy blonde waitress arrived with our dinners, using one hand to support all the plates and glasses on a single large plastic serving tray. Gina had taken me literally, which was fine, and ordered brats with brown onion gravy, sauerkraut, and rösti potatoes for both of us. A large stein of beer for her, water for me. Our waitress wished us a pleasant "*Guten Apetit*" and left us to our meal.

"Have you thought about how we're going to find these gold

bars so we can get out of here tonight?" Gina asked before taking a swallow of beer.

"Yeah, and I don't have a clue—no pun intended. Klaus has a small house and a barn on almost seven hectares of land. What's that, sixteen or seventeen acres? As in, sixteen or seventeen football fields? Christ, where do we begin? The weather says we have to go tonight or things get pretty snotty for the next two or three days. And the longer we stay here, the more likely Miura will find us. Not to mention our Concorde leaves in three days and I still want us to be on it. But if we strike out tonight, we can come back and give it another try after the cruise. Miura will probably be back in Japan by then."

"Look, let's do this, Dane: If we find the gold tonight, we're off. If not, we'll drive back to St. Moritz, put the rifle back, and tomorrow morning, we'll hop a commuter flight to connect with something back to London. We'll have a couple of days to ourselves before flying down to Paris for the Concorde trip on Tuesday. Sound good?"

"The second part, the *if not* scenario, sure does. Screw the gold. Let's go to London. This whole thing's nuts."

"No Bugatti?"

"Oh, right . . . that. Well, I guess since we're here, we might as well give it a shot," I smiled.

"Now that's the Dane I've come to know and love. Go for broke. There's a Russian saying, 'He who takes no risks drinks no Champagne.'"

"You're really getting into this, aren't you? No guts, no glory, huh?"

"It's a little spicier than the ad biz. I wouldn't trade the last ten days for anything. Well, nearly anything. You know." That wink again.

"Yeah, I know. Hey, I offered, but you didn't want your sauerkraut to get cold."

Chapter 19

Saturday night, 22 July 2000

Hotel guests and the *Passing Trade* came, ate, and went for the next two hours while we continued to occupy our table. I spread out the low altitude Jepp chart and penciled in the various en route VOR and ATIS frequencies on a scratch pad for easier later recall. Gina marked on her Michelin maps, highlighting the main roads we'd overfly.

I pulled out the notes I'd jotted down while searching the computer last night for performance data on the Cessna Skylane. Flying at low altitude, we'd be burning almost 14 gallons of fuel per hour at a cruise speed of 165 miles per hour. Figuring our route to be 770 statute miles, we'd be airborne a little over 5 hours, inclusive of the time needed for takeoff and climb-out from Europe's highest airport at the Cessna's maximum 3,100 pound allowable gross weight, and adding in a few extra minutes for a couple of passes over our target field in Radnage. With a total of 75 usable gallons, we'd have less than 20 minutes of fuel remaining in the Cessna's tanks when we landed at Booker Airpark tomorrow morning . . . not a comfortable margin for error.

By 8:45, the sunlight had faded away ahead of tonight's 9:19 P.M. sunset due to the surrounding mountains. It was time to get adventurous. I made one last call to weather which confirmed my earlier briefing: Tonight was the night to fly if we were going to do this. Gina had paid the check before I returned, a tab which included the purchase of two oversized rectangular plastic serving trays. I watched as she stowed them on the rear seat of the BMW.

"Should I ask?"

"You'll see," she said. "And you'll thank me later. Want to drive?"

"No, you take it. I'll navigate. I don't see a black Mercedes, so let's go."

According to Sandrine Laurent's directions, I assumed we'd just exited her "big hotel on the corner," our landmark for turning up into the western hills. "Check your odometer, Gina. Madame Laurent recalled Klaus's place being about two klicks up this road, at the corner of a hairpin turn."

A little more than a minute later, Gina called out the first kilometer before slowing to less than 30 kilometers per hour as she continued to follow the narrow unlit road through the now darkened piney woods. "We're looking for a couple of white wagon wheels. Hit your high beams for a second. I think I see something ahead."

The bright halogens clearly displayed the beginning of a sharp left-hander, with two wagon wheels on the right, opposite the apex of the turn.

"This has to be it," Gina whispered. She turned off the road at basically no miles per hour and stopped on the grassy path leading into the property.

"Turn off your lights, Gina, and follow me. I'm going to walk ahead with the flashlight."

The path was straightaway, with two well-worn parallel ruts in the grass and gravel leading into the pitch-dark. I shined my light to the left and right to see that the path bisected a large grassy meadow with woods on either side; the two tree lines were each possibly a hundred yards distant. Less than a minute into walking the trail, I could distinguish the shiny steel lattice framework of the newly installed power line tower. Twenty steps farther and I made out the outline of a small house dead ahead, a single story stone structure, devoid of any surrounding trees. As I continued to approach, my flashlight lit up the silhouette of a barn a short distance behind and to the left of the house. Gina silently opened her car door, leaving it open, and walked the remaining few yards with me. We climbed the four entry steps to the house; I tried the knob on the solid wood door. Locked, as I would have assumed.

"Okay, Sherlock, what's the plan? A little smash-and-grab job or are we going to just ponce about?" she asked, still whispering, and likely squeezing my hand more out of anxiety than adoration.

"I told you, I haven't any idea. But we obviously have three choices here: inside the house, the barn, or buried somewhere in these seventeen acres of grass and trees. Where do you want to start? And take your time. We've got all of two hours if we're going to drive to St. Moritz and fly out tonight." I turned off my flashlight and sat on the top step next to Gina.

"I'm only thinking aloud here, Dane, but I doubt Klaus would have hidden the bars in his house. So it would be a waste of time for you to start breaking windows. Probably the same for the barn.

Too obvious, and easily found by an intruder."

"Like us?"

"Precisely. Therefore, it's only logical he buried them someplace out there," she said with a grand arm sweep of the grass and forested acreage. "Bloody hell, we might as well be searching for a droplet in a rainstorm."

"You're probably right. And since he buried them fifty or sixty years ago, he'd likely also have buried them again the second time. But where, damn it? C'mon on, let's go take a look in the barn for kicks." I'd check out the barn, and maybe come back to the house and break a window. However unlikely the two structures seemed to be as hiding places, it made more sense than roaming around aimlessly.

The weather-worn barn door creaked open after a few healthy tugs. I panned my light around inside to expose exactly what was supposed to be in a decrepit barn on a non-working farm: an old Renault mini panel truck, a small pile of rusty gardening tools, a tireless bicycle, a dozen or more cans of partially used paint, a stack of manure bags, and a dirty drop cloth covering something maybe two feet high and wide and six feet long. I yanked off the heavy canvas to expose two black steamer trunks laying end to end.

"Aha! Gina, look at these." I dropped to the dirt floor and opened the nearest trunk.

"That old degenerate! Nothing but copies of old Penthouses and porn mags," she giggled.

The second locker yielded a similar library. I tipped over both trunks and emptied them: nothing but dozens more magazines.

"Sorry, Klaus. Didn't mean to pry, buddy. We just want your

gold, you old perv." My Type 35 Bugatti dreams were quickly fading.

We left the barn and silently wandered the meadow between the tree lines for maybe a half-hour, possibly longer, both of us moving our lights from side to side as we walked. Nothing. I slowly began to realize we weren't going to be striking gold tonight. Returning to the house, we resumed our thinking positions on the top step.

"Dane, you told me Arnaud said he and Klaus moved the gold bars to the vault in Neuchâtel temporarily because the electric utilities people needed to do some digging to install that new tower over there. Isn't that right?"

"Yeah. Why?"

"And I remember you laughed when you said they were going to install the tower in the precise location where Klaus had originally buried the gold bars. With all these acres, they coincidentally chose that very spot."

"Yeah, okay. Go ahead." Where was she going with this?

"Well, Klaus was an old man, likely a creature of habit and stuck in his old ways, and he'd want the LGDs close to him, right? So wouldn't it be rather natural for him to put the gold back where it had been before? Under the new tower?"

"I don't like your odds, but it wouldn't hurt to look," I shrugged. We walked the fifty yards to the tower base, and with both flashlights, we completely illuminated the two-hundred or more square feet of ground defined by the four steel legs.

"Look, there, in the center!" Gina burst out, punching me in the ribs to make sure I looked. "That square of grass is dead, but all around it, the grass is green. It probably hasn't rained here recently, and that bit of new grass didn't take hold. Dane, this must to be it."

She dropped to her knees and hurriedly peeled off strips of pre-cut and now brown sod from beneath the center of the tower. I checked my watch as I sprinted to the barn to find a pair of shovels: 11:15 P.M.

At a depth of less than a foot below the surface, my spade suddenly struck something solid. We continued digging, faster now, until Gina's light exposed a sheet of dark green plastic; I reached down to feel the hardness of whatever it was covering. She focused her flashlight on my hands while I ripped a two-foot long tear in the plastic. The unmistakable brilliance of gold radiated back in the bright illumination.

"Holy Moly! Touchdown! Kiddo, we just hit the Eldorado. Hot damn! Regina Domenico, I love you!"

Whoops.

We hastily widened the little hole and cleared the remaining earth from the green sheeting, tossing the dirt behind us—a couple of burrowing dogs.

"Gina, bring the car over here while I pull this stuff out. Back it up with the rear end toward the tower, and open the, uh, the boot."

I lifted the bars from the shallow pit and laid them side by side outside the tower base. By the time she parked the BMW a few feet from one of the steel legs, all twenty LGDs had been exhumed.

I reached into the trunk, gathered up the SIG, the two clips and the ammo box, and placed them on the ground next to the driver's side. One by one, Gina handed me the gold bars, which I began to align in two rows of ten on the carpeted trunk floor.

As she passed me the eleventh bar, an automobile engine

started up from the direction of the road. Its headlights immediately flashed to high beams and the car began accelerating toward us. I raised my hand to shield my eyes, but the lights were too blinding to see anything.

"Gina, come here, quick!" I grabbed her arm and pushed her to the ground next to the rifle. The headlights rapidly neared to within twenty yards of our BMW when a shotgun blast exploded from the car, hitting the ground next to my foot. I instantly graduated from confused to terrified. I picked up the SIG, slammed in one of the magazines, chambered a round, and flipped off the safety. The shotgun fired once more, this time hitting the steel tower leg closest to me.

The car, which I could now make out to be a light colored Mercedes sedan, sped past us as I fired off three rounds in quick succession. I heard one metallic thud: My third round had found its target.

The Mercedes veered sharply to its right, away from us, and then headed down the rutted path back toward the road. I aimed my rifle midway between the two red tail lights and fired a fourth round, but with the noise of the engine and the tires skidding on the gravel, I couldn't hear whether I'd hit the fleeing car a second time. I kept the weapon to my shoulder and the rear red lights in my sights while I waited to see if we were in for another pass. My breathing began to settle.

"*What the hell just happened?*" Gina yelled out, a full octave above her normal voice. "Miura, right?"

"Not unless he changed cars. You told me the car following you today was black. This one was a beige or white Mercedes."

"Then who the hell was it? Now we've got *two* guys trying to kill us?"

"Damned if I know, but he's just now turned left onto the road leading back down the hill to Tiefencastel. Let's get the rest of this crap loaded and get the hell outta here. We probably woke up every farmer within a mile."

In seconds, the remaining nine gold bars were in the trunk, along with the spare ammunition and our two digging tools which I'd dump somewhere between here and the airport. However unlikely, I didn't want to risk the possibility of police checking them for fingerprints.

"Gina, pull out your Michelin map. See if you can find a road that connects with something leading toward St. Moritz if we take a right turn out of here. I don't want to go back the way we came up. I'll be right back."

I ran to the barn, SIG slung over my shoulder, flashlight in hand. Scanning the area where I'd seen the paint cans earlier, I grabbed two rags and a small rectangular can resembling a paint thinner container. With the flashlight tucked under my armpit, I opened the screw top and inhaled slightly: thinner. I doused the rags, wiped down the outsides of the two porn trunks, and then the thinner can itself. I sprinted to the house and cleaned the doorknob, also remembering to hit the painted steps where we'd sat and possibly made hand contact.

Running back to the car, I tried to recall anything else we'd touched; I didn't want to leave any trace of our trespass. Ah, the green plastic sheeting. I reached down into the small pit we'd dug, pulled out all the plastic, wadded it into a ball, and threw it in the back seat of the now idling BMW.

"Ready?" Gina asked through the open driver's window. Two

of her dirty fingernails pointed to the folded map below her flashlight. "If we turn right out of here, instead of left and back toward town, this road starts leading south toward the Julierpass. It goes through a few small villages, Mon, Salouf, and finally into Savognin, where it meets up with the main road to the pass and St. Moritz. We'll be about five miles south of Tiefencastel when we come out onto the highway."

"Perfect. Let's do it. You drive, I'll take shotgun."

"What shotgun?"

"Never mind. I couldn't resist. An old expression I always wanted to use."

She shrugged, and then quickly maneuvered the BMW down the gravel path before turning right onto the hard surface road past Klaus's wagon wheels.

"Gina, I want you to drive this thing as if you stole it, but once we hit the main road, stick close to the speed limit. I don't want to take any chances with the Swiss cops stopping us with five hundred and fifty pounds of gold bullion in the trunk and me holding a loaded rifle."

"Got it. Hold on."

With the halogens brightly illuminating the windy road ahead, Gina's right hand was a blur as she shifted up and down through the gears, her tennis shoes dancing across the three pedals; she navigated the switchbacks with the finesse of a rally driver. We passed through the quarter-mile town limits of the tiny hill village of Mon at over seventy miles per hour, and then through three more darkened hamlets in the next seven minutes before she braked hard and turned right onto the Julierstraße, the main road south.

"Right, how was that?"

"We're still alive. You done good, Slick. What time do you think we'll get to the airport? It's eleven fifty now." I looked back to check for car lights. Darkness.

"I'd say it's less than thirty miles, but it's really curvy through the pass. Maybe another forty-five minutes."

Twelve thirty midnight and change. "We should be all right," I concluded after a few seconds calculation. "Sunrise in London is five eleven tomorrow morning; I checked it on the computer last night. With our five hours-plus in the air, I think we'll be okay."

"But I still have to stop by our house in Celerina and replace the rifle. It's about a mile from the airport. It'll only take a few minutes."

"Wrong, we ain't parting with this thing. There's a good chance your friend in the black Mercedes might be at the airport. Don't forget, he probably saw you checking out the plane before you noticed him."

"If he *is* waiting for us, what are you going to do, Dane? Have a shootout with him?"

"I was kind of hoping we could make it out of there before he saw us. Describe the geography around the airport if you can, Gina. Where's the parking lot in relation to where the Skylane's tied down?"

"So you really do think he'll be there? Bloody hell, Dane, Toru told you this guy's an assassin. We're not walking into that."

"I know, I know. Bear with me. Now tell me about the airport."

"Okay . . . I'll try. The little road into the airport off the main highway is about a quarter-mile long. It ends in the car park, which is adjacent to the office at the south end of the runway. The

Skylane's parked to the north of that, at the opposite end of the ramp area."

"How big's the ramp area? I mean, how far would you guess it is from the parking lot to the airplane?"

"Maybe two or three hundred yards. But if he's there, we'd have to drive past him in the car park to get out to the plane."

"There's no way of approaching the plane from the north side, avoiding the parking lot? Isn't there some kind of airport access road or something?"

She fell silent. Either she'd had it with me or she was thinking of an alternate route into the airport. If she were smart, she'd bail.

"I'm trying to remember back when I used to bicycle around there. As the main road proceeds north past the airport, which is on the right or to the east of the road, I pedaled off to the left on a dirt path which turns back south. The path crosses back under the highway and across a small bridge over the stream that parallels the runway. Are you able to picture any of this?"

"Not really, but keep going."

"Once across the bridge—you're now at the extreme north end of the runway—the path turns into a narrow paved road inside the airport. It passes a glider storage area and continues to parallel the runway down toward the big paved ramp in front of the office. Yeah, that could work, but he might be able to see our car when we pull up next to the plane."

"Not two or three hundred yards in this light. You'll have to drive in the dark, of course. Not even a flashlight shining," I said, trying to convince both of us.

"All right, cowboy, we'll give it a go. But you'd jolly well better be the rodeo of a lifetime if we ever get through this."

233

Chapter 20

St. Moritz

Sunday morning, 23 July 2000

We'd stopped for no more than a few seconds to ditch the digging tools and we were now headed downhill, rounding the last turn out of the serpentine Julierpass; I was relieved to see the lights of St. Moritz in the distance. The terrain ahead flattened, and with a break in the clouds, the quarter moon reflected off the lake to our right. Four miles farther, we passed through Celerina—one more mile to the airport in Samedan.

"Gina, I have an idea: Pull off the road when we reach the airport entrance drive. And turn off the lights before we get there. Didn't you say it's about a quarter mile from there down to the parking area?"

"Yeah, more or less. Why? What are you planning to do?"

"I'm going to see if I can sneak a look and see if Miura's car is there. Maybe we're just being paranoid here."

With no other cars on the road, Gina turned off the headlights thirty seconds before we reached Samedan. Once through the small village, she steered the BMW to the right, across a bridge, and then three-quarters of the way through a roundabout. A small two-lane entrance appeared a hundred yards farther down on the right.

"Okay, this is the airport road. What now?"

"Park behind that tree." I retrieved some more ammunition from the trunk, along with the spare clip. "Leave the engine on and keep the lights off. I'll be back in a few minutes." Despite our still somewhat lengthy distance from the parking lot, I found myself whispering.

I walked quickly along the right side of the unlit road for possibly two hundred yards; four small warehouses shielded me from a direct line of sight view from the lot. I jogged the next hundred yards, across an open grass field, keeping the last structure between me and the parking area. Despite a thin layer of high overcast now muting the already dim slivers of moonlight, I could make out the lot thirty yards ahead as I edged around the corner of the building.

I counted seven cars, four light in color, three dark. All but one were parked opposite of what I assumed to be the airport office. The remaining dark car was parked alone, facing north, away from the office, and closest to the runway. My guess was it had an unobstructed view toward the ramp. And I could see the faint red-orange glow of a lit cigarette moving in the car's interior. Without risking a closer look, I knew Miura was here.

Carefully retracing my steps and remaining out of sight of what I now presumed to be Miura's car, I trotted back to the idling BMW.

"He's there, Gina. He's sitting in what I think I made out to be a black Mercedes. Be careful not to touch the brakes when we pull out of here so he doesn't see the red tail lights."

235

Gina silently moved the shifter into low gear and eased up the access road to the highway. With no other cars visible in either direction, she turned right back onto the main road without slowing and headed north.

"I'm going to switch on the headlamps in a minute so I can find our turn. He won't be able to see us from the car park."

She slowed the BMW to twenty and braked to turn left onto a dirt and gravel path. The headlights went dark again while she followed the track back to the southeast, toward the airport. Within seconds, we were passing under the highway overpass and I could hear water lapping over the rocks on our right as Gina inched the car along, paralleling the stream for another hundred yards.

"Okay, listen," I said. "When you come up on the plane, for God's sake, don't touch the brakes or any lights. See if you can go slowly enough so the car will coast to a stop. And don't close the doors after we get out. Hey, stop the car for a second. I just thought of something."

I reached up for the plastic lens covering the interior light above my door which illuminated when the door was opened. The lens was held in place with two Phillips-head screws.

"To hell with it." With the butt of the rifle, I smashed the lens and the small light bulb, and then reached across Gina to crush the light on her side.

"Okay, we're good. Go ahead."

"Dane, may I be so bold as to mention there's a fuse that switches those off?"

"Oh."

"But your way was much cooler. I'll pull the fuse for the light in the boot so you won't have to break it as well."

"Good thinking."

"And before you tell me, I know to park directed toward Miura so he won't be able to see the red lights on our doors when we open them."

"Yeah, definitely." I'd forgotten about those. It was good having a sidekick, someone to do the heavy thinking. "Wait, it'll be safer if I take care of those now." I stepped out and smashed the lens on my door with the SIG before walking around to Gina's side and taking care of hers.

"You really get off on whacking things, don't you?"

It was kind of fun.

She slowly accelerated and turned the BMW to the right, across a small bridge leading into the airport grounds.

"How far do you think it is from here to the plane?" I asked, back in whisper mode.

"Basically the full length of the runway. About a mile."

We drove the distance in silence for maybe three or four minutes before Gina eased the car onto the grass and gradually rolled to a stop next to the white high-winged Cessna.

"This is it. And here," she whispered, placing the airplane keys in my hand.

I looked ahead toward the ramp and the parking lot. With the minimal moon illumination, I could see only a fraction of the distance to the lot—which meant Miura couldn't see us either. But he would sure as hell hear us when I cranked up the engine. Then things could get exciting.

We walked under the wings and unknotted the two nylon tie down ropes, Gina taking the right wing, me the left. When she'd finished, she proceeded to the tail of the plane to untie the third rope while I unlocked the pilot's left side door.

"Gina, open the trunk and start handing me the bars. I'm going to lay 'em on the floor of the back seat area. I've got the rifle, just in case."

Without a sound, she began passing me the gold, waiting until I'd positioned the first bar in the plane before relaying the second. And so on, until all twenty LGDs were loaded and stacked, ten bars behind each of the front seats.

"What about the car?" she asked after we'd stowed the last of our gold, ammunition, bags and sacks . . . and two serving trays.

"What about it? Leave it where it is, key in it, doors and trunk open so we don't make any noise. I'll call Hertz tomorrow and tell 'em where they can find it."

"Doors open, broken lights and all," she muttered. "Blimey, you're a classic."

Gina climbed into the aircraft through the pilot's door and slid across to the right seat. I handed her the SIG, which she positioned between her knees, barrel angled toward her window.

"I guess this is the moment of truth, darlin'," I ventured once I'd seated myself behind the pilot's control yoke. "I pray to God this sucker catches on the first try when I turn the ignition key 'cause that Japanese son of a bitch is gonna come screaming once he hears this engine turn over."

After dinner in Tiefencastel, I'd studied the notes I'd taken off my computer in Monaco regarding the layout of the Skylane's controls, switches and instruments. Without wanting to risk even the subtle illumination of the red, green, or amber instrument lights, I reached down to the rheostat intensity control knob and turned it counter-clockwise to the full off position. My mind went over the seven steps I'd committed to rote for starting the Cessna's 235 horse Lycoming engine: Cowl Flaps—open; Mixture—pushed in full for rich; Propeller—full in against the wall for max R.P.M.; Carburetor Heat—cold; Throttle—pump a few times, then leave open 1/4 inch; Master Switch—on; Ignition Switch—on.

It was time. I inhaled deeply, held it for a few seconds, and exhaled slowly.

"Okay, let's do it."

The plane's aluminum surfaces shuddered loudly the moment the engine fired up five seconds into the first key turn. The engine noise rose as the R.P.M. quickly climbed. Almost instantly, ahead, across the ramp, car lights came on—first low, then high beams. Aimed directly at us, the headlights grew brighter as they started to approach.

"Put your shoulder harness on and tighten it," I yelled out over the engine noise. With the throttle pushed forward for taxi momentum, I stood on the left rudder pedal until the plane began to turn. We rolled, and then bounced, across a hundred yards of grass toward the runway.

The car's lights were quickly closing in on the Cessna from Gina's side. I turned the airplane more to the left, away from the car, to meet the runway at an angle; the closure rate of the headlights lessened slightly. I glanced to my right and saw three bursts of light coming from the driver's side of the car—muzzle flashes. The odds of Miura hitting us from this distance at night were on our side, but this was going to make for one corker of a takeoff.

"Get your head between your knees!" I shouted as I pushed Gina down.

The Plexiglas windows behind me popped with a loud crack. So much for the long odds.

The Cessna bumped from the grass onto the smooth hard surface of Runway 03 and I hit the landing light for a second to orient myself. With a little more left rudder, we were accelerating through 50 knots straight down the centerline of the asphalt. I knew Miura was closing on us but I was too busy now to look for an update on his progress.

As the Cessna approached 70 knots, I gently pulled back on the yoke until the airplane broke ground contact. Leveling off only a few feet above the runway to gain airspeed, I reached forward to the instrument panel and pulled up on the small round handle to retract the landing gear to maximize our acceleration.

After initiating a climbing left turn, I looked down and saw the car's stationary headlights shining from what I assumed to be the end of the runway. We'd made it. The flashes from the pistol had stopped. And after thirteen years, I was in the front left seat of an airplane again.

"Dane, why are you turning back toward the airport? Miura's still down there!"

"I have to fly over it to get back to the Julierpass. We'll be over five hundred feet above the field with our lights out. No way he's gonna hit us with a pistol," I hoped.

I kept the nose up to maintain the aircraft's best rate of climb speed of 80 knots, the speed which would result in our highest altitude gain in a given short span of time. Once the wings leveled out of the turn, I remembered to come back on the mixture control to lean out the engine and economize our fuel consumption. The lights of St. Moritz glistened below.

"Gina, hand me one of the flashlights."

She reached behind my seat, passed me the light, and I slowly painted the underside of the left wing with the light beam, checking for any evidence of holes or fuel leakage.

"Here, check under the wing on your side. You're looking for fuel spraying out of the wing tank."

"Don't see anything," she reported after several seconds of inspection.

"Good. I can't see around the engine cowling, but the oil pressure's in the green so apparently he didn't hit anything vital up there. I guess he only got us with that one shot through the rear windows."

"That should please Daddy to no end."

I could see the yellow and white headlights and the red tail lights of the scant traffic 300 feet below on the road leading west and south into the pass; the altimeter read 7,900 feet above sea level. I closed the cowl flaps and double-checked to make sure I hadn't turned on the nav or strobe lights out of habit.

"Are you able to pick up any of the navigational radios yet?"

"No, we're way too low for that here. We're below the mountains. I'm going to try to follow this road below us through the Julierpass, up past Tiefencastel, and then we'll take a left turn at Chur. We have a valley between two mountain ridges to follow from there for close to a hundred miles, down to Montana and Sion in the Valais region. We should be able to pick up a couple of the VORs once we get into that area. Gina, grab that low altitude Jepp chart and the paper with my notes. Check the frequency for the Montana VOR."

"It says 115.85 in the box below Montana, with the letters

MOT behind it. Is that it?"

"Yeah." I pressed the five digits into the top nav radio. "MOT is the three letter Morse code station identifier, but we don't really need it." Which was a good thing, since I couldn't remember one letter of my Morse code.

We flew over the Julierpass in five minutes, and within another four, I could see stationary ground illumination: Tiefencastel. I started a descent to drop down to less than 200 feet above the road lights.

"What do my notes say on our distance from Tiefencastel to Chur?"

"*Twelve miles, then turn west.* After that, your note reads, *Check for Montana VOR 20-25 minutes past Chur.*"

"Yeah, okay. I wish I had some more ground elevations for that first leg after Chur. We're down to an indicated twenty-three hundred feet now, but I know it gets a lot higher again shortly. I'm seeing some lights ahead. That must be Chur."

As the minutes passed, my confidence with the Skylane grew. I could feel my left hand, no longer wet with perspiration, applying a lighter finger touch on the yoke, and I briefly thought about actually getting a license again someday if we made it through this.

The thin scattered cloud layer above us dissipated and the road below became clearly outlined against the contrast of the fields and the forests. For half past one in the morning, the truck and car lights were more numerous than I would have expected.

I subconsciously found myself climbing for the next 50 miles to maintain a guesstimated 200 feet above the road west of Chur. By the time we reached Andermatt, the altimeter was reading 5,100 feet above sea level. The moonlight clearly silhouetted the crests of the two black mountain ranges above and to either side of us against the dark skies beyond.

"I have a north-south road below us," Gina said. She shined her light on the Michelin resting on her lap. "Yeah, good. This is the motorway from Luzern to Lugano in Ticino. I've been on that road a hundred times with my parents. I know exactly where we are now. From this road to your Montana VOR is about sixty miles, give or take."

My *borrowed* Skylane had performed perfectly so far, and most importantly, it had started up on the first crank. Without the possibility of a pre-flight inspection or an engine run-up test before takeoff, I'd been carefully monitoring all of my instruments since leaving St. Moritz—and all were reading in the green. The miles passed quickly, a little more than two and a half per minute at our 75 percent power cruise speed of 143 knots. Not trusting airplane clocks any more than I trusted those in cars, I held my watch close to the greenish glow of the instruments: 1:53. We'd been airborne for exactly fifty-five minutes. A little over four hours to go.

Within minutes after starting another terrain following descent, the Cessna's engine lost its smooth throaty purr and began to cough.

"What's wrong?" Gina asked with surprising calm in her voice.

Damn it! I'd forgotten to richen the lean mixture I'd set up for higher altitudes. I shoved forward on the mixture control and the engine instantly returned to its husky drone.

"No, we're okay now. I'm obviously a little rusty at this. Hey, the needle's finally twitching a little; I'm starting to pick up the Montana VOR. Here it comes . . . good. It's indicating we're on a 242 degree bearing to the station. The DME's showing we're sixteen miles out, a little over six minutes away."

"DME?"

"Distance Measuring Equipment. It measures the time it takes for a radio pulse to travel round trip between the aircraft and the station, and gives you a readout in distance and time to station."

"That's brilliant. Will we have these radio stations to navigate the rest of the flight?"

"Yes and no. The VORs are out there but we won't have any long-range reception due to our low altitude. I'm not used to flying low and slow like this, but I'm guessing we'll be able to pick up the signals maybe only twenty or thirty miles out, if that, instead of over a hundred miles at a decent altitude. But I'll get us headed away from the VORs on the right course so you can try to find the roads we're over until we're close enough to pick up the next inbound station."

I held Gina's Michelin map under the flashlight and estimated another six minutes past the Montana VOR to the town of Matigny, my sign post for a right turn to a north-northwesterly heading over the Autoroute de Rhône. Montreux, on the eastern shore of Lake Geneva, lay 24 miles ahead.

"Uh, Dane, I have a minor problem."

"What's wrong?" I asked, shining my light onto her scrunched up face.

"I forgot to visit the loo before we took off. The lagers I had with dinner, you know."

"Well, that is a problem 'cause we sure as hell can't land, Gina. When it gets too bad, hop in the back seat and use one of those plastic bags."

The moment the words left my mouth, the Cessna was hit hard

with two violent and loud shakes, first raising the left wing up almost 90 degrees before tossing the plane into a dive. I immediately pulled back on the power and slowly leveled the wings back to horizontal. We couldn't have been 50 feet above the ground before the aircraft started climbing again.

"*Holy crap!*"

"What the hell just happened?" Gina screamed.

"I didn't see anything, but I think we just got buzzed by a couple of Swiss Air Force jets. Christ, that had to be close."

"They've been following us? They've picked us up?"

"No, I don't think so. Those guys are probably out practicing some low contour night flying and we happened to be in the wrong place at the wrong time. I'll bet they didn't even see us. That's the problem with us charging around out here at night without any strobes or nav lights on . . . let alone a flight plan. We're damn lucky they didn't take us out."

"Yeah, lucky. But that scared the piss out of me. Quite literally. How humiliating."

"One more thing on the list to explain to Daddy, huh?"

With a cute pout, she said, "You're laughing at me! It wasn't my fault. Those planes scared me. I think I'll change clothes now if you can do without me for a few minutes, Captain."

Gina climbed onto the rear seat where I presumed she went looking for some dry pants. I turned right to a new heading of 350 degrees and checked my watch: 2:15. Ten minutes to Montreux, another two hours and forty minutes to the Channel, and a final sixty-five more minutes to Tim's rapeseed field.

By sun up in Buckinghamshire, the Cessna would be 550 pounds lighter.

Chapter 21

Over France/England

Sunday morning, 23 July 2000

That was embarrassing. I can't believe I did that."

"I won't tell if you don't. I think we flew into what's known as an *Oil Burner Route*. They're specially approved low-level routes for jets flying fast practice runs just off the deck. Hey, at some point I'm going to need you to load those transmitters and receivers with batteries and test 'em. Then we need to tape the senders onto the LGDs."

"I'm on it," Gina said. She hoisted my bag of electronic gear off the rear seat and onto her lap.

The scattered car lights on the autoroute 150 feet below led us toward the black void of the eastern reaches of Lake Geneva. I banked the Skylane slightly to the left to follow the northwesterly bend of the lakeshore for another 20 miles before turning to 310 degrees in search of the Dijon VOR, another 80 miles and almost thirty minutes out. At a gradual 600 feet per minute rate of climb, we left the lake behind and flew toward the Juras, the relatively low range of mountains running southwest to northeast along the

French and Swiss border. My charts didn't display any ground elevations in the mountains, but I knew La Chaux-de-Fonds, slightly north of our course, rested at over 3,000 feet in the Juras.

The faint moonlight became temporarily obscured by another overcast layer, leaving us charging toward unlit chunks of rocks hiding at unknown altitudes. I shuddered as I recalled an old flying axiom: *Never let your airplane take you where your brain hasn't been five minutes before.*

I continued to climb until leveling off at 4,000 feet, where I would now be appearing on radar screens as a primary blip without an aircraft number or altitude display. And that wasn't a good thing: No one was supposed to be cruising around out here at night without having filed a flight plan. But I soon sensed we didn't need to be as high as we were. Descending back through 3,000 feet, the signal from the Dijon VOR was starting to come in; we were a little over 50 miles out.

Gina finished energizing the mini-transmitters and moved to the rear seat to strap the devices to the gold bars with strips of duct tape.

"I think I'll need you back up here in a few minutes, Gina. We're coming up on Dijon and I need you to find us some roads to follow so we don't overfly the middle of town."

Butt first and hunched over, she backed up through the tight space between the two front seats. "Sorry, not very graceful," she grunted, and plopped onto her seat. "Now, give me a sec to suss out where we are."

"The DME's showing us forty-two miles southeast of the Dijon VOR. Find it?" I watched as she spread her right thumb and forefinger to measure out the distance on the Michelin's scale.

"Okay, I've got us. In about another ten miles, we'll be passing over what looks to be a motorway, autoroute A36. When you see it, turn left and follow it. It'll take you around to the northwest of the city. Yeah, simply follow route A36."

"I don't like my chances of being able to read the road sign, but I'm assuming you want me to turn over the next major road and follow it to the left, right? I mean, left, correct?"

"To the left, correct, and I think I see it in the distance. There," she pointed, as though I could follow her finger. "Those cars or lorries passing in a line straight across our nose from right to left."

The minutes, then the half-hours, passed while I worked to maintain level flight 150 feet above the highways; the terrain was gradually lowering as we progressed toward the English Channel. Approaching our next waypoint, the Pithiviers VOR, the faint glow of the lights of Paris became visible roughly 50 miles to the north. I wanted to descend lower, down below 100 feet, to avoid any chance of Paris approach radar picking us up. But with Gina now expertly navigating us along secondary routes, we'd soon be passing over Chartres and other towns with towers or similar hazards to flying at these ridiculous altitudes. I opted to stay put.

"I make us to be less than a hundred miles from the coast," Gina announced fifteen minutes later as we flew slightly to the east of Chartres and its clearly visible floodlit cathedral. "I think we've passed the last big town till we hit Deauville on the Channel."

With no more roads going our direction, we'd lost our asphalt compass. I maintained an altitude a little under 200 feet above the ground (I guessed), and flew a 315 degree heading toward the town of L'Aigle. "Do we have any roads between L'Aigle and Deauville?"

She held the flashlight over her map. "Let me look. Right, I've found a road leading northwest out of L'Aigle to a place called Lisieux, about thirty miles from here. From there, I make it to be only another seventeen miles to the Channel."

About 50 miles to the coast, a little under twenty minutes, I mentally calculated as I set the primary VOR receiver to the Deauville frequency of 110.20. Once over the shoreline, I'd seek out a 347 degree northerly heading and pray we kept the signal for a while. Around 55 miles out over the water, we'd hopefully be close enough to pick up the Goodwood station—25 miles east of Southampton—for our inbound course.

It was 5:05—4:05 in England—when Gina's road left us at the shoreline less than 10 miles due south of Le Havre. One final hour to Tim's.

I dialed in the Deauville ATIS as we crossed over the coast with the lights of Le Havre blinking in the distance at our two o'clock position. The recorded information at the local airport reported surface winds from the northeast, 040 degrees at 10 knots, skies scattered, and an altimeter setting of 29.98 inches. Overall, quite favorable conditions for anyone sneaking into the U.K. tonight. I reset the plane's altimeter and noticed a surprisingly small change in pressure conditions since leaving St. Moritz. My Swiss weather briefer had been spot on.

It was now impossible to distinguish between sea and sky; the black hole effect over the Channel erased any semblance of an horizon. Slowly, gently, I applied the subtlest of forward pressure on the control yoke until the altimeter indicated we'd leveled off 50 feet above the water. Actually, it was bouncing back and forth between 40 and 60 feet, either due to the slight turbulence outside or the pilot's unsteady hand inside. I reached forward and hit the landing light switch for a quick three second look at the wave crests below to confirm the altimeter reading.

Gina caught a brief glimpse of the water. "I know we're trying to stay under the radar, but do we have to fly *this* low?"

"Yeah, we do. I only hope any ships out here have lights on their masts 'cause I definitely can't see 'em otherwise." I was confident that little bit of news would cheer her up a tad.

Flying north at a DME indicated 19 miles from the Deauville VOR, the needle on the nav receiver was centered, but as I'd feared, we started to lose the station within short minutes due to our crazy low altitude.

Gina also noticed the needle swing away; we'd already flown out of range of the Deauville nav aid. "Damn. Are we in trouble now that we can't navigate with the radios?" she asked in a clear voice without betraying the fear she likely felt.

"Everything else being equal, yeah, I'd like to have something to navigate by other than a clock and the directional gyro. But we'll be fine. We're just doing this a little unconventionally, you might say. Since we lost the Deauville VOR when it was reading twenty-seven miles from station, we'll keep this same heading for another twenty-eight miles—about ten minutes—and then turn a little left to 328 degrees. We should be able to pick up the Goodwood VOR within another eight or ten minutes after that. So, not to worry." What we should worry about is being picked up on some guy's radar screen . . . or smacking into an unlit ship's funnel.

"How much more time will we have left once we're across the Channel?" Gina asked.

I turned on the map light and looked at the notes I'd jotted down in Tiefencastel, seemingly a week ago. Then a glance at my watch. "About twenty-four minutes to the coast, then maybe another thirty minutes to Radnage. Inside an hour from our present position. Are you okay?"

"Yeah, fine. I want to start organizing the LGD bars in a few minutes so I don't have to muck about with them once we start getting close."

"Got a plan, have you?"

"You'll see."

Soon, a faint string of lights began to appear on the horizon, and within minutes, we'd crossed over the English shoreline. From my earlier perusal of the Jepp charts, I'd noted airport elevations of around 200 feet in the southern coastal area, climbing to over 500 within 15 miles to the north. I settled on an initial quick climb to 350 feet, followed by a more gradual and continuing terrain avoidance ascent as the lights of the scant traffic below grew brighter.

"Gina, we've got twenty minutes. Better start doing whatever you're gonna do."

She touched me on the cheek, climbed back to her rear seat office, and seconds later, I felt her place one of the plastic serving trays on my lap, one of the trays she'd requisitioned from the restaurant. I turned to see her relocating the gold bars to the carpeted deck between our two front seats, stacking them as she proceeded. "I'll need a two minute warning before we reach the field where we're dropping these things."

"And then you're going to place five bars on each of our trays. Very clever. You're kinda handy to have around. Very good, kiddo."

The eastern sky began to lighten ever so slightly by the time I turned away from Compton, our final VOR checkpoint. I set up a northeasterly outbound course of 55 degrees which would put us directly over the Three Horseshoes in seven minutes. Remembering the terrain around the inn to be roughly the same 500-foot elevation as the nearby Booker Airpark, I maintained an indicated 650 feet on the altimeter. The headlights on the M40 motorway became increasingly visible, as did the brightening lights of Stokenchurch, the village marking our one-and-a-half mile point to the target field behind the 'Shoes.

"You'd better start loading up the gold, Gina. We're about five miles out."

Without a word, she leaned down between our seats, and with both hands, she muscled her first plastic wrapped bar onto the center of my lap tray. Then the second, next to the first. She carefully positioned the remaining three 27-pounders in perfect balance on the tray as though she'd practiced the maneuver in advance. In two minutes flat, Gina had finished stacking my tray and hers with a total of ten bars for our first run. The 135-plus pounds of weight on my upper legs was uncomfortable, but manageable.

By reducing throttle and holding backpressure on the yoke to maintain altitude, I set up a level deceleration down to 60 knots. Flaps extended to 20 degrees. Landing gear down. After hearing the whine of the gear motor, I visually checked out my window to verify the left main gear had extended—and it had . . . directly under the window where the LGDs would be exiting the aircraft. What the hell was I thinking? I wasn't going to land the damned thing . . . just throw some gold out of it. Gear up.

"Do you see the Horseshoes yet?" Gina asked.

Now on the last inbound mile, I began to make out the outline of the pub contrasted against the fields behind it. "Yeah, I think so. Dead ahead." I cranked in a steep 60-degree turn to the right to set up a downwind leg parallel to, and opposite, our intended drop path. At a point a half mile south of the road marking our field's southern border, I made a hard 180 to the left and started a slight descent as the Cessna lined up with the field, now hazily visible in the dim grayish-orange half-light. I brought the flaps down to their maximum 40-degree deflection.

"There, Gina," I gestured with my right hand. "We're going to drop these guys to the left of that north-south hedgerow on your side of the airplane. Open your window." I did the same, unlatching my window lock before pushing open the bottom of the hinged Plexiglas flap to a 45-degree outward angle.

I hit the landing light for two seconds, confirming our position positively before we started chucking out gold bars. The field was 200 yards straight ahead, with the hedgerow line 10 yards to the right of our flight path.

"Remember: Not more than three seconds between drops."

One last slight speed reduction and the Skylane crossed the road and started over the south end of the field.

"Okay . . . go! Now!" I shouted over the noise of the in-rushing wind.

With my left hand on the control yoke, I took hold of the first bar with my right, lifted it across my body, out the open window, and bombs away! Then the second, the third, the now heavier forth, and finally, the seemingly heaviest fifth. A quick glance to my right confirmed Gina had also emptied her tray. The north road slipped under us as I added power and reached down to milk the flap switch back up to the 20-degree position.

"Okay, Gina, load up the second batch. I'll be turning us in a long, sweeping 360 degree turn to the left to get lined up with the field again. I'll stretch it out to give you some time to move the gold to the trays."

"Don't worry about me. I'll be ready when you are."

I kept the Cessna low above the trees while I pivoted around the Three Horseshoes in a mile wide arc. Slightly reducing power, I eased the full 40 degrees of flaps back in.

"I'm turning onto final. Fifteen seconds till we drop. Ready?"

"Ready. Yeah, I see the south road coming up."

"Okay . . . drop . . . now!" I called out for the second time.

The second set of 27-pounders seemed to weigh twice as much as the first five bars. My right bicep was burning by the time I let go of the final LGD only yards before passing over the north road. "You get 'em all?" I shouted.

"Yeah, I finished just before you pulled up, but I cheated: I used both hands."

I turned to see her grinning back at me, blowing me a kiss; she was thoroughly enjoying herself. I guessed this beat selling ad space. I applied power, slowly came up on the flaps, and started a climbing shallow left bank back toward Stokenchurch and the M40. I shifted my scan to the altimeter: 550 feet above sea level— barely 50 feet over the ground.

Without benefit of a VOR on its field, I'd decided earlier to locate the Booker Airpark by following the M40 about five miles east toward London from Stokenchurch; the runway was on the immediate south side of the motorway. Checking my notes, I dialed in the frequency for the London Heathrow ATIS. Only 16 miles distant, their surface winds would be fairly indicative for a landing at Booker. The recording reported winds at Heathrow from 330 degrees at 12 knots, gusting to 18. With Booker's single paved runway heading either 60 or 240 degrees, the wind would be at 90 degrees to the airplane on landing from either direction. I opted for the northeasterly Runway 06, only because its approach would be over farm fields, as opposed to coming in low and a little noisily over the housing area to the north of the motorway.

The runway at Booker drew near, now barely a mile away in the dawn haze. It was 5:27 British Summer Time, barely fifteen minutes past sunrise. With the gear down and only 20 degrees of flaps due to the cross wind, I flared, and seconds later, the main gear tires squealed as the Skylane touched down on the asphalt. For my first landing in over a decade, it was a good one.

Dr. Domenico's airplane had performed perfectly for the past five hours. With the exception of empty fuel tanks and a couple of 9-millimeter holes in the rear Plexiglas, I'd returned his plane exactly as I'd found it—albeit almost 800 miles away from where he'd left it.

"And that's apparently how you do that. Overall, quite the sporting excursion," Gina said. "But I must say, the landing didn't have near the sex appeal of our takeoff."

I shook my head. "Thank God. Oh, one question: Have you figured out yet how you're going to explain the bullet holes to your father? Let alone what his plane's doing here in Buckinghamshire instead of being in Switzerland?"

"No, I thought I might gloss over some of those petty details. I've always considered myself more of a big picture girl. Lean over here, Red Baron, I need a kiss."

I taxied the Cessna to the end of a row of six other single-engine planes tied down in the grass, north of the runway and the airport buildings. The three-bladed prop turned its last revolution, and all became quiet. A last quick glance at the fuel gauges revealed they were as dry as I was—the two wing tanks couldn't have had more than ten minutes of fuel remaining between them.

We had the plane emptied of our bags and tied down in minutes. I covered the SIG rifle and the ammo with a sheet and hid them under the rear seats beneath the life vests.

"Very cool," I commented, pointing to the Skylane's vertical stabilizer. "I just noticed your Swiss flag, the red tail with the white cross on it. I'm curious, why's the plane registered in Switzerland if your parents live here in England?"

"Taxes and fees. They have dual citizenship, so my father chose the least expensive way to do it. Can we talk about this later and get away from here within the month? Come on—let's quit arsin' about. Which way?"

I scanned the field for a moment, looking for the shortest route out. The obvious way was across the runway, past the airplanes and buildings, and out the main airport road.

I nodded my head in the opposite direction. "Let's hike out behind us, toward the motorway and away from those buildings. There'd be too many questions if someone saw us walking away from here at this hour. We'll follow the M40 back toward Stokenchurch till we find a bridge to cross over. Then north, toward Radnage."

"How far did you say it was again?" Gina asked as she adjusted the strap on her leather bag to loop it around her neck.

"About seven miles."

"Two hours, eh? Does your friend Tim know we're coming?"

"Nope."

"Right, at half seven on Sunday morning, after they've had the pub open late on the Saturday night. Good thinking there, Dane. So we don't know whether or not he'll have a bed available for us?"

"Damn, you are a randy little critter, aren't you?"

"Normally, yes. But right now, I'm more interested in some sleep. I'm knackered. Aren't you tired?"

"I'm okay now. I took a fifteen-minute catnap while we crossed over the Channel."

Another of her quick jabs to my ribcage.

"Ouch. Damn, Gina. Hey, I just thought of something." I opened the Skylane's left door, climbed into the rear seat area, and pulled out the SIG from under the seat bench. With one heavy blow of the rifle butt to each side, I knocked two large holes in the airplane's rear Plexiglas windows.

"Dane, what the *hell* are you doing?"

"I thought it'd be better to return your dad's plane with broken windows rather than windows with bullet holes through 'em".

Chapter 22

Radnage

Sunday, 23 July 2000

We trekked along a narrow path past endless muddy fields paralleling the motorway, across a bridge, and then through the small hamlets of Piddington and Beacon's Bottom (gotta love the Brits) before finally dropping our bags and collapsing on the kitchen steps outside the Three Horseshoes. I rested my back against the door: 7:40 A.M., sun up, and not a sound from inside. Gina peeled off her soft blue leather jacket, folded it on my lap, and laid down her head.

"I expect you know, Dane, it could be another two or three hours till someone wakes up in there."

"Go to sleep."

Only seconds later, I heard the key turn in the latch, but it was too late. I fell backward onto the kitchen tile, taking the top half of Gina's body with me.

"Bloody hell, mate!" Tim shouted, jumping away from the two of us sprawled at his feet. "What are you lot doin' out here, then?"

"Morning, Timmy. Didn't expect you so early," I smiled up at him. We climbed off the ground and collected our bags from the front steps. "Any room at the inn for a couple of transients?"

"Yeah, sure. C'mon in. The rooms are all occupied now but we'll have them available a bit later after the weekend guests have gone. I'll put the kettle on. Have a seat. What time did you arrive, then?"

"Only a few minutes ago."

"I didn't hear a car."

"Long story. We walked." Now the endless questions for which I didn't have particularly plausible explanations. The truth was not an option.

"You *walked*? From where?"

"I'll tell you all about it sometime, Tim, but trust me, it was one hell of a trip getting here. Promise, I'll tell you later."

"Not a problem," he said as he continued to stare at me. "Gina, good to see you again, old girl. So, how's Dane been treating you?"

"Never a dull moment, I can assure you of that, Tim. It's been a rather exciting week or so since I was out here with my son."

We settled at the oversized "family" table in the inn's kitchen, where Tim, his wife Rene, and their two teen-aged kids would try to take their dinners before opening the pub for the evening. I was still stirring a lemon into my first cup of tea when the metallic clanging of a diesel engine approached and rattled to a stop outside the still open kitchen door.

"Morning, landlord," a man's voice shouted from the lane. "Tim, you won't bleedin' believe what I come across." Without waiting to be invited in, the elderly man in a bowler and a green smock hastened into the kitchen lugging white plastic bags overflowing with fruits and vegetables. "Oh, sorry, didn't know

259

your guests was up yet," the man commented, touching the brim of his hat when he saw me. "Would you excuse us for half a tick, guv?" he said to me before dropping his produce on a counter next to the refrigerator. "Come out here, Tim. I've something to show you you're not going to believe, mate."

Gina stirred milk into her tea and frowned at me across the table. She waited until the two men's voices outside became barely audible before forming her lips to silently mouth the words, "The gold."

I shook my head and quietly whispered, "No way."

Our eyes shifted back and forth between one another and the door for fully a minute before the engine restarted and the converted dairy truck pulled away.

Tim stepped back into the kitchen and dropped into his chair, his mouth agape. "Cor, blimey! You wouldn't believe what I just saw. Mr. Bracegirdle—he's my greengrocer—he told me that when he was driving up to my place a few minutes ago, he ran over a green plastic bag on the lane up by the north of my fields. He felt something hard when he hit it, and he got out and found a brick inside the bag—a gold brick!"

Son of a bitch. One of us had been a half-second late and overshot the field with one of the LGDs. A fraction of a second worth well over $100,000. I avoided looking at Gina and turned to Tim. "You saw it? A gold brick?" I asked without having to embellish my shocked reaction.

"Yeah. A monster gold bar. And it was bloody heavy. I expect it must have weighed twenty pounds or better."

Close. Try twenty-seven and a half.

I immediately thought of the south road where we'd started our bombing runs. Could we have also dropped too soon? I restrained my sudden urge to run down to inspect the road for heavy green parcels. And Mr. Bracegirdle would have found it by now on his way out if anything were there.

"I'll wager every punter between here and High Wycombe will know about this by the time the old geezer finishes his morning deliveries," Tim announced. My hot tea became even more difficult to swallow.

Christ, this is all I needed: Paul Bisno picking up his Monday morning *Times* to read about someone finding an LGD bar within yards of the Three Horseshoes Inn in Radnage.

"Tim, you really ought to catch up with him in your car before he has a chance to tell anyone else about what he's found," Gina calmly offered, staring straight at me as she spoke to Tim. "He doesn't need everyone knowing about it. In the end, it'll only come back to haunt him if he starts advertising."

"That's a good idea, luv," Tim said. He snatched a set of keys out of a drawer next to the kitchen door. "I'll tell him to shut up about this until he decides whether he's going to try and return it for a reward or something. I'll be back in a few minutes." Tim darted out the door, and within seconds, he was tearing down the small hill toward the south road in his dirty green Land Rover.

"What a right cock-up. Not exactly what we needed, is it?" Gina said.

"No. This could really blow up on me. If word gets out before Paul can sell the LGDs, I'm screwed. Even if he hears about it later, it would still be embarrassing."

She nodded and put her hand on top of mine next to my cup. "Tim didn't say anything about the transmitter I taped to the bar."

"Hopefully, the old guy smashed it when he drove over it. We don't need people around here to start thinking about homing devices strapped to gold bars. I'd better run up there and check the road. Why don't you stay here in case Tim gets back before I do."

"Okay, but hurry."

I ran flat out for the first two hundred yards before slowing to a fast jog for the remaining quarter mile. Luckily, it was Sunday morning, and at five past eight, it was likely the locals were still in bed.

Nearing the north end of the hedgerow which had served as my approach path marker, I came across remnants of torn plastic sheeting and the crushed plastic and metal remains of the transmitter box. I carefully policed the area, on and off the pavement, collecting pieces of the radio and stuffing them in my Levi's pockets. I'd hide my collection of road kill in my overnight bag back at the 'Shoes until I could toss it somewhere later.

"Mr. Bracegirdle was most appreciative of the advice, Gina. He promised mum's the word till he reads something about a reward being offered," Tim reported. He'd walked into his kitchen only a minute after I'd returned, and I tried not to let him see I was still a little out of breath from my short run.

The three of us spent the next hour in the kitchen speculating on where the gold had come from, or what it had fallen off. Tim thumbed through the financial pages of his morning paper until he came to exchange rates and precious metal prices.

"Gold's quoted here at 280.35 dollars an ounce as of last Friday. Let me find my four-banger." He reached into a cabinet drawer behind his chair, removed a primitive calculator, and punched away for several seconds.

"It's about seventy-five thousand pounds," I heard myself say, having the simplicity of a convenient 1.5 U.S. dollar to the British pound exchange rate to ease the calculation.

"I make it closer to fifty-five thousand, Dane. That's basing it on the bar weighing twenty pounds, mind you," Tim replied after he entered the equation into his calculator once more.

"Seventy-five thousand. It weighed twenty-seven pounds," I corrected before I realized I was speaking; I had a dumb habit of doing that. I looked over and caught Gina's glare, which silently screamed out, *Shut up, you idiot! What the hell are you doing?* If she'd been closer, I had no doubt she'd have sucker punched me again.

Tim was studying me over his lowered reading glasses. "How do you know, then? You didn't see it."

"Oh, sorry, Tim. I was thinking out loud. I was only guessing. In the watch business, we use one kilo, or 2.2 pound gold bars. I remembered hearing the next size up is a 12.5 kilo, or 27.5 pound, bar. I just assumed that's what you saw."

"Yeah, that must have been it, then," Tim slowly returned, his face resembling a big question mark. He clearly suspected something. "Right, so much for all this morning's excitement with you two walking in from places unknown and my greengrocer finding gold in the streets of Buckinghamshire. A bit of a fry-up, anyone?"

"Yes, please, Tim," Gina jumped in. "I'm starved. May I pour myself another cuppa?"

"Of course, luv. Help yourself."

Tim idly chatted about the local gossip and weather while he deftly worked three cast iron skillets on the commercial grade stovetop. Bulldog Winston made his morning appearance and sat at Tim's feet in hopes of a little spillage. Minutes later, an oversized plate was laid before each of us: a single fried egg, bacon, sausage, fried mushrooms and tomatoes, baked beans, toast and marmalade . . . and black pudding and fried kidneys. Winston inhaled the latter two out of my hand under the table. I always forgot to tell Tim: two eggs, and hold the offal.

"I need to rent a car at some point today, Timmy. Where's the closest place I could find one?" I asked between breakfast bites.

"No need for that. You can use one of mine."

"Thanks, but I'll need to rent something. We'll be dropping it off at Heathrow on Tuesday."

"Oh. Well, I'm sure we can find you one in High Wycombe. Here, let me find a number for you."

* * *

Gina found herself an overstuffed chair in the bar's lounge area and nodded off for a couple of hours before the pub's 11 A.M. opening. I sat across from her and stressed.

I couldn't tell Madame Laurent I'd overshot my target and now her check would be a little light. As unpleasant as the thought was, I'd have to add the missing $113,000 to what Paul Bisno would be forwarding to her. In my fatigued state, it took me fully an hour to rationalize that, at worst, I'd still be acquiring a million dollar-plus Type 35 Bugatti for ten cents on the dollar. I felt myself smiling and dozed off.

The rental agency in High Wycombe delivered the Jag X Type shortly after noon, as requested. The car had a massive trunk and a stout suspension system which could easily accommodate the mass and weight of the gold bars. I offered to buy a couple of pints for the two men who'd delivered the car, but one look at the two deep rail standers in the pub and they decided they'd better return to work.

Drinks in hand, Gina and I wandered out the open rear glass doors and past the picnic tables to the lawn overlooking the rapeseed fields beyond. As anxious as I was to check on our packages near the hedgerow a mere hundred yards away, I knew that would have to wait for another twelve hours.

I reached for Gina's arm and drew her closer. "When I went out to the parking lot earlier to check out the Jag, I tested one of the radio receivers and at least one of the transmitter signals was coming in strong. I hope they're all like that when we start looking tonight."

"Think positive. We'll find all nineteen of them. Have you thought about what you're going to tell Sandrine Laurent about the missing bar?"

"Yeah. I'm not going to tell her anything. She'll receive a check for the sale of all twenty bars from Bisno's. I'll pay him for the one we're missing. I'm only hoping that green grocer keeps his mouth shut so we don't have any publicity while I'm trying to have Paul unload the stuff."

"Stop worrying." She took my hand and placed it on her rear end. "Damn, I can't believe none of Tim's guests has left yet. We need a room!"

"Yeah, I know, tell me about it. But I don't think anyone's going anywhere real soon. These Sunday sessions out here tend to spill on into the evening. By the time things start wrapping up tonight, it'll be time for us to sneak out and walk the hedgerow for a while."

"Great. Another night of being together without *being* together?"

"I know, I know. Later, after we load up the car."

"Promises."

* * *

We waited, hour after excruciating hour, until Tim finally shouted for "last orders." Within twenty minutes, all the empties were on the bar and the last of the crowd weaved out.

"Take any room at the top of the stairs," Tim offered. He emptied the cash register and walked over to lock the front door. "Room number three has the king-sized waterbed as you might recall. Night. See you in the morning."

"You too, Tim. We'll only be a few minutes. I think we'll have one more before bed if you don't mind."

"You know where it is. I'm off, and the honor bar is on. Leave a note by the till when you've finished."

In the quiet of the empty bar, rain suddenly began tapping against the rear glass doors. It was after midnight, and it was pouring. The whole afternoon had been a picture postcard of the Chiltern Hills in summertime: blue skies and light breezes with the occasional passing fluffy cumulus cloud or two. But the moment the last customers pulled out of the parking lot, bam! it opened up.

"This changes things a little, Gina." I walked to the windows. "I was hoping the fields would be dry enough to let me drive out to the hedgerow. But now we're gonna have to walk back and forth and carry the bars to the car."

"We'll just have to suck it up and see, that's all. I saw some pairs of Wellies in the kitchen this morning. Those should help a bit."

"Wellies?"

"Wellington boots. Big rubber rain boots. Boots for walking in the muck. You know, Duke of Wellington . . . Wellies."

Equipped with flashlights, electronic receivers—and Wellies— we started to slog through the mud toward the hedgerow on the eastern perimeter of the field.

"Do we have a plan?" Gina asked.

"Of sorts. I thought we'd stick together and start on the south end and walk north. We'll turn on our receivers, wait for a signal, and then I'll take the bar back to the trunk of the Jag while you look for the next one. Sound logical?"

"Sure, why not? With all this rain, I'm happy I double wrapped the plastic over the transmitters."

"What did you do?" I asked, never having considered the possibility of rain messing with the electronics.

"I wrapped pieces of the plastic sheeting we dug up around the bar once, taped the transmitter on top of that, then wrapped and taped it twice more."

"Damn, you just keep getting better and better. That's perfect. Well, perfect for nineteen out of twenty anyway. Crap. I can't believe I was late on the last drop."

"Actually, I think I was. But perhaps that one will turn up as well."

"What are you talking about? It already has turned up. The green grocer's got it."

"Never mind. Hey, my receiver's beeping."

I looked down at the lighted visual display in Gina's hand. Vaguely working along the same basic principle as the VOR receiver in the Skylane, the receiver's needle centered itself on the small screen when she moved her hand slightly to the right. As she moved forward, the soft beeping sound from the device became more rapid. She stepped to her left to keep the directional needle centered and the beeps became a solid tone. I shined my flashlight ahead a few feet and saw our first dark green plastic wrapped bar.

"Outstanding," I whispered as I hefted the slippery, dripping parcel. "Reset your receiver and continue walking north, Gina. I'll take this to the car and be back in a couple minutes."

"Okay. And you want me paralleling this hedgerow as I walk, correct?"

"Yeah, keep it maybe five or ten yards off to your right. Oh, and when you use your flashlight, try to shield it with your body so it can't be seen from the pub. Be right back."

"Torch," I barely heard her say under her breath as the rain continued to drench us.

"What?" I stopped and turned back toward her.

"It's called a torch, not a flashlight. When in Rome, you know."

"Okay, torch. If you weren't so good lookin' and useful, I might argue about it. All right, be careful to hide the light of your—*torch* —from the pub. Better?"

"Better. Now get going."

I timed my first trip from the field to the car and back to Gina's position: four minutes, twenty seconds. The best we could do would be another hour and a half, assuming she'd located another bar each time I completed a lap. And by returning to wherever she was walking, our system also assured we wouldn't skip an area.

"I have another two for you, Dane. Do you want me to carry one?"

"No, I can do it, but thanks. Stay down here and keep looking for more bars. It'll go faster this way."

Another four minutes, another bar. And another. And another. And the rain continued. My four-minute round trips trudging through the muddy field grew to six, ten, and finally, almost sixteen minutes, as we worked our way north and farther away from the parking lot to the south, something I'd failed to consider in my timing calculus. Progressing slowly but methodically along the hedgerow, we eventually reached the north road boundary of the field, close to the spot where Mr. Bracegirdle had found his gold bar. It was 4:42 A.M. and the sky was starting to lighten . . . another night without benefit of a bed. And we'd only found eighteen of the LGDs.

"What now?" Gina asked from her resigned, legs crossed, sitting position in the mud, her hair stringing down across her face in wet strands. She appeared utterly exhausted; her uncommon energy was spent.

"Well, one, I wish I had a camera to take a shot of you. But two, I guess we retrace our steps. We can't leave that bar out here."

"No, of course not. We have to find it. But, Dane, I was very careful to listen for those transmitter beeps as I came up the field. I'm sure I didn't miss any."

"I'm sure you didn't either, but maybe the transmitter broke when it hit the ground. I'm really kind of surprised all the others were working. Anyway, we'll have a shot at a visual now that the sun's almost up."

"Okay, but we'll have to hurry before someone from the pub sees us. Spread out a few paces from me as we walk back to the south."

"Let's do it," I said, offering my hand to help her up. No go. The suction of the wet muck had glued her in place. A couple more tugs, and finally, pulling with both hands, Gina popped up out of her quagmire. She swore a little, and then started plodding along with me.

"What a bloody mess," she finally laughed.

With the fields dormant until the winter months when the bright yellow blooms of the rapeseed crop blossomed, visual contrast would be minimal between the brown and green of the now grassy acreage and our one remaining dark green package. We slowly covered the five hundred yard length of the field once more, scouring the ground as we trudged, silent beepers in hand. Upon reaching the southern line of hedgerows, we looked at one another, and without a word, we turned back to the north and began another muddy circuit. It was 5:35 A.M. by the time we completed our lap and returned to the southernmost extremity of Tim's land for the second time. We stopped at the five-foot high east-west hedgerow separating the fields from two houses on the south road. Gina's receiver beeped once, weakly.

"Where's it pointing?" I asked.

"Toward this hedge to the south." She took a few more steps toward the bushes. "At that big house on the other side."

Without hesitating, Gina wormed her way through a small opening in the thicket of branches and foliage and into the house's back lawn area. Looking over the hedge, I could see the last of our parcels directly in front of her. She bent over, picked it up, and silently, she triumphantly waved it over her head with both hands as she jogged back.

"There, you owe me. Now let's get out of this damned rain and mud and get a bit of a spit and a lick." She instantly caught the lascivious grin on my face and translated: "Sorry . . . to you, luv, that means our first communal scrub up."

Chapter 23

Radnage/London

Monday, 24 July 2000

Here, let me give your Wellies a bit of a rinse off before you go inside. We don't want to carry in all this mud and have Tim wondering what we've been doing."

I followed instructions and held up my rubber boots while Gina sprayed them down with the hose outside the kitchen door.

"You want something to eat?" I asked after silently closing and locking the door behind us.

"I'm starved, but that'll have to wait. At the moment, I'm into a shower and then to bed. Join me?" she winked.

"Without Champagne, strawberries and candles?"

"Next time. You'll owe me . . . again."

She took my hand and we tiptoed up the stairs, into room number three, the one with the king-sized waterbed bed. The post-dawn glow through the curtains illuminated the room's interior with a soft pink tinge.

Gina reached under her drenched and droopy Cambridge sweatshirt and unzipped her jeans, wriggling around in them until they dropped to the floor. Then she reached her arms back behind her head and struggled with the sweatshirt, finally yanking it off and tossing it down on top of the wet jeans. She stood facing me with a *come and get it* look, her naked body every bit as spectacular as I'd expected . . . with the possible exception of the clumps of muck clinging to her face and hair.

"I'd planned to wear something sexy for our first night together, but as you can see, I didn't bother with a bra or knickers tonight with the rain and all," she whispered, almost bragged, tantalizingly tossing her head to one side, her arms hanging straight down her nude and generally mud-free body.

I was tempted to open the closet door, the one with the full-length mirror. But I resisted. Even the temporary dark slime on her face couldn't keep me from eagerly sliding out of my rain soaked clothes and leading her to the duvet covered bed.

She was fun, giggly, completely open and free, playful, generous, enthusiastic—maybe even a little grateful—and fortuitously, completely unaware of the filthy crud glued to her hair, forehead, and right cheek.

* * *

Come with me," she finally murmured as she rolled over, still breathing heavily. It seemed we'd been tangled up for hours, but the clock radio assured me I wasn't that good; it had been barely thirty minutes since we'd come upstairs. Gina rose, stood by the side of the bed, and extended her hand. "Come, I want to shower with you."

I followed her to the bathroom door and stopped, waiting for her to see her reflection in the mirror over the sink.

"You're a right bastard! Why the hell didn't you tell me I was still wearing half of Tim's field? I hope you enjoyed yourself, because that's the last time you're getting into these knickers." She slammed the door in my face.

I stood staring at the beige paint on my side of the door for a moment, wondering if I should make nice and try for a shower or go back to bed. The bed looked inviting . . . the beige paint didn't. The door reopened. Gina was standing next to the sink, cleaning off her face with a washrag, tidying up before her shower.

"I'm still angry, but get in here. I'm not finished with you yet."

* * *

The sound of vacuuming in the hall awakened me—*hoovering*, as I'd once heard Tim call it. I rolled over for another glimpse at the clock: 11:40, and again, I was the sole occupant of my bed. Gina's white leather overnight bag rested on a chair at the foot of the bed, her wet clothes still in a small pile on the carpet beside it. I reached for my phone and selected Paul Bisno's office number from the contacts menu.

"Paul, Dane Baron here. Good morning."

"Good morning, Dane. Are you back in London already?"

"No, sir, not quite, but I will be in a few hours. I was successful in locating the LGDs we discussed, and I was hoping I might deliver them to you this afternoon."

"Yes, of course, my boy. What time did you have in mind?"

"Maybe something after lunch, say two or three. What's best for you, Paul?"

"Let's make it half two, then. Perhaps we should discuss logistics before you pop over. You'll have the items in your own car?"

"Yes, I've got a rental. They're in the, uh, the boot."

"Fine. You know where my office is. Drive round to the rear entrance when you arrive. There's a small lane named Cheval Place directly behind our building which parallels the Brompton Road in the front. Turn onto Montpelier Street, then left into Cheval Place. I'll have one of our security guards waiting to direct you into our loading bay. I'll be there as well."

"Very good. I'll make a point of being there at exactly two-thirty. See you this afternoon, Paul."

I showered (again), dressed in clean Levi's and my lucky yellow golf shirt, slid barefooted into my deck shoes, and went downstairs for a late and light breakfast . . . two damned eggs, not one, and hold the offal.

"Morning, Dane. Bit of a good kip?"

"Yeah, thanks. That was my first bed since Friday night. Hey, Tim, have you seen Gina this morning?"

"I saw her driving your Jaguar out of the car park a few hours ago when I first came down to put the kettle on. You don't know where she's gone?"

Not a clue, but she has two million bucks worth of my gold with her wherever she is. Oh, Christ, what was that she'd said a few days ago about her future plans requiring more than her recent $100,000 deposit? Impossible—don't even think about it. "Uh, I guess she had an errand to run or something," I finally responded as my brain rapidly clicked through all the nasty possibilities.

"Tea or coffee, Dane?"

"Tea, please. No milk."

I walked over to look out the kitchen door and almost wished I hadn't quit smoking years ago; this was starting to feel like an excellent occasion to fall off that wagon. But only seconds later, a British racing green X Type Jaguar drove up the hill and rolled to a stop in front of me. I exhaled deeply.

A freshly scrubbed strawberry blonde waved from the right seat. "G'day, sailor. First time in Portsmouth? Looking for a good time with a pretty lady?" She blew me a kiss, put the Jag back in gear, and turned into the lot. Working her best fashion runway strut as she walked back toward me, I noticed Gina was wearing a conservative navy blue dress I hadn't seen before—and showing as much cleavage as she had when she'd tamed Klaus in Neuchâtel.

"Miss me? Or worried I'd stolen your car and things?" she sassed. She reached for my head with both hands and gave me a long, wet kiss.

"My, you're in a good mood. Sorry it took me so long to find us a bed. And no, I really didn't have time to miss you. I just came downstairs a few minutes ago. I called Paul Bisno. We have a two-thirty appointment this afternoon at his office in Knightsbridge. C'mon inside and I'll make you a milky tea."

"Where's Tim?"

"I don't know. He was here a minute ago. Maybe he's getting the bar set up for lunch."

"Good, 'cause I've something to tell you. Sit down."

"Should I be worried? Your father's looking for me for messing with his daughter? Someone stole the gold out of the trunk?"

"Shut up. And before I forget, last night was amazing. Earlier this morning, I should say. We've got to set aside time to give that another go sometime soon." The wink. The muddy face crisis was apparently forgotten. "Now, listen." She put a finger to her lips. I took it that meant don't speak.

"I went to see Mr. Bracegirdle—God, can you imagine going through school with that name? Anyway, Dane, I have the twentieth LGD. It's in the boot of the Jag. I think I've finally earned that hundred thousand dollars you negotiated for me from Mr. Toru."

"*You what*? Damn, I should make love to you more often. How'd you get it back?" I whispered.

"Okay, I'll try to make this as brief as I can; I thought of this yesterday. I drove into High Wycombe this morning after you fell asleep, after, well, you know. I found one of those quickie one-hour print shops and had them make me some new business cards. Here, look," she said as she reached into her no-nonsense business purse. I hadn't seen it before either.

I inspected the card: Fiona Atherton, First Assistant Managing Director for the British Isles, Security Division, Anglo-Swiss Investment Trust, Ltd., Threadneedle Street, London, EC2R, United Kingdom, followed by phone and fax numbers I recognized to be in London by their 44-20 prefixes.

"Cool title, but Fiona Atherton?" I was totally confused.

"Yeah, she was the lead character in a series of young girls' books I read when I was little. Now, let me tell you what I did," she said, waving her hands up and down excitedly like a little kid who'd just brought home a glowing report card. "I found Mr. Bracegirdle's shop address in High Wycombe on the plastic bags he used to deliver his produce yesterday. I drove into town early this morning and bought myself—" she stood and twirled around to display her new wardrobe, "bought myself this dress, sensible shoes, and handbag. Quite businesslike and stodgy, don't you think?"

"Your advertising's not very stodgy." I pointed to her mostly unbuttoned dress top.

"Oh, hell. Thanks," she nodded and re-fastened the two lowest buttons. "I meant to do that after I left the old boy. So, now I'm attired in my proper new finery and I stop in to see Mr. Bracegirdle at his green grocer's shop."

"Didn't he recognize you from here in the kitchen yesterday?"

"No, Dane, that's the point. He never saw me. I was sitting at the far end of this table, where he couldn't see me from the door. I heard him, but I never saw him. And he didn't see or hear me."

"All right, go ahead. What did you tell him?"

"Well, first I had to wait about thirty minutes until he returned from his morning deliveries. When he finally came back into the shop, I gave him my new business card and asked if there was somewhere we could speak privately concerning a very important matter. He takes me into his office in the rear of the shop—stuff piled up all over the place, a complete mess. At this point, he's looking very nervous and he goes back to inspecting my card. I told him my firm had lost a twenty-seven-pound gold bar in transit yesterday, and we'd rung up the Thames Valley Police to file a report. The police made inquiries in the area and someone from one of the houses near the Three Horseshoes reported they'd seen a man pick up something off the road and put it in his van. They remembered the name of his shop printed on the side of the van, something I thought of when I saw him drive up this morning."

"And he's buying this bullshit?"

278

"Of course," she beamed. "He was butter in my hand. Want me to unbutton my dress again? No, don't answer that. Anyway, he's scared to death. He's probably thinking he's going to prison for not reporting what he'd found. After a few more minutes in his office, he's in a dead panic. I told him that since I was confident he planned on giving back the gold bar at some point, it would be my pleasure to pay him the reward my firm was offering for its return."

"Jesus, you're a regular little con artist, kiddo."

Squinting her eyes in an *I've been such a bad girl* expression, she said, "Yeah, perhaps a bit. Now listen: As I was waiting for the cards to be printed, I stopped off at a branch of my bank and withdrew ten thousand quid in cash. Once I see Mr. Bracegirdle's all in a bother over his troubles, I pull out five thousand pounds and place it on his desk. I told him if he was to accept the reward, it went without saying he could never speak of this again for the sake of my firm's honor and integrity."

"Five thousand pounds? I thought you withdrew ten," I said, still confused. Happy, but confused.

"The other five was my contingency fund, in case the first five grand didn't close the deal. But now I think he'd have opened that little safe and handed over the bar for nothing if I'd promised not to report him. And maybe unbuttoned a bit more."

"Unbelievable. I'll give you a check for the five thousand. You're sensational—and not only in bed. Hey, I'm curious: Where did you come up with the phone and fax numbers on the card you showed him? Those aren't your real numbers, I hope."

"Of course not, you idiot. The phone number is one I jotted down off a Cadbury's chocolates lorry parked in town, and the fax number is for a betting shop I saw across the road from the printer's. Then I substituted London dialing codes in front of both of them. I'd have been in a spot of trouble if he'd tried to ring either number, but I made sure he was busy concentrating on my tits and the five thousand quid. No chance he was going to call. The sweets and the bookie were rather creative, wouldn't you agree?"

"Right now I'd agree with anything you said. You're incredible. Come here."

Several seconds into showing my appreciation, Tim returned to his kitchen.

"Terribly sorry, you two. This is a bit awkward. I didn't know you were in here. Carry on—don't mind me. I'm only getting some things for the bar. Room number three is still available if you get tired of standing," he laughed.

Gina stepped back to her chair, smoothed out her dress, and ran her fingers through her hair in an attempt to straighten something that didn't really require straightening.

"Thanks, Timmy, but I think I need you to make out our bill for yesterday's food and drink and last night's room."

"You're off so soon, then?"

"Yeah, we have a meeting in Knightsbridge. We should get going."

Tim pulled down his glasses from atop his head, walked to a kitchen drawer, and withdrew a manila file containing various small papers and receipts. He transcribed some numbers from his bar tabs onto a guest receipt and laid it next to my teacup.

"I trust you had a pleasant stay . . . and found everything you were looking for?" he asked with a knowing grin, arms folded across his chest, glasses pushed back up on his forehead.

"Yeah, always good getting out here to see you. But what do you mean, did we find everything we were looking for?"

"Mr. Bracegirdle rang up a few minutes ago from his shop in High Wycombe. Seems a young lady representing a bank and driving a green Jaguar met with him this morning and paid him a tidy reward for returning the gold bar he found yesterday."

I resisted my knee-jerk temptation to glance across at Gina. "That's nice. Good for him. But I'm not clear as to what you're talking about, Tim."

"Well, let's just say after that call I started putting things together. Odd, queer little things. Like the other night, a few hours before you arrived, a small plane flew low over the back fields a couple of times. Then later, but still early that morning, you lot arrive on my front steps without a car. You knowing the exact weight of a gold bar you hadn't seen. And last night, out my bedroom window, I see two wankers with torches mucking about in the fields. This morning, these two pairs of Wellies here are all shiny and clean. I can't remember the last time I washed off my Wellies. Then my green grocer rings up and tells me about this nice young lady, 'a bit of alright', as he described her, with this brilliant set of Bristols. Uh, sorry, luv. Let's just say he approved of your figure, old girl. And she drove a dark green Jaguar. C'mon, mate: It's not exactly bloody rocket surgery. You know, you having flown in the Air Force and all. But not to worry, you two. Not a word, then. Your business isn't my concern. But I'll always wonder exactly how many gold bars were in my fields."

"Twenty. Well, actually nineteen, since Gina got hold of the twentieth this morning. And thanks, Tim. You're a buddy. I owe you."

"Right you are, old son; you owe me exactly a hundred and twenty-seven quid for the bed, booze and nosh." He patted my back as I handed him a small wad of pound notes. "Not a word, promise. And I'll have another go at Mr. Bracegirdle to see he keeps a lid on things."

Gina leaned over and kissed him on the cheek. "Cheers, Tim. Dane has great mates."

* * *

Gina impatiently tapped her fingernails on the steering wheel until the light changed; she chirped the tires off the line and quickly maneuvered the now tail-heavy Jag past Marble Arch and down Park Lane into Knightsbridge and the Brompton Road.

"Where do I turn? We're coming up on Harrods. Bisno's Auctions is ahead somewhere on the right."

"Turn on Montpelier Street. There, I see it, the next street. Then a quick left into Cheval Place."

The moment the car rounded the second turn, I saw Paul standing with his uniformed employee, both motioning madly like traffic cops to turn into their little entrance. It was exactly 2:30. My driver had done her job well. I was starting to believe she did everything well.

As he leaned toward Gina's opened driver's window, Paul said, "Gina, hello, good to see you again, my dear. Follow that gentleman into our loading garage."

She inched the Jag slowly forward behind the guard to a spot next to an armored truck. The overhead door rattled shut behind us.

"Just there, dear. Yes, that's fine," Paul directed. "You had a successful trip, I see. No difficulties in moving the gold from Switzerland into the U.K., Dane?"

"No, I thought it would be a little problematic, but it turned out to be a piece of cake . . . a walk in the park. What's the British term I'm looking for?"

"*Bloody miraculous,* I think might qualify," Paul laughed. "I don't want to know. I'm only happy for your sake you got them here."

Gina pressed the trunk release remote on the key chain. I reached inside and pulled away the pieces of muddy plastic sheeting covering the still aligned LGDs.

"All in all, a most successful trip, Paul. There they are." I stood back to take in the magnificent sight of the gold coruscating under the florescent lights.

"My God, they are beautiful, aren't they? Did you know the London bullion market here trades as much as five hundred tons of these in a given day?" Paul mused, mostly to himself. "Gerald, go ahead. You may proceed and transfer these bars now."

"Straight away, guv'nor," the guard replied, touching the bill of his cap in acknowledgment. One by one, he took the LGDs from the trunk of the Jaguar and passed them to his waiting assistant inside the opened rear doors of the armored vehicle. In less than five minutes, the paperwork was signed and the truck drove off down Cheval Place. Paul checked his watch.

"Where are you staying, Dane?"

"Claridge's. But only tonight. We're off to Paris tomorrow afternoon. Any chance you could stop by the hotel before you catch your train this evening, Paul? I was hoping we might take care of the exchange fees over a couple of drinks."

"Oh, very kind of you, my boy, but I'm afraid I must be straight home after work. But we'll do it the next time you're in the city. And don't worry about the fees. Let's call it my thanks for your bringing the Bugatti Atlantic our way."

I'd been prepared to pay a fee of what I'd researched to be between one and two percent of the gold sale proceeds as a courtesy to Madame Laurent. Now I had an extra thirty grand or so for dinner. What a country.

"Dane, the last gold fixing is at three this afternoon. I'll be expecting a call shortly before that as to the exact amount due from your LGDs. To whom should we make our check payable?"

"Sandrine Laurent." I spelled out her name to be safe.

"Very well. Should we post the check to her directly or would you prefer I give it to you?"

It dawned on me I didn't have her address; I only knew the driving directions to her place in La Chaux-de-Fonds.

"Sorry, Paul, but it just occurred to me that even though I've been to her house, I don't know the address. Could I pick it up tomorrow on my way out to Heathrow? I'll call Madame Laurent later this afternoon."

"Don't trouble yourself, lad. I'll see that our check is delivered to Claridge's within a couple of hours." He looked at his watch again. "By five this afternoon, shall we say?"

* * *

Gina waited until she turned out of Grosvenor Square toward Claridge's before predictably explaining how she needed to spend the night at home with son Willie and the folks before our "fortnight's holiday abroad."

"I know. I only wish I could hear your explanation to your father as to why his airplane's out in Buckinghamshire with the rear windows busted out and his army rifle hidden under the seats."

"Thanks. I've decided to simply tell him the truth," she replied matter-of-factly, apparently serious about fessing up to pop.

"Gina, I'm not sure that's the most brilliant idea you've had all week. Remember: Honesty's the best policy, but not the only policy."

The doorman in front of Claridge's stood at parade rest once I held up my "wait one moment" finger.

"I'm not sure how prudent it would be to tell your dad you were party to the quasi-theft of over two million dollars worth of gold, that you permitted his Cessna to be illegally flown into the U.K., and on two separate occasions within hours of one another, two different people shot at you. Jesus, Gina, think about it."

"What would you suggest I tell him, then?"

"Does he trust you?"

"Until now. But pinching his airplane might be a bit over-the-top, wouldn't you think?"

"Yeah, I guess it is. Well then, darlin', good luck on that." I couldn't help laughing. "Do me a favor, Gina: At least pay your father for the window repairs and the fuel. Let me know what I owe you."

"Okay. Well, I suggested we take the Skylane, so I'll come up with something to tell him."

"I should know shortly what's going on with the travel agent about our Concorde seats tomorrow." I put my hands on both her cheeks and drew her closer. This was as good a time as any. "Gina, I want to tell you something. I—"

"Yeah, yeah, I know. You appreciate me helping with the gold and Daddy's airplane and all. Go on, off with you now. See you in the morning."

That wasn't what I was going to say.

Claridge's reception staff had finally dispensed with the newspaper and beverage briefing, as I was now on my third registration in the past two weeks. Within minutes of Gina's departure, a bellman delivered the two bags I'd left at the hotel last week. I tipped him, waited until he closed my room door behind him, and stepped over to use the phone on the desk.

"Hello, Uwe? This is Dane Baron. You asked me to call you this afternoon to check on our stand-by status for the Concorde tomorrow."

"*Ah, ja*, Herr Baron. *Danke*, uh, thank you. Unfortunately, I still cannot say for certain that you *und* Fräulein Domenico are confirmed on tomorrow's charter. However, I do think it most unlikely the lady *und* gentleman *mit* the medical problem *vill* be traveling *mit* us."

"So where does that leave things, Uwe? We're down to less than twenty-four hours to go and you still can't guarantee a place for us?"

"*Ach*, no, I cannot guarantee, Herr Baron. Let me ask you: Are you in Paris now?"

"No, I'm in London. We'd planned to fly into Charles de Gaulle tomorrow afternoon."

"I understand. *Sehr gut*. Then this is what I suggest, Herr

286

Baron: Since it now appears I will not have a notification *von* the other couple until possibly as late as flight time, meet me at the Air France charters counter tomorrow. That's in Terminal Two, at Charles de Gaulle Airport. I'll be there not later than two P.M. While I can't promise anything, I am quite confident you *und* your guest will be on the Concorde tomorrow. Is this possible for you to do, *ja?*" the German asked in his near fluent but heavily accented English.

I hesitated. The last time I'd flown stand-by, I was in the Air Force, trying to get home on leave on a MAC flight out of Ramstein. But that was free. This time I'd have the pleasure of shelling out damn near $20,000 for our flight and cruise if we cleared the list.

"Okay, Uwe, we'll meet at the charters desk. But if you hear something before our flight out of Heathrow tomorrow, let me know. I'll be leaving my hotel at eleven, London time." I gave him both my cell and the hotel phone numbers. What a half-assed plan this had developed into.

Next, I called Sandrine Laurent, but was told by her housekeeper that madame had left for the evening. She gave me their address in La Chaux-de-Fonds and promised to relay my message to madame to expect a check from England within two days.

I glanced at my watch as I pressed the buttons for Clyde's office number in Paris: 3:20 P.M.—4:20 in Paris, and still duty hours.

"*Mon cher*! I'm so pleased to hear you're still alive. I had my doubts about you this time, Dane."

"Hey, Clyde. Appreciate the concern. Got a minute?"

"*Ah, mais oui. Toujours.* Tell me what's been going on."

I remembered we were talking on an open line in the Paris police headquarters building, and less was better. "I wanted to call and thank you for your help last week, and let you know everything turned out fine. Nobody's chasing me anymore," I hoped. "Actually, I'm not sure they ever really were." That was crap, but this wasn't the time to get into it.

"So you're still not going to tell me what you're involved in, eh? *Et bien,* at least you're safe."

"Clyde, I know I owe you a better explanation, but not right now, okay? Look, there's a small chance I'll be in Paris tomorrow night with my girlfriend. We're trying for a Concorde charter headed for New York to board a German cruise ship, but there's a possibility we won't be able to get on the flight. If we don't fly out, let's meet for dinner. I'd like you Ge the charter."

"*D'accord.* Okay. Call me one way or the other. But if we miss one another, you still owe me a dinner."

"Absolutely, you got it. I'll call you tomorrow afternoon."

"*Très bien.* Bye bye. *Ciao.*"

A quick change into a pair of slacks, jacket and tie (this *was* Claridge's), and within fifteen minutes, I was downstairs sitting at the rail in a medium-busy Claridge's Bar.

"A large Black Label, ice to the brim, sir?"

I smiled broadly and nodded. The barman's memory really wasn't all that remarkable; we'd seen one another only last Thursday night. But it was appreciated.

"Mister Baron?"

I pivoted around to see an assistant manager holding out an envelope. "Yes?"

"This was delivered for you a few minutes ago, sir. After I didn't reach you when I rang your room, I hoped I might find you here."

Yeah, I was pretty predictable. He handed me the sealed robin's-egg-blue envelope bearing the logo of Bisno's Auctions, Ltd.

"Good news, sir?" my barman buddy inquired after the manager left. He'd returned with my drink and evidently noticed my grin as I inspected the contents of the envelope without fully removing the check: 1,484,256.04 pounds sterling. 2.25 million U.S.

"Yes, thanks. Very good news."

Chapter 24

Paris

Tuesday, 25 July 2000

The green Jaguar was waiting outside Claridge's front entrance when I exited the hotel at 11 A.M., sharp.

"You can put those back here, please," I said as I gestured toward the car's trunk while I hunted through my pockets for a reasonably generous tip. "Here you go. Thanks. Oh, I almost forgot." I reached into my inside coat pocket and pulled out the envelope I'd prepared for Madame Laurent. I handed it to the liveried bellman, along with three ten pound notes. "Would you see that this goes out to Switzerland today by Federal Express for overnight delivery?"

"Certainly, sir. Thank you very much. Have a pleasant journey."

Gina was dressed in a white suit, sans jewelry, with nothing visible beneath her jacket other than skin and cleavage; her skirt was hiked three-quarters the way up her tanned thighs. It was the same suit she'd worn the evening we first met, three months ago, and I liked it on her every bit as much today. I leaned over the car's center console for a kiss.

"Dane, please tell me that wasn't Madame Laurent's check for the gold you just handed that man? My God, you are a trusting soul."

"Gina, it's Claridge's. Now, how did it go with Daddy last night?" I was almost afraid to hear.

"Oh, fine, I guess. I simply told him the truth. Well, most of it, anyway. Perhaps I nobbled just a bit. I told him you were a pilot— I've been telling him about you for a while now. I said you were in a spot of trouble, that some very bad guys were chasing you, and I suggested we fly the Skylane back to England to get away from them."

"So he doesn't know about my not having a pilot's license? Our illegal entry? Or about the gold? Or the shootings?"

"Dane, I said I didn't lie to him, but nor did I want to worry him needlessly over some nasty little details. I'd prefer to say I was possibly just a bit thrifty with the whole truth. I told him we'd accidentally broken a window or two in the plane, and you were having it looked after. I reckoned he didn't need to know all the finer points of the weekend."

"Ah. Rationalizing a bit, are we? The old *need to know.* I think I taught that course."

Gina shrugged with the smallest hint of a smile, and aimed the Jag west, toward Heathrow.

"I've already been out to Booker Airpark earlier this morning to collect his rifle. And you'll be pleased to know I rang up and arranged for someone to repair the windows on the Cessna. The man promised he would see to it today and call my father when he finished. I gave him my credit card number to pay for the charges.

291

"I appreciate that. I owe you . . . again."

* * *

Seats 2 A and B, and four bags checked to Charles de Gaulle," the uniformed Air France ticket agent said in heavily French-accented English as she stapled the claim checks to our ticket jacket. "I'm sorry I'm not able to check them through to New York on Concorde, but I'm sure you understand. Once you receive your travel documents in Paris, our agents there will take care of these for you."

"That'll be fine. Thanks."

We walked slowly down the bustling Terminal 2 concourse toward the gates serving flights mostly to and from European cities.

"How confident are you we'll be able to board the Concorde once we're in Paris?" Gina asked, a touch of concern evident in her voice.

"My pal Uwe tells me he thinks we're going, so I guess I'd make it fifty-fifty. Have you given any thought to what you'd like to do for the next two weeks if we don't make it?"

"Negative thinker," she said, feigning a pout and lightly slapping my hand. "If your German friend Uwe is confident, there's no alternative planning required. We'll be making love in our cabin as we sail out of New York harbor tonight."

Well, that was that. We were flying Concorde to New York this afternoon.

* * *

The Air France Airbus braked to a stop at its gate at Charles de Gaulle slightly ahead of our scheduled 2:30 P.M. arrival time. In the next twenty minutes, we retrieved our bags off the carousel, loaded them onto a cart, and made our way to the Air France charters area. The sign overhead the check-in counters read *AF 4590*.

"We're looking for a blonde guy in a lavender Tyrolean hat with a yellow feather in the band. See anyone like that?"

Gina rolled her eyes. "I'm ever so pleased he added the bit about the yellow feather so we can pick him out from all the other chaps wearing lavender Tyrolean hats. Hey, over there." She waved at what I assumed to be an Uwe.

The Tyrolean hat approached us.

"Uwe?" I asked the diminutive bleached blonde man beneath the hat. He was right—we couldn't miss him.

"*Ja*, I'm Uwe. Herr Baron *und* Fräulein Domenico?"

We shook hands as I tried to read the frail German's face for an inkling about our flight.

"Herr Baron, I am very sorry to tell you I have bad news, sir. My other couple *von* Hamburg have arrived for the trip. The gentleman has a full medical release *von* his doctor. I'm sorry I didn't have this information for you earlier to save you the trip to Paris. We have our full complement of exactly one hundred passengers, including myself."

Initially, I felt disappointment, mostly for Gina, but when I turned to look at her, she smiled back.

"Well, that's life in the big city, mate," she said. "We gave it a go, but it wasn't meant to be today. It's fate. Kismet. There's a reason for everything. Perhaps we'll try again when we have more time to plan. I'm sure we can come up with something to do for the next two weeks."

Uwe stood with us and continued to apologize for another few minutes, guaranteeing our passage on his next trip. Finally, thank God, he excused himself, and he and his purpuraceous hat went trotting back toward his group, his arms and voice both raised.

"Let's get a drink and figure out our future," Gina volunteered, reading my mind. She took my hand and shepherded me to a café less than forty yards away.

"*Un Black Label, beaucoup de glace, et*—" I turned to Gina for her drink order.

"G and T. No ice."

"*Et un gin avec tonic. Sans glace. Merci*," I requested from the expressionless white-jacketed waiter who then departed for his bar without any sign of acknowledgment. "Why am I translating my Swiss girlfriend's English into French?"

"Because you absolutely adore me. See, you just called me your girlfriend."

I shook my head, but found myself smiling. "Okay, Slick, where we goin'?"

"What are our options?"

"You pick 'em. The South of France, the Seychelles, Tahiti, the Caribbean? What sounds good to you? Really, I'm open, and God knows, you've earned it the last few days." Our drinks materialized and I took a draw on my airport mini pour of Scotch.

Gina leaned back in the uncomfortable molded plastic chair, slowly stirred her drink with her finger, and then licked off the gin. "Florida. Where you live—in Sarasota. Let's go there. I've never been to America. Maybe pop over to the Bahamas for a few days?"

"Sure, though you may find it somewhat tame after St. Moritz and Monte Carlo. It's the off-season in Florida now, the summer months, when it's hot and humid. But if that doesn't bother you, then Florida it'll be."

Gina slid her chair closer and took my hand. "You know, Yank," she started slowly, swirling the remains of her gin in her plastic glass, "sitting here with my best friend, having a pleasant cocktail, talking about in which exotic place we're going to spend the next fortnight—it doesn't get much better than this, does it?"

"Best friend am I? Hmm. How 'bout this: Let's get one more pop here, then grab a cab to the hotel, drop our bags, and have some drinks at Harry's. I'll call my old detective friend Marie-Claude I told you about, and see if she can join us for dinner. Does that work?"

"Definitely. Sounds fun. I'd like to meet her."

* * *

*B*onjour. L'Hôtel Royal Monceau, s'il vous plaît," Gina instructed our elderly cab driver while I climbed in after her. "You know, Dane, the more I think about it, as much as I wanted to fly on Concorde, the thought of spending sixteen days on a cruise with a mob of Germans we don't know probably wouldn't be my first choice of fun things to do. This all worked out for the best. As I said, it's kismet. We'll do Concorde some other time."

"Oh, so you think I'll still be hanging around with you long enough to do that, do you?"

"You're completely smitten with me and you know it. You wouldn't know what to do without me."

She was close to being right.

The digital clock next to the fare meter read 16:43 as the taxi accelerated out of the airport loop and merged onto the southbound autoroute toward Paris.

"*Jesus Christ! Gina! Look, there!*" I shouted as I pointed out her window, to the east, back toward the airport. "Driver, pull over and stop. Now!" I yelled at him in French.

Without questioning my command, he jerked the Citroën to the right and braked to a skidding stop on the grass beyond the shoulder.

Flames and black smoke were billowing out the rear of the airplane as it lumbered toward the autoroute on a crossing line a quarter mile directly ahead of us. Its altitude wasn't more than two hundred feet and I clearly recognized it to be a Concorde. Our Concorde.

"*Oh my God!*" Gina screamed, grabbing my leg. "*It's going to crash!*"

The taxi driver threw open his door and fell to his knees on the grass, muttering, holding his head with both hands. Gina and I jumped out next to him.

The stricken jet barely crossed over the highway before it abruptly bank to the left; the screaming high-pitched whine of the Olympus engines was ear-splitting. The right wing rose up almost ninety degrees due to the asymmetric thrust—the howling starboard engines were obviously generating more power than the fire-engulfed port side engines. With the belly of the delta-winged plane now facing us, the flames were clearly exposed, trailing out nearly one hundred yards behind the engines and the still extended main landing gear. I guessed the plane to be traveling at about 200 knots; fire and smoke totally engulfed the underside of the left wing. As the Concorde continued to our right—to the west—the noise level dropped dramatically; the pilots had pulled back on the power on the good engines below the starboard wing in an effort to regain control of the roll. But with falling airspeed, the crippled plane's flight path descended below a line of trees to our right. Twenty seconds later and a few miles distant, a telltale black mushroom cloud bloomed up into the afternoon sky.

Gina and I held one another in silence. Our driver sobbed, "*Mon Dieu, mon Dieu. Quelle catastrophe!*"

"That was our charter, wasn't it?" Gina finally asked.

"Yeah. The scheduled Concorde to New York Kennedy leaves around ten in the morning, and I don't think it even operates on Tuesdays. Yeah, that was our airplane all right. God, how awful. And we were nearly on it."

Most of the cars and trucks on the autoroute had pulled over once they'd witnessed the burning SST pass over the highway. I found myself standing between Gina and our driver with an arm over each of their shoulders, the three of us staring at the black smoke continuing to balloon upward from the crash site.

"*Quelle catastrophe, quelle catastrophe,*" the taxi driver moaned repeatedly. Finally, fully four or five minutes later, he slowly returned to the front seat of his cab, his gaze never straying from the west. "*Alors*, le Royal Monceau," he said, repeating his assigned destination before pulling back onto the highway.

Gina rested her head on my shoulder as we rode in silence for the next several miles. My thoughts flashed back to my C-130 crash, and the grotesque sight of its remains. I'd walked away from that one, and was lucky enough not to have boarded this one.

"Are you all right, Gina?"

She didn't comment, but I felt her nod. As we started to enter the city's surface street traffic, our driver tuned his blaring radio to the news reports of the crash: "A catastrophic tragedy for all of France," a government spokesman said.

"Oh, bloody hell!" Gina suddenly cried out, jerking to an upright position. "My God, my parents think I was on that plane. I have to call them immediately."

I caught the driver looking at me in the rear view mirror, clearly confused over the latest emergency.

"Here, use mine." I handed her my phone.

"Damn! They're driving out to Devon today for their fishing trip. I won't be able to contact them till they reach their hotel in Bampton."

"Call the hotel and leave a message that you're all right. You know where they're staying?"

"Yes, at their friend Brian Smith's place, the Bridge House Hotel. Good idea. I have the number here in my handbag. I only hope they don't have the damned car radio on."

"Are you still good for dinner with Marie-Claude tonight or would you rather I canceled?" I asked, thinking back to the recent memory of her reaction to Arnaud's death.

She held up a finger. From Gina's side of the phone conversation, it became evident her parents and Willie had already arrived at the hotel. After endless assurances that we were still healthy and with promises to phone again once we knew where we were going, she handed the phone back.

"Lucky timing. I'm glad I called when I did. And, uh, no, don't cancel with your friend. Let's go ahead and meet her for dinner."

* * *

Thank God the charter was full," Clyde said over the phone. "No, I didn't mean it that way. I meant I'm happy you couldn't get on the flight."

"Thanks, and I understood what you meant."

"Where are you now?"

"Harry's."

"*Merde*. But of course you are. What a stupid question. Look, I appreciate the invitation, Dane, but I don't know what time I'm going to finish up here. They have me covering some things in the office because of the Concorde crash. Where are you dining? If I can break free, I'll check with you there and see if it's still early enough to join you."

"The Copenhague. Upstairs, on the north side of the Champs-Élysées, a block or two down from Étoile. The only reservations they had were for ten o'clock. Kind of late."

"Not for Paris. I know the place. If I can make it, I'll meet you there at ten. If I'm not there, don't wait for me. We'll get together tomorrow if I miss you tonight, okay?"

"Deal. See you later, Clyde."

I'd used the downstairs phone booth at Harry's to call Clyde; I intensely disliked the rudeness of people using their mobile phones in a bar or restaurant, forcing everyone within earshot to listen to their obtrusive and inane conversations. When I returned, a new arrival was leaning across my bar stool talking to Gina. I tapped his shoulder to reclaim my zone, and without a word of protest he instantly retreated back to his space.

"God, what took you so long?" she asked in a hushed voice.

"Sorry. Oh, good, you got our drinks. So, was this character giving you a hard time?"

"No," she grinned, "not at all. As you told me in Switzerland, just a bloke trying to do what a bloke's gotta do. No worries. But I did have a rather bad thought when you were downstairs. I'm worried, Dane. I think we were followed today."

"What?" I saw the genuine concern in her face. "Why do you think that?"

"I could be wrong, but I doubt it. I noticed someone at the airport I thought I'd seen before."

"Where? Here or in London?"

"Here, at the airport, this afternoon, when you were speaking with the German travel agent. A man was staring at us the whole time you two were standing there talking. But as soon as you handed the agent your card, the guy hurried off toward the door."

"I stare at you all the time. You're nice to stare at. So?"

"No, listen, I'm serious. I've been thinking about it and I remember him now from the Crillon Bar the day the cop was interviewing us after Arnaud was murdered. He's an Asian guy, with a tight fitting black suit. Same yellow shirt he wore before, without a tie. Long, straight black hair. Alligator or croc cowboy boots with silver tips on the toes. And gold rimmed oval shaped sunglasses he rests on the top of his head."

"Very thorough description. You're thinking it was Miura?"

Gina took a sip of what appeared to be a very weak orange juice or a very strong screwdriver. She placed the tall glass on the bar, leaned back, turned toward me, and nodded.

"Yes. If the guy at the Crillon was Miura, then it was definitely Miura at the airport today. I reckon he thinks you handed the agent a check for our passage. Dane, he thinks we were on the Concorde."

Chapter 25

Tuesday night, 25 July 2000

I asked Gina to order for the two of us before I walked back to the reception podium at the Copenhague. "I forgot to mention something. There may be a lady by the name of Marie-Claude Perrin joining us. Would you see that she gets to our table?"

"*Mais oui, monsieur. Absolument,*" the hostess assured me with a slight head bow.

My white wine glass was partially filled and my tumbler had been removed when I returned. I guessed that meant someone had decided I'd had enough Scotch.

"What did you order?" I'd dined at the Copenhague several times over the years and thoroughly enjoyed everything I'd tried. Their Danish cuisine was always a pleasant change.

"Eel for starters, along with some ice cold Aalborg akvavit and Tuborg beer, followed by smoked reindeer. Sound good?" Her face was smiley but I feared she was serious.

"Mmm . . . yum." I did in half my wine in one pull. At least the akvavit and beer sounded tempting.

Two waiters arrived to position the plates of eel before us and simultaneously remove their silver serving domes. The starter course was marinated and mixed with little potatoes and onions, and surprisingly, looked quite appetizing. Our conversation naturally dwelt on the shocking events of the afternoon—the crash itself, and our good fortune in not having boarded the flight. I asked Gina again about Miura. I was having her go over her recollections of the Japanese at the airport for the second time when her focus shifted above and behind me. I felt a light tap on my shoulder.

"Sorry I'm late. May I join you?"

"Ah, Marie-Claude." I rose from my chair. "Good, I'm glad you could make it. Marie-Claude, Gina. Gina, Marie-Claude, otherwise known as Clyde."

"*Enchanté*," they both said, then clasped hands as they did the two cheek boogie. Clyde was visibly captivated; Gina blushed. Though I hadn't described Gina to her, Clyde commented on how much more beautiful she was than I'd reported.

"Sit here, Clyde. Let me get you a menu," I offered once they'd broken their embrace. They continued to take in one another for several more seconds after they seated themselves.

"Thanks, but I can't stay long. I'm still working. I'm sorry to do this over your dinner, but something very disturbing has come to our attention concerning the Concorde crash this afternoon. If you don't mind, I'd like to go over a few things with you."

I pushed my eel plate aside and centered my glasses of beer and akvavit. I couldn't imagine what Clyde had to discuss with us about the Air France disaster.

"Sure. What's up?"

One of our waiters approached. "*Mademoiselle. Bonsoir*," he greeted Marie-Claude.

"*Bonsoir. Un Jack Daniels, s'il vous plaît. Un double*," she requested before withdrawing a small notebook from her purse. I could only imagine an American cop declaring herself to be on duty, then ordering a cocktail, a double no less, to help her through her evening.

Clyde cleared away her silver flatware and leafed through her notes until the waiter returned with her bourbon. She took a drink, laid down her notebook, and leaned forward, her hands now laid flat in front of her on the tablecloth. She started slowly, quietly, having inspected the nearby tables to assure herself no one was listening.

"We've discovered some most ominous information regarding the crash near Roissy today. I'm only telling you this because I now believe you were indirectly, but intimately, involved." She held up her right forefinger to caution me against speaking while she peered down at her notes. "This is a most bizarre scenario, and it appears to revolve around you, Dane."

"What the hell are you talking about, Clyde? You think *I* had something to do with this crash? Jesus, you can't be serious! We were trying get *on* the damned plane."

"As I said—indirectly. Now listen carefully, and I'll tell you what we've discovered."

When the wait staff appeared with our main course, I ordered a Scotch and pushed the newly delivered plate to one side.

"Now, it's only been, what?" she checked her watch, "six hours since the crash? But we've been lucky enough to accumulate a lot of information so far. Initially, we have evidence someone shot at the Concorde as it was rolling down the runway on takeoff. Two shots, to be exact. We know this because—and this is incredibly fortunate for us—because there's a small shack on the airport grounds, one of several, which tapes the sound levels of aircraft taking off. That building also has video cameras which show a portion of the southern perimeter fence for airport security purposes . . . live video that unfortunately was not being monitored at the time of the incident. The shooter was positioned about a hundred meters from the structure when he fired the shots."

"And the sound equipment that records takeoffs for noise abatement purposes picked up the sound of two rounds being fired as the Concorde was rolling out," I reasoned aloud, trying to expedite things.

"Exactly," Clyde confirmed.

Gina didn't wait for the sommelier. She retrieved our wine bottle from its bucket, wiped off the residual water and ice with her linen, and filled her glass to the top.

Clyde continued. "Now, it's obviously very early into our investigation, not to mention the investigation by the BEA."

"The BEA?" Gina asked.

"*Le Bureau d'Enquêtes et d'Analyses*. It's our equivalent of the American NTSB, the National Transportation Safety Board. They investigate transportation accidents. They examine the causes of the crash, and we police investigate any possible criminal activity associated with the incident. As I was going to say, we also have video showing the shooter firing the two shots from a prone position on the grass using a bipod, then policing his brass and getting back into his car. By eight o'clock this evening, our sound technicians had already ascertained the shots were fired from a .50

caliber Barrett."

"Jesus. That's an anti-matériel rifle. It's got a sniper range of over a mile," I said.

"That's correct. And from the video, we've pinpointed the shooter's location to be about nine hundred meters to the south and west of the Concorde when he fired the first round. The second shot was fired three seconds later, and obviously from a slightly closer range as the aircraft continued toward him. It was more or less a forty-five-degree angle from his position to the airplane; Concorde was taking off to the west, and the shooter was firing toward the northeast.

"He was near the route Périphérique Sud, the airport's southern perimeter road. He pulled off the Périphérique onto a smaller road located immediately outside the airport boundary and parked where a line of trees partially obscured him from the main route. As I mentioned, the video shows him laying on the grass using the bipod to support the Barrett sniper rifle. They enhanced the video to show not only his car, a Volkswagen Golf, but the license number as well. It also shows the shooter's face to have oriental features. We immediately traced the license to a car rental agency."

"Oh, dear God, no! And you found it was hired by a man named Miura," Gina gasped, putting her hands to her mouth.

"Exactly. Therefore, I now must assume he shot at the Concorde because he thought you were on it, Dane. I couldn't believe my eyes when the fax from the car agency came in with the last name Miura, first name Etsujirou. I didn't trust my memory or the coincidence, so I went back and examined the notes I took when you called me to check up on him last week. The same guy —the *Yakuza* you said was following you. He's already returned

306

the car back to the agency's location at Le Bourget."

Le Bourget, Paris's third level airport after Charles de Gaulle and Orly, and now used for non-scheduled air traffic, general aviation, and the biennial Paris Air Show, is probably best-known as Charles Lindbergh's airport of arrival after his solo Atlantic crossing in 1927. The field is five or six miles southwest of Charles de Gaulle, and less than a mile south of the Concorde crash scene.

"And you're going to tell me he turned in the car within minutes of five o'clock, right?" I now understood precisely what he had done.

"At five fifteen this afternoon, yes."

"Then he flew out in the Kizoku Sabreliner. Son of a bitch!" I almost slammed my hand down on the table before I caught myself.

"What's a Kizoku Sabreliner?" Clyde asked, looking up from her notes.

"The Sabreliner's a twin-engined corporate jet made by North American Rockwell. Kizoku Holdings is a conglomerate based in Osaka which owns the plane. This Miura asshole loosely works for Kizoku."

"I see. Dane, I asked you before, and now I'm asking again. And this time I want an answer: Why was Miura following you?"

The afternoon had started off with our escaping a fatal air crash and it was beginning to appear the evening would end with my arrest for the theft of 550 pounds of gold bullion. I related to Clyde a shortened history of Arnaud's gold, followed by a recap of my most recent conversation with Toru. I told her how Toru had explained that his *Yakuza* "partner" thought I now had his gold, and how Miura would pursue me until he found it or killed me for thinking I'd taken it—or both. He couldn't return to his *oyabun* without satisfaction.

"And you're telling me you didn't steal the gold from the watch company's vault you described?" Clyde asked after I finished.

From the vault? Absolutely not. Most fortuitous wording on her part. "No, Clyde, I had nothing to do with that theft."

"What do you mean, *that* theft? Dane, this is a very bad time to parse words with me. You're not telling me everything. Try again, and cut the bullshit this time. Right now, I'm not particularly interested in whether or not you stole something from this guy. We're a little more concerned with the Concorde being shot down."

My eyes tracked back and forth between Clyde and Gina, with Gina's expression silently telling me to come clean. "Okay. Miura paid cash to the owner of the Laurel Watch Company for twenty gold bars worth a little over two point two million dollars, and —"

"The owner who was your friend, the one who was stabbed in the Crillon ten days ago?"

"Yes, Arnaud Laurent. And through a series of small mistakes and misunderstandings, Miura's gold was stolen and Arnaud was killed. Arnaud's widow asked me to find the missing gold for her, her version of revenge against the Japanese who she thinks were circuitously responsible for Arnaud's death. And, yes, I found and then appropriated Miura's gold in Switzerland, and apparently he tried to kill me for so doing."

"And he murdered a hundred and thirteen innocent people in the process," Clyde commented as she glared at me.

"I heard a hundred people were killed," Gina remarked, obviously missing Clyde's dig.

"One hundred passengers, the crew of nine, and four people on the ground in Gonesse, the village where it crashed," Clyde answered dispassionately, still eyeballing me. "Gonesse is seven or eight kilometers from Charles de Gaulle."

As I tried to think where Miura would be headed out of Le Bourget in the Sabreliner, I excused myself from the table and returned to the restaurant's reception foyer where I pulled up the Hôtel Hermitage from my phone's memory. After the second ring, I canceled the call; I remembered Toru had given me his cell number when we last spoke.

"No, Mr. Baron, I'm sorry. I have no idea where Miura is. Why are you looking for him? That could prove to be most dangerous for both of us."

"Mr. Toru, you've certainly heard about today's Concorde crash near Paris. That sick degenerate Miura killed over a hundred people this afternoon. I need the registration number on your company's Sabreliner. I think Miura flew out on it."

"Registration number?"

"Right. The letters and numbers painted on the wing, and the rear of the plane's fuselage. It'll start with the letter J, as in Japan."

"Oh, now I know what you're referring to. It's JA-27KH. K as in Kizoku, H as in Holdings. Is that what you need?"

"Yes. Thanks. Where are you now?"

Toru briefly explained he was still in Monaco. He'd hired a Swiss plant manager to act as the titular head of Laurel, and this was his final visit to the gaming tables before returning to Japan. I wished him my best if I didn't speak with him again and returned to the dining room. Clyde's chair was now inches from Gina's.

"Clyde, call Le Bourget tower and give them this aircraft

registration number." I passed my notations across to her. "Ask 'em what time the plane took off, and for what destination."

"That's good work." She immediately rose and retraced my steps to the elevator area to make her call.

"What happened to the moose?" I asked Gina, noticing our table was devoid of anything other than our drinks.

"Reindeer. I told the waiter we'd lost our appetites and I paid the check. Sorry."

"No, don't be. That's fine. Gina, I obviously didn't intend for you to get involved in all this crap. God, I almost got you killed this afternoon." I reached for her hand.

"I wanted to be with you. No one was holding a gun to my head. Well, not to my head anyway." She smiled for the first time since we'd left Harry's.

Clyde returned to her chair and stood behind it, bourbon in hand. "Le Bourget checked the flight plan. The Sabreliner filed for Nice, and they took off at 5:42 this afternoon. That would have put them into Nice before 7:00. But where exactly is he now?" she wondered aloud.

I glanced at my watch: nearly 11:00. If Miura had gone to Nice, he'd gone there to find Toru.

"Clyde, if you want this guy, you'd better act quickly. Do you have access to a plane?"

"Of course not."

"Well, it's too late for anything scheduled. Look, let's get out to Le Bourget. I'll charter something over the phone while we're driving out. Do you have a car?"

"Slow down there, Dane. You're not going anywhere. This is a police matter. And I think the Swiss authorities might want to have a little chat with you over the gold you . . . *appropriated.* I'm sorry, but I can't overlook this just because we're friends."

"Oh really? Clyde, I know where the bastard is, and neither you nor any of your crime-stopper playmates have a clue as to his whereabouts. The Côte d'Azur is a big area, *Lieutenant.* If you want to find Miura before he takes off for places unknown, we go together."

I felt a kick to my shin from Gina's direction.

"And Gina comes with. If you want to do something later about me ripping off the *Yakuza's* gold, go nuts. But I don't think anyone's gonna give a rat's ass about my stealing from the assassin of a hundred and thirteen people."

Still standing, Clyde took a slug of her bourbon while she twirled her mobile phone in her other hand. She was obviously trying to decide which way to go, and the possibility of single-handedly nailing Miura had now clearly crossed her mind.

"In answer to your earlier question, no, I don't have a car, but I can have one downstairs in two minutes. *Et bien,*" she mused aloud, "we go together. But don't think for a second you're going to do anything if or when we find him. Understood? Also, there's zero chance you'll be reimbursed for whatever this charter flight's going to cost. Is all this clear?"

"Yes. And I'm not worried about the charter expense. Are you carrying a gun?"

"Always. Let's go. I'll call for a car to meet us outside."

* * *

311

Clyde took the front seat while Gina and I climbed in the rear of the unmarked black Peugeot. The police driver acknowledged a quick word from his front seat passenger, then barreled into the late night traffic on the Champs-Élysées, blue lights flashing and the distinctive European siren warbling loudly. I handed my phone forward to Clyde.

"Get me directory assistance or whatever I need to contact a charter outfit at Le Bourget."

She waved her left hand to shut me up—she was already talking on her phone. "This company has a Dassault Falcon 200 that can be ready to go by the time we get to Le Bourget. Do you want it?" she asked, turning to face me. "And do they wait, or is this a one-way charter?"

I knew the jet she'd mentioned; it was a good airplane which would put us into Nice within an hour of takeoff. I reasoned that if we missed him, Gina and I might as well stay on in Monaco for a few days, and if we found him, I'd let the French police pay the freight to haul his ass back to Paris. In either event, Clyde would be reimbursed for her return ticket.

"Yes, we want it. And it'll be a one-way." I didn't ask the cost, but I assumed it would be something close to ten grand; I'd expense it to my Bugatti acquisition account.

"Clyde, how about getting from Nice Airport to Monaco? It's too late for the Heli Air Monaco shuttle and a cab'll take too long. Can you arrange for a police helicopter?"

Once we left the city streets and joined the northbound autoroute, the Peugeot shot to over a 160 kilometers per hour. Cars weren't able to move to the side when we came screaming up from the rear, but our driver daringly found ways of going around them,

312

avoiding sideswiping a few by inches.

Clyde turned back toward me once again. "I've contacted a private helicopter company. They'll have a helicopter waiting for us in Nice. I told them you'd be paying for it with your credit card once we arrive. Sorry, but I'd have as much pull getting a police helicopter in Nice as you would."

* * *

Within ten minutes of signing my credit card slip, the Falcon was wheels up with the three of us buckled into the jet's sumptuous cream leather seats—they still had that new car (make that, new airplane) smell. Gina and I faced one another across a small table; Clyde sat across the aisle, tucking into the canapés and sipping at her Moet & Chandon. When she finished her third mouthful of each, she reached for the plane's air phone. Gina took the opportunity to lean toward me across the table and spoke in a tone that only I could hear above the ambient noise of the twin turbine engines.

"Do you actually know where to find Miura or are you guessing?"

"Since he had the Sabreliner fly him to Nice, he's obviously going there to see Toru. And yes, I know where Toru is. The thing I just figured out is why Miura's going to see him. Initially, it made no sense when I heard the Sabreliner went to Nice. But now I think Miura has one last item to take care of before he heads home."

Before I could finish verbalizing my thought process, Clyde returned the air phone to its cradle, made a few last notes, and looked across the narrow aisle separating us.

"That was the Chief of Criminal Investigations in Monaco. I told him we'd be arriving in a little over an hour, and I asked for permission to follow some leads there for one of our cases."

"So he'll be meeting us when we arrive?" I asked, fearing the possibility of more people getting involved in something I could have gotten completely wrong.

"No, not the Chief. One of his subordinates. Given the hour, I think the boss wanted to go back to bed. I told him we'd be all right by ourselves, but he wants one of his men with us since I have no jurisdiction in Monaco."

Gina closed her eyes and reclined her seat, Clyde read over her notes, and I gazed out my window into the darkness, wondering if the two drivers up front fully appreciated not having to fly at tree top altitudes to follow the headlights on the roads below. Then, for the first time in over an hour, my mind went back to the Concorde crash scene; I could only imagine the macabre ruins. And Uwe. I shook my head when I considered, again, how lucky Gina and I had been this afternoon.

Before I had time to grow overly morbid, I felt the sensation of our bizjet starting its downhill power glide; our brief flight was nearly over. The Falcon 200 banked left onto a long final, toward a string of glowing white pearls sparkling along the shoreline of the black Mediterranean. A minute later, we gently transitioned from air to concrete; the main gear tires greased onto the runway, followed almost immediately by the chirp of the nose tires touching down. I waited for the Falcon to decelerate and turn onto a taxiway before I went forward to the cockpit. Gina and Clyde were busy smiling at one another.

"Captain, there should be a helicopter waiting for us. Could you ask ground control where it's located on the field and taxi over to it?" I asked from my stooped over position between the two pilots' seats.

"*Oui, monsieur,*" the captain answered before saying something into his headset mic which I didn't hear. "We've been cleared to taxi directly to your helicopter. There, see over there, to the left of the main terminal building? With its lights flashing? That must be it."

It was 12:50 midnight. We'd be in Monaco in less than ten minutes.

I returned to my seat for the final seconds of taxiing when Clyde asked, "Now are you going to tell me where we're going?"

"I know Miura's only contact in Europe is in Monaco, and since he flew into Nice, he's definitely looking for him."

"And why is our shooter looking for this contact?"

"He was ratted out. I think before Miura gets out of Dodge and flies back to Japan, he's planning on whacking him."

"Dodge?"

"Never mind. He's here to kill someone I know."

Chapter 26

Monte Carlo

Wednesday morning, 26 July 2000

The searchlight mounted beneath the Hughes 500 helicopter's fuselage completely illuminated the helipad below. The right-seated pilot came up slightly on the collective with his left hand while simultaneously pulling back on the cyclic control with his right, holding the machine in a momentary hover four feet above the ground before softly laying the skids on the pad.

Through the Plexiglas I saw a uniformed officer leaning against his police car, his white patent leather holster belt buckled over his dark trousers, his hand securing his white hat as the rotor blast tried to blow it off. He gave up on trying to light his cigarette.

"*Bonsoir,*" Clyde greeted the officer in a loud voice as she trotted toward him, instinctively crouching, keeping her head lowered beneath the main rotor blades spinning several feet above her. (Amazing how few people were decapitated each year for failing to duck.) The cop leaned close to her and cupped his hands to communicate directly in her ear.

Clyde shrugged and turned to me. "Where do you want him to

take us?" she asked me in French, forgetting to switch back to English. "By the way, his name is Rizzo." I wasn't sure if that was his first or last name, but it didn't matter.

I climbed in the rear seat of the red-striped white Renault after Gina and told the Monégasque policeman to drive up the hill to the casino. "Hopefully, Toru'll still be playing," I said to Clyde. "If I have this right, Miura will be waiting for him at his hotel."

"Tell me again why Miura wants to kill him?" Clyde asked in English from the front seat. When the driver didn't react, it was clear to me he hadn't understood her words.

"Because he knows he was betrayed. Once we got away from him in St. Moritz, Miura knew his gold was gone, and he logically deduced Toru had tipped me off to him . . . an unforgivable offense to the *Yakuza*."

We sped through the near empty streets for the better part of a mile, from the heliport in Fontvielle to the base of the hill, then up the inclined avenue d'Ostende past the harbor view sides of the Hermitage and the Hôtel de Paris, and into the place du Casino. We'd covered three-quarters of the length of the country in four minutes. In the morning rush hour it would take all of ten.

Our driver stopped at the end of a line of exotics, all parked nose out in front of the casino steps. I counted two Lamborghinis, one Ferrari, a Bentley, and a DB7 Aston. It was a slow night.

We followed our personal cop into the casino and paused momentarily as he spoke with a dark-suited management type who promptly waved us forward without the inconvenience of showing our passports or paying the obligatory entrance fee. Most of the patrons were appropriately attired for the one o'clock hour: dark suits or tuxedos for the men, cocktail dresses or gowns for the

317

ladies. While formal dress was only required in the casino's upper floors' private rooms, the more casual afternoon crowd had either changed or gone to bed.

Rizzo yielded the lead and I steered my little posse toward the cocktail lounge, away from where I suspected Toru would be. "Wait here a minute. I'll have a look to see if Toru's still playing." I turned and walked toward the opposite end of the grand baroque room.

I carefully surveyed everyone seated at the baccarat tables: no Toru. I returned to my waiting threesome who were all still standing exactly where I'd parked them minutes earlier.

"He's not there," I reported to Clyde. "Could you try to find out from someone if Toru was here earlier tonight, and if so, how long ago he left?"

"I could, but they wouldn't tell me anything. I don't have any authority here. Ask our guide."

After listening to several seconds of my explanation in French, policeman Rizzo nodded and led me back to what appeared to be the senior face amongst those overseeing the baccarat tables. Rizzo whispered to the man and pointed in my direction.

The pit manager carefully inspected me as he approached. "*Buona sera, signore.*" I sensed we were carrying some major attitude. "I understand you are looking for a gentleman called Signore Toru?" he asked, switching to French.

"I didn't mention the name Toru. I said a Japanese," Rizzo responded, and turned toward me to shake his head in the negative. I was starting to like this guy Rizzo.

"*Mi scusi.* I thought you said Toru."

"Have you seen him this evening?" I asked, now knowing full

well he'd been here.

"*Signore*, as I am sure you understand, we must very carefully protect our guest's privacy here in the casino."

I turned to Rizzo and spoke loudly enough to be overheard. "I don't have time for this crap, goddamn it! Did you explain to this smug prick how important this is, Rizzo? That it's literally a matter of life and death?"

Before the policeman could answer, the casino underboss held up both hands chest high, palms out, gesturing as to calm me. Having sensed a slight deference toward me from Rizzo, he chose to make nice.

"I'm sorry, *signore*. I did not know the grave nature of the situation. Signore Toru was here until only a short time ago, possibly ten or fifteen minutes only."

I nodded without comment and quickly made tracks back to my two women with pal Rizzo at my side. Clyde was holding a cigarette in her best vamp pose. I assumed she was hitting on Gina, who appeared to be enjoying the attention.

"Let's go. He left just a few minutes ago."

"Do you know where he is now?" Clyde asked, exhaling the last drag of her Gauloise before snuffing it out.

"I'm assuming he went back to his hotel. He'll be at the Hermitage."

Once out the front door of the casino, I took off at a trot to the left, past the Hôtel de Paris, down a block, and into the Square Beaumarchais and the Hôtel Hermitage. I arrived at the glass entry doors only seconds after Gina and the two cops braked to a stop in the Renault.

With Rizzo at her side, Clyde flashed her I.D. at the man

behind the front desk.

"I am Lieutenant Perrin of *la police judiciare*. There is a possibility one of your guests may be in a bit of jeopardy this morning," Clyde advised the assistant manager on duty in classic French roundabout phraseology and understatement. "I need you to accompany us to his room, immediately. Your guest's name is Monsieur Toru."

"*Oui, madame. Immédiatement*," he replied; Clyde didn't bother to correct his calling her madame instead of using her police title. He instantly came out from behind the counter and escorted us to the elevator. "Monsieur Toru is in his usual suite on the second floor."

On reaching our designated level, the elevator doors opened and Clyde motioned for the hotel employee to proceed out first. "I'm going to knock on his door four times," she explained in a distinct but quiet voice. "We wait for ten seconds, and if we don't hear anything, I want you to use your key card to unlock the door. Then step away. Clear?"

"*Oui, madame*," he nervously acknowledged.

"And you two," Clyde continued, turning back to Gina and me. "I don't want you close to this door until I call for you. Clear?"

We both nodded. I'd never seen Clyde in her "go" mode before. Her demeanor was calm and professional, leaving no doubt as to who was in charge. I wouldn't have considered messing with her.

She withdrew her service weapon, a 9-millimeter SIG Pro semi-automatic, pulled back the slide to chamber a round, and holding the firearm with both hands, she pointed it down at the carpeted hall flooring. Without drawing, Rizzo placed a hand on the 9-mil in his hip holster. Gina and I positioned ourselves against the corridor wall, eight feet from the door.

Clyde flipped off her weapon's safety, nodded, and briskly rapped four times on the door. I mentally counted to ten, when she silently gestured to our guide.

The night manager inserted his master key card into the metal slit below the door handle and then quickly withdrew it before moving back as instructed. After a series of small green lights flashed on the lock, Clyde turned the handle, threw the door open, and, with both hands, she pointed her pistol into the room. From my position a few steps to her left, I heard her mutter, "*Merde.*"

Without entering, she shouted in English, "Police! Get up from the table and turn around. Now!"

Silence. She repeated her instructions once again.

I moved to the door. Miura's body was sprawled on the marble-floored foyer, a massive uncongealed scarlet blood spill expanding over the tiles. His yellow shirt was now mostly dark red from the fresh viscid fluid still oozing from his throat. Next to his boots laid a Glock 17 with a seven-inch suppressor screwed onto its barrel.

Toru was seated, his hands palms down on the tablecloth, staring at the body from his chair on the far side of a dining table. A bloodied steak knife rested next to an unopened silver serving dish positioned directly in front of him. He'd aged ten years since our last meeting less than a week ago.

Slowly advancing along the wall to avoid the pooling blood, Clyde tracked through the suite's short entryway toward the sitting room. In lockstep, Rizzo followed immediately behind her, his weapon now drawn and aimed at Toru.

"Drop the knife on the floor," Clyde calmly commanded in a normal speaking tone. "Move the knife away from the table and drop it on the floor," she said once more, this time louder than the first.

"Jioruji, please, either drop the knife or move away from the table," I pled as calmly as I could from my position near the door. He didn't move—he continued to gaze across at Miura's body in the foyer. I'd subconsciously called him by his given name for the first time. Under different circumstances, we might have been friends.

"Mr. Baron," Toru finally said without moving to look at me. "You addressed me as Jioruji. I, too, consider you a friend, and I'm grateful you're here. I cannot begin to express to you how deeply ashamed I am for what I permitted to happen today. And for endangering you over the past week."

I stepped forward, lightly placing my hand on Clyde's shoulder. She glanced back for a moment before slowly lowering her weapon; Rizzo kept his aimed across the room at Toru. With her 9-millimeter at her side, Clyde turned back to Miura's body and knelt to inspect his wound more closely—she didn't bother checking for a pulse. Lowering herself to the marble, away from the blood, she got down on all fours and sniffed the pistol's suppressor without touching the weapon.

"This hasn't been fired tonight, but I assume he threatened you with it?" She rose and looked across the table at Toru.

"Did he threaten me?" Toru weighed aloud, his stare still directed at Miura's body. "Over the past several years, yes, he and his fellow *Yakuza* have threatened me . . . and other executives at Kizoku. I have lived in terror over the *Yakuza's* demands. But no more. When I saw him across the floor in the casino tonight, I knew he had come for me. I phoned room service before I came back to the hotel and told them to deliver a steak to my room as quickly as possible—I ordered a meal I knew would come with a sharp knife because I didn't have a weapon to defend myself. I saw that Miura was holding a gun when I looked through the security eyehole when he knocked on my door a few minutes after I returned, and I sliced his throat the moment he entered. I killed him before he had a chance to kill me. Mr. Baron, he came to kill me for betraying him; he called me from Switzerland on Sunday and told me he knew I'd warned you about him. Once he assumed you were flying off from St. Moritz with his *oyabun's* gold, he knew he couldn't locate you again until you were on the Concorde. I should have guessed what he was planning when one of our pilots told me he'd flown Miura to Marseilles to purchase a rifle. Black market, no doubt."

I didn't look at Clyde for her reaction to his last sentence.

"When you phoned earlier tonight to tell me Miura had brought down that airliner in Paris this afternoon, I finally knew I had to destroy him, even though it was too late for all those poor people. His coming here to kill me before he returned to Japan proved to be most providential." His gaze remained fixed on Miura's body.

"Jioruji, I'm going to walk over to you and take the knife. All right?"

I slowly moved toward the table between us. Clyde grabbed the back of my jacket but I jerked her hand away and continued, one slow step after the next.

Toru held up a hand, motioning me to stop. "You know, Mr. Baron, the minute I received the fax back from Osaka after our first meeting here in Monte Carlo, I knew troubles were just beginning. I never should have relayed your offer to sell the gold.

That was the only reason the *Yakuza* became involved in this business, and why Miura came with me to Switzerland—for the gold. I should have known the mere mention of it would have an irresistible draw for them." Toru's voice was soft and resigned as he spoke. "And you said this gold was stolen over a minor misunderstanding, a misunderstanding that has escalated into this air tragedy in Paris today."

Tears welled in his eyes as he slowly lifted his right hand and picked up the steak knife. Clyde and Rizzo immediately raised their weapons again in one synchronized motion as though they'd rehearsed the move countless times before.

"*Drop the knife on the floor! Do it now!*" Clyde shouted, her two hands steadying her aim at the man twelve feet away.

Toru turned his head to face me for the first time since I'd entered the suite.

"Mr. Baron, I cannot shirk my fate."

He raised the knife and placed his left hand behind his right on the wooden handle, the blade pointed toward his torso. With eyes closed, he lowered his head and then forcefully thrust the bloodied stainless steel through his upper ribs and into his chest, jerking up on the knife as it buried. His body convulsed as it fell forward. His face smashed onto the table; his arms dropped limply to his sides.

Rizzo ran to Toru, felt under his jaw for a pulse, then holstered his weapon and leaned back against the wall, muttering something under his breath, possibly a prayer. Clyde lowered her side arm and slowly shook her head.

He likely wouldn't have been prosecuted; he'd killed a mass murderer in self-defense. But he hadn't committed suicide over killing Miura: Toru Jioruji had brought shame to himself for not stopping him before today's tragedy—and for jeopardizing Gina's life and mine. I felt physically sick. I'd suspected what my Japanese friend might do, but I'd been powerless to stop him.

Rizzo walked to Clyde and spoke for a moment before dialing the phone in the sitting room. Clyde briefly looked back at the two bodies before turning to me.

"There's no reason for you and Gina to be here when the whole Monaco police department shows up. Go on, get out of here. Oh, where are you going to stay tonight?" She checked her watch. "For the rest of the morning, I should say."

Reflexively, I checked mine: Jesus, almost 2 A.M. It had been one hell of a day.

"I usually stay here, at the Hermitage, but I don't think that's such a hot idea right now. Tell you what: I think we'll take a cab down the hill to the old Loews. It's now called the Monte Carlo Grand. Do you want me to get you a room?"

"Not on a Paris *flic's* salary. I'll have the police here arrange something for me after we finish up."

"Nope. Not gonna happen that way. I'll have a room reserved for you at the Grand. I'm paying. No argument."

"Okay. For a change, no argument. Thanks, Dane. Now go, you two. I'll call you in the morning. I mean later, tomorrow. *Merde*, you know what I mean."

"Got it. See you then."

She nodded, she and Gina kissed and rubbed cheeks, and we were gone. We walked through the empty lobby, down the front steps toward a waiting taxi.

"Gina, I'm too hyper to sleep right now. Let's get a drink."

"At this hour? Where?"

"Yeah, you're right. Let's walk back to the casino. The lounge in there'll still be open. Otherwise, it's a club like Jimmy'z or something, and I'm not up for all that noise and commotion."

We passed on the cab and walked the two hundred yards back to our starting point in silence, Gina's arm interlocked around mine. The plain-clothes guard inside the casino doors greeted us with a casual salute and motioned us inside, foregoing the usual formalities and fees, evidently remembering us as part of the earlier police entourage.

Once seated with an iceless gin and tonic in hand, Gina shook her head back and forth slowly. "Dane, I'm afraid I can't take any more. At first, this was exciting, and fun. A bit of a lark: the hunt for the gold, the night flight back to England and all. But we've had two people shoot at us, and then the Concorde crash—Miura shooting down the plane and killing all those people because he was trying to get to you. And the two killings tonight. I've counted: Do you realize that makes one hundred and seventeen people killed since we had dinner with Arnaud? I can't do this any longer. I really can't."

"Hey, Gina, I'm devastated, too. Arnaud, and now Toru. And all those people yesterday. God knows, this is the worst thing imaginable. But it's over now. No one's looking for us anymore. You understand that, right?"

She turned her head away to stare out—unseeing—toward the still active gaming floor. "This is the first time I've ever seen a dead body. Two of them, no less." She twitched her head and shoulders in a shivering motion. "This is all so horrible." She continued her vacant gaze toward the green felt tables. "I'm still thinking back to our nearly having boarded the Concorde this afternoon. Yesterday, I mean. And leaving Willie to grow up without me. My God, all those people killed today, Dane, because some lunatic was looking for you. I'm sorry, but this is more than I can handle right now."

I'd seen this side of her once before, that early Sunday afternoon in Paris at the Crillon, a week and a half ago. There was nothing I could say to comfort her; it really had been a gruesome and scary ten days. But at least I could give her an out.

"Gina, let's do this: Let's get out of here, try to get some sleep, and tomorrow I'll put you on a plane back to London. How's that sound?"

"It sounds like a load of crap! I'm not leaving you now, you twit—not after we've made it this far. Hell, you were with me for God knows how long before we had sex, so you must like me." She leaned forward to take my hand in both of hers, her moist blue eyes focused back on me. "Look, I'm bloody well scared, and I'm obviously still in shock over what's happened today. And tonight. Maybe I didn't say things correctly: I'm not blaming you. None of this was your fault. I'm simply overwhelmed. Kind of natural, don't you think? I'll go back to London when you ask me to, or when our fortnight is over. In the meantime, I'll continue to have bits when I feel melancholic, and properly so. But at the end of the day, I'll be all right. I need to be with you now, but without anymore of this horrific tragedy. Okay?"

"Deal. I promise."

Chapter 27

Wednesday - Friday, 26 - 28 July 2000

With no particular plans pending, Gina and I elected to stay over in Monaco until the weekend to see Arnaud's Bugatti auctioned on Friday evening.

We had a late lunch with Clyde in the hotel on Wednesday: Gina ordered a Greek salad with a chilled split of Sauvignon Blanc; Clyde and I each had a steak sandwich and whiskey—hers bourbon, mine Scotch. Between bites, Clyde had more than a few questions regarding the relationship between Miura and Toru, and how Miura fit into Kizoku Holdings. But not a word about Miura shooting at the Concorde. When I eventually advanced the subject, she explained the investigation would be ongoing in Paris until the exact cause of the crash was determined by the *Bureau d'Enquêtes et d'Analyses*. I felt as though I was listening to a press briefing.

"The Monaco police chief asked about my case. I told him I'd received a tip Miura was here to find Toru, that it was believed he'd planned to kill him for reasons still unclear, but likely work related. There was no reason to get into speculation about his involvement with the Concorde accident."

"Speculation? What are you talking about, Clyde? For Christ's sake, you've got Miura on video shooting two rounds at the plane. There's no speculation here. It's a goddamned fact. And it sure as hell wasn't an accident."

"Listen, officially it's on a need to know basis, and the Monégasque police don't need to know. They have a simple self-defense killing and a subsequent suicide to deal with. They have no reason to know about any connection between Miura and the crash of the Concorde. It isn't relevant to the business here last night. Understood?"

I looked her straight in the eyes for several seconds before answering. "Sure, Clyde. Sure."

"Consider the matter closed. Enjoy your holiday. Now, to other and more pleasant subjects . . . " She turned to Gina and smiled broadly. Then back to me. "Oh, before I forget, Dane, many thanks for the room last night. I only wish I could spend more time here with you two."

I bet she did. While the two women charmed one another in rapid-fire French, I politely ignored them and slowly worked my way through a second drink . . . and a third. Almost an hour passed before Clyde finally announced she was off to Nice for her flight back to Paris. She and Gina said their goodbyes amidst a flourish of cheeks and lips and hugs, exchanged numbers, and promises to stay in touch.

After escorting Clyde out to her waiting car and driver, I stopped at the cashier's counter before returning to the dining room.

"I'd like the bill for Lieutenant Perrin's room, please. Marie-

329

Claude Perrin. My name is Baron. I left my credit card imprint for her room charges very early this morning before she checked in."

With an understanding, "*Oui, monsieur,*" the clerk pulled up the account on her computer screen. I signed the charge slip and walked back to rejoin Gina.

"Aha, I thought so!" I said after a brief glance at the one-page room bill. I flipped it over and handed it across the table to Gina. "See there," I pointed. "At eight fifteen this morning, a nineteen-minute call to a Paris area code. It's the police headquarters number, see?" I held up my phone showing Clyde's office number on one of the memory screens. "I'll guarantee that conversation was a debriefing about Miura, and for some reason, they're covering up any connection between him and the Concorde."

"Yeah, so it appears. Now, do you want the good news?" she asked with a wink.

"What good news?"

"Since, for whatever reasons, they're not linking the two, Miura will not exist as far as the French authorities are concerned, and as a result, they're not going to pursue our taking the gold which technically belonged to him."

"Technically, my ass. But you may be right. I sure as hell hope so. We'll see."

* * *

For the first time since Gina and I had met, we had absolutely nothing to do. No planes to catch, nor to fly—nor to steal. No gold to be found—nor to fence. We entertained ourselves at the hotel's rooftop pool above the rocks overlooking the Med, punctuated by short excursions out of town. We ventured to St. Paul de Vence on Thursday for a most agreeable alfresco meal behind the walls of the Colombe d'Or. Touristy, but still superb. Friday afternoon, we hopped the train for the ten-minute ride along the coast to Beaulieu-sur-Mer for lunch at one of the many nondescript and overpriced fish restaurants bordering the marina. Doing nothing was a good thing. And when we weren't doing nothing, we were in bed doing something. It had been a perfect couple of days.

* * *

*B*onsoir? Monsieur Baron?"

She was standing directly behind me, smiling serenely, decked out in what I assumed to be a most expensive black designer dress. Instantly, I knew I was in for another long session in French.

"Ah, Madame Laurent. Wonderful to see you. But unexpected. This is my friend Regina Domenico. Gina, Madame Laurent. Or have you two already met?" The two ladies shook hands, made a little cheek contact, and stepped back a pace or two to check out one another from head to toe.

"I believe we may have met many years ago, madame," Gina said, breaking the short silence. "When I was in secondary school, near Luzern. I've met your son Luc several times. And, madame, please accept my sincerest condolences on the loss of your husband. I'm so very sorry for you. Arnaud was such a dear man."

Gina's courtesy was accepted with a simple nod. "*Merci, mademoiselle*. But I thought you two were off on holiday for several weeks, Monsieur Baron, no?"

"Well, we had, uh, a problem with our flight, you might say, and we've changed our plans a little. I didn't know you were coming down for the auction. It was rude of me not to have invited you."

"Not at all. It was a rather last minute decision. I had nothing planned for the weekend and I thought it might be a good time to get away from the house, after the funeral and all. So I drove to Genève this morning and caught a plane to Nice. Let me ask you: What time do you expect Arnaud's Bugatti to come up for bids this evening?"

"Mr. Bisno—he's the owner of the auction house in London I mentioned to you—he said because your Atlantic is by far the most significant of the lots, it will appear last on tonight's agenda. With about thirty-five other automobiles to be auctioned before yours, madame, it'll probably be a little after nine before we see it. Gina and I were going to go look at some of the other items being sold tonight in the exhibition hall at the far end of the hotel. Would you care to join us?"

"Very much, if I'm not intruding. And Monsieur Baron, how could I have forgotten to thank you? I received the check from Monsieur Bisno on Wednesday. I cannot put into words how much pleasure I received from taking the gold away from those people who are ultimately responsible for Arnaud's death. You did your assignment well, and most quickly. *Oh, mon Dieu*, what am I saying?" She put her hand over her mouth, grimaced, and turned to look at Gina.

"Not a problem. Without Gina, I couldn't have done it."

"Ah, good. I'm relieved. I trust you didn't have any difficulty in finding the gold?"

"No, none at all. Everything went very smoothly," I replied

without choking as Gina rolled her eyes.

"Oh, monsieur, I didn't mention I saw Luc. He was on a weeklong fishing trip in the Caribbean when I phoned and left him a message about Arnaud's death. After he rang back, I arranged for an airline ticket for him to fly in to be with me last weekend."

"Luc was here? In Switzerland, I mean?"

"Yes, but he was only able to spare a few days. He flew back to America this past Monday. He's buying his own boat."

His own boat? Not from his wages from working second mate on seasonal charters he's not.

"You're probably not aware Luc and Arnaud hadn't gotten on very well for several years now, ever since Luc left the watch business. He's had to work very hard in Florida for not very much money. And Arnaud didn't include Luc in his will."

So Luc hears the old man is gone and gets mama to fly him back to Switzerland for the reading of the will, only to find Arnaud has cut him out.

"Luc was very upset when he heard Arnaud hadn't left him any money."

Oh, really?

Then the fog parted. "Madame, you said Luc flew back to Florida last Monday. When did he arrive?"

"The evening of Arnaud's funeral, a week ago Thursday. Why?"

"Oh, I'm sorry I missed him, that's all. Did he stay with you at your house in La Chaux-de-Fonds?"

"Yes, of course."

"Luc was with you when I called last Saturday morning?"

"Yes. Why do ask, Monsieur Baron?"

"Oh, no reason really. I would have liked to have said hello."

"The next time you see Luc in Sarasota, he'll have his new fishing boat to show you. I don't think he'd mind if I tell you: I gave him a little help with it since he didn't have enough money. Well, in truth, a lot of help. I gave him one million U.S. dollars. He's very excited."

No shit. I'd be excited, too, if someone handed me a million bucks. I turned toward Gina, who I assumed had been monitoring the conversation while appearing to be checking out the items awaiting auction. Her calm told me either she hadn't been listening carefully or she didn't get it.

We ambled slowly down the hall, continuing our casual inspections of the incredible displays of machinery awaiting sale. Beyond the hall was the grand ballroom where the auction would be getting underway shortly.

Paul Bisno's concept of staging his exotic classics sale after the big hitters had held theirs in Monaco during Grand Prix week in May or early June was quite clever. Many of the automobiles which hadn't made reserve in the earlier auctions were placed in short-term storage and offered at Bisno's two months later. If the owners hadn't had any luck earlier, they could either try once more in Monaco with Bisno's or wait for a later and more distant venue.

Lined up on both sides of the carpeted hallway leading to the ballroom were some of the most magnificent automobiles ever produced, far more interesting than current designs. Freshly polished and shining behind blue velvet cordons were more than thirty museum-quality masterpieces, including several Ferraris, the most significant of which were a 1958 250 GT, a 1960 Dino, and my personal favorite, the world's quintessential sports/race car, a

'57 315S. All painted red, of course. Closer to the main salon's entry doors were the Bugattis: a 1923 Type 29/30 Indianapolis racer, and a 1933 Type 55 Super Sports, the latter's classic roadster lines in the same burgundy over black two-tone paint scheme as Arnaud's prize. The final *objet d'art*, parked directly in front of the doors, was *our* coup de grace, the Bugatti Type 57SC Atlantic.

Portia, Paul's director of automobile sales, had created an oversized photo and text history of the "Lost Atlantic" which she'd positioned on easels next to the machine. The props described the sagas of the four Atlantics built by Bugatti, how one was wrecked at a railway crossing, how two others had found good homes, and the lore of this fourth one disappearing shortly before World War II. The hinged split hood was open to view over the right half of the 3.3 liter engine, exposing the pristine supercharged straight-eight which developed all of 220 horsepower, a most prodigious power plant in the mid- to late-1930s.

As the bidders, friends of, and wannabes slowly drifted into the ballroom, the three of us loitered for several minutes to admire the belle of the show from outside the cordon.

"Are you a bit sad having to say good bye to this beauty?" Gina asked Madame Laurent.

"No, not really. This was Arnaud's passion, not mine. I'm just pleased his gem will be going to someone who'll enjoy it as much as he did." Then, turning to me, she asked, "Monsieur Baron, will my automobile be taken away directly by the new purchaser?"

"They'll be responsible for its removal within two days. Bisno's will handle all the transfer formalities. You've already signed the paperwork to permit them to act on your behalf."

"I see. And the payment? How are the funds paid and

transferred?"

"Since you decided not to have a reserve on the sale, the highest bidder will basically own the Atlantic when the hammer comes down. Then, or not later than noon tomorrow, the purchaser pays the hammer price plus an eleven percent commission to Bisno's, who will prepare a check for you for the sale proceeds, less their commission from the seller's side and their advertising and insurance expenses. By law, they have thirty days to make payment, but Mister Bisno indicated you could expect payment as soon as the buyer's check clears his bank. I told him to mail the check to you in La Chaux-de-Fonds."

"Very good. One other question, Monsieur Baron: Will the bidders know I have offered the Atlantic without a reserve?"

"No, absolutely not. We won't know which items were actually sold until after the auction."

"I understand. Well, shall we?" she asked with a nod toward the ballroom.

* * *

The commodious space was alive with people circulating and talking once they'd saved their seats. The male attendees' dress ranged from jeans to tuxes; the females all could have been attired for a reception at the Prince's palace. We settled on three chairs roughly halfway back from the stage, on the right of the center aisle, maybe seventy feet from the auctioneer's dais. On either side of the podium was a large digital electronic tote board, nine or ten feet tall, which would be used to simultaneously display the current bids in seven world currencies: French francs, British pounds, U.S. dollars, Swiss francs, German marks, Italian lira, and Japanese yen—in that order. The bidding was to be conducted in French francs, the official currency of Monaco.

At precisely six P.M., an immaculately turned out Irishman in his mid-thirties called the room to order. Paul had described him to me over the phone, telling me how masterfully his man could work a crowd of bidders. Portia stood to one side of the auctioneer, and thankfully, she'd left her polka dotted dress at home in favor of an equally ill-fitting solid black number. The room quieted, and the auctioneer introduced himself as Jack Deaglan O'Meara.

"*Bonsoir, mesdames et messieurs*," he opened with a loud and pleasant Irish brogue overlap to his acceptable French accent. "Good evening, ladies and gentlemen. *Guten Abend, meine Damen und Herren*." He turned and waved an arm at one of the currency boards. "And with my apologies to those of you who plan to spend obscenely conspicuous sums of lira or yen this evening, please forgive me, for I speak neither Italian nor Japanese."

A small ice-breaking round of laughter ensued from the audience, now numbering in the low hundreds.

"We will start this evening's activities with those lots you will find in your catalogs numbered from one through ninety-nine."

I opened my booklet and leafed through the first eight pages which covered the initial offerings. These were the automobilia collections, the least expensive items of the evening: original automobile sales pamphlets, literature, photographs and paintings, and miscellanea which included hood ornaments, model cars and auto club badges. Auctioneer O'Meara breezed through these items at an amazing clip, completing the entire inventory in slightly over an hour and a quarter. I doubted if any of these relatively inexpensive collectibles were offered on a reserve basis, hence I assumed all hammer prices were the purchasing bids. The final sale prices ranged from a low of $200 for a 1939 Alfa Romeo 6C 2500 Sport sales brochure, to the top price of $60,000 for an *Éléphant Dressé*, the silver and brass elephant hood ornament from a Bugatti Royale which Etorre Bugatti had personally crashed in 1931.

At the conclusion of the first session, most of the room's patrons emptied back into the hall for drinks and cigarettes. I waved down a passing waiter and collected three glasses of Champagne for our little group.

"Monsieur Baron, you appear to be more nervous about the sale of the Atlantic than I am."

With my million dollar Bugatti Type 35B riding on it, you're damn right I was nervous. "And I thought I was doing such a good job of hiding it." I glanced down at my catalog in an attempt to change subjects. "I see your Facel Vega is lot number 107. I'd guess we should see that go up for bids within the next twenty minutes."

As we finished our drinks, the P.A. system began summoning the audience to return to their places for the second and final session.

The competition for the first few items was spirited, with bidders actively pursuing the lesser expensive offerings: a 1972 Jag E-Type, a '63 Ferrari 250 GTE, a '47 MG TC, and an early vintage BMW. The bidding didn't exceed $100,000 on any of these early lots. Arnaud's Facel Vega had generated considerable interest from onlookers in the hall, but when it came up for bids, only two men remained in the running after the tote board displayed the price passing through $41,000.

Madame Laurent, seated between Gina and me, touched my arm. "This is somewhat disappointing, no? Only 70,000 Swiss francs?" she whispered.

I held up my "wait a minute" finger, careful not to have it construed as a bidding gesture by Paul's man at the podium. "The price will go higher. Watch the auctioneer work these two bidders against one another," I answered quietly.

The bidder closest to us raised his catalog and the display board instantly reflected his offer of 350,000 French francs— $49,335. Within seconds, the competition pushed the number to $53,563. One of O'Meara's sexy female assistants on the floor attempted to work the first bidder, but to no avail. The hammer came down with the Irishman declaring, "And sold to the gentleman on the left side of the room for 380,000 francs. Thank you very much, sir."

Madame Laurent gently tapped my arm as a gesture of her apparent satisfaction with the Facel's sale price.

"Next will be lot number 109, as 108 has been withdrawn from tonight's sale. Lot 109 is the 1984 Lotus 95T Formula One Grand Prix Car. We will now be open to bids starting at 3,000,000 French francs."

A tad over 400,000 U.S. for your very own yesteryear Formula One car. And just where was the lucky winning bidder planning to drive this outdated marvel? Someone seemed to know, for within a minute, the race car was hammered down at 4.5 million francs— $634,000. *À chacun son goût* . . . each to their own.

It was a little after nine when auctioneer O'Meara finally came to lot number 137. "*Mesdames, messieurs*. Ladies and gentlemen.

Speaking for all of us at Bisno's Auctions, I now have the unique pleasure and honor of presenting one of only four Bugatti Type 57SC Atlantics ever produced in Molsheim."

O'Meara waved his arm and wowed us all by theatrically and magically parting the curtains behind him and pulling off a white satin sheet covering the elegant machine that had been on display in the hallway only an hour ago.

"This magnificent automobile was thought to have been destroyed around the time of World War Two, but as you see, my honored guests, here is the missing fourth Bugatti Atlantic."

Though they had seen the *pièce de résistance* on their way into the ballroom—the bidders, their guests, and hangers-on alike—they all roared. Auctioneer O'Meara and Paul's assistant Portia had done their jobs perfectly. The crowd was in a frenzy, as frenzied as people can be over an automobile. O'Meara ceremoniously gave the audience a full uninterrupted sixty seconds to ooh and aah amongst themselves before he said another word. He rapped his gavel several times to regain their attention. He was brilliant.

"Some of you may have seen a few of our previous offerings this evening at one of the earlier auctions in Monte Carlo this season . . . at Brooks, Barrett-Jackson, or Poulin Le Fur, most worthy and honorable competitors all. However, my friends, you have never, nor will you likely ever again, see an automobile as significant as our final offering of the evening: lot number 137, a Type 57SC Atlantic—the Lost Bugatti." He'd revved them up again. "Ladies and gentlemen, I will be open for bids starting at 30 million francs."

O'Meara had kicked things off at a near unimaginable level, but it was still more than 12 million francs, or 1.7 million dollars, shy of my target number. I'd already calculated I needed to hear 42.4 million French francs out of O'Meara's mouth before he used his gavel again and for the final time this evening. My reward was depending on it. The next four or five minutes would be excruciating.

I turned in my seat to scan the room, and I felt almost physical ill when I saw but one lone hand raised. I was screwed.

O'Meara thanked the opener, and then asked the room for a bid of 35 million francs. Again, only a single taker. I looked at the tote boards displaying the latest bid and the three currencies below the French franc quote, the only three I was following: 3.283 million British pounds, 4.933 million U.S. dollars, and 8.265 million Swiss francs. I needed almost another 2 million Swiss francs. I also needed a Scotch. A double.

"Ladies and gentlemen, I have 35 million. Do I hear 40?"

After an interminable five seconds, another new bidder raised a catalog over his head.

"Forty million from the gentleman in the straw hat. Thank you, sir. I have 40. I'm looking for 45. 45 million. Do I hear 45?" he expertly worked the bidders. A single twitch from anyone in the room and I was home free.

Silence and immobility.

"*Mesdames, messieurs*, I need a bid of 45 million. Do I see 45?"

They were goddamned statues.

"All right, do I hear 43? 43 million French francs? Please, anyone? Anyone at 43?" he asked.

I was dead.

"Very well, 41 million. I have 40. I'm looking for 41. Anyone?

Last chance at 41 million." He visually swept the silent room, his eyes momentarily stopping at each of his associates working the three bidders on the floor.

"And yes, I see 41. Thank you, sir. I have 41, looking for 42 million. 42? 42? Going once . . . twice . . . and *sold*! for 41 million francs to the gentleman in the fourth row. Thank you very much indeed, sir. You have purchased a most extraordinary automobile."

The sound of the gavel striking its wooden block as O'Meara closed the auction exploded like a hand grenade detonating in my gut.

I gazed at the electronic currency boards' final numbers: 41 million French francs, 3.846 million British pounds, 5.779 million U.S. . . . and 9.682 million Swiss francs. Damn it! A measly 318,000 Swiss francs short. Less than 200,000 bucks. I should have run over and given one of the other bidders a check for the difference to put us both over-the-top.

The poor bastard in the seat in front of mine turned around with a sneer after I unconsciously kicked the leg of his chair. I didn't apologize.

Gina leaned forward around Madame Laurent and squinted her eyes at me, giving me one of those *poor baby* looks—our incredibly risky gold flight to England had been for naught.

I started to rise from my chair when I felt something touch my hand. Madame Laurent handed me an envelope.

"Monsieur Baron, watching you during the bidding for the Atlantic was better than cabaret," she gleamed. "I only wish I'd had a video camera to capture the torment you were experiencing. I'm sorry, I shouldn't laugh, but you were absolutely enraptured. It was hilarious."

I attempted to feign a slight smile, but couldn't; I'd lost out on my million dollar prize.

I looked down at the sealed envelope.

Still grinning, Madame Laurent prompted, "Go ahead, open it."

I tore off one end of the envelope and pulled out the single paper inside: the title to Arnaud's Type 35B Bugatti.

"But . . . " is all I could feebly muster.

"Monsieur Baron, you've earned it, and I know you appreciate it, so please don't say anything. By telling you I wanted to receive a minimum of ten million Swiss francs, I simply assured myself that all possible would be done to realize the best price for the Atlantic. You did that, and your facial expressions during the final minutes of bidding were well worth the small shortage. Now, I'm taking you two to dinner at the Louis XV in the Hôtel de Paris to celebrate. I should think my proceeds from Monsieur Bisno might just cover it."

Chapter 28

Paris

Saturday, 29 July 2000

In one long sentence, she machine-gunned, "I borrowed your swimming costume; it's more comfortable than my bikini bottoms; I hope you don't mind; would you like me to order you some breakfast? so where are we going? or would you rather relax and stay here in Monaco a bit longer?"

I opened one eye to see Gina sitting cross-legged beside me in my swimming trunks, topless, holding a cup of something in one hand and a jammy croissant in the other. Clearly, her day had begun and it was time for company.

"My shorts become you. *Très chic*."

"How would you know? You haven't taken that eye off my boobs yet."

"Busted—pun intended. And as to your question, do you mean where are we going today or for the next two weeks?" I asked, now with both eyes open to better take in the view. "What time is it anyway? Shouldn't we still be asleep?"

"It's past seven, we're awake, and it's time to plan the rest of our holiday," she answered, bouncing her rump on the bed like a little kid waiting to open her birthday presents. I decided I liked it when she bounced. "I only insist that whatever we do, it be completely without drama. No more shootings or killings. I'm tired of hardships—it's time for some easyships."

"You want some *easyships*, do you?" I chuckled, and partially sat up to snag a wedge of orange off the room service tray laying on the bed. "Okay, if you're still up for it, how 'bout we head off to Florida? Then maybe over to the Bahamas for a few days. Sound good?"

I took her jumping across the bed to crash on top of me (after removing her loaner swimming trunks) as an indication of her approval. Again, ever the quick study. Twenty minutes later, she dragged me into the shower behind her. The day was starting off well. It was a good day to be Dane.

As the proud new owner of a Type 35B Bugatti, my first call was to an automobile transporter in Nice, a company Portia had suggested. Madame Laurent had asked if I would arrange for Arnaud's Mercedes to be shipped to Florida along with the Bugatti, and while I was confident Luc could wait a month for a sea shipment, I couldn't. The forwarder said he'd arrange to pick up both machines in La Chaux-de-Fonds for air transport to Miami, after which the autos would be loaded onto an enclosed semi-trailer transporter for the four-hour drive across Alligator Alley and up to Sarasota.

By eight o'clock, I was on to my second call, this one to the concierge for our airline reservations. He assured me he'd see to things and phone back within ten minutes.

"Monsieur Baron, I have completed the arrangements for you

and Mademoiselle Domenico. I have you reserved on Air France leaving Nice at ten twenty-five this morning, with an hour and a half connection at Charles de Gaulle to another Air France flight, arriving in Atlanta at five twenty this afternoon, local time. Finally, you will connect to a Delta flight which will land in Sarasota at eight fifteen this evening. You have seat numbers two A and B on all segments, per your instructions, sir."

"Perfect. Thanks very much. Do me one more thing and arrange for the Heli Air Monaco van to pick us up downstairs at, what? Say nine?"

"Very well, sir. I'll arrange for the van to be here in forty-five minutes."

We were a blur, Gina dressing and repacking the four bags the Royal Monceau had sent down from Paris, me taking off downstairs to the checkout desk and then over to my concierge friend who seemed pleased with the fifty-dollar bill I folded into his palm. Between prepaying the auto forwarder, checking out of the Grand, and paying for our two first class tickets to Florida, I'd managed to make over a $21,000 dent in my credit card. Someday soon, I'd have to give some powerful consideration to setting myself up on a budget—soon, maybe the same day I quit drinking. Seriously.

Once checked in at Nice Airport, I popped for a couple of disgusting lukewarm canned orange juices while we waited for our gate to open.

"Okay, this is my plan: We'll spend a few nights at my place and I'll show you around Sarasota, then we'll fly over to the Bahamas. I never asked: Do you dive?"

"You're referring to SCUBA, I presume," she answered with a

sexy wink at my unintended double entendre. "Yeah, I earned my certification card on a trip to Greece several years ago. So we're going diving. Great. Where exactly?"

"The big island of Andros in the Bahamas. There's a place there I've been several times called the Small Hope Bay Lodge. They have some amazing diving just off shore—a wall, for example, which goes down to something close to a mile deep. The lodge is nothing fancy, just great diving, and total relaxation. No phones or TVs. Nothing but those *easyships* you were looking for. Sound all right?"

"Perfect."

* * *

I looked up at the noisy overhead flight arrivals and departures board to find the gate number for our connecting Air France flight to Atlanta. Each time a flight was updated or added to the board, little white on black metallic number tiles clicked away annoyingly.

"Monsieur Baron?"

I nodded at the two men standing to my right. One wore a dark green sport coat, with tie; the other, a black leather jacket, sans tie. Sport coat held out his opened identification wallet.

Christ, what now? It was supposed to be time for no more drama.

"You are Monsieur Baron and Mademoiselle Domenico?" he stated, more than inquired, in French.

"Why? What do you want?" Gina asked curtly.

"You will come with us. Our car is outside," black leather

347

jacket ordered.

"Let me see both of your identifications again," I requested for no particular reason other than to gain some thinking time.

"I've shown you my identification. Now you will come with us without delay."

"Look, our luggage is being transferred onto our flight to the U.S. that departs in an hour. We're not going anywhere until one of you tells us what this is all about," I stated defiantly, as though I had the horsepower to refuse.

The two detectives glanced at one another for a second before sport coat pressed a selection on his cellular, mumbled something, and then handed it to me. "It's for you."

"Hello?"

"Dane, this is Marie-Claude. You need to follow the instructions of the detectives. Do as I ask and save us all a lot of trouble. I'll see you shortly. Now give the phone back. I have something to say to him."

"Listen, Clyde, goddamn it: Gina and I are getting on our flight to Atlanta in less than an hour. Our bags are being loaded as we speak. I don't know what the hell this is all about, but we ain't going anywhere until you tell me what's happening."

"I'll explain everything when I see you, and your luggage will be taken care of. Give the phone back to the detective, and do as he tells you," she said brusquely, without a hint we'd ever been friends, let alone occasional lovers.

Gina leaned closer and whispered, "This is about the gold, isn't it?"

"Hell, I guess so. The hits just keep on comin'. I can't believe she's doing this. That *bitch*!"

348

Once out of the terminal building, the attitude of the two cops deteriorated from rude to surly Gestapo. We were unceremoniously shown into the rear of their car, the doors slammed and locked from the outside. There were no interior handles, and a thick Plexiglas partition separated us from the front-seated detectives. My perfect day had smashed headlong into a ditch.

The unmarked police car sped south down the autoroute, retracing the path of our cab ride last Tuesday when the crippled Concorde flew past us in smoke and flames. I could never have fathomed the possibility I'd be connected with the disaster, but at the moment, I didn't like our odds of sleeping in Sarasota tonight.

I checked my watch as we turned onto the Champs-Élysées and drove downhill and away from the place de l'Étoile: Our plane to Atlanta was now in the boarding process. My anger at Clyde for yanking us off our flight was only surpassed by my fear and incredulity . . . fear of being prosecuted for the theft of the gold, and incredulity over my pal Clyde selling me out.

We turned right, toward the Seine, then, passing the Grand Palais, the car slowed and came to a stop before starting across the pont Alexandre toward the Left Bank. The leather-jacketed detective exited and opened the rear door, motioning us out. Without speaking, he pointed to Clyde, standing twenty yards away, facing us from the bridge. Gina took my hand as we walked toward her.

"What's this all about, Clyde? And how did you find us?" I asked, and immediately realized my words sounded as if we were consciously trying to duck her.

"Simple, really. I phoned for you at your hotel this morning and was advised you'd checked out only a few minutes before my call. I identified myself, asked if they knew where you'd gone, and I was put through to the concierge who filled me in on your flight details."

And after I'd given the prick a fifty.

"Now, don't speak, and follow me." She began across the bridge, down the busy sidewalk on the west side of the ornate span. With its adornments of Art Nouveau era lamps and gilded bronze statuary of nymphs and rearing horses, I'd always considered the pont Alexandre to be the most beautiful of the city's thirty-two bridges. But I sensed that opinion would be changing shortly, and I was certain I'd rather be sitting in seat 2 B on an Air France 747 than going wherever Clyde was leading us.

Upon reaching the center of the span, Clyde stopped behind a man who was leaning against the railing with both arms, puffing on a cigar, and looking down the river to the west, toward the Eiffel Tower. Across the broad sidewalk, a driver sat in a highly polished black Citroën idling by the curb in one of the southbound lanes. The car's blue emergency lights were flashing.

The man flicked some ash into the Seine and slowly straightened himself. He turned to face us, resting his hands behind him on the bridge's railing.

The man was tall, well over six feet, in his late fifties, wearing a navy blue suit ($2,500, minimum) with a light gray shirt and a solid pink silk tie. He could have passed as easily for an haute couture fashion house owner as the policeman or government official I logically suspected him to be. Clyde remained silent. She clearly was not at ease in the man's presence.

"I am Bertrand Rondelet. You may call me Monsieur Rondelet, or preferably, remain silent and do not call me anything. I am the

Préfet de Police for Paris." He spoke in perfect and only slightly accented English. His speech was painfully slow, undoubtedly for the effect he was successfully seeking. "Are you familiar with the title *Préfet de Police*?" Without waiting for a response, he continued: "It means to you that I am the top cop around here. Understand? Good, I like being understood. Now, let's talk a bit." He turned and flicked another ash overboard.

I grasped he meant *he* wanted to talk a bit. A meeting with the Paris police chief, on a Saturday, in the middle of the pont Alexandre, had a certain *you're in deep, deep, shit* feel about it, and he did nothing to dispel my perception.

"Lieutenant Perrin has filled me in on the details of how you came to know a certain individual named Etsujirou Miura."

"I didn't know him, I—"

"Be silent!" Rondelet shot back. "When I want your comments, I'll ask for them." Gina's grasp on my hand became firmer. Clyde stared down at the river.

"We are here in regard to the crash of the Concorde. I am going to give you some information you may not be aware of, Monsieur Baron. And you, Mademoiselle Domenico, you are unfortunately involved due to your association with Monsieur Baron. If I didn't know you two were already aware of certain details about the disaster, I wouldn't be telling you these things you are about to hear. And when I conclude my comments, I have full confidence you both will have a clear picture of my expectations.

"Now, and without regard to what you do and do not know about the accident last Tuesday, let me tell you a little about what I know so far, and what the BAE knows. You know the BAE?"

I risked another scolding and answered. "The *Bureau*

d'Enquêtes et d'Analyses. Yes, I know what they do. Your equivalent of our American NTSB."

"*Et voilà!*" the boss of all cops replied, almost pleasantly, touching his nose, as if we were playing a lunch time game of charades on the pont Alexandre. "Since the crash last Tuesday, we have carefully gone over the audio and video tapes from our monitors around the airport. I understand Perrin has told you about these. We have surveillance materials showing Miura driving on the route Périphérique Sud at four twenty-two that afternoon. This road parallels Roissy's south runways. Then we see him on the tape pulling off onto a smaller, but parallel, road that borders the airport perimeter fence.

"He stopped his car in a line of trees between the two roads, exited the vehicle with a rifle and a bipod, and then took up a prone position on the grass next to the chain fence. He was only one hundred and thirty meters from one of the airport's audio recording stations used to measure takeoff sounds for purposes of noise abatement. This small building also serves as one of the video camera locations. It was fortunate for us he chose this location, as it gave us very clear sound recordings and good images on the video. Through analyses of these recordings, we were able to determine the rifle he used was a Barrett .50 caliber— a most significant weapon. This was confirmed once we found the remains of one of the bullets. The videos show his face, as well as the license number on the car he used. A rental."

I stared at Rondelet while he spoke and wondered why the hell the Paris Chief of Police was bothering to relate all this to us. I was confident it wasn't to enlighten us as to the diligent workings of his departments.

"As you are now aware, Perrin here remembered you had previously asked her about the identity of a certain Etsujirou Miura. She permitted herself to be used in your unofficial inquiries regarding this man you thought was following you." He turned to glare at Clyde, whose expression now resembled the kid whose teacher had caught her cheating on an exam.

"Our tapes, both audio and video, confirm your friend Miura fired two rounds from the Barrett, exactly three seconds apart. The first shot hit the front right tire of the Concorde's left main gear bogey, causing the tire to explode and split into pieces. The second round, three seconds later, was fired at the Concorde after it had traveled three hundred meters farther down the runway. We found projectile fragments in the metal landing gear from this second shot."

Where was he going with this?

"After Perrin related the details of her trip to the Côte d'Azur with you two, she also told me about your involvement with this Miura individual—that you had stolen gold belonging to his company."

"Now wait just a goddamned minute," I almost shouted at the *Préfet de Police*. "Do you also know Miura was *Yakuza*, and the gold I supposedly stole from him was first stolen from its true owners by the German Schutzstaffel? And I don't like the implication that I was somehow involved in the crash of the Concorde. You know damned well I didn't have anything to do with it. Shit, I was trying to *board* the damned plane! Miura was clearly nuts, and the tragedy is he killed all those people in looking to get to me. Now, why don't you tell us why you've had your goons take us from the airport? You wouldn't be here over the alleged theft in Switzerland of some gold of questionable origin from a known and habitual criminal in the *Yakuza*."

After a deep inhale on his cigar, Rondelet flicked another ash into the river. Not once did the icy stare from his gray eyes stray from me as I waited for the explosion.

Calmly, he continued: "Patience. I haven't finished my story, Monsieur Baron. You see, I have a liaison man I work with, or more correctly, to whom I report now and then, when the situation arises. Unofficially, of course. This liaison man works in the Palais de l'Élysée. Do you know the Palais de l'Élysée, monsieur? Mademoiselle?"

He asked the question with a condescending smile, as an arrogant parent might quiz a slow child. "The French White House, the French Number Ten Downing Street," I responded, mostly for Gina's enlightenment in case she was unfamiliar with the address.

"*Bravo*," he said, keeping his smirk, clearly most satisfied with the progress we were all making here. "You see, my friends, my liaison has suggested—and he tells me this thought originated from the absolute highest authority in his building—he suggested Miura didn't exist. He said a Continental Airlines DC-10 took off on the same runway, Runway 26 Right, shortly before the Air France Concorde started its takeoff roll. He suggests Concorde's tire was ruptured as a result of its striking a titanium shard the American airplane had dropped onto the runway. This caused a large piece of the resulting tire debris to fly up into the underside of the left wing area and puncture the internal fuel tank located immediately above the landing gear. The fuel ignited and, well, the rest you know."

He stuck the cigar in his mouth and crossed his arms as if to say, *so what do ya think about them apples?* He paused for another draw on his cigar. And effect.

"You sons of bitches—so you're going to try pin this on the Americans, aren't you? Yeah, I guess it would look pretty crappy to have to admit the security around France's premier airport is so lax as to have been penetrated by a single Japanese wiseguy who subsequently caused a hundred and thirteen people's deaths in the crash of France's, and the world's, premier aircraft. Yes, that would be rather embarrassing for the French government, wouldn't it? But you have a major problem, Monsieur Rondelet, don't you? There's too much evidence. Like the audio and video tapes. And all those people investigating the crash. It'd be kinda tough to cover up Miura's rifle shots, wouldn't it? So again, why are we here? Are you going to put us in some far away island prison so we can't screw with your little cover-up scheme? Or how about killing us? That would shut us up."

"Ah, but you Americans are so melodramatic, Monsieur Baron. My solution is far more civilized and simpler than all that."

Rondelet reached into his inside suit coat pocket and withdrew a small clear plastic bag. He raised it up for both Gina and me to inspect: an evidence bag containing the twisted remains of a large caliber bullet.

"You see, there are no longer any tapes. They have all been accidentally misplaced or inadvertently erased—I've forgotten which. And the technicians and security personnel working on this incident all fall under the umbrella of our National Secrets Law, specifically article 413-9 of our Penal Code. They can never speak of this case or they would be treated as traitors to the state. Isn't that correct, Lieutenant Perrin?" he asked with a smirk.

"*Oui, monsieur,*" Clyde replied, succinctly voicing her understanding of the situation, her eyes still looking down at the concrete sidewalk.

The P*réfet de Police* replaced the cigar in the right side of his mouth, and, using both hands, he unsealed the plastic bag to remove the remains of what I presumed to be a .50 caliber slug.

"And nor will either of you ever speak of this again. For two reasons: First, you'd have absolutely no evidence to support your insane assassin theory. And second, if you ever did speak of this incident, I would find a crime to charge you with and have you extradited back to France from wherever you were, at which point you'd be turned over to the Swiss authorities and charged with the theft of the Kizoku company's gold bullion."

Rondelet held up the bullet. Displaying it between his left thumb and index finger, he waved it in front of each of our faces for fully five seconds. He pulled the cigar from his mouth and turned to extend both arms out over the bridge's railing. With his right hand, Rondelet tossed the cigar into the Seine, and with his left, he dropped the bullet. He rubbed his hands over one another in a washing motion, moved away from the railing, and stepped across the sidewalk and into his waiting Citroën.

"*Et bien. Bonjour, et bon voyage, mademoiselle, monsieur.* My two detectives over there will return you to the airport," he said through the car's opened rear right window as he checked his watch, "or take you to a hotel, since you've unfortunately missed your flight. Good-bye. I would say *au revoir,* but I seriously doubt we'll ever meet again."

Chapter 29

Sarasota

Thursday, 3 August 2000

Neither Gina nor I slept on Sunday's nine-and-a-half-hour daylight flight to Atlanta; mostly, we rehashed our bizarre rendezvous on the pont Alexandre. We ultimately concluded we had no choice but to let Continental Airlines continue to be the scapegoat in the Concorde disaster—Préfet Rondelet and his chums had either destroyed or long-term temporarily mislaid all meaningful evidence of Miura's existence. But should things ever change, our visiting an updated version of the Bastille or Devil's Island wasn't really a possibility since there was also no evidence of any gold we'd purportedly stolen.

Our three days in Sarasota since we'd arrived had been glorious: long days and longer nights together, mostly spent in the prone position, either in bed or across the street at Lido Beach. We'd unknowingly settled into a routine of short tours around town, long, wet lunches, siestas at the beach, cocktails, dinner, and back home for another ten hours in bed.

My Type 35 Bugatti (God, I loved the sound of that) was

dropped off late yesterday afternoon, and this morning, I attacked the blue beauty with a pile of clean rags and a new plastic bottle of Mothers Car Polish. First, the dreaded alloy wheels and hood louvers, then the larger, and easier, flat surfaces. In truth, all the machine had actually needed was a quick trip around it with a dust cloth.

By 1:30, we were crossing the Ringling Causeway in my 308 Ferrari, which had now been relegated to *other* car status with the arrival of its 1927 vintage garage mate. From my place on Lido Key, it was less than five minutes to the Marina Jack yacht basin at the foot of Main Street on Sarasota Bay, where I was confident we'd find our choice of charter boats available for an afternoon in the Gulf. It was August, and things wouldn't start getting busy for the skippers until well after Thanksgiving. Once parked, I remembered to pop in the Targa top in case of a summer afternoon downpour, while Gina lubed up with more sun tan lotion than there is grease in a Christmas goose.

As we walked through the parking lot toward the line of fishing vessels, I noticed a light cream-colored Mercedes C280, maybe four or five years old.

"Uh, Gina, go on ahead over to the boats. I'll be right behind you." I wanted to do a little private sleuthing to confirm my suspicions.

"Everything all right?"

"Yeah, I'll only be a minute."

With a nod and a shrug, she sauntered off toward the docks. I waited for a few seconds before turning to examine the Mercedes with the Swiss tag, the distinctive license plate with the Swiss shield on the left, an NE for Neuchâtel followed by six numbers in the center, and the Neuchâtel cantonal shield on the right. It was Arnaud's old car; the Mercedes had been delivered yesterday, before the transporter had come across the causeway to Lido.

I didn't have to look closely to see that two pieces of duct tape adhering to the car had been painted over with a non-matching cream-colored paint. The small pieces were taped to the left rear passenger door and the vertical portion of the trunk lid, two inches to the right of the Mercedes silver star emblem. Scanning the parking lot and seeing no one, I knelt down, slid a fingernail under a corner of the painted tape on the door, and peeled it back halfway.

"Son of a bitch!"

I moved to the rear of the car to pull back the other square of tape: identical. I didn't bother to smooth the tape back over either spot.

I joined up with Gina on the dock where she was doing her best to ignore one of the fishermen ogling her in her shorts and bikini top as he played at washing down his boat.

"Dane! Dane! Down here."

Farther down the platform, Luc, bare chested and appearing suntanned and fit, was waving from what appeared to be about a 40-something-foot sport fisher.

"And is that you, Gina? My God, I haven't seen you since school days back in Switzerland. Hey, Dane, good to see you, man. Come on aboard." He was completely relaxed and at ease.

Luc's mother had given him the million dollar advance on his inheritance only two weeks ago, but he'd already purchased his boat and had the new name *Miss Suisse*, and home port, *Sarasota, FL*, painted on the white transom in gold and black lettering. I'd heard it was bad luck to change a boat's name, but apparently, Luc hadn't been listening that day.

"Gina, what brings you to Florida?" Luc asked, extending a hand to help her aboard.

"Good to see you, Luc. I'm here at Dane's invitation. A bit of a holiday in the sun."

"Let me show you guys around. A kind gift from my mother. But I'm sure you guessed I couldn't have afforded it myself from what I was making as a second mate. She's a forty-five-foot Viking Sportfish. A 1995 model. Twin Detroit diesels, six hundred gallons of fuel, a hundred and twenty gallons of fresh water, and berths for four, not counting the owner's stateroom forward. And my new eight thousand dollar fighting chair," he commented as he proudly pointed to the center of the fiberglass aft deck. "What do you think?" he glowed. He redefined chutzpah.

"She's beautiful. You done good, Luc. And your English has really improved since I last saw you."

"Yeah, I guess it's from working with an American crew and dealing with the American and British tourists on my old boss's boat. I knew I had to get better in English to pass the test for my captain's license. I just got my six-pack ticket last week, so now I can legally carry up to six passengers plus the crew. I'm ready to go, but I haven't had any charterers yet. Hopefully things will pick up in a few months when the season kicks in."

"Well, Luc, this may be your lucky day. We're looking for a few hours in the Gulf for a little fishing. Gina's an experienced trout fisherman, but you'll need to teach her a few tricks about open water fishing. You available this afternoon? We could be your first passengers."

"Now? Absolutely! I have a lot of beer and Cokes and chips aboard, but if you'd like something else, I could make a quick trip to the store."

A kid on Christmas morning.

"No, we'll be fine with whatever you have on board. Thanks," Gina said.

With two of us managing the lines and Luc handling things from the flybridge, we eased out of his slip within fifteen minutes of coming aboard the sparkling white Viking. Luc slowly guided *Miss Suisse* out of the Marina Jack slips, under the Ringling drawbridge, and out through New Pass. Once clear of the cut between Lido and Longboat Keys, he accelerated the two massive diesels until the hull came up on plane; the Viking steered a westerly course into the Gulf of Mexico at close to twenty-five knots.

Gina found her way through the sliding glass door to the salon and the galley. "I have Coke and Coors Lite. Which would you prefer?" she asked a minute later when she reemerged, holding the two cans to her bikini-topped chest while she closed the slider behind her.

"I'll see what Luc wants." I took both drinks and climbed the seven teak steps to the flybridge, holding the tubular stainless railing with my left hand, and the icy cans in my right. I took the seat next to Luc's captain's chair and handed him the beer.

"Thanks, man," Luc said, taking a swig before placing the can into a drink holder on the fiberglass helm console. "It's an incredible coincidence running into you today, no?"

I hesitated for a moment before answering. What the hell?

"No, not really. Your mother told me she'd given you money to buy a boat, and I thought I recognized your dad's Mercedes in the parking lot last night when we came over to the marina for dinner. I was hoping you'd be here today."

I turned to check for a reaction, but he stayed focused straight ahead, his mirrored sunglasses hiding any possible tells. He took another pull on his beer and continued his gaze toward the forward horizon without comment. Then a final tug at the can, draining it this time. We sat in silence for the next twenty minutes until he pulled back on the throttles and the Viking slowed to trolling speed.

"Tell you what, Dane: I'll go down and get Gina set up with her gear. Can you hold this course for a while? Maintain your two hundred and sixty degree heading." Without waiting for a response, Luc was down the steps and onto the aft deck.

Keeping my right hand on the stainless steel wheel, I turned in my seat to watch the activity behind and below me. On the port side, I watched as Luc helped Gina with her bait. If she suspected anything, her actions didn't show it.

Luc had taken us about eleven miles out into the Gulf. We were floating over an artificial reef in fifty feet of water, a spot he said he hoped would yield some good amberjack and grouper possibilities. His hunch was good. Within five minutes, Luc jumped to Gina's side the moment he saw her rod bending.

"Should I get in the fighting chair, Luc?" she asked hopefully.

Luc looked up, caught my eye, and smiled. I took it he didn't think Gina's hit required the full dog and pony show, but why not? "Absolutely. Here, let me adjust the foot rests for you."

Gina leaned back and began to reel in her monster. I'm sure it took all Luc had not to burst out laughing when he leaned over the side and netted what appeared to be a three-or four-pound Spanish mackerel. Good thing he'd invested in the fighting chair or she might never have landed the leviathan.

Another two hours in the sun, another two Spanish macs, a smallish gag grouper, a nearly landed three-foot baby blacktip shark, and Gina was finally pooped. Luc climbed up to the flybridge and I yielded back his helm.

"Why don't we start heading back in, Luc. I think she's had it. And you and I can have a little chat."

With a nod, he pushed the two throttles all the way forward and the engine noise rose as the Viking accelerated onto plane.

Minutes later, Gina appeared at the top of the ladder; I reached for her hand to steady her.

"I was going to take a nap in the cabin but I think I'd rather be outside in the fresh air. Mind if I join you?"

"Please do. Luc and I were about to discuss hunting in Tiefencastel."

Luc barely broke his pose. He leaned forward and continued to gaze out over the bow, both forearms now stretched out across the wheel. Gina gaped at me wide-eyed from her standing position behind Luc and put a hand over her mouth. She finally got it.

"Your mother told me it took her several days to get in touch with you after your father died. I understand you arrived in La Chaux-de-Fonds only a few hours after the services."

Playing for time, he hesitated before he spoke. "Uh, yeah, my mother said I just missed you. She said you flew out directly after the funeral."

"That's true. And she told me you stayed at her place in La Chaux-de-Fonds for a few days. She mentioned you were there when I called on the Saturday after the funeral to ask her for directions to Klaus's farm in Tiefencastel. Did you overhear her phone call?"

"I don't know what call you're talking about."

"Sure you do. When she explained to me in detail where the farm was. And you also heard I was going there that night, didn't you? How am I doin' so far, Luc?"

I looked down at the GPS display on the console: a little over five miles out from New Pass, and another three to the marina.

"So what did you do? Tell your mother you were going to see some friends, then sneak the shotgun from Arnaud's gun case, borrow the Mercedes, and drive the two hundred miles to Tiefencastel? What'd that take? Maybe three or four hours each way? And you were back home at mama's house snug in your bed before dawn . . . with two of my bullet holes in your dad's car. C'mon, Luc, help me out here. Feel free to jump in any time."

"You don't seem to be needing any help. Your little story is fascinating. Please continue." The smug bastard was actually smiling. He needed a good bitch slapping. Another three miles and the little shit could swim back.

Gina moved from her standing position to a leaning pose against my armrest, between my chair and Luc's. "I'll take it for a bit if you don't mind, Dane. Your daddy cut you off financially after you abandoned his business. Arnaud told me this, Luc. I'm not guessing here. Despite your endless pleas for money, your father wouldn't give you a single franc. So after you found Arnaud hadn't left you anything in his will, you thought you'd try to get your hands on that gold he'd told you about."

Luc's white knuckles contrasted against the tanned back of his hands as he visibly gripped the wheel harder.

"You probably couldn't believe your good luck when you overheard your mother telling Dane how to find Klaus's place. And you assumed we knew where the gold was buried there, didn't you? You arrived at the farm before us and hid out in the dark until we unearthed the bars. Then all you had to do was kill us and collect your stash."

The Viking slowed as Luc pulled back on the throttle levers; we were approaching New Pass Bridge and coming up on a no wake zone. The boat wallowed in the water momentarily before moving toward the marina at a crawl relative to our earlier speed. Luc leaned back in his chair and lit up a Marlboro, his first of the afternoon.

"Now I want to say something," he started. "You're right about my father and me. As I told you over three years ago, Dane, when I first arranged for you to meet with him, his business wasn't for me. I hated it. You knew that. But he wouldn't discuss it with me. He said if I left Laurel, he would disown me. So after he died, I decided to take my share of the gold. I was going to split it with Klaus, but after I heard he was also killed, the bars belonged to me, one hundred percent.

"You were right, Gina, I didn't know where the bars were, and as I watched the two of you from the woods that night, apparently you didn't either. But you got lucky, and you found them under that electrical tower. Please believe me: It wasn't my intention to shoot either of you. I didn't want to hurt you. I only wanted to scare you away before you had a chance to take off with my gold."

I went nuts. "*Your* gold? Jesus, you moron, it wasn't even your grandfather's gold—he and Klaus stole it. And your father sure as hell didn't bequeath you his share—he sold the bars to the Japanese. Man, you're a piece of work. And I don't take kindly to assholes like you taking shots at me or my people. Understand?" I stood up and grabbed him around the throat with one hand. "You fired a shotgun in our direction, twice, with one hand, from a moving car, at night, and you were only trying to scare us? You're a goddamned social disease. God, you're stupid. And greedy. Shit, you knew your mother would give you a ton of money. You're just a downright evil piece of crap."

I released my grip and returned to my seat before my borderline physical attack on the little crud constituted grounds for charges of mutiny. A couple of the fishermen on the nearby seawall gave me a thumbs up after my tirade—sound carries well over water. As we slowly approached the Ringling Causeway drawbridge, I opted to wait on my ultimatum until we tied up.

"Tell me, Luc, how much is a boat like this worth?"

"What you're really asking is how much my mother gave me."

"No, I'm not. I already know that. She gave you a million bucks."

"All right, so you know. I spent about half of it on the Viking. Now I have a question for you: How did you get hold of my father's Type 35 Bugatti? I saw it in the transporter yesterday when they dropped off my Mercedes. Why didn't my mother sell it at the auction along with the Atlantic?"

If Madame Laurent hadn't told junior about our little deal, it wasn't my job to enlighten him. Obviously, he'd been counting on the proceeds from the sale of the Type 35 to eventually trickle down.

"Let's just say she made out better having the machine go to me than she would have done at auction. Basically, she made twice as much. If you've got any more questions, ask your mother."

I rose, took Gina's hand, and walked to the ladder. "I'll help you with the lines when you pull in. After that, you can go to hell."

Luc said nothing. He slowed the Viking to a stop, spun it around with the bow thruster, and backed into his slip as if he knew what he was doing. I jumped onto the dock, Gina threw me the stern line, and once I had it secured on a cleat, we both walked forward and she tossed the bowline across.

I reached out for Gina's hand as she hopped off the boat. She muttered something very dirty under her breath before turning back to her fellow Swiss, and cleaning it up a tad, said, "Ta ta, Luc . . . you bloody arsehole."

"Here—" I reached across, handed him four C-notes, and pointed at his freshly painted advertising. "Your sign on the dock here reads, '*$400 for a half day*.' Plus gratuity, I assume. Well, Luc, here's your tip: I want you and this boat out of here and out of Sarasota by tomorrow morning. If you're still here after that, your shiny Viking will be sitting on the bottom of this basin, and your mother will be told about your little escapade in Tiefencastel with Arnaud's shotgun. I don't think she'd like to hear her little boy, who stands to inherit everything, is a failed double assassin, do you?"

Luc stepped back, leaned against the fighting chair, and pushed up on the bill of his Tampa Bay Bucs cap. His face was redder than the bit of sun he'd picked up this afternoon.

"And where do you suggest I go? I've already paid three months advance rent on this slip."

"Luc, I don't give a damn where you go. You're just lucky I don't throw your scrawny little Swiss ass into the business end of an Everglades airboat. Move the boat up to Clearwater, Tarpon Springs. Hell, go over to the other coast, the Fort Lauderdale or the Miami area. And don't give me that crap that you're worried about a few months of lost rent and having to repaint a new home port on your transom. You have plenty of money left. Just don't be here when I drive by tomorrow. Got it?"

I took Gina's hand and we started down the dock.

"Dane, Gina, I'm sorry," I heard Luc yell out with a cracking voice. "I know you don't believe me, but I wasn't trying to hurt either of you."

He sounded genuinely sincere. We continued to walk away as I held up my right hand with the middle finger extended. I genuinely didn't care.

* * *

It was a little after ten when we returned from dinner. The thick, sticky air outside was still in the high eighties. Before coming back into the garage, Gina changed into shorts and slipped on one of the gaudy aloha shirts I'd bought her. She walked to the right side of the Ferrari before she saw me going to the right side of the Type 35, the driver's side. After a few cranks, the unmuffled straight-eight engine thundered to life with a heavy cloud of blue-gray smoke, enveloping the automobile and its hand-waving occupants.

I drove north, over the New Pass Bridge and up Gulf of Mexico Drive, thinking some live jazz and cocktails at the Haye Loft on Longboat Key sounded like a pleasant way to end the evening. I only hoped if I was pulled over tonight, the cop would be so fascinated with the Bugatti he'd let me slide on little details such as my lack of registration, tags, or insurance.

Gina didn't seem to mind her hair waving frantically in the open wheel racer, even tangling on the fuel filler cap behind her head. I'd have been surprised if she had. She was like that: As long as it was fun or exciting, she was up for it.

"Gina, you remember back on the boat today when I referred to you as *my people?*"

After a somewhat lengthy hesitation, she nodded. "Yeah, and you'll notice I didn't ask about the implication."

Not one to be put off by a little sales resistance, I continued. "Well, I didn't realize I'd said it until later this evening, but it means people who are important to you, people you care about. Family, people you'd never want to see hurt—people you're reasonably madly in love with."

There it was. I'd finally thrown it out there and there was no way of ever pulling it back. And I was okay with that.

"Dane, before you go and say something stupid, no, I won't marry you. You've already told me you're not good at it. Look, you're a man with very simple priorities: You just want to eat and drink well, make a lot of money, drive a Bugatti, and make love to me . . . in whichever order. And that's all fine. But let's not complicate things. Okay?"

At first I thought I'd been insulted, but then I reconsidered and decided these were all good things. "Alright, but now you'll never know what I was going to say."

"Quite, and nor would I care to. Now, let's talk about something else." She leaned over a little, kissed her finger, and touched my nose. "I have a question: How are we going to stay busy and amused after all we've been through the past few weeks?"

369

I gave her my best Groucho leer. She gave me her best poke to my ribs.

"Damn, woman. Those punches hurt."

"You mean my little love pats? Poor baby, you should have said something earlier. Sorry. No, I'm serious, Dane. We can't just sit at the beach all day drinking Margaritas and strumming ukuleles."

"Scotch, thank you. Tequila's another thing I'm not good at. But maybe when we're not at the beach, we could write about what we did over our summer vacation."

"That's brilliant. It would also make for a smashing film."

"We can hope."

Afters

Friday morning, 4 August 2000

I wandered out of the bedroom to join Gina. As I neared the kitchen, the phone rang on the living room desk.

"Hello?"

"Morning, Dane."

"Gina? Where are you?"

"Sorry I couldn't stay for breakfast, luv, but I'm a bit pressed for time. Thanks awfully for a brilliant holiday . . . and an amazing last night."

"Gina, where the hell are you? What's goin' on?"

"Dane, don't talk—just listen. First off, remember my telling you I'd be needing a lot of money in the near future? Well, I'm afraid that hundred grand from Toru didn't quite cut it, so I took the liberty of electronically transferring two million dollars from your Credit Suisse account into mine at the Cayman Islands Bank in Georgetown yesterday morning when you were in the garage polishing your car. You kindly left your account number in the top desk drawer below the computer, along with your personal identification number. You really should keep those two separate, you know. I did have a spot of trouble with your account password. I must have tried three or four before I thought of *hARRY'SbAR*. The reverse case-sensitivity was actually quite clever.

"And, Dane, my parents don't fly. I nicked the keys for the Skylane off the board in the airport office when the girl went in the back to look for the charts I'd requested.

"I'd originally planned to relieve you of the gold once we moved it to England, but later, it occurred to me a little computer embezzling would be much easier . . . and require far less heavy lifting. Regardless, you may want to avoid visiting Switzerland or the U.K. in the near future. You know, the pinched airplane and all.

"Dane, I will miss you. You're an incredibly sweet and clean-hearted man. Gullible, and a bit overtrusting perhaps, but sweet. I must ring off now; they're calling my flight. Cheers. Enjoy your Bugatti. I'll give Marie-Claude a big kiss for you. Bye bye. *Ciao*."

Author's Notes

Versailles, France

Thursday, 29 November 2012

(Reuters) — A French appeals court on Thursday absolved Continental Airlines of blame for a 2000 Concorde crash that killed 113 people and cleared a mechanic at the U.S. airline of the charge of involuntary manslaughter. The verdict comes over a decade after the accident helped to spell the end of the supersonic airliner.

A previous court ruled that a small metal strip that fell onto the runway from a Continental aircraft just before the Concorde took off from Paris, caused the crash.

Continental was originally fined 200,000 euros and ordered to pay the Concorde's operator, Air France, a million euros in damages. Continental appealed the verdict which it described as unfair and absurd.

(BBC News) — "We are going to fight it and establish that the Concorde caught fire eight seconds before this scrap of metal met with the Concorde – so about 700 meters before," Continental lawyer, Olivier Metzner, said.

Oxnard, California

Monday, 7 April 2014

(**Los Angeles Daily News**) — Mullin Automotive Museum guide Warner Hall said they don't like to talk about how much the cars cost, but the 1936 Bugatti Type 57SC Atlantic is an exception. One of four produced, the gleaming silver car, once owned by Lord Victor Rothschild, has twice been the most expensive car in the world. In 1971, Dr. Peter Williamson paid an unprecedented $59,000 for the car, which later won best in show at the Pebble Beach Concours d'Elegance in 2003.

In 2010, the Williamson family sold the car for a new record price, something between $30 million and $40 million.

Made in United States
Orlando, FL
27 December 2022

27786526R00211